LOUISA

LOUISA

SIMONE ZELITCH

G. P. PUTNAM'S SONS

NEW YORK

This is a work of fiction. Names, characters, places, and incidents either are the product of the author's imagination or are used fictitiously, and any resemblance to actual persons, living or dead, business establishments, events, or locales is entirely coincidental.

G. P. PUTNAM'S SONS
Publishers Since 1838
a member of
Penguin Putnam Inc.
375 Hudson Street
New York, NY 10014

Library of Congress Cataloging-in-Publication Data

Zelitch, Simone.
Louisa / Simone Zelitch.
p.   cm.
ISBN 0-399-14659-8
1. Righteous Gentiles in the Holocaust—Fiction.   2. Holocaust, Jewish (1939–1945)—Fiction.   3. Daughters-in-law—Fiction. 4. Mothers-in-law—Fiction.   5. Jewish women—Fiction. 6. Palestine—Fiction.   7. Hungary—Fiction.   I. Title.
PS3576.E445 L68   2000   00-026766
813'.54—dc21

A portion of this novel was published, in an earlier form, in *The Long Story*, No. 15, Spring 1997.

Printed in the United States of America.

1   3   5   7   9   10   8   6   4   2

This book is printed on acid-free paper. ∞

Book design by Marysarah Quinn

IN MEMORY OF MY FATHER,
MY BEST READER

PART
ONE

SMOKED MY FIRST CIGARETTE
when I was six years old. I found it on the kitchen windowsill, though the railway platform proved more reliable. The butts I gathered on that platform made terrible, gritty cigarettes, hardly worth re-rolling, yet to my mind, they're all mixed up with where I smoked them, by the tracks. I loved the trains, window after window of Budapesti smokers who would carry cigarettes to theaters, lectures, and cafés. I'd do those things too. But later there would also be smokes passed, like gifts, between strangers in the dark.

Now where the hell can I get a cigarette? Everyone in Israel is a smoker, but nobody gets something for nothing, and what do I have to trade? Not that my head's the clearest. We're just off the boat, Louisa and I, and we expected my cousin, Bela, to meet us at the dock, but he wasn't there. We went through customs, and there were so many of us piling in at once that we were backed up for hours. By the time they let us go, it was dark. Rain fell by the fistful. No Bela.

So we were forced onto a government truck parked by the gate, a flatbed full of Poles. Some young clods in wet leather jackets unfastened the tarp and hoisted us on board, and those Poles reluctantly made room between their trunks and carpetbags and feather mattresses. The rain slapped on the tarp and cut through a stream of aromatic Yiddish. It was hard to tell where the luggage ended and the humanity began. There is a kind of Jew who looks deep fried, a chinless sloucher. Here was a happy family of them.

Louisa whispered, *"Ich verstehe kein Wort."*

The Poles fell silent. A woman to my right asked, in Yiddish, "What is she?"

"My daughter-in-law," I said.

She asked, "What is she doing here?"

"The same as me."

"She's not the same as you."

It was no use saying no, here in the truck skidding through mud that would take us to a transient camp where we would share close quarters. Could I begrudge them curiosity?

Ah, the trouble was, I could. I had no use for these people. I had no use for this country. If Bela had met us at the dock, I would have understood why I was here.

HE EASY ANSWER WAS: WHERE else did I have to go? I'd lost my parents and my husband and my son. I had only Louisa. I owe her my life. It was Louisa who had kept me hidden during the German occupation. This was five years ago, in Budapest. Louisa stayed through a siege under a rain of bombs and steady gunfire, and she kept me in the cellar of her family house through the winter, in constant danger of discovery and death. The latticed vent under the piano of her music room was our lone gateway, and through it she passed water, rolls, canned meat, and cigarettes. Often, she would sing a composition by my son.

What is lost, what is lost
We can not have back again.
It is like a breath we've taken.

We can not breathe it again.
It is like good bread we've eaten.
We can not eat it again.
It is like a heart we've broken
Or our own heart, lost in vain.

Some days, I could hear nothing but a constant roar in my ears. It must have been the sound of my own blood which, my cousin Adele the nurse once told me, renews itself once every three weeks. In that case, in that cellar my blood was renewed four times. I don't doubt it made a noise.

After the war I didn't seek out Louisa, but she found me. I was at the border station on my way to Italy, and she grabbed hold of me and cried out, *"Mutti,* I'm going with you!"

She wore a rabbit-fur coat and she gripped me so hard that I could feel through the fluff straight to the skin. "What do you want from me?" I'd demanded then. "You've done enough. Let go."

But she didn't let go, even as the train pulled from the station, and though she didn't have the proper papers, somehow we were rolling through the mountains of Slovenia and then to Trieste, where after some time we secured passage on a boat bound for Haifa to the Holy Land, and during our months on the road, not once did she let go.

WHY DID SHE CLING TO ME?
She said she loved me. "Dear," I said, "that's not a reason."

"You're all alone."

"I'm going to my cousin."

"I want to be where you are."

"And what if they don't want you?"

In fact, they all knew: Poles, Slovaks, Romanians, Greeks, even the British at Cyprus. Everything about Louisa told them she was German. They'd start with questions, and I'd answer, "I owe her my life."

On the boat, she sought out a rabbi. It is Louisa's way to look for things without hesitation or embarrassment. She wanted to convert before we reached the Holy Land, and she cornered anyone who looked like he might do. There were few contenders. The emigrants were young and sullen, and none of the men had beards. Sometimes, Louisa would catch a fellow with a hat on, who was staring at the sea with an expression that she chose to read as prayerful, and she would ask him to baptize her and make her a Jew.

One fierce girl gripped my arm and asked, "Does she know where the boat's going?"

I couldn't keep pace with her Yiddish, and again I only said, "I owe her my life."

"You owe her something? Work it out with God. Don't bring us such a burden. Don't bring it to Israel. You know what she is?"

She pressed close, chin all but indenting mine, and her hot breath steamed all over my face so that I had to ask, mildly, "Do you have a cigarette?"

"She's their daughter," the woman said. "Even here we can't escape them."

So much for Yiddish. To me, it's greasy black hats, the smell of fish, wet eiderdown, that truck. My own emerges a resentful mouthful at a time. I prefer German. In Budapest, our set spoke German, and it was in German that I wrote my letters to my cousin Bela. The telegram I sent Bela from Trieste was in German, and in German I received his answer. *Das gibt's doch nicht! Wann? Wo?*

That answer met my expectations—joyous, tender, and inquisitive. It was printed in blue type so faint it might have floated, and only after I'd replied with the details of our arrival did I notice the unfamiliar Haifa address on the bottom of the page. So had Bela left Kibbutz Tilulit? That seemed impossible.

Bela had founded Tilulit. I imagine it the way it was in a photograph he sent me in '25, a photograph I lost: himself and two comrades in front of the kibbutz chicken coop. Dori sat on a spool of wire, legs stuffed into shorts, elbows on thighs, blond hair blown back. Bela and Nathan knelt on either side. They were substantial people, muscular and happy. They had just finished building the coop that day. Sunlight or overexposure filled their hair and glanced off bare knees into the camera. Bela would be grizzled now, and his hair would have gone gray, but he would whip open the tarp over the truck full of Poles with that same happy, frank expression, as though it were the gate of a chicken coop he'd built with his own hands.

*I*F I HAD SENT THE DATE OF our arrival to the wrong address, it stood to reason that Bela would not have received it in time to meet our boat. It would be futile to try to contact him that night, but until I saw him, everything around me would feel impermanent, the camp, mud underfoot, Poles, Yiddish. Also Louisa. She jumped off the truck, pulling both myself and our luggage with her.

"*Mutti*," she said, "we must thank God we have arrived." She bowed her head.

"We'll be trampled," I said to Louisa, for by now there was a push for bedding and ration-books. Such were our numbers that the camp administrators made no attempt to keep records, but they sprinkled us with disinfectant powder and handed out papers no one had the equilibrium to read. What with the rain, the ink of the documents was running.

No one paid attention to bed assignments, and by the time we reached our block, Louisa and I had to make do with a single cot under a window that didn't quite close. Around us, the Poles emptied carpetbags and fought over the space around the fizzling electric heater. The barracks were a shell.

When the British left Palestine in '48, they'd stripped them down to a few walls of corrugated tin that more or less held up a roof. On that roof, rain slapped and the light hummed like a mosquito, and between those high and low notes ran the Yiddish, a tongue no cultured person speaks. The Poles were all old friends. They had been liberated by the same battalion, and at the same American DP camp in Belsen they had attended the same Labor-Zionist meetings and would probably settle into the same apartment block in Tel Aviv and turn it into Warsaw.

Louisa made up our bed matter-of-factly, as though all of this were just as she'd imagined. She opened our little suitcase and pulled out our dressing gowns, modestly climbing into her own under the sheet, and kissing me before laying her head down and at once falling asleep. She curled there, with the bedding tucked around her and a crescent of disinfectant powder clinging to her cheek. Her hair fanned her arm, and the softness of that arm, the fairness of that hair, stirred as she breathed. Her breathing put me in mind of her singing voice, which is moving and a little uncanny and implies an intelligence you can't see in her face. I watched her for a while, and then I heard a voice close to my ear.

"*Csodálatos!* Excellent human material."

Hungarian. I turned, and inches away on a neighboring cot sat a Pole in a leather jacket. He addressed me, but his eyes were on Louisa.

"They'll never let her stay in Israel. Who knows how she got this far." He introduced himself. "Yossel Berkowitz. A man of business."

"You're not Hungarian," I said. "How do you—"

"What don't I know, *Nagymama?* There are businessmen in Hungary, in Italy, in Greece, in all the mighty nations. Now Hebrew, that's another matter. All Zionists must learn Hebrew."

I took him in: dull eyes under a fur cap, broken nose, stained teeth. I said, "You don't look like a Zionist."

Amused, he said, "*Nagymama,* do you look like a Zionist? We're all Zionists now."

I had to laugh, in spite of the foul air, my lack of sleep, perhaps even because of them; they're both narcotic. Maybe hearing my mother-tongue disarmed me, because for the first time in who knows how long, I put more than four words together. "In this room, then, I'd say there are more Zionists than there were in all of Hungary before the war, and what a likely bunch of recruits, God help us. Do you include my daughter-in-law?"

"Give me your daughter-in-law," he said.

I didn't answer. I only stared.

"You want to be rid of her. Of course you do. How can she sleep?"

Then I could only say, "I owe her my life."

Berkowitz laughed or coughed. A light blazed, and with a brief, dismissive gesture, he placed a burning cigarette in my hand. "You break my heart with your gratitude. So she saved your life. She gave you yours, and you give me hers. A fair exchange."

I inhaled. It was my first smoke in a week, and confusion peeled away, allowing me a clarity impossible without a cigarette. My circumstances arranged themselves. I was in a cold room with a lot of strangers. Why should it concern me? In the morning I would find Bela at the new address he'd sent me. One night. I had passed worse nights, and with Louisa. I touched the place in my stocking where I had put Bela's telegram, and a shot went through my bones. It was gone.

Berkowitz broke through the silence. "There's something you're not telling."

Forcing some equilibrium, I managed to ask him, "Why do you want Louisa?"

He smiled and replied, "Do you realize how much people would pay to fuck a German?"

2

_M_Y HUSBAND, JANOS, HAD SOME strong ideas about raising children. Even while we were courting, he would say, "Nora, if you're a sentimentalist, I should know now."

I asked him, "What do you mean by a sentimentalist?"

"No fairy tales, no silly stories," Janos said. "No illusions."

So my son, Gabor, grew up in a temple of Realism. This was partly circumstantial. Consider our flat on Prater Street, hardly a dreamy sort of place. It vibrated with a nearby tramline, and what windows didn't face the street looked dead-on at a courtyard full of other people's laundry. We could never manage to heat it in the winter. Janos moved a stove into the tiny nook he used for a study, but even then he worked in several sweaters and a long, yellow scarf. He would read Gabor passages from his engineering journals. Gabor couldn't bear the cold, so he would wander off, tuck himself somewhere inside the coatrack, and pull everything on top of him until the rack itself came crashing down. Then he would laugh.

Understand, Gabor was completely irrational. His hair stuck up. He turned my music box backwards and sang along. He never ate what I had in the pot but he had no qualms about climbing out of bed at three in the morning and trying to bake himself a cake, and at dawn, I would find him standing in a circle of eggshells, peeling strings of hardened batter from his forearms with a look of concentration. He loved noise, especially the sound of trains. Early on, Janos would take him to Nyugati Station to try to explain the mechanisms of the locomotives, and he would break free and rush straight into a puddle of oil, whooping with joy.

He was also beautiful. That made no sense. I look, to be frank, like a woman who smokes too much, and even when Janos was pleased, his features drooped a little. And through our flat ran this black-haired angel of a child, who left behind him a trail of gasoline, broken glass, and flour.

As years passed, Gabor learned to depend on his charm. Janos found work abroad, and although at first he sent money through the post, those envelopes stopped coming when the war began, and we had to live off of my income as a school receptionist. That didn't bring in much, and Gabor liked nice things. He wouldn't eat bread when he could get cake, or milk when he could get cream, and as for clothes, you can imagine that he wasn't easy on his coats and trousers, and he wouldn't wear what I mended, let alone accept castoffs his father left behind. By then, quotas kept Gabor out of the university and more or less out of work. Then there were the Labor Battalions. The government had been sending boys like him to clear minefields in the Ukraine. We didn't talk about that.

So my son was at loose ends and in constant need of things I couldn't give him. Fortunately, there were women. He'd write them poems or sketch their portraits or read their palms. It couldn't have been more effortless. The palm-reading had certain psychological advantages, but music proved most lucrative. He'd taken piano lessons years before and played just well enough to give a novice lessons; every lady pupil fell in love. Without exception, the girls sat at the keyboard, watching him with such fixed expressions that it was possible they didn't blink. He would sing out notes in a conversational tenor. Somehow, he always managed to time his lessons around supper, and the mothers were charmed enough to make him stay. More often than not, he'd return before our own supper with a little cake for me.

There was a strong bond between Gabor and myself, less tender than conspiratorial. I confess, I loved his stories. He gave those poor girls names:

Boiled Cabbage, Snowflake, Giraffe, Kali. He had a warm and nasty laugh, and there was something cozy about sitting there with my coffee and cigarette and listening to him chew through those poor girls like marzipan.

So, imagine my son's future before him. It is 1943. He is nineteen. He strides through the lobby of the Music Academy, below high eaves of gold, his portfolio of music tucked under his arm, his open angel-face lengthened into a man's, but still warm and intelligent. His shoes are expensive. He bought them himself a month before and they are already in shameful condition because I refuse to polish them. Though Gabor is not a student, no one at the Academy challenges him because he is so sure of where he's going. On the afternoon in question, Gabor heads for the practice rooms.

The rooms face each other across dull maroon tiles. He is supposed to sign with the lady at the desk, and of course, he does no such thing, but simply swings his way into an unoccupied room and fills the rack above the piano with notes for a composition.

There are three songs in all: *Rocket One, Rocket Two,* and *The Booming Rocket.* All were in their initial stages. He'd been beginning compositions for years; the first pages of torch songs, comic duets, operas, and choral works littered his room and sometimes overflowed into the hallway to the point where I used the fair sides for grocery lists. He didn't mind. He even tried to set the grocery lists to music.

It was the third unfinished song Gabor looked at that afternoon. He had already completed two measures: *Boom, Boom! The Happy Missile Sings!* For a tenor, he thought, with the bass family breaking through. Then where should it lead? Up, probably. He had a rudimentary knowledge of theory, enough to take the form of a faint headache and some frustration.

His room was snug, just big enough to fit a bench and an upright piano. The door was padded with a leather cushion embedded with a tiny pane of crosshatched glass. Gabor had raised the piano lid and spread his papers on the stand, and he was rolling the nib of a pencil between his thumb and fore-finger when he heard a tapping.

He turned. There was the face of a girl, divided into twenty-four small squares. Her voice was faint and she said: *"Entschuldigen Sie bitte."*

Or it might have been, "Come hither," or "Bedsitter," or something equally absurd. With all hope of a morning's work gone now, Gabor hoisted himself from the bench and with elaborate resentment, opened the door a crack and answered in frankly rude Hungarian. *"Nem szabad."*

Of course, though Louisa had been living in Budapest for three years, she knew no Hungarian, so she smiled over her blue canvas schoolbag, and replied, *"Ich habe ein Zimmer reserviert."*

This time, Gabor answered in German. "That doesn't mean a thing. No one with a brain in his head follows those rules."

Louisa took his fluency as a matter of course, and didn't seem to think him worth an argument. "You'll have to leave."

"I'm staying here," Gabor said. "You don't need a piano. Your father's rich as Croesus and you've got a grand at home."

She turned a little pink then. "I don't see how you know."

"I know everything," said Gabor. In fact, he hadn't been sure. Louisa was dressed in the green pinafore of a schoolgirl and might have been at the Academy on scholarship, but her manner was so unapologetic that she had to have some money. Besides: She was German. In Hungary, every German was a millionaire. He added, "You don't even play piano."

Here, he was on firmer ground, as he knew most of the serious girl pianists at the Academy and had never seen this specimen before. She wasn't a bad specimen at that, straight-backed and slim with a clear complexion and fine, light-brown hair. Her age was hard to pin down. She had a very young girl's seriousness, but there was something knowing in the curl of her frown that had appeared when he'd said he knew everything. He made her a proposition.

"We could share the room," he said.

Louisa shook her head. "I need the whole room."

"Depends," Gabor said, "on proximity." He swung the door wide open and moved back, not too far. "What do you play? Tuba?"

"I sing," said Louisa.

"Well, then, you sing and I'll accompany you. Hand over the score. Don't be shy."

"I'm not shy," said Louisa. "But it's impossible."

Gabor took possession of her Schubert. He gave it a dismissive glance. "This old thing?"

Louisa did not reply. She watched Gabor as he opened the score, and after a moment, asked, "Can you manage it?"

And of course, it was too late for Gabor to say no. The score was, in fact, well beyond his strength, a task for a real pianist. Now he had to slap the music over *Booming Rocket* and plunge right in.

It was worse than difficult. It was impossible. The notes piled on like cord-wood and his right hand had to pump the keys while the left found its way to a sequence of notes against the rhythmic grain, and so complete was his absorption that the voice took him by surprise.

Who rides so late through night and wind?
It is the father with his child.

It wasn't what he had expected, not like her speaking voice at all.

He has the boy in his arms.
He holds him safely, he keeps him warm.
Father—father—

A shiver shot up Gabor's neck. He stopped dead and turned, as Louisa trailed off:

Do you not hear
What the Eorl-King softly promises me?

Gabor asked, "How old are you?"

Caught off-guard, Louisa paused before answering, "Seventeen."

"The hell you are." It felt right to belittle her now. It put things in perspective. "What are you doing in Budapest?"

"It's obvious that I can't work here," Louisa said. She reached for her schoolbag. "I have a lot of work to do. In three months, I tour Europe."

"And you're singing Schubert? No you're not," Gabor said. He pushed the piano bench back, scraping the floor so violently that Louisa flinched. "You're going to sing my music."

"I can't," she said, so taken aback that she lost a grain of composure, and her voice broke. In that break, Gabor heard a note, a trill, so like that other voice, her singing voice, that it renewed his determination.

"You can," he said. Now he turned on her the full force of his charm. His black eyes, below all that thick, black hair, sparkled, and he leveled them on her own, conscious too of how close they stood, breath-distance. "Don't lie. There's nothing you can't do. I've heard you sing."

Louisa said nothing for a moment. She lowered her bag and almost shyly asked, "Do you compose?"

Gabor thrust into her bag the page of *Booming Rocket*.

Louisa said, "It's not up to me."

Gabor only laughed, for in fact, she was correct. It wasn't up to her at all. He let her go. As for Louisa, she stepped out of the practice room into air which must have felt unearthly clear and open, as it wasn't filled with my son. It might not have been until she met her teacher that she realized she had left her Schubert score behind.

The realization hit Louisa so suddenly that she didn't know what to do. Under the clear brown eye of Professor Istvan Lengyel, she searched her bag: a half-filled notebook, her harmony text, and a bag of lemon-drops she'd bought a month before that lay among the lint and paper in a yellow, gummy ball. Then there was something she tried to hide under the notebook.

"What's that there?" Professor Lengyel asked. "It looks as though it was copied by an epileptic."

Louisa had no choice. She had to hand it over.

He let his eye pass across a few measures and he asked, "Is he making love to you?"

Blood rushed to Louisa's face, and she said, "Of course not!"

"That's fortunate," said Professor Lengyel. He set the manuscript aside. "This young man is a Jew."

3

TURNED OUT EVERY SET OF
stockings I had worn between Trieste and Jaffa, but there was no sign of the
telegram. Louisa stood over me, watching with maddening detachment.
"Mutti, I need to make up the bed. They told me I could bring our breakfast
here, so long as I kept clean."

Through the window sunlight streamed in, dappling everything and
making it impossible to sort through the mess I'd dumped on top of our
sheet. I thought I found it, once, twice, but it was some obsolete paperwork in an alphabet I couldn't even recognize. I said, "It couldn't just
disappear."

"You mustn't worry," Louisa said. "You mustn't make trouble for yourself."

"How can I make more trouble than we're in?" I said. How could I make
her understand? Without Bela, we might as well have landed in the Wild
West surrounded by Red Indians.

Louisa laid out our rolls and margarine on a fresh handkerchief, and she
broke my roll and buttered it for me. "Eat something. You'll feel more at
home."

All the while, I wondered if the telegram had slipped out of my stocking
when I disembarked. Such a little piece of paper, why hadn't I put it into my
bag? Why had I wanted it where I could touch it?

Louisa munched on her own bread, careful to gather the crumbs into a napkin. "Leave it in my hands, *Mutti*. I'll just fold up your nice things," she said to me. "Then you can have a little rest."

I said to her, "You want to do something useful, dear? Walk back to port and swim until you see something floating past that looks like a telegram."

At once I regretted the suggestion, because it was easy enough to imagine her rising and walking straight to the Mediterranean to do just that. She is a very serious girl.

*I*T TOOK A DEEP, ARRESTING seriousness to set up housekeeping under our circumstances. She arranged what little we had in a couple of clean crates under our bed, establishing a kind of pantry where she kept our own soap, jam, plates, and cutlery. She even hemmed a blue cloth that could cover yet another crate she called our "breakfast table." I did not know where Louisa procured these things. They were spotless and smelled of sawdust.

"She gets what she wants," a Pole said to me. With the boldness of a street walker, she yanked a jar of jam out of the crate and held it out for inspection. "How do you think she got this, eh? Plum jam. You think we get plum jam? No, they say to us, you can live with a little margarine, you're used to it, but they take one look at the German girl and they stand up straight and give her jam."

Louisa must have known she was the subject of our conversation, but she went on hemming that cloth. I couldn't help but wonder where she'd found the thread and needle. "She's resourceful," I said.

"You've got that right, lady," the woman said, giving me a strange little smirk. "She's a girl who gets just what she wants." The words somehow produced a lump like a plum that lodged in my throat. How was I supposed to talk to these creatures? Why did she keep on standing there, waving the jam? It would have been better if she'd gone and cracked the jar on my head. Maybe it would knock something loose, like my cousin's new address.

Louisa looked up from her sewing, and asked me, *"Mutti,* what does that lady want?"

"Nothing we can give her," I said.

But Louisa asked, "Does she want a little jam? We need to be good neighbors. This is our home now."

I MANAGED TO DISLODGE MYSELF from Louisa's protection long enough to make my way to the Jewish Agency office, where I tried to put in a call to Kibbutz Tilulit. I made my request to a youth in khaki and was met by a level glance and this reply in Yiddish:

"No such place."

I kept my head and addressed the young man behind the metal desk who had given me the information without so much as picking up the phone. "I sent a wire."

"From where? Here?"

"Trieste."

He said, "They sent it back. You said you have a Haifa address?"

"I lost it. But they'll know my cousin's whereabouts at Tilulit."

That boy couldn't have been more than nineteen. He tipped back his chair and lit a cigarette; what he said next was wreathed in smoke. "Look, I fought in the Galilee. I know every settlement, village, and sinkhole in the Galilee. There's no Kibbutz Tilulit."

Without the telegram from Bela, what did I have to throw in his face? I said, "For eighteen years, I wrote him here in Palestine."

"The name of this country is *Eretz Yisrael,*" he said. "Look, do you think you have some kind of special case? You people, you *sabonim,* you come here, you're like children. Place the call yourself."

He thrust the black mouthpiece at me, and of course what came out was Hebrew. In my life, I have learned my mother-tongue, German, some Yiddish, and a few words in Russian. If I can't be addressed in any of those languages, you don't need to address me at all. I shrugged the telephone away. He didn't look surprised.

"Yofi. Nice," he said. "Wonderful. Goodbye."

I persisted. "There must be a record somewhere of a Bela Hesshel."

He glared dead at me and said, "He changed his name. Sure thing. No one would run around Israel with a name like Bela Hesshel."

WHO CHANGES HIS NAME? Someone who commits a crime or has something to hide or wants to be forgotten. My husband, Janos, changed his name when he left his father's house for engineering school in Budapest. Perhaps when he left me, he changed it too. The people in this camp would probably all change their names. The parents of that weasel of a desk clerk probably went through a dozen names since the day he was born. What can he know about my cousin?

I've called him many things: Hesshi, *Bélácska*, *Borzas Medve*, but all the while I knew that he was Bela; he was satisfied with being Bela. No one would want him to be anyone else. He looked the way he was, like a bear picking apart the bark of a tree to see what was inside. It is impossible to think of him without his chin in his hand, and on his face an expression of bewilderment as he asked his impossible questions. His work, scholarly and otherwise, complemented his nature; it had everything to do with asking questions, listening closely, and drawing straightforward conclusions. He was a linguist. He was also a Zionist, which meant, in his own terms, living in Palestine. Therefore, in Palestine he lived. Such was Bela, who was the most earnest person in the world, and with whom I could never be earnest.

How could I help myself? What was this Zion? Throughout our years of correspondence before the war, I would ask him: How could you cripple yourself with a dead language and travel to a land where nothing much had happened in a thousand years?

E MET WHEN I WAS NINE, THE summer after his father drowned in Lake Balaton. In spite of my mother's letters, I think my Aunt Monika assumed we lived on an estate. Things being what they were, the lady and her two children could hardly vacation at the lake again, so every June, for three years, they took the train from Budapest, and it was impossible to ask them to leave Kisbarnahely before September.

Kisbarnahely lay two hours east of Budapest. Summers, it was ringed with fields of shoulder-high sunflowers, but by late August they had withered into shrunken heads. The town was a railroad junction with a main street that extended in a straight line from the tracks for a kilometer before ending abruptly at an empty lot where someone piled manure. My father kept books for the brickworks, and our house was no more than fifty meters from the cooling shed. It was a narrow house, with nothing between us and the train tracks but a blind wall. The house measured fifteen paces end to end. I knew because I measured it again and again from the time I could count.

Now into that house each summer were crammed three carpetbags, two trunks, a lot of leather-bound German novels, and a phonograph, as well as a cigarette case which I'd empty while Aunt Monika slept. They were English Ovals, very good cigarettes. The lady herself was a source of fascination, with her big black eyes and breathless vulnerability. She never talked about her husband, at least not around me. I suspect she found amusement and distraction in my mother's stream of complaints about the mud, the dust, the brutes they had for neighbors, no proper gaslights, no paved streets, and nothing available in the shops but mule-harnesses and boots full of beetle-droppings. But that is life, my mother would say, tragedy if we don't make it farce, isn't that so, Moni?

Aunt Monika would agree. In short, the two of them had a terrific time. They would sing together to the phonograph, and my mother let me make them coffee, which I poured into peach-pink china cups I hadn't realized we'd owned.

Altogether, the children held less interest for me. There was Adele, a girl my own age. She always seemed to be writing letters to her three-dozen best friends, and on the long table beside the bed we had to share, she lined her doll collection shoulder to shoulder, in a row, as though they were about to face a firing squad. They were arranged by hair color, and their dresses were sewn onto their bodies, which I knew because I tried to pry them off. Really, I preferred Bela.

He was eleven. I had been told he could speak German, so I recited a Heine poem I'd learned in school. He replied with a fluency that knocked me backwards. When I prodded him, he told me that German was what his family spoke at home, and in addition, he knew a little French, and, of course, Hebrew.

"Why 'of course'?" I gave him a look. He was still dressed in tweed knickers and a clean white shirt, and there wasn't a muscle in his body. I had never seen such a Jew.

By then, I'd led him to the cellar to show him a mouse-hole. He had a middle-class boy's interest in vermin and actually got on his hands and knees to peer inside. I struck a match so he could see, and of course that scared the mouse away.

"I teach Hebrew," he said as he rose from the mouse-hole. He had gotten mold all over his Budapest clothes, and looked so forlorn that I was moved to offer him one of his mother's cigarettes. He refused with a slightly shocked expression.

The best thing about Bela was that he made me feel daring, and he believed everything I said. He'd never picked an apricot, and I told him the only really sweet fruit was on the crown of the tree, so we climbed on the roof, and he grabbed my ankles as with a swimming head I hung upside-down and reached out to the tree in the courtyard to pull an apricot free. I swear, it was the sweetest fruit I'd ever tasted. Afterwards, he just sat up there, watching me lick the juice from my fingers and shaking his head.

*W*E SPENT A LOT OF TIME WITH my father's brother, Oszkar, a watchmaker who also tinkered with spectacles and music boxes. When Uncle Oszkar worked at his bench, his eyes would turn inward in a bewildered, Bela-like way, and he'd rub his mustache in the wrong direction. Uncle Oszkar was an old bachelor. He never left that shop. He even lived there. The workbench stretched along one wall, the bed along the other, and a tub-sized kitchen was crammed into a corner blackened with twenty years of his cooking. The WC was outside, and so was a little kitchen garden and an arbor strung with grapevines, where he'd serve us supper.

Those were easy hours. Bela and I would sit up on high stools and watch my uncle as he unpacked tiny cogs or lenses from their nests of cotton-wool. Uncle Oszkar took to Bela in a way that made me jealous. One afternoon, Bela went out back to the kitchen garden where Uncle Oszkar was weeding, and the door closed before I could follow. I sulked, fiddling with the tension on a music box until the melody curdled. Before long, they both appeared with their arms full of under-ripe tomatoes. Uncle Oszkar said, "Your cousin wants to be a farmer."

Bela shook his head. "I didn't say a farmer. I said Pioneer."

"Pioneer. Farmer. No matter what, talk sense into him, Norika. He's got a good head on his shoulders. Why would he want to be a peasant?"

"Because peasants know how to pick apricots," I said.

"Because," Bela said, "Dori and I are going to Palestine."

"Who's Dori?" I asked.

"Dori Csengery. She's going to be a doctor. I call her Mouse."

"Why?" I asked Bela. "Is she scared of cats?"

Bela laughed and said, "She isn't scared of much."

By then, we were all peeling tomatoes and chopping peppers for *lekvar,* and I had a thousand questions about Dori but just kept chopping harder and looking grim until Uncle Oszkar told me to go out and lay the table.

We ate our *lekvar* under the grape arbor as Bela talked about his father's friends who'd moved to Palestine three years before and were working alongside Arabs on plantations until they could afford to buy land of their own.

"There's a song," Bela said.

"Well, sing it," said Uncle Oszkar.

"I've got an awful voice," said Bela, and he was right, but he sang anyway. It was the first time I'd ever heard Hebrew. He translated: *We've come to build the land and be built by it.* "It goes with a dance," he said.

I imagined Bela picking apricots in the middle of the desert with some lady-doctor giving him instructions. He'd never manage to pick them on his own.

*W*HEN BELA WASN'T IN KISbarnahely, I had no friends. The girls in school played games they seemed to have learned on days I wasn't there, and I suppose that if I'd asked, they would have taught them to me. But patience has never been my strong point, and it was easier to make up my own games and play them by myself. Sometimes, I gathered pebbles and turned a paving stone into a topographical map. I would compose national anthems for these imaginary countries and send them through the air to Bela in Budapest.

The only one who would give me the time of day was my uncle's assistant, Laszlo, a boy ten years older than myself with broad shoulders and thick golden hair and a sly way of looking up from the workbench that made me want to bite him. One afternoon, my mother had sent me to town to pick up some lemons. As sullen as ever, I set off with the coins in my pocket and the little net bag hanging from my arm. It was April. Where was

I supposed to find a lemon? She always wanted things she remembered buying as a girl in Pest.

Given my state of mind, I was grateful when I heard a bell, turned around, and saw Laszlo on his bicycle. He was a man by then, but he still looked like an overgrown boy, waving and grinning and swinging himself over the bicycle frame. "Nora, don't you even say hello? I passed you by five times."

He made me wonder how I could have looked so sour. I said, "Maybe you should make me a pair of glasses."

"Try this," Laszlo said, and he reached into the pouch slung over his shoulder and drew out something wrapped in cotton-wool. It was an octagon of cut glass set in wood, and as I leaned in to see, he pressed it to my eye, and my mouth turned into a round, round O. He said, "It's called a prism."

I asked, "What makes it do that?"

"Light is actually a lot of different colors," Laszlo said. "We got a model in from Switzerland, but this one your uncle cut himself. And look."

He took it from me and drew it some distance from ourselves. Against the dry yellow wall, it threw a spray of rainbows.

We sorted through the lenses, and he showed me how one flattened images, another worked with a twin to turn them upside down, and on a third they seemed to float to the surface like oil on water. He used a fourth lens to light a cigarette. I asked for a puff, and he frowned and said, "You must be nuts."

"I smoke all the time," I said.

He said, "Don't show off."

"It's true. I do."

"You're just a kid. Who'd sell them to you?"

Boldly, I said, "The gypsies."

"You are nuts," he said again, and of course he didn't believe me. "Anyway, girls shouldn't smoke."

After he rode away, I saved his cigarette butt and carried it in my pocket, wondering if I ought to smoke it all at once, save it for later, or not smoke it at all. By the time I'd made up my mind, it had fallen apart, and I had nothing to show for the encounter but a little loose tobacco.

BELA WASN'T AFRAID OF GYPsies. One summer, I took him to their encampment just past the brickyard, and he walked right up to a woman hanging wash, picked up her basket, and followed her down the clothesline. She gave him a cup of something, and he drank it without hesitation. Me, she ignored. Bela also wasn't afraid of the dark. We would spend the hottest part of the day in the cellar of our house, where we would dig and find strange coins or pins or bits of teacups. Bela would wrap what we found in a handkerchief and clean it in the kitchen sink, and months later he wrote and told me that the coin was two hundred years old.

I showed him the Jewish cemetery. He asked, "Is your family buried here?"

"I don't know," I said. "I've never been inside. There's a dog and I don't think it's chained."

Without hesitation, Bela rang for the porter and the old man actually appeared, a squat, wry, clearly Christian gentleman who asked us what our business was and said to Bela, "If you know where her grandfather's stone is, get her to clear off that ivy. What was that name? Csongradi? Oszkar's niece? Fourth row, to the far right. Grandmother's there too. Nice stone."

So we passed his shack where the dog was held by the collar so hard that the bones in his neck strained through the skin. Beyond it, maybe three or four dozen graves were lined along a knoll. Bela stopped before each one, cleared off a little underbrush, and read the Hebrew.

"What a funny alphabet," I said to him. "It looks like something you'd make out of sticks. You can't really read it, can you?"

But he could. He found the two stones, just where the man said they would be, and in fact my grandmother's was a handsome stone, red marble and an arc of Hebrew broken by a bird with outstretched wings.

"Csongradi Naomi," Bela translated. "Died at peace, surrounded by her sons."

"I didn't even know I had a grandmother," I said.

"But aren't you named after her?"

"Maybe," I said.

"What's your Hebrew name?"

"Why would I even want a Hebrew name?" I offered Bela a cigarette, pretty sure he'd still refuse, which was a good thing because I only had one left. It was damp among all those stones, and it took a while to light my match. Bela watched me with the edge of wonder which always drove me to greater acts of boldness. Was this a sacred place? I blew the smoke out of my nose and said, "So you've got a Hebrew name, I take it."

"Boaz," Bela said. "But I don't like it. Sounds like a giant in a children's book."

"*Borzas Medve,*" I said. Shaggy bear.

He blushed, and I felt light-headed, thinking of all the languages in the world, the bird in flight, wild possibilities. Back then, it would have thrilled me to think that I would travel through a dozen different countries and sleep on train platforms and in ditches and share barracks with people who spoke languages that even Bela never knew.

"*Borzas,*" I said to my cousin, in the presence of my grandmother Naomi's stone, "what was the dance that went with that Pioneer song?"

The afternoon was waning and in the dark green light of the Jewish cemetery, on a knoll overlooking the town hall, Bela leaned forward and grabbed hold of my forearms, saying: "Just put a foot behind, a foot forward."

"Foot behind what?" I asked, but then he started pulling me along, at first just enough to make me stumble. Then he whipped on one heel like a top and my arms stretched tight, all my breath rushing out until there was nothing to me but a little thing going around and around, feet leaving the grass altogether. Bela sang something badly, but I couldn't hear. It all sounded like wind as I shouted, "Let me go! Let me go!" and he abruptly fell and took me with him.

Dizzy still, heart beating fast, I stared up through the trees for a while. The sky was Prussian blue, the way it is just as the sun sets. I knew I was lying on top of a lot of dead people, and I didn't care. Bela lay maybe arm's length away, and when I turned my head a little, there was his hand almost touching my face. I reached out, turned up the palm, and said to him, "You know, I can tell fortunes."

"What do you see?" Bela asked, still out of breath.

That palm was indistinct. Where was the life-line, and where was the heart-line? A grass stain ran along the base, and I touched it and said, "You will have a great fall."

*H*IS FEARS WERE LESS PREDICTable. There were trains. At midnight, I knew the Szeged express would be passing by, so I woke Bela up and made him join me outside. We both wore our nightshirts and stood with our backs to the wall, and as the foundation began to vibrate, I felt the thrill rise from the bones of my hips. I turned to Bela and saw he'd gone all pale.

I said to him. "It doesn't go off the tracks."

Yet once, the headlamp of the train seemed to swing so close that I was abruptly blinded, and my hand reached sideways for Bela's and hit nothing at all. I found him sitting on the stoop of our front door, breathing hard. His head was turned and I couldn't see his eyes.

Bela was also afraid of bridges. I didn't find out until his last summer in Kisbarnahely, the day before he was due to leave for Budapest, when, after three years, he finally gave in to my pleading and joined me to see the sun-flowers.

"They're the only beautiful thing in this town," I said to him.

Bela smiled, but he didn't tell me I was beautiful. Even at twelve, I had the face I wear today, flattened and squinting. My black hair was so thin, it puffed in the slightest breeze. Bela followed me over hard, yellow mud, beyond the boundaries of Kisbarnahely. Then he stopped walking.

The plank bridge across the ravine was perhaps ten paces long. He looked at me and said, "Is there any other way around?"

"No," I said. "What's wrong with you?" I wasn't about to turn back. We'd already walked three kilometers and the flowers were at their peak.

He told me that he had always been that way about bridges, big and small. Even the mighty constructions across the Duna in Budapest, he had to cross with his head down. He couldn't explain it. Perhaps it was because people jumped off bridges. He asked, "Do you believe in ghosts?"

He asked it the way he'd asked if someone had taught me to pick an apri-cot, with the same earnestness. I said, "I'm not a baby."

"My father fell out of a sailboat. That's how he drowned. And some-times, when I'm on a bridge, even if it's not over water, I see his ghost. And others."

I didn't say anything for a moment. Then I caught his arm, and before he could stop me, I'd pulled him onto the bridge which lurched with our weight, and as we scrambled to the far end I could feel his fear pass through his arm and into me. When we reached the other side, I realized what I had done, and I was ashamed. When I let go of his arm and dared to turn to him, Bela looked at me as though I were a stranger.

I wanted to apologize, but instead, I spoke German: *"Gehen wir."*

He didn't answer. We walked on, and eventually, of course, he forgave me for pulling him across that bridge. We reached the sunflowers. They were high, yellow and lovely, and I took us back by a route that circled the ravine, though it meant adding two more kilometers to the walk. Our talk was easy as ever; Bela taught me the German word for sunflower (*Sonnen-blume*) and how to say "My legs are sore" (*Meine Beine tun weh*). Still, once in a while, I caught him giving me that look: disbelief, betrayal.

I didn't like knowing Bela Hesshel saw ghosts. A girl from the provinces collects her share of superstitions, but Bela was a Budapesti. It had the feel of a confession. Later, I found out he hadn't told Dori Csengery, and that gave me satisfaction. He never did reveal to me what he meant by "others."

FTER BELA BEGAN TO STUDY
through the summers, his family stopped coming to Kisbarnahely. I wrote
him once a week. It helped me practice German and improved my penman-
ship until it was as exact and blotless as his own. He lived on Dob Street.
One day I'd know that big apartment well. I would spend a winter in its parlor, reading all of Bela's books on a green sofa, with a lumpy throw across
my shoulders and a cheek pressed against a pillow embroidered with straw-
berries.

Yet all of that was still to be imagined. Abandoned, I wrote in broken
German: *Wie geht's?* I don't know how many pages I filled and rejected
before I would consider the letter ready, and I saved the versions I'd discarded in one of my mother's sturdy Budapest shoe-boxes and kept it under
my bed. By the time I turned fourteen, the letters Bela saw were written in a
dry, economical style that left little room for error.

Bela's German was a different story, headlong and overflowing. Later, I'd
know the desk where he had written his letters, a scarred warhorse, blackened
with varnish. I could well imagine him hunched in the chair with one hand
deep in his hair and a little ink on the joint of his right thumb. When he got
one of my letters, he always wrote back the same day.

Bela was a heroic writer of letters. At the same time that he wrote me, he
corresponded with Zionists in Palestine, Berlin, and Minsk. When he wasn't

writing letters, he was attending secondary school at the Budapest seminary, frequenting lectures or concerts where he could do a little fund-raising for his youth group, and trying to teach himself Arabic.

He took on the last task with nothing but a dictionary, a grammar, and a newspaper one of his father's friends sent him from Jaffa. It was lonesome work. Once, walking along the promenade by the Duna River, he saw two Arab gentlemen well-settled on a bench, smoking cigars, and a few sentences drifted by that made him jump out of his skin. He threw himself upon them and blurted out a salutation: *"Taeshaerrafna!"*

They stared.

He tried: *"Sabah ael-kher."*

This made more of an impression. The stouter of the two produced a line of German. "Sir, you are addressing us in Arabic?"

Bela turned purple and tried to speak again, but the man raised his hand for silence.

"It is a beautiful language, young man, and it is very admirable that you approach it with such zeal, but I am afraid I do not understand a word you say. Do you plan to go into the foreign service?"

Startled, Bela said, "No, sir."

"Well, in any event, learn English. It's a tougher bird than Arabic and will stand more abuse. Good day."

After that encounter, Bela redoubled his efforts and haunted the docks in search of conversation partners. When I read his letters, I could see him, wandering around Budapest with all those dictionaries, listening hard for languages he didn't know. His clothes, though clean, were never pressed, and when the weather turned warm he would take off his coat and leave it on the chair of a café or on the hook by someone's door, or folded behind a throw-pillow. Hats were worse. He had too much hair to keep a hat. Once he left something behind, he never bothered to find it again, and you were forced to run after him or to simply accept it as a gift.

His work at the seminary involved the commonalities between the verbs of Middle Eastern languages and Hungarian. In his letters, he would keep me abreast of the latest trends in scholarship. I skipped those parts. What I read instead, over and over, were simply the accounts of his days. First, a breakfast, over which he would make corrections on a translation while sister Adele cleared his plate out from under him and Aunt Moni boiled fresh coffee. Then, a last-minute dash for the trolley where, still refining, he would turn the translation into something like prose just in time to hand to a professor, who by the way invited him to dinner as there would be a guest from Palestine, and so Bela must arrange for that guest to speak at his Zionist club before he left town: a flurry of visits to households, more coffee and cakes—I imagine all the cigarettes and light one of my own—more arrangements and a room confirmed and then the man himself: the phlegmatic owner of an orange plantation, a Hungarian-Ukrainian named Mr. Manuel Lorenz who was, in fact, anti-Zionist.

So much the better, Bela wrote, though by now his squarish handwriting had little points, like waves. They never got to meet anti-Zionists who actually lived in Palestine. Lorenz was told they were a walking club with an interest in botany. Bela asked him about fertilizers and backed off when it was clear he knew nothing about them. Then Bela turned the conversation towards climate and steered a friend away from the obviously sensitive point of labor relations. Muttering answers under a dirty-white mustache, Lorenz made it clear that Palestine was a dead-poor country for hiking, and they would all catch malaria. Later, he took Bela aside and said, "My boy, I hear you know some Arabic. Come by tonight at ten. I have something to show you."

After the meeting, over more cake and coffee in a friend's kitchen, Bela and his comrades speculated. Had they misjudged the gentleman? He had been in Palestine for so long that something of the land must have rubbed into him and made him a new man.

Well, with some trepidation, at ten precisely, Bela went to call on Manuel Lorenz. Lorenz was staying at a spinster sister's in a well-appointed flat on Josef Street. He appeared in his dressing gown and slippers, as though he hadn't been expecting company. Bela was ill at ease, and kept his coat on, which wasn't in his nature.

Lorenz settled into the most comfortable chair in the room, offered Bela a cigar, and lit his own before rather abruptly beginning.

"Young man, you realize, don't you, that Hebrew is on its way to becoming the lingua franca of the *Yishuv*. What's your opinion on the matter?"

The question took Bela by surprise, and he answered it honestly. "It's the language native to the land."

"You're planning on settling Palestine, of course," said Lorenz. "I've seen enough of these Pioneers. They all look like you. They're not bad workers if they live through the first few years, but you can't pay them the same as blacks, and in the end it just makes trouble. Take a look at this." He passed Bela what looked like a handwritten broadside. "You know the language?"

"Arabic," Bela said, but at close range it didn't look like Arabic at all, at least not the Arabic he'd read in grammars, dictionaries, and newspapers. In fact, it didn't look like anything he'd seen before.

"Who knows?" Lorenz said. "I'll tell you the truth. None of the Arabs I know can make out more than half of it."

Bela beetled his forehead and spoke softly. "The script is beautiful."

"What they did understand was seditious." Lorenz drew on his cigar. It looked queer and big in his sunken, soulless face. "Something about a strike. Now there had been some trouble, but I know the ringleaders can't even write their names, let alone this."

Bela had less than half an ear for Lorenz as he struggled through the text. *Will we not walk out together like Men?*

"You Pioneers, you think it's Zion," Lorenz said. "But it's no different from any other backward hole. You have your land, and on that land you have your brute labor, and they're not poets. They're brutes."

Bela read on. *What are these orange groves? Imported weeds! We will not fertilize them with our Blood. We will not Slave for another man's Profit!*

"Not that I'm worried about a strike. The blacks can no more organize than jackals. In the end, it's all about the tribe, the clan. If someone gives you trouble, send him back to his village. But I need a smart boy who understands Arabic."

"Can't Arabs?" Bela asked him.

Lorenz looked exasperated and said, "Look, son, you know how to ride a horse, don't you? You can handle a rifle."

"Tell me," said Bela, "why did you emigrate to Palestine?"

The question couldn't help but seem uncharitable. Lorenz didn't answer at once. He sat back with the cigar burning down between his fingers. Then he said, "You want to know why I emigrated? Because it was impossible to live in the Ukraine. Impossible."

"But you didn't go to Hungary. You didn't go to America. You went to *Eretz Yisrael,*" Bela said. "What good is living in Zion if you act as though you were living anywhere else?"

Lorenz stubbed out his cigar and decided there was no further purpose in the conversation. "When you get there," he said to Bela, "come see me. We may find we have more to say to each other."

As Bela rose, he said, "You know, you can't send him back to his village."

"Who?"

"The Jew," said Bela. "The one who wrote what you gave to me. The vocabulary lapses into Hebrew more than once."

After that, Bela was shown the door. He took the broadside, though he left his hat behind. He spent the whole of that night in translation: *If we demand Wage Parity between Pioneer and Peasant and make common Cause against the Exploiters and Imperialists we can create here in Palestine a Worker's Paradise. What can stand in our Way?*

The grammar was erratic, and entangled in the Arabic and Hebrew were a few stray words of Russian. As for the script, it was unpracticed but visually stunning, like stems, roots, wings, and bursts of water. The whole of the page he copied time and time again, and he sent one to Dori Csengery, who by that time was in medical school in Szeged. She told him that it smacked of Internationalist Infantile Romanticism. She must have been a pretty serious girl. To me it looked more like an artist's rendering of birds stripping an orange grove.

That night, Bela said in closing, *I missed my sleep. I need my nine hours or I am impossible, so off I go to make up for lost time. Adele and my mother send their love. Regards as ever to your mother, father, and wonderful uncle. Affectionately, Bela.*

By the time I finished Bela's letter, a second cigarette was worn down to a nub. In the solitude of my room, I lulled back on my bed in my half-unbuttoned nightgown, and the letter fell from my hands as I stared at the ceiling, purely happy. Drawing the cigarette to my lips for a final drag, heedless that my mother would smell smoke, I'd think: How long before I write him back? A day? Two days? The waiting was a luxury, and I let it gather just long enough for my cigarette to burn my fingers. Then I pulled out my German dictionary:

Cousin, I think you sleep too much. I would prefer to be impossible. Just now, it's past two, and I have been planning our future. You will become a producer of orange marmalade and I will bottle it in Barnahely. Maybe then you would visit as you promised. I put that page in the shoe-box, started again: *Cousin, sleep or no sleep, you are impossible.* But that wouldn't do either, because somewhere along the line I wasn't sure what I meant by the word impossible.

WHO COULD I DEPEND ON IN life? You can't get things back, not the things that matter. Laszlo got married. She was a girl he had been courting for a year, and the wedding took place just after the Great War was declared, a week before he was called up for the army. We were invited to the church ceremony but not the reception, and my mother was so insulted that we didn't go at all. It couldn't have mattered less. I sat in my room with my chin on the windowsill, figuring my life was over.

At midnight, there was a rattling at the gate, and to general astonishment, there was Uncle Oszkar, almost too drunk to stand, holding a lumpy napkin. "Hello!" he shouted. "Gyorgy, open up!" My father shuffled out in his spectacles, nightshirt, and slippers, and Uncle Oszkar clapped him on the shoulder. "I brought some cake for Norika."

Of course, by then, I was in the front yard too, half-hidden by the flowering apricot tree, dazzled by the sight of Uncle Oszkar so entirely out of context, in a snug suit and tie. My father hesitantly opened the front door, and Oszkar stumbled inside and dumped himself on the velvet couch. He unwrapped the wedding cake, and we all had some.

I remember that night well because it was so different from every other night in that house. Uncle Oszkar made my father pull out playing cards. They were Hungarian-style cards, the fine type you don't see nowadays: the suits of bright, round bells, the spade-like leaves, the hearts and acorns. Then there are the face-cards of the seasons: Spring dipping her hand into a bouquet, Fall sipping from a wine-vat, Summer lazy, though he holds a scythe, craven Winter.

We played a few hands, and my father asked Uncle Oszkar if he still told fortunes. He shook his head.

"I've lost the touch," he said. "But your daughter could try. Laszlo tells me she spends her free time with the gypsies."

I shot my uncle a look, feeling some superficial anger, though I'll admit the thought of Laszlo actually mentioning my name made my blood sing. My mother said, "Nora runs wild. I've given up where that girl's concerned." She poured my uncle more tea, and my father, as oblivious as ever, set his cards down on the table so that everyone could see them. He would lose.

"I can read palms," I said.

I was used to saying things I didn't mean; my parents never noticed. But that night, Uncle Oszkar was there, looking at me with both eyes. There was a moment of rich silence, as my mother took a sip of tepid tea and was about to change the subject. But then my uncle presented me with his palm.

I held it with both hands as though it were an enormous slice of bread and lard. It was square, white, and unevenly callused. More than the palm itself, I was aware of him waiting and listening.

"So tell me my fortune, Norika. Will my life be a long one? Will I find a buried treasure? Will I miss my little Laszlo? Will he visit me, now that he's a grown man with a wife?"

My voice seemed to come from a distance. "I don't know. I can't read palms, really."

"Then why did you say you could?" Uncle Oszkar asked. "I think you can, but you don't like what you see. It takes a hard heart to read fortunes. My heart's too soft." His voice broke then; it startled me, as though a plate had broken. "Nora," he said, "I want to read your cards."

"We're playing," said my father.

"Playing? You've already lost. Why waste our time? I need to think about somebody else's troubles tonight," Uncle Oszkar said, and with a few clumsy, disruptive gestures, he managed to gather the cards from my parents, shuffle them, and knock them straight against the table. He said to me: "Cut the deck."

Shamed, I would have sooner gone to bed. I took a long time figuring out where to cut until I was all turnip-faced like my father. Then I just did it without thinking. Uncle Oszkar turned the topmost card over. It was the card of Winter. The suit was acorn: Four bright nuts floated around the figure and her reversed reflection. She was a crone who walked through a pale blue landscape studded with broken trees. One hand reached across a shoulder to pull the strings of her shawl a little closer. The other held a walking stick.

I didn't want to ask him what it meant. Sobering a little, he said, "I can't read cards, really, Nora."

"Yes, you can," I said.

"Well, I can then. And I promise you a long life." Then he said something more surprising. "But not here."

"Of course not here," I said, trying to sound offhand, though my heart was beating like mad.

He shook his head. "I see a child, a grandchild, in another country."

Now this was past imagining. It was as though the walls melted away and outside flowed the world in all directions. I couldn't pretend not to care, and I spoke with urgency. "What country? Can you tell me?"

"I can't tell you," Uncle Oszkar said. And how could he, when that country was not yet invented?

NEVER IN MY LIFE DID I IMAGINE I would be living in Israel. Yet Bela's kibbutz, I imagined. How couldn't I imagine it? For years, I sent my letters to Kibbutz Tilulit and got my cousin's letters in return. So steady was our correspondence that I could trace the progress of the kibbutz, month by month: the first harvest, the purchase of another hundred dunam from the Arab village of Taell al-Taji, Gezer born, the clinic open, and so on. Or rather, I could have traced it if I hadn't lost his letters back in Budapest.

During the winter when Louisa lived with us on Prater Street, she would spend most of the day on the old sofa with the bedding tucked around her. She wasn't well. When I'd return from work, I'd fix her a pan of warm milk with a little sugar in it and watch her eyes fog over the brim. While I was gone, what did she do? She went through my papers. Once, she found my letters from Bela, and when I came home she thrust them forward like an accusation:

"*Mutti!* You're going to leave me!"

I was still half-out of my coat and didn't know what to make of this wobbling girl with my bedding draped around her shoulders and both hands stuffed with letters. My first impulse, frankly, was to give her a smack. But this I could not do. She was my daughter-in-law. I took a low breath, walked her to the couch, and with as much gentleness as I could manage, said,

"These are very old letters. I haven't heard from him in years. Besides, leaving now is out of the question."

She shook her head and drew my attention to the photograph he'd sent in '25: Dori, Nathan, and Bela in front of the chicken coop. Their ease, their solidity, the way the whole scene swam in light yet was defined down to the tender specificity of Nathan's bootlaces and the ribbon in Dori's hair, all of this was not lost on Louisa. "You could be there now," she said. "I wouldn't be such a burden to you."

That was the sort of thing I couldn't answer. During those months on Prater Street, I gained a talent for knowing when I didn't need to speak. Louisa said all sorts of things when she was ill. She meant some of them. Others simply fell from her mouth like the frogs or the jewels of the princesses in fairy tales. She would ask questions and answer them herself. She would say something and take it back. I learned to let her be.

"WHY," RABBI SHMUEL NEEDLEMAN asked Louisa, "did you follow your mother-in-law to Israel?"

Louisa answered, "Because I love her."

Shmuel gave her a long look before asking, "Do you take anything in your tea?"

Louisa hesitated. "Do you have cream?"

"We have cream," the rabbi said. "We have lemon, we have honey, we even have white sugar. We are completely civilized." He smiled enough to soften the last remark, and walked off to the staff canteen, where he spent too long trying to find two clean cups and compensated with a plate of cookies filled with jam.

Louisa picked up a cookie and put it down again in a manner that could have been read as arrogant had her hand not been shaking. The little barracks office where they met was unheated, and a broken window had been repaired with masking tape that rattled. She sunk deep into her sweater and pulled towards her the milky cup of tea. The rabbi was surprised to see she wasn't even pretty. She looked like a washed-out bit of nothing.

The young Israeli who'd referred her had made much of her resilience. She'd had some trouble with the Poles in the camp. There was one lady who'd thrown her in the mud outside the shower, shouting some rubbish about how she'd been a guard at a women's barrack at Treblinka. Louisa had stepped out from that mud-puddle and taken her place at the end of the line for her shower with a straight back and high head, the young man had said, like an angel. She made that mud look like gold.

All of this high drama had led the rabbi to expect a beauty. *The Book of Ruth* was foremost in his mind; how could it not be? Here she was, the daughter of a cursed nation, far from home, clinging to her mother-in-law and taking on her people and her God. But this Ruth was more a Leah, a defeated girl with weak eyes and a forgettable face.

"Frau Gratz," he said, "why do you want to be a Jew?"

Louisa said, "It's because of my mother."

"Your mother? She was a Jew?"

"My husband's mother."

The rabbi suppressed a sigh. "You must say things right out. Your parents, I take it, are not Jews. And your husband?"

"My husband," said Louisa, "is dead."

Shmuel poured himself some more tea and ate a cookie he didn't want, all the while knowing that he was making himself look more ponderous than he wanted to be. "Which brings us," he said, "back to the question at hand. Given what you know, given the past ten years on your continent, why on earth would you want to be a Jew?"

Again, Louisa said, "It's because of my mother—mother-in-law."

"What about her, then? When you married her son, did she want you to convert?"

"No," Louisa said. The question clearly left her puzzled.

"She wants you to convert now?"

"I can't be separated from her."

There was a note in this girl's voice that moved Shmuel, but moved him like a piece of furniture, by force, in a manner he didn't trust. He said to Louisa, "Your loyalty is commendable. It's a good deed, a blessed thing, what you've done. But it's not a reason."

Louisa took this in without a word. She didn't look surprised and didn't argue. The cup of tea lay centered on her knees, and above it her symmetrical face hovered, framed by lank hair.

"There is only one reason to be a Jew," said Shmuel. "Because you are born a Jew. If you have felt yourself to be one, acted and lived as one, then you must convert. Otherwise, you are commendable, but your application will be rejected."

Softly, Louisa spoke at last. "How can I know a thing like that?"

"A good question," said Shmuel. He felt relieved to be able to give frank advice. "Two ways. First, study our history and our laws. Learn *kashrut*, learn about family purity, learn about the Sabbath. If you're accepted, you will keep those laws for the rest of your days. Second, review your own life. You've been drawn to Jews. You married one. You followed one to *Eretz Yisrael.*"

Throughout this speech, Louisa stared down into her teacup as though she expected something to float to the top. After he had finished, she asked, "What happens after?"

"What do you mean, after?"

"After I learn the laws and review my life," she said.

"You're called before a council of Rabbis, the *Bet Din,*" said Shmuel. "They examine you. And if you're accepted, you're immersed in the ritual bath."

"And I stay here?"

"Do you want Israeli citizenship, or do you want to be a Jew? Do you know," Shmuel said, "the *Bet Din* has received a record number of applications since the state was established last year? They've rejected half."

That made her sit up. So she thought it would be easy? Or was there some-thing else in that abrupt attention, a note of panic? "Would they deport me?"

"You would go home," said Shmuel. "To Germany. That still is your home. This is our home. Two years ago, we didn't have a home. Would you have wanted to be a Jew if you had nowhere to go, Frau Gratz?"

Louisa didn't answer, but she stared into that teacup which seemed to have swelled between her hands into enormity. That pale, still tea must have been cold by then. Shmuel resisted the impulse to warm it with a little from the pot.

*L*OUISA AND I HAVE CERTAIN things in common. We were both only children who led isolated lives. Her father, like mine, pored over columns of numbers, but, unlike mine, he had means, and cause to travel. He worked for German Railways and had been sent to Hungary to make a study of our transportation system and to coordinate trade routes for shipments of bauxite between eastern Hungary and the Reich.

When Louisa's family moved to Budapest, she was just thirteen, a sensi-tive girl. Her father wondered if she ought to be pulled from secondary school in the middle of the winter term, and it took her mother to point out that it was not wise to refuse government posts these days. Furthermore, she'd looked into the matter and found that Budapest had a decent conserva-tory. In fact, the city seemed like the ideal place for their girl to, as she put it, "bloom and grow."

"Bloom? Budapest's no place for a girl like our Lu," her father said. "Gypsy music. That's all they've got there."

"You're wrong. She'll meet some very cosmopolitan people," Frau Bauer said, "and she won't be taken for granted."

She didn't say this in front of Louisa, who would have taken it the wrong way. It wasn't that she doubted her daughter had talent. It was only realistic;

Berlin was full of talented girls, and Budapest, when all was said and done, remained comparatively provincial.

Louisa's voice first called attention when she joined a children's choir, and by her tenth birthday, she was performing solos in a fluted bandstand in the public park surrounded by fourteen gifted but inferior girls. Her governess, though hardly tone-deaf, proved inadequate. So did the director of the choir.

They tried several teachers before settling on the most reluctant, a Madame Twersky, Russian and barrel-bellied and aristocratic. After the lessons, Madame Twersky would take coffee and brandy with Louisa's mother. She confided that Louisa would never sing opera. "Her voice," she said, "is too intimate. She's meant for *Lieder*. It is the sort of voice that makes you hear your own heart beating." Yet in that flattery was a note of condescension; Madame Twersky herself once sang opera and at points released a mezzo-soprano like a hurricane.

After Madame Twersky there was a dull mother hen who insisted on teaching Louisa with four other girls, and after the dull mother hen was a dreadful patriot who told the twelve-year-old Louisa that singing in public would make her infertile. Really, they couldn't find a proper teacher for Louisa anywhere, until they came to Budapest and happened upon Istvan Lengyel.

Lengyel taught at the Music Academy, but he was at liberty to take as few pupils as he chose. His heroic chin and brow made him look like an actor, and in fact, like Madame Twersky, he had once appeared in operas in Budapest and Vienna, though generally in minor roles. "Who has time," he said to Louisa's mother, "to be second rate?" Later, he moved on to composition, and finally to music criticism, and by the late thirties he had found his niche at the Academy, where he taught a little bit of everything, primarily voice.

After listening to Louisa sing, he addressed her in flawless German. "Do you have a hobby?"

Louisa thought she ought to say something, so she replied, "I press flowers."

"Let them wilt and die," said Lengyel. "From now on, you have one hobby, and that is your body. Your voice lives there. It doesn't come down from heaven. It rises from your lungs. I'm glad you are still slim."

"Slim?"

"Ah, I like the way you echo back the intonation. Your ear is not half-bad. And if we build your muscle-tone below the breast, we'll force out something worth hearing. Just now, you might as well be made of match-sticks."

Lengyel's hands came up behind Louisa and abruptly cupped her rib cage. She took her breath in sharply, staring forward at her mother, who sat watching this performance without a word. Lengyel addressed Louisa's mother. "You have no idea how many hysterical Belladonnas tell perfectly sound young girls to get fat because they themselves got fat, and you have no idea how many perfectly sound young girls believe them."

All the while, his hands sexlessly kneaded Louisa's ribs and then moved back to her spine. He pushed both thumbs up at the base.

"Uff," said Louisa.

"You felt that?" Lengyel asked her. "Good. Your body is more than the seat of your soul, my young friend. Madame," he said to the mother, "does your daughter attend church?"

"We have not yet found a suitable church in Budapest," she said.

"Then she will walk with me on Sunday mornings," said Lengyel, and in that manner, he admitted her not only as a pupil but as a part of his inner cir-cle, a group of no more than five intimates who joined him for long hikes around the Buda hills. Summer and winter, they would meet early at Lengyel's house near the castle and spend a full day either on the tramp or sitting in the frosty shade with volumes of Goethe.

The language spoken on those walks was German. Lengyel was ruthless about pronunciation, correcting even Louisa, and in the middle of a chapter of *The Sorrows of Young Werther,* he would make her stop short and repeat over and over the most trivial line about the color of the hero's hose.

He would clasp the sides of the book still in her hands as though it were a rib cage, and say, "Those hose are presented in the purest German. If you don't keep them clean, I'll ram them down your throat."

How could his pupils help but love him? They were a mixed multitude, Louisa, another German girl, Hungarians, Austrians, and even a Spaniard. Each he worked with alone, only occasionally scheduling all of them at once and springing on them an ensemble piece in a language none of them knew, like Russian. In spite of his preference for German Romantics, he threw his net wide. Only Louisa was given a strict diet of Schubert.

At first, she took it as a rebuke. Madame Twersky was right. She was a parlor singer. But then Lengyel said to Louisa, "Do you know what your voice is?"

Louisa admitted that she did not know.

"It isn't sound," he said. "It's light. You are a clear vessel, and *Lied* is a light in you. It generates through your lungs as though they are a set of fuses, and it sparkles through your throat. Your voice," he said, "is infinite and formless. It will take the shape of any music, take it so completely that no one will know where your voice ends and the music begins. Keep two fingers on your mouth, Louisa. Like this."

Then he took Louisa's middle and index finger and placed them on her mouth.

"Sing *lu lu lu,*" said Lengyel.

Louisa sang, and she felt, on the tips of her fingers, the spire of the *L* and the curve of the *U,* and it was as though she were made of thin, blown glass, and *lu* after *lu* generated in its heart. Arrogance kindled then, awareness of what lay within her.

If she could just sing *lu lu lu* all day, she would have been happy. Such was not the case. She hated the German girls' school that sat between the Lutheran Church and Castle Hill. She arrived there mid-year and none of her classmates included her in their intrigues. Sometimes their green jumpers seemed like a wall and sometimes like a literal forest where she would lose herself. She hated Budapest where everything was covered with a film of soot. Sometimes, as her father's driver took her from Rose Hill to the Music Academy, she would press her finger to the window and wonder that even ten minutes on the road could make the glass so filthy.

Three years after she arrived in Budapest, she had settled into a persistent homesickness that had nothing to do with Germany. Even in Lengyel's circle, she felt distinct, holding herself apart even during those walks in the hills, wandering ahead with those two fingers on her lips and her eyes full and distant.

*S*UCH WAS LOUISA'S CONDITION the day she met my son and found herself before her teacher without her Schubert. When the lesson ended, she rushed straight home and wandered around the house, trying this or that measure of *The Eorl-King* to see if she could recover it from memory.

Over dinner, she asked her mother, "Are there Hungarian composers?"

"I believe so," her mother replied. "Some people consider Liszt a Hungarian, after all."

"I mean living composers," Louisa said. "Young men."

"I'm sure I don't know," her mother said. Louisa barely ate, and afterwards found her way to the practice room, where she played a few chords on the piano and sang out fifths in a voice that throbbed and carried. After a while, the servant, Eva, brought her a cup of tea.

Eva was five years older than Louisa, and she worshipped her. She approached the piano as though it were the altar of a church, and she hovered there, whispering in her excellent German, "Do drink this, *Fräulein,* please. You look so pale."

Louisa glanced up. "Eva, are there a lot of Jews in Hungary?"

The question was so unexpected that Eva had to get her bearings before she answered, "Unfortunately, yes, *Fräulein.*"

"Do you know any?"

Eva said, "One can't help but see Israelites on the streets."

"What did you call them?" Louisa asked.

"Israelites," said Eva. "That is the polite term."

Louisa took up the word. "I've never met an Israelite. So I would know one if I saw one? On the street?"

Eva said, "Surely."

Louisa took a sip of tea, and, gathering courage, she told Eva everything, how she found the young composer in her practice room, and how he put her in such a state that she abandoned her Schubert. Then, with a shiver, she told Eva what she had heard from Professor Lengyel. Eva was so overcome that she began to take anxious sips from Louisa's own cup of tea. She broke in.

"The professor's a liar, *Fräulein.*"

"What makes you say that?"

"It's nothing but jealousy. He must have taken one look at the music and knew he was a genius." Then Eva said, "You never told me his name."

"Oh—Lord—I don't know his name." Louisa despaired now. "I don't have my Schubert or the manuscript or even the name of the Israelite—"

"He's not an Israelite," Eva insisted.

"How can you know?"

"They don't let them into the Academy anymore. We haven't let them in the universities for years. We're not barbarians," Eva said.

Louisa conceded the point, but she couldn't believe that her teacher would tell such malicious stories. She drew her hand across the piano.

"What a shame that old man has the *Lied,*" Eva said. "He'll probably burn it."

A new weight fell on Louisa. Was it possible she had the only copy of that song? She wanted to weep. Eva put her arms around her, and her face was soulful like the face of my son, and her hair was dark and curly like the hair of my son, and Louisa said to her maid and bosom-friend, "I have to find him."

"You must," Eva agreed. There were tears in her eyes. She couldn't believe that Louisa was in such a fascinating situation.

*T*HAT'S HOW MY SON CAME TO show up an hour before supper one evening with a note in his hand: *To Gabor Gratz, return my Schubert to me.*

"Return, my Schubert, to me," Gabor sang out as he swung himself into the kitchen chair. "She already has a pet name for me. I've never been called Schubert before. Should I be flattered?"

I was peeling potatoes, and over the bowl, I gave him a hooded look. "Do you still have her score?"

"Somewhere," Gabor said. "It doesn't matter. If she bothered to find out my name, not much can matter. It's a good thing you made me work on my German." He grabbed a potato from the bin and peeled it idly. "Maybe I should marry the girl," Gabor said. "Then I'll have German citizenship."

Take that as proof of Gabor's innocence. He never opened a newspaper. With the competence that came on him when he chose, Gabor peeled three potatoes for my every one and all the while he imagined his future. The most likely future, that he would be drafted and die in a Labor Battalion in the Ukraine or Serbia, did not seem to cross his mind, and I wasn't about to press the point.

He said, "I'll bet her father is an ambassador. When they draft me, I'll take refuge in the embassy. I've always wanted to live in an embassy."

Gabor did not stay for supper. As usual, he had a full evening ahead of him. These days, he rarely came back before midnight. I couldn't help but wait up for him, but I'd stop letting on, waiting until he went to bed before I would get up to gather the trail of discarded coat, shoes, socks, and trousers between the front door and his bedroom. The shoes were sometimes caked with gravel from the railway yard or even slippery, as though he'd waded across the Duna. I did not like the thought of Gabor wandering in those places after dark, but I had the sense to keep my worries to myself. Besides, he told me more than most mothers have a right to hear from their sons.

I knew, for example, that on the night in question he had scheduled two piano lessons, a date with a lady painter who wanted to use him as a model, and a possible tryst with Louisa. He had arranged for the last by pinning a note of his own on what he already thought of as *their* practice room: *Engel, ich verstehe nicht. Could I have something you'd want?* Then he had written a time: ten o'clock, too late to have anything but romantic implications.

Gabor had to admit that all through the lessons he could barely concentrate, and he actually left over half of the sour-cherry pastry one mother pressed on him. Even as he stripped and posed for the painter, he searched for a clock and discovered that she didn't have one. He occupied his mind by wondering how the girl would slip away at that hour; he had no doubt she would manage it somehow. Would she have to bribe a servant to call her a taxi? Would she actually go so far as to take a tram? Would she arrive early and hide behind a letter-box, peering out every time someone approached?

As it turned out, Louisa was waiting openly, right in front of the locked doors of the Academy. She was quite pale. Gabor's first thought was: She isn't all that pretty. Then, a second thought eclipsed the first: She doesn't even have breasts yet. But then she started towards him with the electric lights of the street burning across her face.

"*Veloren,*" she whispered. "*Ich habe das Lied verloren.*"

Gabor almost asked what song she'd lost, but he caught himself and laid a warm hand on an arm that felt like ice. "Don't worry. I'll write another."

"But it couldn't have been your only copy!" She sounded appalled, and in her voice, Gabor heard enough of her old arrogance to remember why she had interested him in the first place. Still, how could he reconcile that with her little ribbon, her white smock, her tie-up shoes?

He asked her, "Would you like an ice cream?"

By now, they were walking side by side under the streetlights, and Gabor was trying to remember what shops might still be open; his late-night meetings, as a rule, did not involve ice cream. The whole situation set him on edge, to be offering her candy and soda pop and so on. She could at least have kept up with him, but she meandered behind, staring up at the lights of Pest as though she'd never seen them before.

When they at last found a little *cukrászda* and sat with dishes of vanilla ice cream in front of them, she said, "You must be so upset with me, Gabor." She said his name so tentatively that he almost laughed, but instead asked her:

"How did you find me?"

"The lady at the desk," she said. Gabor couldn't help but smile. The pinch-faced porteress was no friend of his.

"How did you describe me?"

"I told her I was looking for a composer. And I said—"

"Did you tell her I'd stolen your score? The police could use a full description."

Louisa frowned. "What do you think I am?"

"Someone who signs with the lady at the desk. Someone who loses manuscripts."

"But I didn't lose it. It's with Professor Lengyel," Louisa said.

There was a pause. Then Gabor said, "Istvan Lengyel? Well." He lifted a spoonful of ice cream to his mouth. "It's lost all right."

"So you know him?" Louisa asked.

"Sure. I mean, years ago. I was a prodigy. Hung around his circle, got a little attention, learned a thing or two. See," Gabor said to Louisa, "I was his pet, but I wasn't domesticatible, if you know what I mean."

"No," Louisa said. "I have no idea what you mean." She looked so agitated then that Gabor gave her a warmer smile than he had before.

"I mean that I don't sign up with the lady at the desk."

Louisa sat straight up. "You think I'm a superficial girl?"

Gabor took Louisa's hands from where they gripped the edge of the table, and he held them for a moment. "Angel, calm down. You'll break your knuckles, and then you'll never use another practice room."

Louisa retrieved her hands and said, "Don't make fun of me." But Gabor could feel the way she had vibrated when he touched her. He thought: She's not so young.

No, she wasn't so young, but he probably shouldn't push it. It wasn't worth the risk. Still, he felt as though he ought to walk her home; my son is not so badly trained. By then, it was close to midnight, and the walk from the Academy to Rose Hill was long indeed, west to the Duna River and over Margit Bridge, long enough for Gabor to wonder whether he wanted to see the girl again. Quite naturally, he put his arm around her as they walked; her spine was like a band of steel, but she didn't pull away.

As they crossed the bridge, Louisa spoke unexpectedly. "Gabor," she said, "stop a minute."

Gabor felt an uneasy premonition, as though his nerves were piano strings Louisa had touched. He gave a shrug and said, "Do you want me to carry you the rest of the way?"

Louisa disregarded his tone. She stepped into the center of the empty bridge. Never had silence felt so complete to Gabor than at that moment, and that silence seemed to wrap itself around the girl like a blue oval, curling up from her ankles in their small white socks, around her gray skirt and her hips, closing over the crown of her head. Then she began:

She entered in the full moonlight;
she looked towards the sky.
"Distant in life, yours in death."
And gently, heart broke on heart.

The notes ran the length of Margit Bridge. Gabor felt his arm reach to hold something steady, and he thought: How can I walk this girl the rest of the way home? Who is she and who am I? What does she want from me?

He didn't even know when the song ended until he felt Louisa's presence at his side and heard her say, in a very ordinary voice, "How can you not like Schubert?"

"Did I say that?" Gabor shook his head out like a dog by way of coming to his senses, and he thought that he had never really been in love and never would be, things he'd known before, but which for the first time struck him as unfortunate. These thoughts managed to take him and Louisa the rest of the way over the bridge and most of the distance to her house.

Louisa touched his arm. They had been walking apart since she'd sung. She whispered now, with a slight, pained smile. "I'll have to go in through the cellar door."

"Bad girl," Gabor said, absently.

"But you must promise me you'll write another *Lied*."

"Sure," Gabor said.

"How long will it take you?"

"A week, maybe," Gabor said. He had never in his life finished a song.

"We'll meet in a week, then," said Louisa, and she stepped back, putting between them the same distance there had been on the bridge. It was daring of her; she was in full view of the house. That house was substantial: stone front, peaked roof, green shutters, and two first-floor window boxes stuffed with perfect white geraniums. It looked displaced, as though even the flowers had been imported from Germany.

Gabor did not stay to see how Louisa would manage to get in through the cellar. He turned up Castle Hill and began his own long walk back to our flat on Prater Street, wondering what sort of song he would write in a week.

ONE YEAR LATER, IN 1944, I
would unlock that same cellar door; it would be slanted and either weather-
beaten or damaged by flying shrapnel. The heaps of coal below would look
soft and not quite real.

I would climb down and find myself swallowed by damp. The door
would close from the inside and a match would throw enough light to make
the walls glisten and to sugar-glaze the grate that led to Louisa's practice
room. When Louisa was home, that grate gave off a bent square of crosshatched light.

In one corner, Louisa would provide me with blankets, and a bucket full
of water and a wooden crate. If I stood on the crate, I could easily reach the
ceiling and even free the duct; a tight squeeze would force my head and
shoulders through; I would be underneath the piano.

Louisa would sing the song my son had written for her:

What is lost, what is lost
We can not have back again.
It is like a breath we've taken.
We can not breathe it again.
It is like good bread we've eaten.

We can not eat it again.
It is like a heart we've broken
Or our own heart, lost in vain.

Three months, I'd hide there, and the cellar door eventually would be sealed from the outside by snow, layered with dirty ice, and piled to buckling point with rubble. Not one house on the block would be intact. From Pest, Soviets would spray streets with gunfire and blast every roof and window until handsome old Buda would be pretty much gone. Three months would draw from those damp walls generations of stench, coal, wine, horses, and the fishy Duna. Wrapped in Louisa's blankets, with my head against the crate, my eyes would be as round and stupid as the eyes of a fish, gazing up through the grate to the belly of the Bauer piano. At first, the blasts would make the strings vibrate, but then they didn't vibrate anymore, and on the day I would finally abandon my hiding place, I didn't think to look at much of anything at all.

AND FIVE YEARS LATER, AT THE border station, inside that train, Louisa cried, "I won't leave you!"

Midday, full sun, crisp air cut with coal smoke from the train, and Louisa in the reeking fur coat she'd soon abandon, with her arms latched on my waist like clamps and her face filthy and distorted with hysteria. "You don't know where I'm going," I said.

"Yes I do."

"How can you?"

"Where else could you go?" She struggled against my attempts to dislodge her, and I could feel her quick, sharp heartbeats through all that rabbit fur and at the same time the acceleration of the train that I must move her from at all costs.

I spoke with conviction. "It's no place for you."

"It will be."

By then, there was no logical way to make her go unless I flung her through the open door, and at the rate we were moving that would probably kill her. How had she even found me? Who had she bribed? What had it taken? Her hair dripped with perspiration and hung in strings before those soft, gray eyes, and I thought: When we're across No Man's Land and we face those border guards again, that will be that.

But Louisa clung to me.

*W*ITH LOUISA'S HELP, I MAN-aged to get hold of a Haifa telephone directory and decipher the Hebrew, but we found no Bela Hesshel. As far as Louisa was concerned, that was the end of it. "I've put us on a waiting list for flats," she said. "Then *we'll* be in the telephone book, *Mutti.* Wouldn't that make it easier?"

I'd heard about those flats. They were in abandoned villages, huts sprinkled with bits of furniture left over by Arab occupants. A Rumanian woman told me about her sister who thought she was going to get a house in Tel Aviv and ended up in a gutted mosque.

In fact most of the places were refused by self-respecting Europeans. They stayed put. I would run into mobs of them everywhere, complaining in Yiddish about the rationing, the beds, the wait for a shower, the Arab-speaking Jews, the children always underfoot, the strain of dragging buckets of water back to the barracks. There was something about the camp that encouraged dislocation: caftans, fur coats, dusty sack-suits, embroidered blouses, khaki shorts, and just about every stench and language in the world.

Then there were the Transylvanian girls. They were considered excellent human material because they were young and hadn't been sterilized. Their ages ranged from ten to seventeen and they were so commonly dark and rat-faced that they might have been sisters. Rumor had it that they'd crossed the border in a pack and negotiated their way through Serbia by selling themselves to Tito's partisans. In Greece, they'd stolen sheep and corn, and some of them still wore sheepskin. It smelled like rotten meat. Maybe that's why they liked it.

Before the war, they'd lived in Szatmar and had never gone more than thirty paces from their front doors. They had never heard a word that wasn't Yiddish or Hungarian or met a soul who didn't keep the Sabbath. Now they'd appropriated a shack which had been meant for bed linen and had decorated it with advertisements for face cream torn from American magazines they had gotten from the Red Cross. Some of the younger girls had also received dolls. They buried them in different corners of the camp to be sure they weren't stolen.

These girls were fascinated by Louisa. They would follow her around or sometimes waylay her between the barracks, calling in their weirdly innocent Hungarian: *"Szép lány, szép lány!* Sing a little song for us!"

Louisa didn't know what to make of the girls. She seemed to vacillate between disgust and pity and managed to focus somewhere above their heads, not always easy if, for instance, one of them hung upside down from a rafter like a bat. It was instructive to watch her face at such times. It struggled towards a discipline and symmetry that must have been a lot like the face she wore when she sang on stage.

Once, she asked me, "Who takes care of those little girls?"

"They're old enough to take care of themselves," I said.

Louisa said, "No one is that old."

There was no answering Louisa on that particular point. I lay back on the bed and streaks of sunlight fell across my face.

She sat beside me, took my hand between her own, and pressed it. "Everyone needs someone. What if you died alone and no one ever found you?"

"Girls like that don't die," I said, still looking up, but I wasn't thinking about the Transylvanians now. I was thinking about never being found, about my cousin.

"You make life so hard," Louisa said.

There was justice in that remark; I do make life hard. But what I want doesn't come easily. Here is Louisa. She exists. So do the camp's cold showers and plates of strange cold salads and those gruesome girls. But none of those things exists in the same way Bela does. Or certain longings.

I found a Lucky Strike that afternoon. It had been balanced, deliberately, on the metal foot of my bed, untouched and already burning. I had not seen Yossel Berkowitz since that first night, but that cigarette was like a tap on the shoulder or a wink. Was it a gift? I took it up, inhaled, and tried not to think about the consequences.

I didn't ask for much, just a little arbitrary human kindness, nothing grand, nothing epic. I needed something that wouldn't cost me much. Sometimes, that's asking for the impossible.

*T*HEN ONE DAY I HEARD A rumor that telegrams could be traced. Louisa offered to look into the matter. It made good sense. After all, with her inborn talent for persistence, surely she could do anything to which she set her mind. When she wasn't scrubbing our dishes or doing our wash, she attended patriotic and vocational lectures, she volunteered time at the dining hall and laundry, and she took classes in everything from language to geography to needlework. How hard would it be for her to trace a telegram? Yet I had a suspicion I could not shake; Louisa would sooner the telegram wasn't traced at all.

When I brought it up, she would break in and ask, illogically, "Please, *Mutti*, are you unhappy with me?"

"It has nothing to do with happy or unhappy," I said. "My cousin is the reason I came here. When we find him, he'll know what to do."

"But I know what to do," Louisa said. "We don't need him. He's just an old man."

"Two years older than I am," I said. "Not much past fifty."

Louisa didn't answer, pointedly I thought. She opened her book on the laws of family purity. Bela would have taken that book from her, glanced at the awful wood-cut illustrations and the sentimental German text, cocked his head to one side, and asked what was meant by "purity." What would Louisa answer? I could not imagine. The two were of such different make that they could not exist at the same place at the same time. It was as though if Bela stepped into this barrack, Louisa would have to disappear.

Perhaps Louisa knew. She let the matter drop and buried herself in her lesson, with her girlish lower lip thrust out, and a line forming between her eyebrows. She wasn't going anywhere.

ONE AFTERNOON, OUTSIDE THE administrative barrack, I was approached by an Israeli I hadn't seen before, an older man with thick grayish hair, who wore the lightweight shirt and khaki trousers of an official of the Jewish Agency. He extended a hand and addressed me in Hungarian: "Nora Gratz? I am Dov Levin. Come with me, please."

He moved us through a crowd of Poles and Rumanians who were waiting to complain about something or other, and who glared at me and sputtered out Yiddish in righteous disbelief. I barely heard them. I was unable to take my eyes off Levin, whose Pesti accent made my heart pound. This man could have been Bela's brother. He had his build, his eyes, even his plodding walk. He motioned me towards the staff office, and as he opened the door, I asked him, "Is there some news?"

"Nothing to worry about. Just some routine questions," he said.

"About my cousin?"

"Cousin? I thought she was your daughter-in-law," he said.

So much for that. What could I do but let him sit me down in his stuffy cubicle. I said, "You want to know about Louisa? She saved my life."

"Yes, that's what I hear," said Dov Levin. "Apparently, it's a remarkable story. But you must realize, Mrs. Gratz, that there have been other stories going around."

"Oh yes," I said, suddenly exhausted. "The stories."

"Some people in the camp claim they've seen her before," said Levin.

"I take it you've noticed that the stories contradict each other," I said.

"It's true, the details are admittedly a little shaky," Levin said to me, "but we know so little about her. How old is she? What brought her family to Budapest? Do you know anything about her background, what her father did for a living?"

His desk chair creaked, and he laid his elbows on his old green blotter and set his chin in his hand. It was such a Bela-like gesture that I had to fight back vertigo. I asked him, "When did you come to Palestine?"

"This isn't Palestine. It is called *Eretz Yisrael*. I came here in 'twenty-six," he said.

"From Budapest?"

He hesitated and then said, "Yes. From Budapest."

My throat knotted abruptly. "Then you must have known Bela Hesshel." The urgency in my voice made me ashamed. I half-believed that if I'd pressed that Budapesti hard enough, his outlines would have blurred and deepened and I would be sitting across from my cousin.

But that wasn't so. Dov Levin wasn't Bela. He was a Hungarian bureaucrat such as I'd met before in countless forms. "Your daughter-in-law came here," he said, "the same way as everyone else in this camp. She is not a Jew, but that's no novelty. Many refugees bring Christian spouses. The trouble is, Mrs. Gratz, is that her presence is seen as a direct affront. We don't know why. Nor are we so simple as to believe that where there is smoke there has to be a fire. But these people are insisting that we take them seriously."

"She wants to be a Jew," I said.

He ignored me. "It's a delicate matter. Frankly, we would all like to see this problem disappear. No one wants to open old wounds or bring up the past."

I said, "What past, Mr. Levin? You mean my son who died? She was with him when he died. What do you want? For her to slit her own throat?"

He didn't answer. But my words seemed to have some impact on him because he dropped the stiff manner with a little half-shrug and seemed, abruptly, rumpled and unhappy. He opened his top drawer and felt for something, and for a moment I thought he would pull out a pack of cigarettes. He would have offered me one; I was sure. Then he said, *"Figyelj, mit szeretnél?"*

He had used the informal, less a sign of disrespect, I think, than helplessness. I almost smiled. *"Mit szeretnék, Levin úr?* What do I want? I want my cousin's address. It was on a telegram I lost. A phone call, two phone calls, and I get out of this camp, my daughter-in-law gets out of this camp, and the whole thing stops being your problem. In fact, the problem disappears. You only have another million or so *sabonim* to worry about."

He asked, "Where did you pick up that word?"

"It's what the kids in the shorts call us. What is it? An obscenity?" He didn't answer. Instead, he pulled out a pen and notebook.

"Write down," he said, "everything you know about your cousin. Can you remember any part of the address on the telegram? A street name? How old is he? When did he make *aliyah?* Would there be military records? Maybe I can do something for you. But for *you,* Mrs. Gratz. I can't help your daughter-in-law stay. You understand?"

I gave this Dov Levin a long look. I said, "You have an army, trucks, guns. Why don't you just send her back to Germany?"

He ignored the question. "The kibbutz is worth a try," he said. "What was that name? Tilulit? That's just the Hebrew word for hill. Galilee is all hills. See if you can remember some of the industries, and give me more names. Have you tried looking for him on the radio? That can be very effective."

I took the notepad. It was spiral-bound, the sort of pad I'd used for dictation during my secretarial days at the girls' school. I said, "He wouldn't listen to the radio."

"Everyone listens to the radio," said Levin.

"Then he isn't everyone."

Levin nodded. "All right. Then who is he? Fill up this notepad. Tell me about him, about the kibbutz. Give me all the details. But you must promise me something in return."

Without hesitation, I said, "You know I can't make the girl leave."

But that wasn't what he'd meant. He leaned forward over the green blotter on his desk, suddenly mild and foolish, like a sick sheep. I wasn't surprised when he used my first name. "Nora," he said, "take some advice from a fellow Hungarian."

I turned my face to the window; the sky was the color of wheat.

Levin said, "Don't stake everything on him. Start making a life of your own. You won't regret it. I've been working here for a year now. I should know."

The road to Galilee, northeast, would take me through the Valley of Jezreel and towards the sea where those Budapesti Jews had been so determined to walk on water.

Levin said, "Nora, some cousins don't want to be found."

7

WHAT NAMES COULD I REMEM-
ber? Dori Csengery, of course. Then there was Nathan Sobel: He'd been in
that photograph of the chicken coop, stocky, compact, and square-jawed
with thick black brows that met in the middle and an iron-hard grin. Bela
had mentioned him in his last letter, some argument about buying more
land. Nathan also must have been part of the group from the start because
they held fund-raising dances in the ballroom of his father's Buda hotel.
Bela would write to me about those dances, enthusiastic calculations of how
many tickets Dori sold. *Most of them were to kids in Szeged who had to spend
half the day on a train to get up here. Mouse can be very persuasive.*

I replied, *So why didn't she try to sell me a ticket?* Then I didn't mail it
because I was frankly afraid that Dori would take that as an opportunity to
introduce herself. I also added to that letter, *Nobody ever tries to persuade me
of anything. This sounds like a complaint, but really I ought to be grateful. If
they persuaded me of anything, it would be to kill myself.*

What can I say? I didn't mail that either. The shoe-box of unsent letters
filled, and I began another. Those letters were written front-and-back on the
cheapest possible paper. *If those kids can spend half a day on a train to go to a
dance, why can't you spend half a day to visit me? Do you know how often I've
watched trains between Budapest and Szeged and wondered if you were on them?
If I did see your face, what would I do about it, Borzas Medve? Throw myself in*

front of that train so it would stop here? One afternoon, I worked myself into a state and actually stuffed a number of those pages in an envelope addressed to Bela, but somewhere between our front gate and the post-office, I stopped dead. If he got that sort of thing from me, he'd never write again.

I was nineteen, three years out of secondary school, and my self-pity was only matched by my intolerance. The world seemed to me petty, alien, and full of gloom. I was not half-wrong. Since the Great War, a pall hung over Kisbarnahely. The park by the town hall was occupied by loafing veterans. Train service was cut back, as was construction, and men who might have found jobs with the railroad or the brickworks returned to their family farms only to find no market for the crops. Crown currency was worthless. No one went to the market square anymore. Instead, they bartered at the train station, villagers arriving on the slow, local trains, carrying sacks of yellow peppers or crates of eggs to trade for parts of plows or sacks of coal.

As a watchmaker, Uncle Oszkar was the only Csongradi who produced something of value, and he kept our family larder stocked. I still stopped by his workshop, not as often as I once had. In fact, I felt a little guilty. It was clear he'd thought I'd make more of myself. My future was uncertain. Three afternoons a week, I apprenticed to a pale little lady stenographer at my father's office, but I could already best her at shorthand and typing and found the entire enterprise embarrassing. Uncle Oszkar said, "You ought to make some friends, meet some fellow who can make you laugh."

I said, "With Laszlo spoken for, what's the use?" I was sitting on the stool which no longer felt so very high. I did still see Laszlo occasionally. Since returning from the war, he had become a full partner in my uncle's shop and he no longer rode a bicycle. Sometimes I would catch him and his wife and little son on their way to church. His wife always waved. I wondered how marriage had turned him overnight into such a dull old man.

When I came home, I would find my mother sitting on the couch, knitting tight cylinders that eventually turned into hard covers for cushions. Although the factory sometimes shut down for weeks at a time, my father still worked late, and dinner was kept in the stove for him until it was inedible. I would cross the length of the house: fifteen paces. Such were our evenings. Then I'd hear the train.

The humming came up through the floorboards. Instantly, I would run outside and wait for the first sign of the signal light over our wall, pale as water. I would wish on that signal light the way that other people wished on stars, the way you can just say, "I want, I want," without being able for the life of you to say anything more.

*T*HEN I'D GET ANOTHER LETTER. Bela was training with the other Pioneers in the Bakony hills just north of Veszprem. A Youth Leader who trained them was the cousin of somebody's sister-in-law, a fellow whose name was so outlandish that I remember it perfectly: Ami Chai Jezreel. It meant: My People Live in the Jezreel.

Why is that so strange? Bela asked me. *Your family name is Csongradi. Your people probably used to live in Csongrad.*

My first name isn't My People, I replied.

Bela let the comment go and told me more about this Ami Chai Jezreel. He had spent five years on a kibbutz called Gan Dahlia, but as far as I could tell that was about all he had to recommend himself. Most of the time he spent trying to find some shade, eating meat-paste sandwiches out of a paper bag, and adjusting the Primus stove to make what he identified in a condescending way as authentic Turkish coffee. From beneath the nearest tree, he called out orders to the boys and girls who labored in the sun.

The work lasted from sunrise to sundown. Ami Chai Jezreel was in his sleeping sack by ten, but the rest of them boiled coffee, lit a fire, and kept the day from ending for as long as possible, singing and dancing the old dances or the new ones Ami Chai Jezreel had brought over from Kibbutz Ma'Otz: two steps forward, two steps back, clap twice over your shoulder. The Yemenites had danced this way since the days of Alexander the Great.

So that was another name, Ami Chai Jezreel, and there was Bernadette, the star milker, and her brother Eleazar, who read a lot of poetry, and Tibor, who played mouth-organ and wrote songs in Hebrew. I could see them as Bela had described them in his letters, sweaty and tenacious, wearing broad hats and short trousers, the girls dressed like the boys, outlandish creatures. The Bakony hills were scattered with vineyards, lush and green. It was enough like how they pictured the Galilee to make them homesick for the future.

Dori would sometimes pull Bela away from the rest and the two of them would try their hand at duplicating Ami Chai Jezreel's "authentic Turkish coffee." While the attempt boiled in the pot, she would check Bela's bandage where he had fallen off the stool trying to milk the cow. Her concern was like her dancing, correct, but full of self-parody.

Dori would say, "Authenticity is an imposition. Things aren't authentic because we think they are, but because we don't think at all."

"Stop using your doctor voice," Bela would say to Dori. Maybe he gave her a kiss then. I don't know; he didn't say. He did tell me that there wasn't enough coffee to go around, so they ended up sprinkling it on the staked tomato plants to see what it would do to them.

They had been permitted to plow a fallow field, but first the stones had to be cleared away. They couldn't find a wheelbarrow, so after much debate, it was Bela who was asked to approach the nearest neighbor and borrow what he could.

The nearest neighbor turned out to be a convent, and it is easy to imagine Bela taking a few steps towards the front entrance and hesitating there with his hand cupping his chin before he thought to try the back. He could make out the crowns of fruit trees over the stone gate, and as he approached, the leaves gave a shudder and a dozen blackbirds burst out and flew straight for the belfry.

He'd figured on a nun, but he was greeted by an old man in felt trousers and a floppy hat, the gardener. He made his request. The man asked, "What do you plan to do with the stones?"

Bela answered honestly. "I don't know."

"I thought Jews were supposed to be so clever," said the gardener. Then he took Bela by the elbow and led him among his raised soil beds where he'd grown rows of velvety lettuces, and the walls of tiny stones were just about the size of the pebbles the Pioneers had pulled from the dirt. He pointed out the value of chrysanthemums and drew Bela's attention to the local pests, particularly the blights common to fruit trees. His own cherry tree had been pruned so ruthlessly that it looked like a fist. "Prune and prune. Don't think it won't grow back," he said. "It will. You say you're going to the Holy Land? To farm? Like Father Abraham?"

Bela could have pointed out that Abraham had been a nomad, not a farmer, and for some reason he felt suddenly foolish. He said, "That's right. Like Abraham."

"I'll let the sisters know. They'll pray for you," he said. Then he led Bela to the storage shed and from a pyramid of garden tools dislodged two wheelbarrows.

Bela thanked him and was about to drag each of the wheelbarrows by a handle when the gardener set a hand on his arm and hoisted the smaller of the two into the larger.

"Half-wit," he said to Bela, obviously feeling pleased with himself. He gave Bela a smack on the shoulder. "God protect you. You'll need it, you half-wit Jews."

HUS BEGAN BELA'S CAREER OF neighborhood diplomacy which would extend for at least twenty years. He always claimed it was because it was all he could do well. He couldn't plow straight. The tents he pitched fell down. Whenever he tried to lay his hand on any animals, the rest of the collective were wise enough to leave the barn.

I wrote, *You're such a Jew, and you don't even know when you're being insulted.* Or I wrote, *If you're so fond of mice, come back to Barnahely and I'll trap a few for your amusement.* I was proud of this reply. It was just the sort of Nora he expected—teasing, bold, dismissive. Also, I had managed to include an invitation in a way that didn't smack of desperation. I continued in that vein. *Why do you think that being a peasant is any more authentic than being a Budapesti?*

Bela replied, *I live in Budapest because someone has granted me permission. As Jews, we're here on borrowed time.*

Speak for yourself, Borzas, I wrote. *As far as I can tell the only thing that makes me a Jew is that I'll be buried in that cemetery.*

Bela replied, *You won't be buried in that cemetery if you come with us to Palestine.*

I read that letter on a cold night in March of 1919. It sent a shiver through me. I thought of the day he swung me round and round until we fell and breath blew out of us there on the knoll where Grandmother Naomi Csongradi was buried. I wrote: *You'd better watch what you say or I'll actually go.* Then I stuck that version in the shoe-box and tried again. *I can't be as sure of everything as you are, Borzas.* That wouldn't do either. Another attempt: *All I can see in your asking me along is that you're serious and you'll really go. And all I can read into this talk of burial is you're going to die somewhere and I won't know it.*

My mother came in as I was writing and said, "You've got to do something about all these papers. They attract dust."

"What do you want me to do?" I asked her. "Burn them?"

"You'll burn down the house one day. Don't think I can't smell smoke," my mother said. As I got older, my mother and I took on each other's mannerisms down to persistent scowls. I didn't like it. Neither did she. She would glare and I would glare until I had to either hide in my room or leave. If I was home, my mother would say, "Nora, stop lurking." If I left, she would say, "Don't go out like that without telling me where you'll be." In that last demand, there was a note of panic.

I would say, "How many places are there for me to go? This isn't Budapest."

"I know this isn't Budapest," my mother would say. "In Budapest you would have been a different sort of girl."

I felt sudden vertigo. My mother had grown up in Budapest, just like Aunt Moni. She had been my age once, not long before she met my father and returned with him to Kisbarnahely. I thought about that first cigarette I had found on the kitchen windowsill when I was six years old, and I knew it had been hers. I had finished what she started. And she could smell it on me. The knowledge made me tremble.

I WOULD USUALLY END UP AT the Kismacska, where I had my own little table which may well have been designed for the likes of me. It was solitary, unsteady, and never quite clean. The waitress didn't even take my order anymore. She just let me wait until she decided to bring me my coffee, cream-cake, and pack of cigarettes and let me be, knowing I'd put my money by the ashtray.

Once, one of the patrons brought out a fiddle and played badly; it must have been a birthday or a name-day. Old men shouted requests and sang *Jaj De Szépen Harangoznak* or *Szép a Fekete Barany*, songs about beautiful bells and beautiful black lambs, and refugees from Transylvania would sing out in yearning voices:

> *Little dog, little dog*
> *You will lead the sheep to me*
> *But my love has grown so wayward*
> *She will never come to me.*
> *Oh my black-eyed love's a bold love.*

She will wander, she will stray
But my blue-eyed love's a true love.
She will never go away.

"Little dog! Little dog!" one squat man sang out, crossing the dark, slippery floor and leaving brown boot-tracks. He made his way to me. He was the uncle of someone I knew from school, a bricklayer from Koloszvar who'd fled west when his city fell under Romanian rule after the Great War, a melancholy man who grabbed my arm and whispered, "Little black-eyed love, come dance. Come make a party with me."

And why couldn't I simply rise on my hind legs and dance? He would be happy. I even had little heels on my boots, like a good country girl. My black hair was tied back with a white ribbon. We would stomp from one end of the grim Kismacska to the other, and maybe I'd marry him. How terrible would it be to keep house for a bricklayer? He would come home from work and bathe in an iron tub. I would scrub his back with birch-twigs. In December, in the heavy snow, we would take a carriage to his brother's farm for a pig-killing, and I'd join the other women as they boiled the blood to pudding. Wouldn't that make for a good letter to my cousin in Budapest? And then I'd bite my lower lip to keep from crying.

M Y FATHER WAS HAVING AN affair. I don't think my mother knew. I saw him leave the Hotel Oasis with the same secretary who had taught me shorthand. It was three in the afternoon, and they must have dined together; the girl had a fresh gravy stain on the front of her blouse. That the matter went further than supper was speculation on my part. I did notice that she took his arm rather than the other way around, and that it was she who guided him unsteadily past the Town Hall towards the brickworks where, no doubt, she would unlock the office door for him and make sure he was seated comfortably before she took dictation.

I took to waiting for them there. The secretary's name was Ibolya, and whenever she saw me she forced her lips into a faint, terrified smile and at once commenced filing whatever was on my father's desk. Father himself took off his glasses, rubbed his eyes, and then looked at me with that warm, brown candor and said, "What's the matter, Nora? Does your mother need anything?"

"I just came to help you," I'd say, against my better judgment. "There must be something for me to do."

More often than not, there I'd be, side by side with my father's mistress, sorting out receipts for goods or copying inventory lists. At least, then, I would walk my father home. Mother would open the door, clearly startled to see him back so early, and the three of us would knock around the house, shy of each other. It would pain me to see the fuss she'd make over supper, chopping the onion until the whole kitchen swam with fumes. He had already eaten, after all, and I couldn't force down a thing.

But to Bela, I wrote, in my most sardonic German: *I must refuse your invitation. How can I leave Kisbarnahely now that it's summer and the* Sunnenblumen *are* blumen? *Besides, I don't for one minute believe you're actually going to that awful place. What if you milk a cow and it explodes? What if you get less than nine hours sleep a night? Not even Dori the Wonderdoctor can help you then.*

H AD I BEEN A DIFFERENT SORT of girl, I might have been a Communist. That was the year of Bela Kun and the Commune, which reached full strength by early spring. The day that Kun was freed from prison, a Szeged newspaper made the rounds of the *cukrászdu,* and there was his photograph: tousled hair, sly eyes, a soft mustache. He looked more like an actor than a criminal, although one hand was thrust under his suit-jacket, as though he were about to draw a gun.

I wondered if my cousin knew this Kun. The man who read that newspaper out loud to us made much of the Jews who held positions in the Party. "And they say Kun's a convert. But he's no more a Christian than I'm a Turk." To Bela I wrote: *Why do you need to go to Palestine? The Jews rule here.* No answer came. The post had become unreliable.

In fact, as time passed, it became difficult to get so much as a newspaper from Szeged, and such was our isolation in Kisbarnahely that we did not even know that Kun had taken over parliament until we were told that a representative from the Commune would meet with local farmers and answer any questions about land redistribution. A steam locomotive pulled into the station one hot April afternoon. On board was a Komsomol, smallish and swarthy, and he disembarked and stood on a station platform hung all over with red bunting. He was met by a crush of men in thick, felt coats and hats, some of whom had walked all day, from distant villages. They had been told they'd own the land they worked, and expected to leave with leases in their hands. They looked a little sunstruck.

I wondered what he said. He didn't have a carrying voice and before long, the villagers were joined by unemployed men from the brickworks, and the mood was turning ugly. The pistons of the locomotive started and the last of his words was lost in a cloud of steam. I think he called out, "Goodbye, Comrades!" as he stepped back on the Red Train. The men might have mobbed the tracks, but they seemed cowed by the sheer size and presence of the train itself as it pulled away and started east towards Szentes.

My mother had her own opinion about the Commune. She feared for Aunt Moni and the children in Budapest. "They shoot people in the streets for believing in God."

By May, the first and second floor of the Oasis Hotel had become the offices of the Worker's Tribunal, and my father started coming home for dinner regularly. In fact, he was usually in by four, and we saw a lot of him, enough to notice changes. His glasses had been broken and badly repaired with twine, and his hairline had receded. It was July when he admitted that his job had been given to the brother of a Komsomol.

My mother smiled, stiffly. "What have you been doing all day, then? Hiding at Oszkar's?"

"Helping the new man learn the ropes," my father said. "It's a rather complicated system."

I asked, "Couldn't Ibolya help, or has she also been replaced?"

"She went back to her brother's farm," my father said.

I said, "Good. At least there she can eat." Then I went outside for some air. The house felt impossibly crowded. That night, I walked its length and counted fifteen paces, as I had when I was nine, when I was twelve, when I was fifteen. What did it matter who ran the trains, the Reds or the Whites? I still watched them pass by.

*A*S IT TURNED OUT, THE COM-mune didn't last through fall. A White Army marched up from Romania. Word of its arrival drew out neighbors from their houses and they stood at the crossroads, whispering: They are three days off, they are fifty kilometers away, they will reach Kisbarnahely by dawn.

It was maybe four in the morning when I heard a crack at the door. Then another. Mother answered in her robe. On the threshold stood a drunkard who pushed her aside and blundered through our overfurnished living room, calling back: "Hold the dogs! I'll get him!"

In fact, he easily pulled my father from between the covers and dragged him back outside. Father wore a nightshirt and he kept feeling his way through empty air as he crossed the little courtyard, and Mother trailed after to give him his spectacles. "Gyorgy! Tell them you don't even work there now! Your name is clear!"

From my window, I could see them frog-walk my father up the road towards the market square; the three men and two yapping dogs made a parade. I could have told her: They were not Communists. They were local men I'd seen in the Kismacska , or coming out of the brickyard in dirty overalls. They had waited out the summer of the Soviet to see which way the wind blew. Now they were anticipating the arrival of the Whites. They were killing Jews.

It stood to reason. Kun was a Jew. The Komsomol on the train was a Jew. And my father. And Uncle Oszkar.

My uncle they could not dislodge from his shop. The men found him at work with Laszlo. Uncle Oszkar and Laszlo had already had a morning shot of *pálinka*, and maybe it gave them strength because when the man came at my uncle, he dodged them and Laszlo hiked up his stool and aimed for their heads. The stool cracked and split, and the men fled, leaving Laszlo to turn to see to Uncle Oszkar. My uncle had fallen on his bed. Laszlo gave him a shake, but he didn't respond. He'd had a coronary.

Laszlo stumbled out of the workshop and found himself ankle-deep in fog, a fog typical of September. He faced the square. Maybe two-dozen Jews shivered there, my father among them. There were not many Jews in Kisbarnahely. Other towns had more, also more Communists. The Communists were shot, hanged, or exiled. As for the Jews, their treatment was less systematic. In some towns, they burned the Jewish Quarter. We had no Jewish Quarter, just the cemetery and a modest synagogue some distance from the park. I could see smoke from my window, and a little ash floated across the yard and clung to the apricot tree.

Later that day, Laszlo sat in our kitchen, the blood still on his hands, hair, and apron, and he told my mother how my father had died. Some of the Whites had rifles, and three were on horseback, in their old uniforms from the Great War. They cocked their rifles at the Jews and one called out: "Here's the road to Budapest! Go run to that Red bastard! Run to Kun!"

Then the horses broke into a gallop straight into the line of Jews and the Jews ran, nightshirts, bare feet, and all. Some fell at once and were trampled by the horses. The rest were shot in the back. My father reeled well off the road and fell with a bullet in his neck.

"Did you see the body?" my mother asked Laszlo. "How can you be sure he's dead?"

Laszlo shook his head. "He's dead. As for the bodies, they cleared them off, Mrs. Csongradi. There's a lime-pit near the brickyard. But I wouldn't go there."

My mother set off at once for the lime-pit. She found it empty, save for some broken brick. In the market square, she picked up a pair of glasses, but they didn't belong to my father. That night, we stayed with Laszlo's family, which was brave of them. The next day, I found out why our house hadn't been burned. Someone wanted to claim it. Apparently, it had been purchased through foreclosure by my great-great-grandfather, and a fellow with an enormous red mustache had the documents to prove his family had owned the property since the time of the Turks. He brought the paper to Laszlo's house and gave my mother some advice.

"You and your girl had better leave the country anyway. Go to Vienna."

You would think my mother would be beaten down, but she said to him, "If you put your faith in an army from Romania, what kind of Hungarian are you?"

That touched a nerve. Blood rushed to the man's head, and he shouted: "I'm a true, full-blooded Magyar, and you shits don't know how lucky you are to be alive!"

Laszlo interjected. "The house is Mrs. Csongradi's by right."

"What's she paying you?" the man asked Laszlo.

"Get off my property. We'll settle this in court."

"Are you fucking the daughter? Or maybe you're still buggering the old watchmaker. I hear he likes it in the ass!"

Somehow, Laszlo kept his temper; maybe his head still hurt. At any rate, the man with the mustache left, and what followed was six months in court; in the end, my mother did get to keep the house she'd never liked, and she also inherited Oszkar's share of the workshop. The house, so dearly won, would be where she would spend the rest of her life until she was transported east.

As soon as things calmed down enough for Laszlo to have a coffee with me alone, he said, "Oszkar remembered you in his will."

That brought on tenderness and guilt. "You should have everything," I said.

"I have enough. Now look, Nora," Laszlo said. "There's nothing for you here. Don't you have family in Budapest?"

"My mother—" I began, but he interrupted.

"Your mother can take care of herself. Why don't you go stay with those cousins? You liked them, didn't you? I remember that girl with all the dolls."

Then he pressed something into my hand. It was a velvet sack, and when I opened it, there were three crystal prisms and a variety of lenses, thick and thin.

"I put this together for you," said Laszlo. "Just a keepsake."

The glass felt smooth and cool; by now, it was March of 1920, and I was twenty years old. I held one of the lenses to my eye, and Laszlo shrank back to a pinprick.

"Get on a train to Budapest," said Laszlo.

In an unsteady voice, I asked him, "Do you have a cigarette?"

He rolled me one and lit it for me. "See? You can smoke in front of me now."

I did. The smoke felt tender going down. I blew it out of my nose and looked through a second lens. Laszlo turned into the earth and sky, and his brassy hair and pink face were so overwhelming that I had nothing more to say.

8

BEFORE I LEFT FOR BUDAPEST,
I sent Bela a letter written in such a rush that I leapt straight into Hungarian:
*So now you're in for it. So far as I can tell I'm entering a whirlwind, and if every-
thing you led me to expect is true, my life is going to begin, which will include
protecting you from cows, collecting your stray hats, and keeping you honest. I
have both invented and applied for this job. Meet me at the station.* I mailed that
thing before I could think better of it and ran out the door of the post-office
to double-check the schedule of the train.

I took the Szeged Express. The second-class compartment had brass
ashtrays, wood paneling, and velvet cushions. I opened the window a crack.
The fringes on the curtains fluttered. I had worn a traveling suit that matched
the green upholstery. What did I have in mind? To become the car itself?
Who knows? I could have closed my eyes and still named every village on
the way: Lajosmizse, Orkeny, Dabas, westward to Cegled. Above me was a
new brown cardboard suitcase with leather trim, at my feet a carpetbag. We
picked up speed. I had a deep sensation of fitting into my life like a hand into
a glove—that exact, that wonderful.

The feeling lasted until I got to Nyugati Station. Aunt Monika stood on
the platform. "Nora, dear. You have so little luggage."

I looked past her, but I think I already knew.

She gave me a kiss. "I'm so glad you're here. You can have his room."

Bela and his friends had left for Trieste the week before. The departure had been sudden and at first Aunt Moni was vague as to the circumstances, but later my cousin Adele told me that some members of the group were under investigation as Communists and had to leave the country in a hurry. I demanded to know why the idiotic boys and girls in question didn't emigrate to Vienna like everyone else, why they had to drag the whole group off to Palestine, and who Bela thought he was to leave his widowed mother and little sister alone at a time like this.

"A time like what?" Adele asked, and she tactfully ignored the fact that my own mother had been widowed less than a year before. "Honestly, Nora, you'd think this was a surprise. He's had his passage paid for since last January."

I spent my first week in Budapest ignoring the electric lights, the avenues, even the trams. I couldn't bring myself to ask if Bela had received that letter before he'd gone, and sitting on the couch that served as Bela's bed with its yellow crocheted cover, I pulled down the blinds of the window and stared at the bookshelves, reconstructing line after line of that letter until there seemed no question it had driven him away.

Yet before a week had passed, I got a letter: *Take the train to Lublijana or the express straight through. Either way, you can make the boat to Jaffa. Don't worry about the ticket. Dori will throw something together.*

I wrote: *I don't want Dori to throw something together.* I put the pen down, knowing that I would have to write something, but no words came to me. For the first time since arriving, I raised the blind and looked out the window. The room that had been Bela's had a view of the onion dome of the Great Synagogue. Of course I had the shoe-boxes, three of them now. If I pulled them out and poured their contents on that yellow cover, could I piece something together?

Adele came in just then and asked, "Are those Bela's old letters? Can I see them?"

I pushed the boxes under the bed, probably rudely, and she looked a little shocked.

"Nora," she said, "won't you come out with me to the cinema? There are some people you should meet."

"You Hesshels are always asking me to do things," I said to her.

"That's because we like you," said Adele. She'd grown up into a conventional beauty, with soulful eyes and lush black curls, and she spoke so graciously that there was no way I was going to believe her.

In fact, Adele had plans for me. She'd always wanted a sister. There was a closet full of clothing we could share. In a stupor of misery, I allowed myself to be taken up, taken up, I must add, like a dress with a low hemline. Adele spent a whole afternoon trying to figure out the best way to do my hair. I sat on the edge of her bed, digging my nails into the chenille spread as the comb raked this way and that.

"You have a gamin quality," said Adele when she'd finished. She'd combed everything forward, right over my eyes. "You ought to wear a raincoat with the collar turned."

"Good," I said. "Then no one will be able to see me."

"Honestly, Nora, I'm so glad you're here. We're going to have so much fun this summer. We'll cheer each other up."

When she said that, I was forced to realize that she too missed Bela. Then all was lost. I had to do exactly as she said.

*S*O THAT WAS HOW I FOUND myself rushing all over Budapest with a troop of mostly Jewish girls and boys. The girls were fashionable, talkative, and from good families. Many of them were Adele's friends from nursing school. The boys were, for the most part, just a little too young to have fought in the Great War or to have taken an active role in the Commune. They were younger brothers and they couldn't fight battles or have strong opinions. Worse yet, after the Commune fell, a law had been passed that made it almost impossible for a Jew to get into a university. These boys wandered around Pest like pimpled ghosts and attached themselves to fun so desperately that they made it look like hard work.

There was one named Kalman Nagy, a tall, white-haired boy who always buttoned his collar to his chin and had a way of ending every sentence with a nervous giggle. I think he'd tried his luck with every girl in the circle before I had arrived, and he latched on to me almost at once, offering cigarettes from an oily-looking leather case and trying to take my arm when I got out of the tram. He took to calling for me at the Hesshel apartment every afternoon until I took a course in advanced shorthand just to avoid him. Even Adele admitted Kalman was a bit much. But, of course, she always had to open the door for him and offer him coffee.

"You can't just write somebody off," she'd say to me. "I met David because I was nice to his brother, and his brother is honestly the most unbearable person I ever met."

David was Adele's steady beau, a medical student. He was older, serious, dazzlingly handsome in a wavy-haired matinee idol way, clearly of a different class than the rest of the boys. Yet I never remembered a word David said. As for the unbearable brother, he tagged along one afternoon when we went to the cinema and proved his unbearableness by actually walking out of the film because he didn't like it. Until that point, he hadn't struck me one way or another, but afterwards I felt a stir of interest and asked Adele his name.

Adele's face lit up. "Do you want me to arrange something?" All interest vanished on the spot.

"Look," I said to Adele more than once, "I'm a lost cause. I'm not a social animal."

"You really are a scream, Nora," Adele said. "You should have known Bela's circle from the Youth Group. They said the most horrible things about themselves but they all had egos big as houses. David went to school with Dori Csengery. You know she dresses like a man? Would you like me to arrange something?" she asked again.

"I can't marry Dori Csengery," I said to Adele. "Bela has to marry Dori Csengery."

"Oh, everyone's in love with Bela," Adele said. She tossed the sentence off, and afterwards, I sat in that room that used to be his, stretching my legs out on his bed, and wondering if she had been fair. How could he help it if everyone was in love with him? At least he asked them all to join him in Palestine. Or he asked me.

Throughout the years, Bela would continue to write as though he assumed I would take the next boat to Palestine. Even when I met and married Janos, his opinion didn't waver. When I had Gabor, he wrote about how much my son would like life at Tilulit.

Although I had no intention of leaving Budapest, I let him go on trying. I was flattered. After all, the boys and girls of Tilulit were remarkable by anybody's standards—intelligent, brave, original, good-natured, witty, and, on the whole, good-looking. After their arrival, Ami Chai Jezreel helped them find an adobe house on the outskirts of town, and they got jobs on a road crew, working through the blazing heat with wet handkerchiefs draped over their heads. They shared rough Arab bread and handfuls of olives and drank a lot of coffee. Eleazar developed a taste for British cigarettes, but the group couldn't afford them, so he settled for loose tobacco and rolling paper. But after a day of picking stones, his hands were so cramped that most of the tobacco fell on the floor.

We are completely unprepared, Bela wrote me. *The months with the cow and the wheelbarrows were a joke. There are Pioneers here who have spent two years in training camps, and I won't even mention the Arab workers who get paid a fraction of what we do and have families to support.*

Then there was the afternoon he ran into Manuel Lorenz. Bela had gone to the office of the Jewish National Fund only to find that their request for land had, again, been denied, and when he stepped outside, the sunshine and heat had fallen on him like a mallet so that he had to sit down on what proved to be the stoop of a little restaurant with a verandah. The voice that called down in German was half-familiar:

"It's the linguist! And brown as a nut! Well, don't be shy, young man, unless you think you're too good to have a cold drink with me."

Bela looked up and could barely see the figure under the canopy, but recognized first the mustache and then the narrow jaw and small, bright eyes. "Well, sir, I can't—"

"No money? I have money. Come on, young man. It's only lemonade, not cognac. I won't compromise your principles."

Bela stood on shaky legs and managed to make his way onto the verandah. At once, he regretted his decision. Lorenz was not alone. He shared a table with a gentleman Bela recognized as the manager of the road crew and an Arab in a robe and headdress who raised his cup of Turkish coffee in greeting.

Lorenz did not bother to introduce the two men, but said to them of Bela: "See? He calls me sir. That's very typical of his type. They call each other Comrade, but put them before their elders and the Prussian manners surface. Well, young man," he said to Bela, "do have a seat. There's a real Arab here. Won't you address him in Arabic? Or perhaps you'd like to write him a seditious leaflet."

The Arab twinkled at Bela, who remained tongue-tied and did not sit down.

"My dear boy," Lorenz said, "I did offer you a cold drink. Did you just come up here to stretch your legs?"

Bela spoke deliberately in Hebrew. *"Ha shemesh chazak."*

Lorenz smiled. "Well, so it is, very hot. Stay under this nice cool awning for as long as you like. Would you care for a cigar?"

"He's too pure for cigars," said the owner of the road crew. "He'd want to divide it into fifty pieces and share it with his comrades."

"This is really fascinating," said the Arab in excellent German. "He doesn't have that stunned look you see in most of them. I'm familiar with the Russian type. From before the war. Worked alongside the coolies and fell into a dead faint half the time. We buried at least a dozen of them."

"At your own expense?"

"Naturally. What money did they have?"

"There's a patron for you, young man," said Lorenz. "As good as Rothschild. It certainly is one way to get yourself some land."

Bela put up with this for a moment longer before taking his leave. Lorenz did make a final attempt to make him stay for lemonade, and in fact, a fat, sweaty glass pitcher sat at the center of the table, clinking with ice. Bela shook his head.

"Are you always planning on acting against your own best interest?" Lorenz asked him as he turned to go.

Bela said his last words in German to be certain he was understood. "No, sir. But you won't be the one to determine my best interest."

"That's too bad," said Lorenz, but he turned back to his drink and conversation and let Bela leave the restaurant in peace.

*I*T WAS NATHAN SOBEL WHO eventually returned with the news that the Jewish National Fund had granted them a thousand dunam of land in the Galilee. He'd run to the office during lunch and returned with the documents raised up in his fist in a gesture of victory. They dropped their shovels and let out a whoop that made the other laborers drop their own tools and walk over to find out what had happened.

One young Arab said, "I know that part of the Galilee. The soil's no good."

By then, most of the comrades understood a little Arabic, but Bela had to translate Nathan's response. "Soil can be fertilized."

"Well, what will you plant there?" the man asked.

Sobel answered, "Whatever we choose to plant, we'll plant. We're not afraid to work."

Bela found the simultaneous translation tiring, and eventually he took the man off to the side to ask him about the region, what his own village planted, how they fertilized, what water sources they found and how that water was transported, and he pressed a little too hard. The worker stopped him with an upraised hand.

"Listen, you think that if that land gave anything back, I'd be here clearing stones?"

Bela shrugged and said, *"Aesef sadiq."* He felt a brief, quick sinking of the heart but made himself speak again and asked him, *"Momkid taeqolli aeynae . . ."* Midstream, he pulled an old map from his pocket and shook out its folds. The young man squinted, and his finger climbed along the ridges to a point just south of Safed.

"Taell al-Taji," he said.

Taell meant hill. As they debated names that night, it was Bela who pushed for a Hebrew variation: Tilulit.

They gathered all their old and new friends in their favorite ice-cream shop—a dilapidated storefront with its screen door half-off the hinges—and they overtook the place, polishing off whole tubs of strawberry, lemon, and tutti-frutti. Sandor climbed on a stool and turned an empty tub into a drum, and Tibor took up his mouth organ and played. Completely drunk on cream and sugar, they pushed back the flimsy tables and danced, gripping each other's shoulders, knocking over chairs, rattling the walls.

"I want you to call me Arielle!" Dori screamed in Bela's ear. "I want to be a daughter of Zion!"

Bela gave her a squeeze. "You're still a mouse."

"Mice are vermin! They're *Galut!*"

Eleazar grabbed her then and spun her at the center of the circle. The owner despaired, announced he was going to bed, and let them close the shop themselves at dawn, when they fell asleep in a fragrant and slightly sticky heap in that adobe house they would soon leave forever.

*T*HIS HISTORY OF TILULIT CAME
to me by way of Bela's letters, hardly the most reliable of sources. Bela
doesn't lie, but Bela tends to overlook divisions, petty squabbles, and everyday annoyances—a quality which, at points, drove me mad. The first years
couldn't have been easy. Yet Bela wrote about the first working shower, the
Hebrew poetry Tibor set to melodies he'd heard in the Arab village, the village itself, Taell al-Taji, which lay just over a gully, white and silent.

Bela was the go-between. He must have been a spectacle, appearing in
that village in his worn gray trousers with the cuffs rolled up and a half-
buttoned white shirt, one hand steadying his bicycle. Palestine hadn't cured
him of his fear of bridges, and he had to ride that bicycle kilometers out of
his way to find a land-crossing. In Taell al-Taji, he paused by an open doorway where two old men crouched. They offered him coffee which he drank
down at once; it had been a long, dusty ride.

The older of the two had a jaw like a nutcracker and only a few teeth in
his head; his Arabic almost eluded Bela. "A very beautiful machine you
have. The British make beautiful things."

"It's German," Bela said, and he felt foolish; what difference did it make?

The younger man broke in. "There are how many of you Muskovites in
those tents?"

Bela accepted the name. It was better than what the Arabs commonly
called the Jews: the Children of Death. He said, "There are seventeen of us."

The man was silent for a moment, running his finger along his mustache
and letting it linger at the edge of his mouth. "You plan to do what?"

"We plan to farm," said Bela.

The man waved his hand dismissively. "Farming won't make you rich.
You should keep bees."

Bela crouched beside the bicycle and set his chin in his hand, settling in
to listen as the man unraveled the mysteries of bee-keeping, of hives, honey,

beeswax, and also of the intricate and fascinating lives of the bees themselves. This, Bela outlined in a letter that reached me not so long after I married Janos. The bee-keeper, Ahmad, invited Bela to see his own hives. Remarkably, Ahmad wore no net, and as Bela watched from a respectful distance, he allowed his front and forearms to grow fuzzy and yellow and alive with bees.

Honey from the honey-comb, Bela wrote, *is nothing you can get off a shelf. I brought it back to where I knew it would be treasured. Vera made a honey-cake but most of it we just ate with our fingers. We had a long meeting about something afterwards—some of those meetings last all night—and Mouse took notes and kept the honey-pot next to her. The pages got all stuck together.*

Ahmad agreed to train some of the boys in bee-keeping. He came at first on foot and then took pleasure in the kibbutz gift of the bicycle. He became a fixture near the foundation of what would become the dining hall, sitting on a blue three-legged stool surrounded by David, Sandor, Eleazar, and a few more wondering, adolescent boys, speaking Arabic Bela would translate. He helped them build hives and allowed those hives to be painted yellow, though that seemed, to him, ridiculous. He saw them through their first harvest and admitted that the honey was acceptable. His motivations seemed, to me, obscure. Why would he want competition? Bela attributed to him an altruism which seemed ridiculous. *He's a neighbor,* Bela wrote, *and knows what a neighbor is.*

I wrote: *He must like bossing Muskovites.*

But Bela replied, *You're thinking like a Galut Jew. He's at home in his life. Can you imagine?*

That line must have been the only hurtful thing Bela ever wrote to me, implying that I was not at all at home. I started a few letters back, some sharp, some simply base justification. Finally, I wrote: *No, I can't imagine. I have a poor imagination. Send me physical evidence or I won't believe you.*

In a package that contained a beeswax candle and a letter twelve pages long, Bela described the first anniversary of the founding of Kibbutz Tilulit.

They still lived in tents, but they had built a cowshed and a dining hall, and there was talk of a generator, which would mean hot water for the shower and eventually electricity. Soon they would start a nursery. Bernadette and Tibor were expecting a child. Eleazar's school fellows were on their way, twenty of them by all accounts, maybe more.

*W*HEN I RECEIVED THE CANDLE, Janos had just started his first semester at the Polytechnic. Those were the best days of our marriage. He came home straight from his class to study in our tiny dormitory room. Wintertime, we moved his desk right up against the gas heater, and as he read me bits of his engineering textbook, I would keep my stocking feet on his lap and he would rub them absentmindedly. Once in a while, he would dislodge the bag of lenses I had received from Laszlo, and he would tell me how glass fractured light.

One day, he turned one of the lenses towards the window and sent a beam of light straight at the candle.

"But your papers," I said. The room was overflowing with things that could catch on fire.

Janos was in an unusual mood, almost playful, and he said, "Do you think you married a pyromaniac." I held my breath, but the beam was exact: the wick smoked, sizzled, and took.

The candle had a steady flame and it smelled good. Janos stretched back his neck and frowned. Then he took out his measuring tape. There was a lot of afternoon sun in that room and he made a careful calculation of the angle of the shadows, the height of the flame. All the while, the wax dripped down. I was afraid he would set the room on fire, so I leaned over and blew the candle out.

9

*L*OUISA HAS NEVER ASKED ABOUT my husband. One would think that Gabor sprang out of my head, or out of that piano in that practice room. The winter Louisa lived with us on Prater Street, she seemed to have opened every drawer, and pulled out every photograph, postcard, and letter I possessed, but she found no sign of Janos. In this regard, she lacked imagination. Granted, by then he had been gone for six years, but his engineering journals still lay piled in his study, and for economy's sake, I couldn't bring myself to give his clothes away. His yellow scarf hung on a coatrack by the door.

It's true he left us, but most of the women in my situation were left by their husbands. Some of those husbands were transported east, some slaughtered during a forced march. I could count myself lucky that my own found work abroad before something else took him from me. As things stood, I could tell myself that he would return. After all, he'd taken no more than a single suitcase. He'd even left his pipe behind.

*W*HEN I FIRST MET JANOS, WE were both employed at the Katona Jozsef School for Girls, and I saw him at a faculty meeting, bent like a pretzel in his seat, knocking that pipe against the table in a way that wasn't endearing him to me as I was trying to take notes in shorthand and found it hard to concentrate.

I had been secretary there since the school re-opened in 1921. It was a gaudy, pink-white pastry of a place with neo-classical pillars and slippery floors. Two years before, under the Commune, it had been The Institute for Proletarian Education, and in the foyer was a mural of blue-skinned, wild-eyed seamstresses with their arms stretched towards a red horizon. The school was reluctant to paint over the mural because the artist had fled to Vienna and there was some chance he might turn out to be famous, but at some point someone added the Crown of Saint Stephen where the horizon used to be, thus giving the rapture of those seamstresses an acceptably patriotic object.

I did not actually speak to Janos until one afternoon when I was drinking a cup of tea at the *cukrászda* across from the school. I looked up and there he was, standing a foot away and staring. I started to get up, and almost irritably he waved me down again.

"That's a big cup," Janos said. He sat down. "They hold twice as much as coffee cups. I've measured them. I take it you're not independently wealthy. No rich husband."

I blurted out, "Who'd marry me?"

He pulled his tape-measure from his pocket and drew my cup across the table. Wrapping it around the rim, he frowned. "Yes, twice." His mustache was damp, and he wiped it with a napkin before saying, "Do you want me to buy you more tea?"

"Why should you pay for my tea?"

"It's a bourgeois custom," Janos said, and from that I understood that he was courting me.

That courtship lasted for perhaps three months and involved a small wading pool of very bad tea. We always met at the Hovirag, a tea shop with gilt-trimmed mirrors, lace-trimmed tablecloths, and limp peonies in bud-vases. On the whole, the cheap sentimentality suited Janos. To me, he seemed like a real thing in a false place. He was too tall to fit himself comfortably into the wire-backed chair, and his hands were too big even for the handles on the teacups.

He liked to compare teacups; apparently sizes varied. He would guess circumference and jot down the number on the tablecloth. Then, I'd hold the lip of the measuring tape while he pulled. If the true figure matched the estimate, half of his mouth would turn up, which was the closest he would get to a smile. "Good to train your eye," he'd say, "but there's no substitute for measurement." All of this would be said with his pipe between his teeth, and it was some time before I could make sense of it at all.

I will admit that I kept waiting for Janos to measure me. It seemed possible. At points, those estimating eyes would settle on me, almost accidentally. They were gray-blue, slanted, deep-set, and miserable, presented across a table like a couple of old coins. He was ten years older than me, a grown man who had gone through the Great War and the Commune, and now he was spending his afternoons in my company. There had to be some reason why.

*A*S TIME PASSED, HE CHEWED HIS pipe a little less and said more to me. He had been born near the Slovakian border to an Orthodox family, given the name Jochanan ben Ezra, and was made apprentice to a tinker at fourteen. Most of the work was dull and meticulous, done in a cellar underneath an inn. By sixteen, he already had a stoop. Even the synagogues were cramped and musty. As a journeyman, Jochanan sometimes went to bigger towns, and at the sight of a church spire, gaslights, and carriages, he would almost instinctively tuck his side locks behind his ears and try to see how long he could mix with a crowd in a café before he lost his nerve. Janos told me that he knew even then that he did not believe in God, that the knowledge was inborn, like a talent for mathematics.

One day, a German engineer passed through on his way to Debrecen, and because he was Jewish, he stayed in the quarter, though he was like no Jew anyone there had ever seen, with hair shaved well above the temples and a neat mustache. He spoke Yiddish, of course, but awkwardly, and as it was well known that Jochanan spoke some German, he was commandeered to show the gentleman to his room. There they spent most of the night in conversation, and in the end he gave the young man three engineering journals and the names of some good textbooks, as well as a few addresses in Budapest.

The journals were hard going; at first it would take Janos half the night to work his way through a paragraph. But as he persisted, page after page opened, and language and content drew him further on until there was no question what ought to happen next. The morning Janos finished the third journal, he took a carriage to Debrecen, where he got himself shaved down to a mustache and bought a new suit of clothes. Then he took the train to Budapest, the center of the world, home of Andjos Jedlik, the Father of the High Voltage Capacitor Battery.

He formally declared himself to be without religion. The ceremony took place on the Sabbath and was witnessed by his landlady and a student Janos had pulled in from the street. The student was good-natured because Janos was going to pay him. The landlady, a good Christian, disapproved, but she had a full month's rent in advance, rare in that district, and so she was willing to placate her new tenant.

Janos made them both stand in his furnished room where he had not yet unpacked his suitcase. He handed the student his mint-fresh electrical engineering textbook, and set his right hand on it, saying, "As of this day, I cast away all ignorance and take on the mantle of human knowledge and human progress."

To mark the occasion, he offered each of the witnesses a cigarette which he lit with such aplomb that they might not have noticed that his hand was shaking. It was the first time he had broken the Sabbath.

*J*ANOS STILL HADN'T MANAGED TO get his degree. The war had interrupted, and then, after the Commune fell, there was the quota on Jews entering universities. Yet before Christmas, he planned to take the exams again and he would do so well, the Polytechnic would have to readmit him, and within five years he figured he could write his own ticket. An engineer could work anywhere in the world. Numbers were a common language. Janos pulled from his pocket the silver measuring tape and drew a length across the table. "A meter and a quarter wide in France, in India, in Australia. One world. The rest is mindless superstition."

He ran through measurements with a driving optimism that seemed at cross-purposes with his hangdog face, as though those numbers had to do with the life he would live one day, and his expression with his hangdog present. Why was he telling me all of this? Then, abruptly, he would ask something like: "What do you think of the name Gabor for a son?" Floored, amused, shy, horrified, I would agree with everything he said. I think that's why he considered me sensible.

At night, I'd sit cross-legged on Bela's bed and open up his maps. First, I found Janos's village, north of Eger. It wasn't in Hungary anymore; we'd lost that territory after the war. Now even its name would be in Slovak. What was it like, to be from a place that no longer existed? Did it make you homeless, or did it make you free?

It was so strange to sit on Bela's bed and think about Janos, who was as different from Bela as a broom was from a bear. Bela had left me here with all these maps, roll after roll: Hungary, Central Europe, the Western Hemisphere. One world: Berlin, Rome, Paris, London. Another map took me across the sea to New York, and from thence to San Francisco, and back east again. Map after map lay across my legs like dry, light blankets. Hadn't I long ago drawn from the deck the card Winter, carrying everything she owned wrapped in a little ragged bundle?

So it seemed settled; I would marry Janos. Admittedly, I wondered how it would come to pass. There was our life together in all of those far-flung countries where we would live with the son named Gabor. Then there was the grubby little lace-trimmed table where we both sat smoking now. How could we get from here to there?

It didn't help that we only saw each other in the Hovirag. After we'd finished our tea, or sometimes even in the middle of a conversation, he would abruptly push his chair back, mumble an apology, and head out the door. Every afternoon, I promised myself I would leave with him, but when he rose, he seemed to shake off any knowledge of my presence, and he left our table without so much as a backwards glance. I will admit, I found him, at those moments, powerfully attractive, as he tucked his pipe in its case, buttoned his overcoat, and strode out onto Andrassy Street. I watched him through the window. He was taller than everyone else, and walked faster.

Of course, given the circumstances, a less callow girl would have assumed that Janos was already married. Why else the mystery? He'd leave a little loose tobacco in our ashtray, and I'd lean in and take a whiff; it made my eyes water. Maybe he'd even told me where he was going. After all, half of the time, he still spoke through his pipe-stem and I wouldn't understand a word.

MEANWHILE, I WAS STILL LIVING at Aunt Monika's. Though my income could have paid for a room at a boardinghouse, the idea struck both Aunt Moni and Adele as absurd, even insulting. They fluttered around me, pretty, charming, gracious ladies who had lost the boy they'd spoiled and probably found me a poor substitute. Adele had given up David and was keeping company with a dashing surgeon named Andras. She tried to introduce me to Andras's younger brother, a regular bohemian, she said, but all through the intimate dinner at the expensive restaurant, I felt myself rise slowly to the ceiling and watch us from that height as though it were a play called *Young People Having a Delightful Time*. Andras knew all about the Riesling we were drinking and made a series of German puns. The bohemian brother recited Brecht from memory, still a daring thing to do back then as real Communists had fled to Austria or rotted in jail all over Hungary. Adele flashed me look after look below her glowing curls, and I could tell that she assumed the smile pinned on my face was genuine, so I allowed my spirit to leave the room entirely.

After the boys had put us in a taxi, Adele said to me, "I think Andras's brother likes you. You can be charming when you want to be, you know. But did you really have to smoke so much? While we were eating?"

"Some men don't mind a girl who smokes," I said.

"No, I suppose not." She leaned back into the depths of the taxi cab's upholstery and looked suddenly wistful. "Do you ever wonder where we'll be in twenty-five years? I mean," she said, "Bela always knew he'd go to Palestine. But honestly, I don't know what'll happen to me, if I'll be a nurse or not be a nurse, or marry Andras or someone I don't even know yet, or no one at all."

I leaned in close and said, "Give me your palm."

She gazed up through her eyelashes. "Where did you pick that up?"

"Gypsies," I said. I held the slim right hand Adele presented and turned it towards the passing streetlights. The lines were faint, the soft skin just above the wrist almost transparent. It felt unfinished. Still, I could not tell her that, so I said, "Very subtle lines here. There's more to you than there seems."

"What does that mean?" Adele asked, rather sharply.

"It means," I said, "that you've got a good mind, though you work hard to hide it. Also, you'll be an excellent nurse."

But those were commonplaces. As the taxi turned up Dohany Street and passed the synagogue, I knew I had to say more, so I asked for her left hand, squinted, and saw the smooth palm divide itself into braided lines that flowed up from the base.

"So, Nora," Adele said, "tell me. Where will I be in twenty-five years?"

That would be 1946. I touched my forefinger to my cousin's wrist as we cut past a streetlight and abruptly, each fine line burst into flame. I said, "I can't read palms, not really."

Adele retrieved her hand. "I don't believe you. You can. You just don't want to read mine."

Fortunately, we'd reached our house by then, and Aunt Monika spread out some coffee and cakes and turned on the gramophone, and Adele either forgot to press me or she had tact enough to let the matter go.

What would Adele and Aunt Moni make of my young man, that is if he was my young man at all? I wrote to Bela, who was still in Haifa then: *What would you think of a child named Gabor? I suppose you and your Dori would go for something Hebrew.*

I imagined that when Janos and I actually married, I would write Bela with the news. It never occurred to me that anyone else would have to know.

I OWED THE JOB AT THE KATONA Jozsef School to Bela; he'd written to the headmistress about me soon after I arrived in Budapest. She had been in charge before the Commune, when the school was simply called the Rakoczi Gimnazium and had no pretensions. Back then, Bela had taught a little German and Italian to replace men drafted during the Great War. It was right around the corner from his home on Dob Street. Bela had been absurdly young, but he must have made a strong impression because the headmistress hired me on his recommendation, sight unseen. When I arrived the first day and asked where she kept the typewriter, she admitted it had been tucked away somewhere but she hadn't thought it necessary. She was a mild lady with short hair and a loose gown, a little too old to try to look so modern.

"I've always done up the correspondence by hand," she said. "It is more personal. Still, I suppose you could give the old girl a try. If you think it would be faster. We are a little pokey around here, what with the changes."

In that office were at least a dozen boxes of loose correspondence and contracts and ten-month-old tuition checks, a few unsigned. These I sorted as best I could. Then there were reams of old materials from the Commune about the plight of Pesti seamstresses which sat under a leak and were infested by mites. I found two strong men on the street and offered them both beers if they would clear the mess away.

The school had no filing system to speak of; the headmistress had stuffed everything she could into the drawers of a beautiful rosewood desk, and when I told her we needed metal cabinets, she said nothing. At first I thought she disapproved, but when the cabinets appeared the next day, I realized the poor woman was terrified. Of me.

Given those circumstances, it was no surprise that I outlasted the head-mistress and four others. In fact, I would be a fixture at the Katona Jozsef School right through the early forties. Students would pass through the office, cadging change for the *cukrászda* or complaining about this teacher or that, but on the whole I wasn't a favorite with the girls. I was too efficient about passing on records to their parents and I did not take bribes. Once, someone let slip that they called me Old Shylock. Interesting, given that most of the students had been drawn from the surrounding neighborhood, and were Jews themselves.

Janos was not popular either. As one of the few male instructors, he should have held some fascination for the girls, but he spent most of his class facing the chalkboard where he scraped out problems and solutions, and when he would turn he would be coated, head-to-toe, with chalk as though he'd fallen into a lime pit. If they made a mistake, he would wag his finger at them and back up, knocking his head against the board. Sometimes, I would overhear girls in the hallway doing Janos Gratz imitations, muttering and clearing their throats.

One said, "Did you hear about him in the cafeteria?"

"Cafeteria? I thought he ate chalk."

"He was in the cafeteria last week, Reka says, and he bends down while we eat lunch and right in the open he looks up the girls' skirts at their panties."

I suddenly threw open the door, and said, "The floor."

The girls froze. They had been all bunched up in a cluster like a body with three heads, and they turned their round, stupid faces in my direction.

I clarified. "He's measuring the floor. That's why he kneels down."

"Yes, ma'am," one of them said, and from the way her lower lip trembled, I could tell she was about to burst.

I turned and closed the door.

$\mathcal{T}$HAT AFTERNOON, WHEN I MET Janos at the Hovirag, I asked him, "What do you think of the girls?"

He took a long draw on his pipe. "I don't think of them at all."

"They think of you," I said. Then, I braced myself and added, "They think of me and you. There may be problems."

"Problems?"

"I don't—" I hesitated, and leaned back in the chair, glancing through the window at the school across the road where girls emerged in their blue pinafores. Finally, I said, "I don't understand girls."

"The whole class is embalmed," Janos said, and I didn't know if he meant his math class or the middle class. I also knew that I had been wrong. I had nothing to do with the future Janos had planned for himself. I didn't have good sense, not an ounce of it. Who couldn't see right through me, if he took the trouble? I had the strangest sensation then that Bela was observing all of this, standing, bemused, in the doorway of the *cukrászda,* shaking his head. Janos was muttering something now, into that hateful pipe-stem, and I told myself that there was no one in the world to whom I was not a stranger.

"Janos," I said, as though saying the name out loud would prove me wrong. But he was rising to go.

Then, he was out of the chair and through the door of the Hovirag, walking briskly up Andrassy Street, with his shoulders bunched up and his hands in the pockets of his overcoat and the back of his brown hair sticking up like a coxcomb. But this time, I ran behind him, taking two steps for his every one, and then I did a very foolish thing. I grabbed hold of his sleeve and pulled until it tore. He turned around.

My face was red and my eyes smarted. I said, "You're ashamed of me."

Janos said nothing. He dislodged his sleeve from my hand and held the torn gabardine, staring at it with wonder.

I said, "I'll mend it for you."

"Now? You carry around a needle and thread?"

"No," I said, and I started to cry.

Janos just stood there with the patch in his hand and he said, "Look, don't. I'm no good at this. I wouldn't care, only the coat's a loan from a friend and he doesn't have another one."

"Who is the friend? Why can't I meet him? Why don't you ever take me anywhere?" Even as I spoke, the questions struck me as completely reasonable. I felt startled that I'd never asked them before.

"Nora," Janos said. His voice had dropped back to that hateful whisper. Now he moved in close of his own accord, though my head was buried in my hands and I couldn't see him anymore. "I'm a Communist. My friends are Communists."

Now my head was pressed against his chest, and his hands were buried in my hair. What he had just said wouldn't sink in for hours, both the substance of it and what it meant that he had told me. Yet all I could say was, "That doesn't matter. You're ashamed of me," just so he would stroke my hair again.

*Q*URING THE COMMUNE, ON THE first of May 1919, in Budapest there was a grand parade. The streets were strung all over with red bunting imported from the Soviet Union, and proletarians gathered under banners and marched on the Great Boulevard. Railway workers led a plaster locomotive expelling real steam; the film industry was represented by a twenty-meter film canister pulled by six white horses; girls in red neck-kerchiefs sang folk-melodies and a pensioners' band played a rather ragged version of the *Internationale;* children tossed red confetti hither-thither into people's hair.

Janos didn't like parades. By then he was twenty-nine, too old to be an enthusiast. He had returned from the Great War to find the Polytechnic in a shambles, and he had found a position at the Institute for Proletarian Education only because he claimed his mother was a seamstress. He was put-off by the impossible prospect of crossing the Great Boulevard, and the confetti made him sneeze, so almost by chance he stepped into what turned out to be a local chapter of the Party.

The office was lively, full of brisk young men in leather jackets writing up dispatches for this and that newsletter. Janos sat sullenly in a hard chair until a pretty girl asked him if he knew how to type, and when he shook his head, she asked him if he knew how to run a printing press, and when he didn't respond at all, she said, "You must be good for something, you're so serious," and she kissed him on the nose and walked away.

Then Janos got up and took a step towards her, but, as was his way, he stumbled, this time straight into one of the boys in the leather jackets, and Janos said to him, "This parade is obscene! How can you justify spending that kind of money on red bunting when your revolution is bankrupt?"

The boy laughed, and he said, "Comrade, why do you say to me, *your* revolution? It's yours too. You make me think of the rebellious son they talk about at the Passover Seder who said to his father: 'Why did the Lord lead *you* from bondage?'"

"I don't care for religious references," said Janos.

"I'm born Catholic myself. Just keep good company," the young man said. Then he shouted out, "Hey! Balazs! Sign this donkey up to do something or other. He's an accountant."

"Teacher," Janos said. Then with the sense of making a confession, "And student of engineering."

"Very good, very good," said Balazs, a boy with twinkling eyes who couldn't have been older than seventeen. And that was how Janos became a member of the Communist Party.

T   WAS   THAT   SIMPLE.   YOU filled out a form and they kept a copy for their files, and you were a Party member. They gave Janos an assignment, to teach elementary economics to a group of workers in a dismal suburb an hour east of Pest. After the first class or two, the only regular attendees were a blind old man and his illiterate daughter. Half the time, Janos ended up in the old man's flat pretending to drink homemade *pálinka* and nursing a guilty conscience.

The daughter's devotion to Bela Kun and the revolution was fierce and genuine. She made Janos read out transcripts of the debates in Parliament, and she learned parts of them by heart. Her pox-scarred face always looked a little unclean. When she talked about the Commune, she'd sweat as though she had a fever, and she'd grip Janos's hand across the rickety table and say, "We're so lucky to have lived to see this."

What could Janos say to that? It couldn't be answered. That daughter had lost her husband in the war. Janos was afraid to ask where he had fallen. Janos himself had overseen the construction of temporary bridges on the Russian Front. As they had worked under pressure, he had doubled as surveyor and taken photographs of the area with a portable box-camera. There was something clean and scientific about setting up the tripod, snapping and developing those photographs, and overlaying the prints with faint cross-hatches in pencil.

Yet it seemed that measuring a photograph was no substitute for measuring a site, and they distorted the height and width to the point where the materials ordered might as well have been paste and pick-up sticks. The moment men started across, bridge after bridge collapsed. As a consequence, Janos ended up in the infantry, where he tried not to think too hard about what he had done.

Janos told that story to the woman, whose only response was: "Could you take a picture of me?"

Reluctantly, he dug up the old box-camera and took it to the block of flats the next afternoon. He photographed the father and daughter together. The father's cataracts had turned his eyes completely white, and his skull had visible brown spots. Even as Janos took the photograph, he wondered if the woman knew what she would be forced to see. Her hand was folded over her father's, and she stared into the camera without smiling.

After that day, Janos stopped teaching economics altogether. Instead, he became something of an official photographer for that block of flats. Into that grim kitchen came old women in embroidered blouses and kerchiefs wanting a picture to send to family in the provinces, young girls with waved hair and lip-rouge hoping to send a photo to a film director, and veteran after veteran in their uniforms. One of the veterans seemed too old to have served; his hair was already white and the teeth he had left were brown with tobacco. He looked as though he hadn't taken off his uniform since the war, and it was only when he put his crumpled soldier's cap on his head that Janos saw he was missing an arm.

"You take my picture," said the man. "People should know." He took a long suck on a cigarette then, and Janos gave in to weariness. What should people know? Economics? The sight of their own faces? How to build a bridge? How to forget?

One afternoon, as Janos was pretending to drink another glass of *pálinka* and smoking his pipe, someone knocked on the door. This, itself, was unusual because nobody usually bothered knocking. The woman answered and before Janos could even see who had arrived, he could tell by her expression that it was someone she recognized and also feared.

In fact, it was a Komsomol, a man around Janos's own age, though he looked younger. He wore a leather jacket, but his rank was clear in his carriage and in his voice as he said, "You're Janos Gratz? The engineer?"

Janos lowered his pipe and looked the fellow over. He didn't look unfriendly. Still, Janos hesitated as he said, "I'm not an engineer."

"That must have been why your bridges always collapsed," said the Komsomol. Then he took Janos's hand and gave it a shake. "I'm here to take you to the district headquarters. We need a group portrait to send abroad, and obviously, you're our man. After all, you're the reason I became a Communist."

Speechless, Janos blinked, and the Komsomol's face went a little out of focus as he went on pumping Janos's hand, and he told Janos how he had been on one of those bridges when it fell apart, and how he had been taken prisoner by the Russians, and there joined a Marxist study group, along with Bela Kun, and so on, and as he cheerfully went on, he led Janos down the hall to a waiting automobile where he was driven to a well-appointed office in the Buda hills and asked to take group and individual portraits of most of the members of the Kun's inner circle.

It turned out that three of the Komsomols Janos photographed were what they called his "front line recruits," captured by the Russians because of a flaw in Janos's designs, and converted to Marxism as prisoners of war. "They ought to erect a statue to you in front of Parliament," one said to Janos, and another suggested that he move to Romania and build bridges for the Whites.

Yet none of this banter was ill intentioned. In fact, they had a confidence that they gladly extended to Janos. It was assumed he was as happy with himself as they were with themselves, and they expected him to make as many jokes at their expense and seemed baffled at his silence. After he'd finished taking the photographs, the Komsomol who had fetched him led him to a restaurant and ordered pork, and when there was no pork to be had, he ordered cakes, and when there were no cakes to be had, he ordered vanilla ice cream. Indeed, with no food coming from the provinces, they all seemed to live on vanilla ice cream that spring. It made Janos light-headed and slightly sick, but seemed to have the opposite effect on the Komsomol, who scraped his plate.

"So what are you doing now?" the Komsomol asked Janos.

"Teaching mathematics to seamstresses," he said.

"Ah, very nice, useful to know that sort of thing," the Komsomol said. He ordered more ice cream, and then he turned to Janos again. "Don't tell me you've given up on engineering."

"Shouldn't I?" Janos felt himself go red up to the ears. "My bridges fall down." Then he surprised himself by going on. "You joke, all of you, but there were men on those bridges who didn't become Communists. They drowned or they were shot or they were maimed."

"History," said the Komsomol, "is a process. Bridges fall down. So build better bridges, Comrade Gratz. Be on the side of the builders. Are you a Nihilist?"

Janos stared down at his plate of melted ice cream and said, "No, I'm not."

"You look like a Nihilist. You look like a donkey, frankly. No wonder I found you up there drinking. Get something in your stomach. Don't you like ice cream?"

"It's too sweet for me," Janos said. "So is all this talk about being on the side of the builders. So is your manner. Men died because of me, and they're going to die because of you, because of this thing you call a process. Look at these," Janos said, and he pulled out his photographs of the residents of the block of flats—the veterans, the disappointed old women, the gaunt girls, and the blind man and his daughter—and he fanned them across that sticky table, all the while wondering why he was bothering. The Komsomol put down his spoon and picked up first one, then another. He threw both back on the table.

"Well, then, you're just a Romantic," he said to Janos. "A donkey and a Romantic."

"You're the Romantic," Janos countered, and the men argued like two boys, closing the restaurant and walking off together. Eventually Janos took another photograph of the Komsomol. His uniform was half-unbuttoned, revealing the medal of his patron saint. A smile was smeared crookedly from chin to cheek. As for the cap, it was frankly off-balance, and a lot of clean hair sprang from it and caught the gaslight by the entrance of the subway station.

 ASKED JANOS, "DO YOU STILL have the photograph?"

He leaned back on the public bench where we'd settled together, and shook his head. If he had been running from me to an appointment, he had missed it long ago.

But I asked, "What about the other photographs?"

"Gone," Janos said.

"Where did they go?" I asked, without quite knowing why.

Janos stuffed his pipe and lit it, buying time. As he sat with his neck bent and a cable in that neck throbbing, I tried to detect in him something of the spirit he must have shared with the young man when they had argued through the night.

I asked, "Do you still take pictures?"

In a flash, Janos turned his head. "What do you mean by that?"

"Nothing," I said, and my voice shook a little. "It was just a question."

Janos was looking at me now, unmistakably looking at me with eyes like lenses, and I don't know what he found in my face, but when he spoke again, it was with hesitation, but more gently. "Nora, I don't mean to seem, well, how I seem. It's only, those photographs, they're out of my hands now. They were taken from me."

"By the Komsomol?" I asked.

"By the new government," said Janos. "By the Whites, the reactionaries. And, well, how smart are you, Nora?" He paused to catch his breath, and he was still looking at me, as though if he broke his gaze, he'd know what he risked in speaking. "How much do I have to spell out for you? What do you think happened to the people in those photographs?"

That brought a lump to my throat. "Look," I said, "I'm sorry. You don't need to tell me anything."

"They were good people," he said.

Then I had to ask, "You say *were* good. Are they dead?"

"Some of them," said Janos, "and some in prison, and some in exile, and some, well, what do you want me to say? You're a young girl, Nora. These aren't trivial concerns."

I broke the gaze, at last, myself, because otherwise, I would have asked him about the blind girl and her father, whether they were implicated too, and the longer I delayed, the more my thoughts kept racing, until I was wondering why the people met those ends, but he was free. Had he turned in those photographs to spare his own life? Had he been considered too unimportant to pursue?

Janos said, "Look, do you want me to lie to you?"

He allowed me silence. I used it to keep on staring at my hands, which looked small and white.

"I can't tell you everything. I could lie to you, but I don't want to lie to you."

What could I say to that? By now, it was twilight, and Janos's torn coat was damp with perspiration. Sitting so close to me, he looked younger, lean, anxious, giving off a scent of panic. What I knew now was like the tear in that overcoat, something that couldn't be undone. My head rang with too many thoughts at once. Finally, I asked him, "Janos, if you don't trust me, why did you tell me this much?"

"It's not a matter of not trusting you," he said. Then, with something approaching tenderness, he added, "I want to protect you."

And I thought: I want to protect you too. From what? From sorrow, maybe, or a deep loneliness, from having to lie to me. "Janos," I said, "I'm not so fragile."

After some hesitation, he said, "I know." But that was all he would tell me.

MIGHT BE ACCUSED OF LOSING
my husband the day I got him, that afternoon on Andrassy Street. I compensated by treating the matter of Janos with a Janos-like reticence. Adele and Aunt Moni didn't know I was engaged until the day I got married when I took them to the courthouse to serve as witnesses.

Aunt Moni wore one of her pre-war hats for the occasion, a white-plumed boat that made her look tiny and old. She laid a hand on my arm, maybe to steady herself against the sight of Janos knocking his pipe against the mahogany bench in the judge's chambers. She leaned in close enough for me to smell mothballs and whispered, "He seems like a very steady boy."

Adele held Aunt Moni's arm and kept a bright smile pinned to her face. Afterwards, Janos had to study for the entrance exam to the Polytechnic, so I went back to the apartment to get my things. Adele followed me into Bela's old room and asked, "Why didn't you ever bring him home?"

"To Barnahely? To get my mother's blessing?"

"I meant to our apartment. To us."

"To get your blessing?" I think my tone was a little wry. "I don't suppose he's what you might have for a husband, Adele. He isn't a doctor, for one thing. I don't think he's tasted Riesling in his life."

By now, of course, Andras was history. Adele let my insults pass over her, and she sat me down on Bela's bed and tried to talk to me seriously. "It's done," she said. "That's that. You're married. He ought to make a decent living if he's an engineer. And if he looks like a scarecrow with a mustache, maybe that's what you like in a man. But do you really love each other?"

"What do you think? He married me."

"Has he said it?"

Now I felt as though Adele had stepped into territory where she wasn't welcome. I let a telling silence build as I tucked all those dresses Adele had given me into a carpetbag. The late-afternoon sunshine slanted across all those rows of dusty books Bela had left behind.

Adele watched me pack for a while, and then she got up to help. She was far more efficient than I was, folding the better underwear and stockings in tissue, and even throwing in a handful of lavender, "like the fancy ladies do," she said. "What do you want for a wedding present?"

I said, "You don't have to give me anything, Adele."

"Not even my blessing?" She rubbed a little lavender between her fingers. "Hmmm. You'll need this. That boy doesn't bathe. You think I'm jealous?"

"No," I said.

"You want me not to tease you about him?"

"I don't know." I closed the carpetbag before she could put anything else in it, and I turned towards the window. "I never told him I love him either," I said. "We don't talk like that."

"Maybe I talk like that too much," said Adele. "To me, it doesn't feel like such a hard thing to say."

"Lucky you," I said. How could I help, just then, but think of Bela, who probably was just like his sister, spreading his love around like apricot jam. I had spent most of the night before trying to write him a letter about the marriage, and typically, settled for writing one I couldn't send. *Well, then, Borzas Medve, shaggy bear, you weren't here to give me away. Maybe you wouldn't have given me away. Maybe you would have kept me.* Like all the letters in the shoe-box it felt as though it were in code. Either he'd understand or he wouldn't, and either possibility would be unbearable.

I allowed myself to accept a token gift from Adele, a lamb's-wool coat that she'd bought for herself, but which, she claimed, was much too short, so she really must have been thinking of me all along. And, she added, it could be a man's jacket if I reversed the buttons; it would do for Janos as well. It was a very good coat, dark and soft, with a square collar, horn buttons, and black silk lining. As I fastened the buttons, I felt protected and glamorous. It would suit some men, I suppose, but I could no more imagine Janos wearing it than I could imagine him wearing a monocle.

Aunt Monika meanwhile had filled a crate with preserves, biscuits, sausage, and most of her good hand-painted Herendi china tea-set wrapped in the same tissue Adele had used for my underwear.

"I can't take the pot," I said.

"We have another pot," said Aunt Moni, and then she started to cry. "It's not Herendi, but we have another pot. Norika, I wish your mother were here. I know I can't take her place, but she would want you to have nice things."

Faced with the sight of Aunt Moni dabbing her eyes with a bit of tissue paper, I found her a handkerchief. She blew her nose. "Thank you for the tea-set," I said, trying to mean it. "We'll have you over for tea as soon as we've settled."

I cabled my mother. We'd written each other regularly since I'd moved to Budapest, though the letters were rather telegraphic. To me she did not seem badly off. Uncle Oszkar's shop was under Laszlo's care and earned a decent income. She had become friendly with the porteress at the Száras Gimnazium dormitory, and they took a trip to Szeged to hear the orchestra.

She replied: *Now that you are married and will want to settle down, I will make arrangements for the deed to the house to be placed in your name, as I trust you will not turn me out onto the street.*

I said to Aunt Monika, "She can't seriously expect us to move to Kisbarnahely."

"Maybe not," said Aunt Monika. Then she paused and set the lid on the crate. "She'll want to meet him."

"He'll be what she expected," I said to her. "No social graces." At once I regretted the flippancy because her eyes teared up again, and I wasn't sure if it was from happiness this time. Adele threw her a look I didn't want to understand. I took the opportunity to give the two of them a quick kiss goodbye, call the porter to carry the suitcase and crate, and be on my way.

I GOT ANOTHER CRATE FROM Laszlo. It arrived the day Janos took his entrance exam for the Polytechnic, and it was Janos who opened it, prying the slats apart with the back of a hammer. Encased in straw was a music box made of cut glass so one could see the works.

Janos turned the handle, and out came, of all things, *Little Dog, Little Dog*. I'd never heard that tune come from a music box before, and it made me think of the drunk old Transylvanian, but also of Laszlo himself whistling on his bicycle or Uncle Oszkar laying the table in his backyard. The melody was infectious, slight, the dog, the sheep, the black-eyed love a bold love, the blue-eyed love a true love. I wanted to say all of this to Janos, to tell him about Kisbarnahely and the sunflowers, about the way I would pass by dances in the town hall, hear the fiddle play *Little Dog, Little Dog* and feel a pinch in the heart. But Janos was completely engrossed in the workings of the box.

"This is remarkable," he said. "He must have done it by hand. There's no other explanation. I'm going to open it up."

I caught my breath. "Janos, it's glass. Be careful."

"Careful?" He smiled. "Nora, I used to be a tinker, remember? Trust me." He was in high spirits. The exam had gone very well. I think he enjoyed my obvious anxiety as he produced a tiny screwdriver and removed the bottom of the box as precisely as a surgeon.

We both lay on our bellies on that dormitory floor, and he took me, step by step, through the workings of that small, clean device Laszlo had made. We spent the afternoon there, breathing in dust and the smell of the straw from the crate, my husband lying next to me and tapping, with a pencil point, gear after gear of the music box. He didn't whisper, didn't need to, we were so close. The light waned, and after a while I could not imagine that my husband actually could see a thing he was describing. Nor could I listen. It was enough to hear the tapping of the pencil and the sound of his voice.

Then it got so dark that he couldn't even pretend to give a lesson. He turned the handle: *Lit-tle-dog-lit-tle-dog-you-will-bring-my-sheep-to-me*— so slowly that the notes divided and lost meaning, and I thought back to those afternoons in Uncle Oszkar's workshop where I turned those handles backwards and made random music spark and sing. I looked at Janos, a man Laszlo's age, and like Laszlo, he had blue eyes, and like Laszlo, hair the color of straw, and just as Laszlo brought my past to me, this man would carry me forward just as clearly as those careful hands moved from the works of the machine and found me. I felt his mustache brush against my ear, and I thought: Time moves on, thank God.

*J*ANOS DID SCORE HIGH ENOUGH on that exam to enter the Polytechnic, and not long afterwards, he found us the flat on Prater Street. It was grim, but I'd figured that it would do for a while. I couldn't have known then that I would live there for the next twenty years. It had some good features: ample space, French windows looking onto the street, and a courtyard with a live tree in the middle. It was also a short tram-ride from Aunt Monika's. I would stop there, sometimes, after work, when Janos was studying, and when he had business that kept him out late, I would often stay through supper.

I never did manage to follow through on my own invitation to tea. Frankly, it was easier to go to Dob Street and pour from the non-Herendi teapot into the mismatched cups. Janos might have joined me once or twice. I don't remember. His schedule was erratic, and it was sometimes difficult for him to know where he would be from one hour to the next. There was his teaching at the Katona Jozsef School, his course-work at the Polytechnic, and also two or three nights a week when he wouldn't come home until well after dark and would crawl beside me in bed, smelling of mimeograph fluid and cigarettes.

If you do not ask once, you cannot ask again. I don't know why that is the case, but it is so. I did wonder about the work he did, why it was dangerous, why it was worth the trouble. I speculated: Surely there was a girl Comrade who worked beside Janos, a bouncing, healthy working girl for whom none of this was a mystery. There were nights, even early in our marriage, when I wondered if my husband would come home. Yet he came home.

Once, there was paste in his hair, and I combed it through with vinegar without asking how the paste had gotten there or if the anti-Horthy posters he had plastered everywhere would be scraped off by the police by morning.

I did let slip, "You're a little old for this."

"Will it all come out?" he asked me, as though I combed paste from men's hair every day.

I answered, "With your hair, I don't think anyone will notice."

He let himself smile then. "Nora, why'd I drag you into this?"

I would reply, "You didn't. Go to sleep."

Sometimes, he'd sleep. More often, he would lie with me for a while, and then get up and study those engineering books that he had promised would take us right off the map of Hungary to Vienna, to London, to America. When I woke up, he might have his head on his desk, and I would wake him up by turning the music box backwards the way I had when I was a child in

Uncle Oszkar's workshop. I'd pour him coffee from the pot hand-painted with blond shepherdesses and white doves.

*J*ANOS WASN'T HOME THE SUNDAY Adele finally decided to visit our flat. She appeared without warning, carrying three hairy-looking red flowers, and as she took the place in, I could see her heart drop to her feet. Compared to the elegant clutter of Dob Street, it must have looked like a warehouse, bare and cavernous. To make matters worse, I was drying laundry, and linens and towels were draped across every piece of furniture we had. There was even a bedspread hanging from the kitchen cabinet. As for me, I had been leaning over a laundry basin, wringing out Janos's underwear.

"Where should I put these?" Adele asked, meaning the flowers.

"Just empty the cold water from the pot by the window. Thanks. They're nice," I added. I couldn't think of why she'd turned up at all.

She did find the pot, which of course was the Herendi china. It was too short, and she hunted for scissors to cut the flower stems, all the while trying to hide the fact that she was appalled at what she saw. She asked me, "Don't you have a maid?"

"A maid owns the building," I said. It was true. Prater Street No. 30 was owned by a retired housekeeper who had managed to buy the property for almost nothing when the owner left for Vienna during the short-lived days of the Commune. The woman must have been close to ninety, and occasionally I came across the terrible sight of her on her knees, scrubbing the hallway.

I took my hands out of the laundry basin and wiped them dry before lighting a cigarette. Adele asked, "Where's Janos?"

"He must have heard you were coming," I said. "You're not serious, Adele. You actually came to see Janos?"

"Well, I wanted to catch both of you," she said. "We're going to a lecture."

I laughed. That was a new one. "I can't leave looking like this," I said, thinking that got me well out of it.

But Adele was surprisingly emphatic. She opened the wardrobe and managed to dislodge a decent dress, and even a pair of shoes I had forgotten I owned, and she bullied me into changing, even going so far as to buckle the first shoe before I thought to ask her:

"Are you kidnapping me?"

"That's not such a bad idea," said Adele. By now, she had my other shoe on and seemed to be deciding if I would need my coat.

Helpless, and admittedly curious, I asked, "So what's the topic of this mysterious lecture?"

Adele said, "The Idea of Zion."

$\mathcal{M}$Y FIRST SURPRISE WAS THIS: The lecture took place in the auditorium of the Katona Jozsef School. Many of the girls I knew were in attendance, not in their school pinafores but in bright, crisp party-dresses. They called to each other across the auditorium so cheerfully that they might as well have been in the courtyard of a block of flats. Every seat was taken, and Adele and I were forced to stand in the back. I couldn't have felt older or more out of place.

"You rushed me out of there so fast that I forgot my cigarettes," I said to Adele.

She ignored my tone, in fact, suppressed a smile. "Good," she said. Then, everyone started shouting and clapping, and onto the stage of the auditorium walked Bela.

My stomach dropped to my toes. I had not seen my cousin in eleven years. He was a grown man now, in a badly fitting sack-suit, but unmistakably it was Bela, with that mop of hair, those outsized hands and feet, the way that even at the podium he took a moment to cup his chin in his hand and stare out at the crowd of girls, too bewildered to acknowledge their applause.

Adele tugged my arm and whispered: "So?"

I brushed her off and strained up to get a better look. Bela was trying to calm down the crowd, particularly the girls in the front row who seemed about to storm the stage. It was then I remembered that he used to teach at that school years before; he must have retained a following. He blushed and grinned as he recognized face after face, and then he managed to quiet them down enough to address them.

"I see my old students are here. Now what did I teach you? Hebrew or German?"

"Lashon Galut!" one bold girl called. It must have been Hebrew.

Bela said, "I feel ridiculous. I've given this speech in five cities in eight days and this is the first time I've been put in my place. How old are you now, Rozsa? Sixteen? Want me to speak Persian?"

"Chatul!" she called.

Adele whispered, "That's cat." I had forgotten she knew Hebrew. I thought: Bela sounds different when he speaks than when he writes, more like a boy, or maybe it's because the last time I heard Bela speak at all, he'd been fifteen years old. And he's here, here now. How can he be here now?

In fact, Bela himself rubbed his face as though to make sure he really did exist. Then he said, "All right. I won't talk about Tilulit. Or about Nathan or Dori. They send their love. You should know Bernadette and Tibor's baby Gezer just said his first word. And it was in Hebrew."

That got them whooping again, and that got him blushing again, but there was something studied in his embarrassment, I thought. He'd acquired a firm jaw, and his suntan made his teeth look too white. I didn't think I liked it, nor did I like the way he was playing the crowd. I would give him hell afterwards. Then I went cold. I would see him afterwards. What would I say?

He went on. "The man we are going to hear today is less advanced than Gezer. He will be speaking German." When no one laughed, he quickly added, "No, to be honest, let me tell you a story. Recently my kibbutz built some bookshelves and turned part of the dining hall into a library. We had an argument. Should every book in the library be in Hebrew? In the end, we reached a compromise. We would allow one book in German. That book is called *Ich und Du* and it is by the man I'm introducing tonight. Comrades, girls, ladies, gentlemen, friends," he said, "I present to you Doctor Martin Buber."

That was all Bela had to say. He fell back, and the girls deflated with an audible sigh as a soft-eyed gentleman with an enormous beard rose up to take his place. Doctor Buber's cultivated German rose and fell, liturgical. He probably said a lot of wise things. He probably would have made a Zionist out of me. But my eyes rested on Bela, who had managed to free up a seat somewhere at the end of the first row and who seemed almost as unconcerned with the lecture as I did. Frankly, he looked exhausted.

Doctor Buber spoke for two hours. He managed to wear down the girls, who not only stopped whispering to each other, but seemed to stop breathing altogether. After it was over, there was a rush for the reception hall, and I lost sight of Bela. Adele said, "Come on. There's cakes and coffee."

"I'd sooner not socialize with schoolgirls," I said.

"But don't you want to meet Doctor Buber?"

"Do you think he'll have any cigarettes on him?"

Adele rolled her eyes. "You don't have an ounce of patience. Bela knows we're here. He'll find us."

Then I had a stroke of luck; a stream of schoolgirls pushed Adele against a wall and I used the excuse to break out on my own. I knew a shortcut out of the auditorium through the boiler room, a way familiar to any teacher who wanted to escape a crowd. I slipped behind the stage, opened the door that said FORBIDDEN, and as I suspected, there was Bela.

It was a startling moment. Up close, he looked completely different than he had on stage, browner, taller, broader, and he took a step backwards and said: "What's this?"

"What do you think it is, *Borzas?* My God, you're enormous!" I said, having no idea what was coming out of my mouth and only aware that I'd gone pink all over.

Bela crushed me up against him and didn't quite release me before he said, "And you're no bigger than a girl."

I felt like crying. Any attempts at cleverness melted off with the forceful heat of those big boilers. "I'm married," I said, foolishly. Of course he knew I was married. We managed to disentangle ourselves and to pry open the basement exit and head out into the afternoon sun.

Bela stretched, taking in the sunshine and open air as though he'd just emerged from a cave. "Those girls. I never know what they expect of me."

"You do so know," I said.

"I don't," said Bela. We started towards Andrassy Street for no particular reason. Leaves crunched underfoot, and I realized for the first time that it was autumn. "I don't know what they expect," he said. "You tell me."

"You know what they expect," I said, "and you give it to them. Face it. You like little girls."

I regretted what I said. It broke the mood, made Bela a little thoughtful. We turned north, towards Vidam Park, and Bela stared off into the middle distance in a way that let me know there was another question coming. But I wouldn't have been able to guess its nature.

Bela asked, "Would you call yourself a little girl?"

I kind of lost my footing. Then I said, "You still don't smoke, do you?"

Bela smiled like an idiot. "It's so good to see you. After these weeks, just to have some time to myself."

We managed to find a bakery and bought a few rolls with jam inside. Bela ate one in three bites and started another, and I saved mine, as though the bread were something from a fairy story and as long as I didn't finish it, the afternoon would not be over.

Bela asked, "So where's Janos? I wanted to meet him."

"He's not around much," I said. I didn't know why I said it, as it seemed to imply problems that didn't exist. Of course he wasn't around much: On top of the teaching, he worked twice as hard as students half his age, and as a consequence, he'd gained a reputation at the Polytechnic and might be permitted to complete his course-work a year ahead of schedule. I'd meant to say these things to Bela, but somehow, I didn't.

Bela said, "So, what's it like, being married?"

By now, we had settled on a bench somewhere deep in the park, and I curled my legs up under me. I took my time about replying. "It's all right," I said. "You ought to try it, you and Dori."

"Dori?" Bela smiled in a way I couldn't read. Then he took another big bite of that roll, swallowed, and said, "No."

"No, what?"

"No, I'm not going to marry Dori. People in kibbutzim don't marry. Sometimes they share a room."

We sat beneath full boughs, and even with a meter of bench between us I could feel warmth radiate from Bela, and mingled smells, the damp wool from his sack-suit, the yeast and honey of that broken roll. I did not know what time it was, and didn't care. A few leaves fell on me. I said, "*Borzas*, I need a cigarette."

"Here," Bela said. Without rising from his place on the bench, he shifted his weight to dig into his pocket and drew out a rather crushed cigarette.

I propped myself up on one arm and leaned towards him to get a better look. "You've been holding out on me."

"They always offer them, you know, during receptions. And what am I supposed to do? Turn them down?"

I managed somehow to get the thing lit, and I took a long drag before I said, "I think it's mean of you to take them all and let them accumulate."

"From now on," Bela said, "I'll pass them to you."

He would stay only for a week. He had arrived two days before and had barely slept, which explained the way he seemed to be nodding off now. I took off my shoes and lay back with my head on the bench and my feet on his lap.

"So, do you like being married?"

"You asked me that already," I said.

"You didn't answer, really."

"It's fine," I said. I could have said more, too, but I didn't. "Do you have another cigarette?"

"Maybe half of one," said Bela.

"I'll take it. Listen," I said, as the afternoon turned dark and green, "how are you going to pass them all on to me if you go back to Palestine?"

"Because you'll come with me," Bela said.

We stayed on the bench until twilight, and by then I had long finished that half-cigarette. I knew I could talk or not talk, that it didn't matter, and I stretched all the way back and tilted my head upside-down until the blood rushed to my ears. I wanted a physical sensation to mark the moment when I was so happy.

PART
TWO

N O KIBBUTZ TILULIT ON CURRENT
lists," said Dov Levin. "It might have dissolved or merged with another kibbutz. Those names you gave me didn't help. You must realize, Nora, nobody
keeps a *Galut* name unless it's a matter of principle, and these people's principles are along different lines."

I asked, "What about Kibbutz Gan Dahlia?"

"What about it? Send them a wire or call them. But to be frank, Gan
Dahlia is enormous and they've just taken in a busload of newcomers. They
may not be up to doing you any favors."

"Ami Chai Jezreel?"

"That," said Levin, "was the one name on your list I recognized. He
moved to America in 'thirty-six. Last I heard, he was in New York, driving
a taxi."

The air in Levin's office was like sour cream. He presented me with a big
cup of sweetened coffee. I felt thick-headed and sullen. "What about Taell
al-Taji? That's not a European name."

"It's also not on a standard map. You know how many Arabs fled the
Galilee during the war last year? By now, that's probably a Jewish village.
You could live there."

The thought gave me no joy. I asked, "Don't they have files on these
things somewhere? In German?"

"Learn Hebrew," said Levin. "Your daughter-in-law is making excellent progress, I hear."

I said, "She's got a good ear."

"That's right," said Levin. "She was a singer, wasn't she? *Lieder*. This is a very strange place for a singer of *Lieder*."

Something in his tone made me ask him, "How did you know she sang?"

Levin hesitated. Then he said, "Something else they've all been saying. A little more consistent than the other rumors. I take it, this one's true."

I didn't want the subject to linger on Louisa, so I raised my coffee cup and said to Levin, "You know, in Budapest after the war we drank boiled chestnuts that weren't much worse than this stuff. Do you have a cigarette?"

"No, Nora," said Levin.

"Then what good are you?"

"I can't answer that," he said. He smiled, and that smile was far more wry and melancholy than anything Bela would have managed. For all his years in this country, Levin was still a European; Israel hadn't knocked that out of him. But what was the good of irony? How far had it gotten my son? Maybe if Gabor had been pure and selfless he would have gone to Palestine like Bela and would have been alive today.

I was alive, of course, but that had nothing to do with me. I was alive because of Louisa.

N OW LOUISA WAS PART OF THE labor pool. Early in the morning, she would wait at the camp gate with the North Africans. It was ludicrous. Europeans simply didn't do that sort of work, at least not the Europeans in the camp. None of the Poles would have been caught dead fighting for a place in one of those plantation trucks.

To my mind, her effort was doomed. No matter how eager she looked, no matter how much she would insist that she had picked fruit before, who would believe her? And though she used her Hebrew, as soon as she opened her mouth she might as well have said *Güten Morgen.*

"Dear," I said, "I don't see the sense of it. You'll only faint and then some poor North African will have to carry you back."

"I must work so you don't have to, *Mutti,* " she said. At that point, the prospect of work was theoretical. By breakfast time, she would return to study one of those books on Jewish family purity.

I overheard one Romanian say to her friend in Yiddish, "Sure she's willing to do black work. The girl's done worse." They were sitting by the primus stove, prattling together as though they were in some café, although Louisa sat no more than a meter away with her nose buried in that book.

"A lovely voice though," said the woman's friend. "Like a nightingale." She turned to me, who stood at the foot of the bed where Louisa studied. "Nightingales sing best in the dark, I hear." She gave a low-pitched laugh then.

Louisa looked up, and her eyes flicked across the room, and back to the book again. She turned a shade paler, and moved her lips as she read, as though to force concentration. There are times when it made little difference if she understood Yiddish. She heard enough. I thought: No wonder she wants to work among North Africans, where she would be spared all of this. Yet she could have spared herself completely had she not clung to me. She had come to a country where she was cursed. No matter how many books she read, or how many rabbis she visited, or how many young Israeli men she charmed, the curse would remain.

HEN, ONE DAY, THEY LET HER onto the plantation truck. She returned just before supper in a pair of baggy shorts and a blue blouse. Her hair was tucked into a round, white cap. She'd pulled that cap down as far as it would go, and her ears stuck out below

the brim; I'd never known they were so big. I asked her, "Have you joined the army?"

"*Es gefällt mir.* It's an orange grove. And they're harvesting," she explained. "They were shorthanded."

"And they dressed you like a little boy?"

"They all wear this," Louisa said.

"Who are they, dear?"

"*Meine Freunde,* the others, the ones who work with me."

She was vague about those others and about the work she did, though when I pressed her, she admitted that she was not a picker but a sorter, and she spent her time not on a ladder but in a warehouse, separating bruised and perfect fruit. The other workers were North Africans who spoke neither Hebrew nor German and classed her as a European who had somehow fallen to their lot in life. By all accounts, those workers treated her with respect, and maybe a little fear. I cannot speak for the management.

So, during the day, Louisa left me, and three nights a week, she studied with the rabbi. She would slip into our cot late at night. Even after a shower, she still smelled of oranges, and the juice clung to her hair.

*R*ABBI NEEDLEMAN ASKED HIS wife, "Why did Ruth follow Naomi?"

Sharon said, "You could still withdraw the offer."

Shmuel shook his head. "Who else would take her on? She's not among friends here, after all."

They spoke in Yiddish in the kitchen. The children were asleep. This was their quiet hour together, kept, traditionally, since the first years of their marriage. Though early on, Shmuel had hoped to spend the time teaching his wife Hebrew and a little German, eventually it lapsed into conversations about the budget or the children. During the past few years, after Sharon had their fourth child and Shmuel took on duties at the camp for new arrivals, the hour was often the only time they'd have to themselves, and the talks took on the feel of reports from the front lines.

He'd married Sharon not long after he had escaped from Germany to Palestine, in 1937. Her father had initially turned down the match, as Shmuel had a secular as well as a religious education, and seemed to him tainted by the outside world, but his grandfather and great-grandfather were well-known scholars, and in the end, Sharon herself put her foot down. She was not a girl to be crossed.

Shmuel himself was initially in awe of Sharon's family, who had lived in Palestine since the 1870s. Yet in the course of his work with new immigrants, Shmuel grew less tolerant. The members of the Old *Yishuv* went on with their lives as though there were no state of Israel. They believed Hebrew to be a language meant for prayer, and they conversed exclusively in Yiddish. It was as though they were the newcomers, isolated in a foreign country.

That isolation took its toll on Sharon. She was still young, but her face had been merrier once. Now she looked, in turns, stunned and exhausted. Funny to think that she was not much older than Louisa. An idea occurred to Shmuel. He asked Sharon, "Would you like to meet her?"

"You want me to tell her how to be a good Jewish wife?"

"I didn't say that," said Shmuel.

Sharon took a sip of fruit-juice and lowered her eyelids, in case he hadn't noticed how tired she was. "I suppose she plans to marry one of us."

"All right, all right. I'll drop the subject," Shmuel said, with more good humor than he felt. "But that's not what I meant."

"You'd better figure out what you do mean," said Sharon.

"I only wonder," Shmuel began, but then he thought better of it. He'd meant to say he wondered if Louisa knew her own mind. Why did she leave her home and her life and take on the life of someone else? Is there a reason for an act so rash and selfless? Perhaps it was in the category of those lines in the poems he admired which, if examined too closely, would break down into nonsense.

*H*E'D MAPPED OUT A PROGRAM OF study. It wasn't hard to find good texts in German, but he also wrote out transliterations of the Hebrew and was stunned to find she didn't need them. She had already mastered Hebrew characters. Her memory was outstanding. From her seat in the office, she would recite the texts down to the subtle vowels.

"Very good, Frau Gratz," he would say. "And now, please, tell me the purpose of these laws."

"These are the beasts which you may not eat," Louisa began again, this time in German, and she counted them off on her fingers. "The ox, the sheep, the goat, the hart and the gazelle and roebuck. You must not eat abominable things—"

"And to what purpose?" Shmuel asked again.

"Purpose?" Louisa turned pale. "To keep clean," she said. "Not to eat anything abominable."

"What is meant by abominable?"

"Camels and hares," she said. "Rock badgers."

"What makes a rock badger abominable?"

"It doesn't have cloven hooves or chew cud."

Shmuel said, "You don't chew cud, Frau Gratz. Are you abominable?"

Louisa's face contorted. "I don't understand."

"Prayer and observance of the law," Shmuel said, "are duties, and we do them at first without knowing why. But if you want to understand these laws, you have to know their purpose. Why all these details? Why the separation between Israel and the other nations?"

With some hesitation, Louisa said, "To keep clean."

"Are you saying, then, that Israel is clean and all other nations are dirty?"

Then came the silence. Shmuel had learned to think of that silence as Louisa's natural element, strange given that he heard she was once a singer of *Lieder*. Sometimes the silence felt fertile, a place where new things could grow, and sometimes it felt like a void. That silence paralleled the gradual darkness of the room. He did not turn on the light.

"Rabbi," Louisa asked him, "what if I do and I do and I still don't understand? Will they send me back?"

"I've told you before, I can make no guarantees."

"But I can't help not understanding. It's not my fault."

The panic radiating from the girl unnerved him. He fought against the urge to reassure her and make promises he couldn't keep. Again, he wondered why he felt so pessimistic about her case. "No one is blaming you," he said. "No one is asking for the impossible." Yet somehow neither of those statements felt quite true.

Then he tried to imagine me, the *Mutter*, whom he had not met. The biblical Naomi was not a sweet old lady. After the death of her sons, she had asked her fellow Israelites to change her name to Bitterness. There was, Shmuel knew, plenty of guilt to go around.

$\mathcal{J}$ MET LOUISA FOR THE FIRST time in August of 1943 when I sat on my bed surrounded by a pile of my husband's trousers, jackets, wool socks, ties, and dress shirts; they had not been moved in years, and they smelled of dust and silverfish droppings. I did my best to sort through them. I knew the brown sweater with the moth holes would have to be discarded, but what could I sew up again? It was then that Gabor came in unexpectedly with Louisa.

I must have lacked some dignity. As I rose from the bed, three pairs of trousers fell to the floor. I extended my hand. Louisa took it. Her handshake was weak, and her eyelids fluttered slightly, as though against rising dust. "I'm so sorry," she said. "We're interrupting."

"Oh, Momma, hell!" Gabor pushed us apart and held up, for inspection, my ancient lamb's-wool coat, the wedding present from Adele. "What do you expect to do with this? Pawn it?"

I said, "I'm too stout to get it buttoned these days, but it's in good condition. I thought we'd reverse the buttons and make it a man's coat. You could wear it this winter."

"Winter? Winter's not going to come. Trust my mamma," Gabor said to Louisa, "to spend a day like this sorting through garbage." He threw the coat over Louisa's head and held her at arm's length. "Angel, you'd make a splendid nun."

Louisa kept the thing on for just a beat too long before letting it drop to her shoulders. Something about me made her lose her composure. In any case, Gabor and I soon stuffed everything back into the wardrobe. I offered them a cup of something, but Louisa insisted on taking us to a local *cukrászda* for a plate of overpriced sandwiches and some lemonade.

Here was my first impression of Louisa: transparent. Her color came and went through skin like fine stationery, and her hair was so light that it looked like an optical illusion. Also, she was obviously younger than Gabor had led me to believe. Honestly, I didn't know what to say. I'd never before met one of Gabor's girls. I knew it would be all too easy for my son and me to settle into our natural camaraderie, so I forced myself to address Louisa directly in German. "So, dear, do you like it here in Hungary?"

"Perfekt," Louisa said. "It really is the best place for an artist at this stage of my development. My father travels for the *Deutsche Reichsbahn,* and he tells me trains pass through villages that have not changed in a hundred years. You have no High Culture. You have only Folk Culture. It exposes me to new influences. Like, for example, your son."

Gabor's mouth was full of meat-paste, but he pressed a few teeth sideways in a lazy smile.

Louisa clarified. She reached across the table and laid a cool, weirdly throbbing hand on my arm. "Your son is a genius," she said.

"Is he?" I took up my glass of lemonade, and over the rim, I locked eyes with Gabor.

"He is a genius of the Hungarian kind. He comes from no tradition. He is his own tradition." She gave my arm a condescending pat. "Of course, we have a great master in common. Professor Istvan Lengyel."

I took care to swallow what was in my throat. Gabor said, "Small world, hey?"

If Louisa knew a thing, it didn't show in her face, though it did turn just a little pink as she swallowed the iced lemonade.

LATER, I WAS DIRECT. I SAID TO Gabor, "I don't want you to get yourself or that girl into trouble."

Gabor seemed startled. He had returned from walking Louisa home, and he'd expected a few laughs at her expense. "You should know me better than that. I don't get girls in trouble."

"I'll make myself clear," I said. "That she's too young, you know. And that's your business. But Lengyel's another matter. You're the one who said you wanted to keep out of his circle."

"The Queen of Sheba? He's old news. Frankly, I'm flattered he recognized that manuscript," said Gabor.

"How could he have recognized it, if you haven't seen him in all those years?" I asked him.

"Well," Gabor said, "I must have made a lasting impression. I do, you know." He straightened and wiped the last traces of meat-paste from his mouth with the side of his hand. I'd meant to launder napkins that lost afternoon and now had nothing to show for it but worry. That worry made me furious, and I dumped the dirty dishes in the sink, all the while wishing I could give him a smack now that there was no one here to tell me to be reasonable. But Gabor was nineteen. I couldn't tell him what to do.

$\mathcal{T}$HAT SAME MORNING, IN A fashionable district in the Buda hills, Istvan Lengyel's maid laid out his long underwear and hiking gear for the weekly excursion with his students. He shaved, cleaned his spectacles, and combed his hair back from his brow. Lengyel loved to walk. He'd spent the best days of his early manhood in the Austrian Alps, where, with his boon companions, he'd conquered mountain after mountain, and in the frost they would wrap blankets of hide across their shoulders and read Schiller to each other by the light of a kerosene lamp. At dawn, he would practice his voice, which was nearing its prime, and it would echo back against the margins of those mountains.

What did he have now? Students in their little shorts humoring an old man. At nine o'clock, he expected Louisa and a tenor named Laci. Laci arrived half an hour early and was so enthusiastic about the walk that he had brought along a pad and pencil for sketching flowers. Recently, he'd taken to carrying a staff like his master's, though he was such a big boy that it had weapon-like proportions. Laci unpacked a roll from his bag and chewed most of it in his left cheek. He looked like a squirrel. He would leave crumbs on the furniture.

"We will have to go without Louisa," Lengyel said. "If we wait for her, she will never learn discipline."

The day was cheerless. Without Louisa there, Lengyel's insistence on German felt all the more artificial. They didn't reach the countryside until noon, and the morning chill soon gave way to far too much sunshine, so the two of them had to stop and rest. Never before had Lengyel noticed how boring the tenor could be. He would sit there and sneeze, and then he would lapse into Hungarian to apologize.

Well, he hadn't taken Laci on for his charm but for his remarkable voice, and as he suspected, he had caught a cold. By the time they returned to the house, Laci's nose was beginning to drip, and when he said, "Goodbye, Professor," his voice broke.

"Goodbye yourself!" Lengyel shouted, losing his temper. "You sound like a bullfrog. If you don't take care of your throat, you'll end up working as a cobbler."

It was not in Laci's nature to answer back. Lengyel knew he would do anything to please him, wrap himself in hot scarves, make his mother steam the bedroom, even bribe him with some homemade brandy. But Laci said something surprising. "Louisa sure kept warm." Lengyel was struck by the note of insinuation. He hadn't planned to press, but Laci added: "She's got a boyfriend. Everyone knows."

"I must congratulate her when I see her," said Istvan Lengyel, "and I'll be sure to let her know you were the one to break the news."

Then he turned his back on the young man, stripped off his damp coat, and deliberately ignored him so as not to lose his temper and dismiss him altogether. He settled onto the one comfortable chair in his study for a brandy. After a moment, he asked his maid to dial the Bauers' number. She handed him the receiver and at once he asked for Louisa, only to be told she'd been gone since morning.

"But I'd assumed she was with you," said Frau Bauer.

"Indeed she was," said Lengyel. "But she forgot a certain manuscript, I think. A short piece, not finished. By a friend, a composer."

"Composer? I don't believe she's mentioned a composer. Eva!" Frau Bauer called, and after a moment she returned. "Yes, Eva says she knows a composer from the Academy. Funny, the way she'll tell a servant what she won't tell her own mother."

He said, "Do let the matter drop. Girls need their secrets." Then he took his leave, and sat for a long time, turning the glass of brandy around and around in his hand.

*A*s for Gabor, he'd brought Louisa home because he had run out of things to do with her. They met once or twice a week, at the Academy or at an ice-cream shop on either end of Margit Bridge. Once, they spent the afternoon on Margit Island, and they walked among the gardens and rented a tandem, rounding the parameters until Louisa was breathless and Gabor light-headed with boredom.

There were a thousand other things he could have been doing. The artist still had the portrait to complete; a friend had told him about a stunt pilot performing in a field in Ujpest; a girl whose brother wrote plays wanted him to read for the part of the Young Man. Yet this Louisa's light breath blew on his back as she sang out: *Would that I were a fish so nimble and swift—*

Then, touching her vibrating throat to his shoulder, her mouth brushing his ear, she'd whisper:

"Is it for my voice?"

"Ja," Gabor said. She was referring to his song.

"But, you know, it's not a big voice. Perhaps you want a Dramatic Soprano."

"Nein," Gabor said. "I want you." He didn't turn around, but the faint flutter in her throat and the warm hum along her lips reminded him. He could pedal and pedal and he wouldn't lose her. Then she'd sing again:

If you came angling, I'd not keep you waiting!

That voice was smooth, bright, fully formed. She'd release it without warning, as if she couldn't help it, and he knew that the Schubert was for his benefit. With every day, her expectations and impatience grew. It had been a month now, and no song.

"Gabor," Louisa said once, as they were walking with their ice-cream cones, "why don't you work in my practice room at home? That way, you won't have to worry about getting past the lady at the desk."

"You would disturb me," Gabor said. "You have a history of disturbing me, Angel."

"You'll never let me live that down," Louisa said.

"I never said I minded being disturbed."

"Don't worry, I'll be out of the way before you know it. By November, I'll be in over my head with rehearsals. We'll never get to see each other. Then it's off on tour and you're rid of me altogether."

Gabor didn't dignify that claim with reassurance, but he walked on, considering, as he often did in Louisa's company, just what he wanted from her. The ice-cream cone made her face sticky and filthy. Even her ordinary skirt and blouse looked like a schoolgirl's uniform. "Angel," he said to her, "the pressure doesn't help."

"What would help?" Louisa was pleading now. "Maybe if you didn't live in that awful flat with your mother. Did you see how she looked at me?"

"She looks at everyone that way," said Gabor.

"Even you?"

"Especially me."

"I'd never look at you like that," said Louisa.

"Ah, but you already have," said Gabor, pleased to catch her out. "Every time you ask me about that song, you look at me like that."

This was said at the very threshold of her neighborhood, where they parted ways. Was she honest with her parents? A stupid lie could cause a lot of trouble. Perhaps he ought to give in and use that piano in her house on Rose Hill, make the friendship public, at least walk her to the door to show he meant no harm. But every time the impulse overcame him, he thought better of it. The tidy street, the window-boxes filled with puffy white geraniums, the green shutters and the arched doorway swallowed up Louisa. It was no place for him. She was, frankly, no girl for him. And he would shake her off soon, as soon as he gave her that song.

He would turn his back on Rose Hill and start for his next destination, the wine-cellar up the street, or a card game in the park, or the wharf or rail-road yard, nowhere in particular. He thought: What song?

He asked a friend, a porter in the Hotel Astoria, "Have I ever written a poem that I could set to music?"

"I don't know," he'd reply, buttoning his uniform. "I thought you were an actor."

To a girl pianist, he said, "Play that piece I composed last year."

"Must I?" The girl snuffed out her cigarette. "Why must I remember everything you do?"

Weirdly, the whole world seemed to be united against him, narrowing from indifference to hostility and leaving him walking across the Pest which not so long ago was very much his oyster, and trying to reconstruct a few measures of *Rocket*.

Boom! Boom! The notes, like two tin pellets, hit his gut. Two schoolgirls dressed in green jumpers passed by, and to Gabor's eye, they were pointing and laughing. He realized, with wild anxiety, that he had come close to Louisa's school and the girls were pointing because she'd mentioned him, described him in detail, and very probably every German girl in Budapest knew who he was and also knew what he was, every girl but Louisa.

*A*S A RULE, I DIDN'T INVOLVE myself in Gabor's affairs, but the mention of Lengyel had thrown me off. Also, there was something about this one, maybe her youth or her German-ness or even the way her hand vibrated when it touched my arm. I got the strangest sensation: as though the girl were made of nitroglycerin.

After Gabor and Louisa had gone, I turned back to sorting through my husband's clothes. I wish I could have said that his memory was a comfort to me, but it wasn't. He was not the sort of man to whom I could have spoken what was in my heart. I shook out a pair of what I always thought of as his "professor pants," loose, tweedy things with ample pockets. Janos always filled those pockets with scraps of paper covered with equations or notes from engineering journals, and long after he'd left the Polytechnic, in fact long after he had given up hope of finding a position anywhere but at the girls' school, he would still carry those arcane notes everywhere. I was always washing them along with the trousers, and they'd form little pellets and bleed ink all over everything.

I used to find folders of his notes, carefully dated, stuffed not only in his desk, but in the linen closet, underneath the breakfront, apparently anywhere he could find room for them. After Janos had gone, I went through a period of hunting for those folders on a regular basis and attempting to arrange them chronologically, trying to hear his voice in them somehow. Perhaps because that flat was so enormous, I kept too many things: Name Day cards, student newspapers from the Katona Jozsef School, twine from parcels, and everything Gabor ever scribbled on a piece of paper.

I also kept the shoe-boxes full of letters I never sent Bela. Later, of course, I lost everything. Some of the lines from the letters come back to me, the sort of things you write when you know no one will be reading, senseless, sentimental, in a private language: *the breath we took together, before you dropped me in that cemetery full of stones, all of those birds in flight, that's you, flying off, and I'm the stone.* Or *What is lost, you can not have back again, not a breath we took together or bread we ate together. I can not join you any more than I can make bread out of a stone.*

There was a sock of Bela's in my hand, just then, darned with yellow thread. He'd left it in the flat years before. It had probably been mended by Dori Csengery. I pulled it over my hand, and, onto it, sunk my chin.

*C*ONSIDER THE PHOTOGRAPH I'D mentioned previously: Dori, Nathan, and Bela. Louisa knew it well; she'd found it one day when she riffled through my private papers on Prater Street and held it towards me like an accusation, sobbing out her heart.

"You'll leave me. All I do is make you unhappy, and look at the three of them," she said. "Look at all the sunshine."

Indeed, the Pioneers swam in light, but the effect was probably the consequence of poor photography. Really, it was a mundane place. The settlement was set in real earth and its membership was flesh and bone, as unhappy as the rest of us. All this, I knew from Bela's letters, sent along with the photograph of Bela, Dori, and Nathan posing in front of the chicken coop.

Each of those letters began and ended with a plea to join him in Palestine; most of the invitations were light-hearted, some direct, and a few in 1939 a little pointed. *You say the Jews of Europe are flocking to Hungary? They're running in the wrong direction. I've written the same to Adele and to my mother, but you must make them go. You have the stronger will. You could convince them. At least think of your son.*

It was that letter that Louisa held out that afternoon, along with many others, and that photograph, as she said, "You're going to leave me and go to the Holy Land."

"Dear," I said, by way of consolation, "he wrote that five years ago. There's no way to get there now."

By 1944, Hungary had long since sent those Jewish refugees back to Poland and Austria, and my flat rumbled beneath American bombs, and on my couch lay Louisa, sobbing her heart out for fear I'd go to Palestine.

"But you're an Israelite," she cried.

I stroked her hair and whispered, "Shh, shh. There's no such place."

As I've said, Janos put no faith in photographs. When Gabor was two years old, I asked Janos to come with us to a studio on Andrassy Street to take a family portrait. He refused. "Photographs reproduce perceived perspective. They have nothing to do with objective truth. For example, look at our son." Aside from three hours of work in the afternoons, I had done nothing but look at Gabor since he was born. Janos said to me, "How big do you think his head is, Nora?"

"Counting hair?" I asked.

"You could factor in the hair."

"He has a lot of it."

"Theoretically, hair doesn't matter."

"You would say that," I said to Janos. "You're losing yours."

"I'm serious," he said, in case I doubted it. Frankly, I'd hoped to drive him out of the house, because I'd almost, and I mean almost, gotten Gabor to take a regular nap, and I knew that Janos would be pulling out his tape-measure in a minute and wrapping it around Gabor's head.

"Look," I said to Janos, "all I want is to take a little picture of the three of us to send to my cousin in Palestine."

"That's the whole point," Janos said. "Photographs only reproduce individual perception. There's no objective reality to a photograph. A photograph would tell your cousin more about the photographer than it would about our son."

He shook his finger at me while he said this, and he stumbled back a little in his agitation, looking no different than he had four years before, like a pipe-cleaner with a frayed end, like a lost soul, like someone schoolgirls would snicker over in the hall. As time went on, the oddness felt increasingly like affectation. He couldn't possibly think that shaking his finger would make me pay more attention. Eventually, I got the photograph taken without him, by a man who had a little shop on the Great Boulevard, and I mailed it off to Bela with a short note in German: *Measure Gabor's head. According to every study I've read, it's the right shape for a Cossack.*

What I did not send Bela was a longer letter in Hungarian that I wrote around that time, in 1926: *It was his sadness that made me marry him. What is it like to be married, you asked me. It is like knowing you're being watched, then wondering how he can't be on to you. I think I am a mystery to him, Bela. It's like I speak another language. I wish I was a linguist, like you, and understood everything.*

I had reverted to them again, those letters, the way another wife might revert to drink. Although I hadn't time enough to fill the pages at the rate I had as a girl in Barnahely, there were six boxes now. I kept them in a deep drawer in the living room, under a lot of bedding, and took them out sometimes to read through while Gabor napped. I would put my legs up on the couch and pile them on my lap, smoking and reading, and it was as though the flat were crowded with myself at fourteen, eighteen, twenty-five. I didn't keep them hidden, really. I told myself I wasn't the one with something to hide. I wasn't Janos.

I THINK GABOR'S BIRTH MADE ME less tolerant. Once, Janos decided to use our flat for storage. Of course, there was no warning. At eight, when he'd already left for the library and I was making Gabor a pancake, a boy showed up at the front door with a handcart piled with parcels.

He squinted up at me. "I'm supposed to leave these."

He pushed right past, dragging that wretched, squeaking cart to the center of the flat and dumping the parcels. There were maybe thirty of them wrapped in thick brown paper and crisscrossed with lengths of twine, each around the right size to hold thirty or forty contraband magazines or a hundred leaflets or half a kilo of explosives.

"All right, then," said the boy. Then he left. So there I was, and there was Gabor, and there were the parcels. Was I supposed to line them up neatly against the wall? Was I supposed to hide them under the bed? The only thing I knew I wasn't supposed to do was open them. I went to the window and looked after that boy, a spindly, dead-pale creature who dragged that empty cart behind him so carelessly that one of its wheels dislocated and scraped along the road. Then I looked at Gabor.

That afternoon, Janos got home before I did, and I noticed that he'd put the parcels somewhere out of sight. He was leaning over his bowl of soup and the spoon was just in front of his mouth when I said, "I want those things out of the flat."

He put the spoon down. "What? You mean my papers?"

"They're not your papers. They might as well be rat poison. They're out of here tonight."

Janos did not say anything for a while. He looked into the bean soup and moved the stem of his spoon first one way and then the other. Gabor sat in his high-chair, observing the movement of the spoon with more interest than the expression on his father's face. Then, Janos said, "All right. But it's not possible until morning."

"You could throw them in the Duna," I said.

"Nora, be reasonable."

"Not here," I said to Janos. "Reason stops here."

I didn't even let him finish his soup. He had to knock on a neighbor's door to borrow a handcart, claiming he had to move some books to his cubby-hole in the library, and I think that was where he stored the packages that night, though that meant getting them past the guard who was a reactionary and suspicious. I do know he came home without them, just before midnight. He dragged in the empty handcart and stood, sweating, in his coat. He said, "Can I at least leave the cart?"

I came up behind Janos and removed his coat, setting it on our coatrack next to my lamb's-wool jacket and Gabor's little winter parka. He didn't shake his bad humor that night or the next, but I did notice that he was home for supper for the rest of the week, and when he returned the handcart next door, he made a great show of complaining to the neighbor about how a woman never understands the importance of a man's work, and he actually let himself get invited in for a glass of *pálinka* like any other husband drinking with a husband to make common cause against their wives.

*I*N 1927, WHEN GABOR WAS three years old, Janos graduated from the Polytechnic, and it was then the future he had laid out for me in the Horivag *cukrászda* was supposed to begin. It was June, the end of the semester at the Katona Jozsef School, and I had never seen him so close to profound happiness as after that final math class. Not once had he complained about the girls, mind you, not once had he said a word to make me think he knew what they thought of him, but that afternoon, he burst into my office with a demonic grin. His style was telegraphic.

"Done," he said. "Over. Gone. Never again. Say," he added, looking down at my paperwork, "can't you get out of here? I want to show you something."

I followed him outside into the milky sunshine, and when we were in the open, he took my arm and guided me to a side-street where workers were drilling through the cobblestones. I said, "I can't stay away long. I've got a full afternoon's work ahead."

"An afternoon? An afternoon?" Janos turned full around to face me, and then he laughed, surprising me to the point of panic. I had never heard him laugh before. Then he pointed to the drillers and said, "Molten iron switch-boxes. All over Budapest. Mains-fed. Activated by an astronomical clock." Then he drew me to a lamp-post and said, "See that? It'll be timed to come on at sunset, whether that's four in the afternoon or ten at night. And that's my job," he said. "Ganz Electrical Works. Complete overhaul of the circuit system. Tear out the old equipment, bring it up to date, and when Ganz asked around at the Polytechnic, they got my name."

I never did get back to work that day. Janos measured the distances between the future switch-boxes and made me hold one end of the tape as he walked backwards with the other. The brilliant metal strip extended like a band of light, and when he shouted out a measurement, I'd let myself be pulled forward to meet him, giddy and bewildered. I don't know what pedestrians made of the two of us, all doubled over and sweaty in our good clothes with that tape-measure, making our way up Andrassy Street. Janos wrote numbers on a little pad and pointed out the lamp-posts that would be timed to dim at midnight and the lamp-posts that would burn until dawn. By the time our knees gave out, it was twilight, and we were perhaps a mile from where we had begun.

Janos lit his pipe. "You know, they'll probably climb on the boxes, those schoolgirls." As ever, when he spoke around the pipe-stem, I could barely make out what he said, and I moved in a little closer.

I asked him, "Do you want to sabotage the boxes and electrocute them?"

"As a class?" Janos asked, and then he took his pipe out of his mouth and kissed me.

By then we had been married for four years, and I didn't know at first why that kiss seemed to run so deep and turn the world fuzzy and green. I fell back hard against something but didn't care. Janos dug his hand under my little suit jacket and pulled it halfway off, and it was so dark, no one could see or mind, and little Gabor was at Aunt Monika's and wouldn't be the wiser, so what made me abruptly pull away? We were on a bench in Vidam Park.

"You knocked your head," Janos said, not looking at me.

"A little," I replied, gently. "Not much. You know, I'd better put our things in to soak. They're filthy."

"Yes, soak the jacket. I won't need it. It's a warm night." He handed it over, and I bunched it up in my arms and held it so tightly as we walked home that it had to be pressed later. I laid it out under our mattress. That did the trick.

*J*ANOS DID NOT GET THE JOB AT Ganz. They never contacted him again, and when he gathered enough nerve to go to their office, he was told that they had given the position to another recent graduate who had more "hands-on" experience. "What was the Great War if not experience?" Janos said, but then he pretended not to be surprised. "Something will turn up," he said. By then, it was early July.

I worked through summers; Janos did not. Thus, in theory, he would have all day free to look for a job. Every afternoon, I would pick up Gabor at Aunt Monika's, have a cup of tea with Adele, and return to find Janos sitting hangdog at the kitchen table cleaning out his pipe, with his good suit-jacket slung over the back of the chair. I didn't even ask if he'd had luck.

"I need to throw a wider net," he said at first. He had stopped calling himself an electrical engineer and tried to spread word that he could take on any project. No one was interested. Then he thought it was because he was too old, but the other war veterans his age were hired by firms that valued their maturity. One morning in early August, Janos said to me, "How do I look?"

"The same," I said to him. He was wearing the coat I'd pressed and a pair of very baggy trousers, and he had made an unsuccessful attempt to slick back his hair.

"The same? What I mean," Janos said, "is do I look, well, like . . ." His hesitation seemed to pain him. He wanted to get it out. "Do I look suspicious?"

"Suspicious?" I'd picked up his own habit of echoing back questions.

"I overheard them," Janos said. "They said I was suspicious." He dropped his voice. "I can't risk it."

He muttered something else, but to be honest, I was getting tired of having to get close to hear him. Why be so conspiratorial? Who was going to listen in now? Gabor? The boy had already climbed out of the trousers I had put on him, and now he was opening the kitchen drawer and dropping cutlery on the floor a handful at a time. I had to stop him before he got to the big knives. I didn't have time for this sort of conversation. What was I supposed to say to him? That he was right not to become an ordinary man without politics who could get an engineering job? The Katona Jozsef School would be opening in less than a month. Janos had still not officially given notice. I could see the beginning of the new term rushing towards him like the floodlight of a train, and he was miserable to the point of paralysis.

"Maybe," he said, "I could just become an electrician."

"A suspicious electrician? Wouldn't they be afraid you'd blow things up?" I asked him. I think I was trying to make him laugh. Sometimes, I could get that little half-smile out of him, but not that day. He didn't even answer. In the end, I dressed Gabor, and off I went to work. I took my time about getting home, and in fact stayed at Adele and Aunt Monika's for supper. I sang to Gabor about exploding cows, about a giant bear who danced with boys and girls in cemeteries, about magic bread that wise people know better than to eat, and though I did my best to put off the inevitable, I was met by Janos, who told me, in case I didn't know, that he would be teaching at the Katona Jozsef School again that fall.

*A*FTER THE TERM BEGAN, ADELE was not at home as often as she had been. She'd fallen in love. The man in question was not a surgeon, not even a pharmacist. He was an unassuming little fellow from Szeged named Matyas who owned a shoe factory. The first time I met Matyas, I could tell by Adele's pleading look that she'd been afraid to have the two of us in the same room. Well, what could I do? Bite his head off? Gabor was on my lap most of the time, so I could barely make it off the sofa. They had met the day of the Martin Buber lecture. Apparently, that walk I'd taken with Bela had served some purpose.

"So are you moving to Szeged?" I asked Adele.

"Nora, it's not as though we're getting married," she said, but of course, they did, after a leisurely courtship. The worst of it was that they were going to take Aunt Monika south to live with them, and I didn't know who would watch Gabor, let alone where I would go when I wanted to avoid conversations with my husband.

The wedding itself took place in Budapest in December of 1929 in an Orthodox synagogue. It seemed that this Szeged fellow was a Jew in the old style. The ceremony was brief and incomprehensible, and the chanting sounded like gypsy music. From my perspective on the women's balcony, I could make out no more than the top of the embroidered canopy. Around me sat guttural-accented Szeged provincials in their dresses from before the Great War. There were also a few girls from Adele's old circle of nursing students, straining to see the ceremony like anthropologists. I knew Bela had not been able to come, but I still found myself searching for him among the men below.

After the wedding ceremony, there was a reception at a supper club, and I shared a table with some of my companions from the old days. Most of them were married by now. Andras the surgeon was there with a sweet little girlfriend who might have been Adele's younger sister. Kalman Nagy took a seat across from me; he was still single and so unchanged that he might have been preserved in formaldehyde. He gave a weak giggle at the sight of me and kept trying to light my cigarette with a faulty lighter.

There was a surprise. Seated to my left was Laszlo. At first, I didn't recognize him. Somehow, in the years since I'd left Kisbarnahely, he'd gotten fat and had grown a thick, blond mustache. "Well, Norika," he said, "where's the engineer?"

"Prior engagement," I said. Janos had said he'd try to go, but I knew better. I'd seen him literally shrivel at the sight of a synagogue.

"You two should move back to Barnahely," said Laszlo. "They're wiring the whole town for electricity. The man we have working on it now is no good. He's the mayor's brother-in-law."

"Does he look suspicious?" I asked Laszlo. He gave me a bewildered smile, then rose and pulled out a seat beside him. I got the second surprise of the afternoon. There was my mother.

She didn't greet me, just looked at me across the tablecloth with her pince-nez glinting over her little hard eyes. I straightened and said, "Well, you finally made it to Budapest."

"I was finally invited," my mother said. "Where's my grandson?"

"I fed him to the wolves," I said. Actually, he was with the landlady.

She ignored me, which was her own way of telling me nothing had changed. She took a long time about removing her hat, drawing out at least five pins before she managed to place it on the table. "I can't even take off this thing without it being a production with all the trimmings. It's arthritis. Watch for it, child. You'll get it as certain as you're sitting here."

"Nothing in life is certain," said Laszlo.

I felt as though they expected me to take sides. Really, it was just too strange, seeing that little beetle of a woman looking just as she had eight years ago, sitting there replacing the pins in her enormous hat. I tried to master myself. "How are you, Mother?"

"I told you. Arthritis," she said. "Where's my grandson? I came here to see my grandson."

"Anna," Laszlo said, taking hold of my mother's arm, "you've got days and days to see them all—Nora, Janos, little Gabor."

Days and days? I swallowed hard and said to Laszlo, "You're staying—"

"I'm going home tonight," Laszlo said at once. "Your mother booked a room near the train station. She wants to take Gabor to the zoo."

"The zoo?"

"I am a grandmother," my mother said, not nicely, I thought. "Grandmothers take their grandsons to the zoo. Of course, grandmothers generally don't stay at hotels."

"You'll stay with us," I said. And all the while I was trying to remember the condition of the flat, not to mention how easy it was for me to bear my mother. Not so easy. Even as we ate the fish course with our little forks, I could feel my worst self surface.

"I was making a joke," my mother said. "Of course I'll stay at the hotel. Who just appears and moves in?"

"You do, apparently," I said to her, and then I managed to smile. "Laszlo," I said, "why don't you stay too? You could take the couch."

"No, me? I'm going home."

"Please. Stay," I said, trying hard to keep my eyes pinned on his.

"I've already got the ticket. It's a reserved train," Laszlo said, clearly taken aback. "I've got my own son waiting for me. Daughter too, did I write you?"

"Apparently, Nora likes to write letters," my mother said to Kalman Nagy. "To everyone but her mother."

"Mother, that's not fair," I said.

"A line or two a month? On a postcard? Well, that's to be expected. After all, after all this time, aren't we practically strangers?"

Kalman giggled, and said, "I'd know you were her mother anywhere. You two are like peas in a pod!"

I had to excuse myself from the table then, rush outside, and take a few gulps of air. Then I had a smoke and felt a little better. My head cleared, but I couldn't take the invitation away.

*A*FTER THE SUPPER ENDED, MY mother put her hat back on, and as I couldn't see myself putting her on a trolley, I had to hail a cab, something that brought back memories of long, stupid evenings with boys like Kalman, and also, admittedly, made me feel wistful about Adele.

"Who would have thought it?" my mother said. "You, in Budapest. You must have quite the apartment here if you give up a perfectly good country house."

I rolled my eyes. "How could I forget? The healthful fumes from the express trains. All the peace and quiet. And such a rich cultural life there. Just the place to raise a happy child."

"Nora," my mother said, "you haven't changed. You always say the wrong thing at the wrong time and call it honesty. And you don't have a feeling heart. How could you let those years pass without visiting?"

"You never invite me to visit," I said. "You just tell me to move back." How could a cab ride take this long? How much worse could I get? I tried to think, was there someone, anyone, with whom I was a human being? I was a human being with Gabor. No, I was a mother with Gabor. Was the driver taking a long route? What was wrong with me?

We pulled up, and my mother made a long, insistent ceremony out of pulling the correct change from her purse. I led her up the two flights, and as soon as I reached the landing, stopped dead.

"What's going on?" my mother asked. "Don't tell me you left your key at the supper club."

"I did," I said.

"Well, then, we'll use a hat-pin."

"Um," I said, as she pulled one from that hat; I should have known my mother would be an expert at breaking into flats. I could have thrown myself against the door, I suppose, or had a fainting spell, or otherwise caused a diversion, but I finally said, flat-out, "Mother, there's a meeting going on inside. I can hear them."

"A meeting? Whose meeting? What meeting?"

"It isn't supposed to be here," I said, though I don't know why I said it, as it made no difference. I took out my own key and turned it. The door held firm. Obviously, someone inside had locked the dead-bolt.

"I'll go knock on the window," my mother said, and before I could stop her, she'd hurried up to the window that faced the courtyard and gave it a sharp little rapping like a woodpecker. My heart stopped.

The front door opened. There was Janos gazing out from a cloud of cigarette smoke, looking so terrified and angry that I was struck dumb, though believe me, I had plenty to say.

But he spoke first. "You weren't supposed to be home until after nine."

"My mother's here," I whispered, though of course she could hear me.

"Your what?"

"Mother. I have one. She's here. My God, Janos, tell me Gabor isn't in there with you."

Janos didn't answer. Then, I heard a peal of laughter and an unmistakable crash—Gabor had pulled down the coatrack. I forced my way past Janos and, without looking right or left, went straight for the pile of strangers' coats that covered my son, who by now was screaming. There were cloth coats, fur coats, coats with lush collars and cuffs, worker's coats without linings, and I threw aside coat after coat until I reached the hard rack, under which lay Gabor with a little blood on his head, screaming his lungs raw.

I held him and spat a little on the edge of my sleeve to wipe the blood away, and he struggled free and tried to dive back under the coats, but people were collecting them now and quietly filing out the door into the hallway. Gabor grabbed hold of one fur collar, hard, and wrapped himself in that coat so tightly that there was no getting it off of him. The owner, a short fellow with a bald head and soft eyes, just stood there for a moment with his hands loose at his sides. Then he said to Janos, "Well?"

"Take mine," Janos said, and he handed the man his overcoat so he could go.

That left Janos, my mother, and me. He was so tall, she was so short, he looked so scared, she looked so angry, and all at once what I wanted to do more than anything was join my son inside that coat. I said to Janos, "Get out."

"You're not serious."

"Get out," I said. "Go to another meeting. There must always be one running somewhere, like a crap game. But don't bring your shit here again."

"Nora—in front of the baby!" my mother cried out. Then, she knelt and gathered up Gabor, coat and all, in her arms. She couldn't lift him; he was five by then, and a good size. Still, after a struggle, he settled on her lap with his eyes peeking out of the coat and was too curious to keep on crying. My mother looked up at Janos, who showed no sign of leaving. "Well," she said finally, "the child's a beauty. Looks like my side of the family—he's got Moni's curls. But obviously my daughter's temper. Young man, get me a cup of something hot, preferably tea with a slice of lemon."

"We have no lemons," I said to my mother.

"Well, then, I'll make do," she said, "with my own sour nature."

I followed Janos back into the kitchen, gathering ashtrays full of cigarette butts on the way, and then I almost stepped on a wide fan of diagrams, sketched with a ruler on lined paper, crowded with figures, taking the shape of who-knows-what. I gathered them up, and when we were out of earshot, I slapped them down in front of him and said, "So you were passing these around? What for?"

"They're engineers," Janos said. "The information's valuable."

I couldn't bring myself to laugh. "What do you do? Sneak into Ganz at night? Too bad you can't do it on their payroll."

Janos turned to face me. "What do you want me to say? I'm not doing anything illegal. I read the journals. I make a few notes and share them with my friends."

"Friends in Russia, I suppose."

"That's absurd. You think they don't have technology far beyond this in the Soviet Union?"

"If it's so advanced, why don't you get an engineering job there? You can't get one here. All you get here is trouble. What on earth do you think you're doing?"

"You want me to lie to you?"

"Yes," I said. "Lie to me. Like the time you said you wouldn't bring your shit home."

Janos sighed. The kettle was on now, and I think we both hoped it would start whistling, but the water had been cold; it would take a long time.

"I don't understand why you keep this up," I said. "The Commune was, what? Ten years ago. You don't want to be a worker. You want to wear a suit and tie and light lamp-posts. Is it because of those men in the photographs?"

"Nora—" Janos began, but I kept going.

"They're in better shape than you. I hear Bela Kun's in Russia now. I'll bet he doesn't have to teach a bunch of girls arithmetic. I'll bet he thanks the White Guard every day for getting him out of some clerk's job in Budapest. At least he's not stuck! You may as well have stayed in that village and been a tinker! We're just as trapped!"

I don't think I even noticed when I stopped shouting and started sobbing. What I wanted was for that kettle to whistle or for Gabor to cry or for something, somehow, to break through. I managed to control myself, and silence thickened.

From the other room, I heard it: *Little dog, little dog—*

My mother had found the music box. It had been a long time since I had turned the handle, and given the erratic melody, there was no question: It was being turned by Gabor. Was it possible for a heart to break and melt at the same time?

Little dog, little dog, you will lead the sheep to me. Janos was searching for the teabags, and I looked up at him and said, "I'm sorry."

Janos didn't look at me.

"I just don't want to turn into my mother," I said.

The kettle finally whistled, and he took it off the burner, letting that comment pass. I had a terrible feeling that he hadn't understood a word I said. And honestly, did I? What was I afraid of? Really, as seen through the archway of the kitchen, my mother looked almost regal, like Queen Victoria, with her neat little body and her dark hair. Gabor seemed to like her. He had played with the music box years before, and now he was discovering it all over again. My mother held it between her hands, and he lay belly-down on the floor. My mother sang the words: *Oh my black-eyed love's a bold love, he will wander, he will stray—*

I approached slowly. From behind I could hear Janos trying to pick up the hot teacup, but I didn't come to his aid. Rather, I crouched down next to my mother. I said to her, "So do you go to many dances these days?"

She jerked her head around and said, "Who'd dance with me?"

"Laszlo," I replied. "He likes you, for some reason. Too bad he's married."

"Ah, you should have been the one to marry Laszlo," my mother said, and that more softly, barely managing to finish the sentence before lapsing back into: *But my blue-eyed love's a true love—*

But I wouldn't let that pass. "Mother, don't judge him. He's been going through a hard time. This is all he has left."

"Since when do I judge?" my mother asked, smiling at the same time down at Gabor, who took the music box from her and stumbled off towards the door. My impulse was to follow him, but I was determined to make my point.

"He's remarkable in his own way. He's stuck to his political convictions, and they're unpopular, unfashionable. They cost him his career."

"Convictions?" Without Gabor there, my mother was free to stop smiling. She rose, slapping her gray dress back in place, and she said, "Convictions didn't cost him a career, Nora. Look at the man. Look at his name. Maybe you think I'm provincial, but there are laws in this country. You think they'll hire a Jew?"

*A*LTHOUGH BELA COULDN'T COME in for the wedding, he sent his sister a stiff, embroidered gown. She mailed me a photograph of herself in that gown, another one I lost years later when I was forced to abandon the flat. The cotton was so white that it made her skin look swarthy, and with her curly hair and shining eyes, she looked less like a Jewess than an Arab boy.

He'd gotten the gown from a friend in Taell al-Taji. I liked to say that name: Taell al-Taji. Sometimes, when I held Gabor, a sweetness would fill me, and I would whisper to my dark-haired son, "Taell al-Taji, Taell al-Taji."

I found that village more interesting than the kibbutz, and I pressed Bela for details, claiming I was his conscience. *You say the Arabs work as day-laborers? And have you passed them that old leaflet written by the Jew? Maybe they'd take his advice and organize a strike.*

I used to be a pretty arrogant kid, Bela wrote. *Now I wouldn't approve of a Jew telling Arabs what to do.*

So what do you do with your Arabs then? I wrote.

You ask me about our Arabs, as if we owned them. You make a funny sort of conscience.

Sometimes he would go on at length. *The one thing they used our hill for was grazing and now that we've plowed it under, they'd like their sheep to keep on grazing there, impossible of course. And then there's the water hole. We worked like mules setting up the irrigation system, and not everyone was happy when the people in the village started dunking in their buckets, especially since the water isn't really meant for drinking. So their intestines react and they overcrowd the clinic. That clinic is Dori's pet, but it's a drain on time and resources and it was clear from the start that it brings in a lot of strangers, people we can't be so sure we trust. Remember: none of our doors have locks.*

So it wasn't an easy friendship. But maybe, he wrote, the best friendships are the most difficult. They are the ones that can transform you because you must come from such a great distance to know each other.

*G*ESTURES OF DIPLOMACY COULD not help but feel a little forced, though the spirit was genuine. Ahmad's daughter brought the kibbutz a lamb for Easter. In turn, his family was invited to the Passover Seder. In 1932, it was held in the new dining hall, a cement square with a modern aluminum kitchen, and in addition to the regular members, there were twenty newcomers from Poland who stayed in tents stretched out by the laundry room. In contrast to the regular kibbutzniks, these Poles were white and stunted, still in their European clothes.

Tibor and Eleazar had worked on the Seder for weeks. They'd produced a series of handwritten guides to share among the tables. Seder plates held new symbolic items, olives, a grapefruit, and tamarind. The five children did a dance to represent the ten plagues, and then Dori read a poem about a girl who killed her rapist during a pogrom and lived to ride with the kibbutz Night Watch, disguised as a man.

There was matzo baked in the kitchen; after years of practice, they managed not to burn it. There were four questions, rewritten by Tibor and asked by little Gezer, now a sturdy boy of eight. "On all other nights, we sit unsupported. Tonight, we lean on others and remember the strength of our comrades during hard times."

The Poles watched all of this with mounting confusion. They had come, almost without exception, from religious families. Perhaps it was when they reached the mixing of the bitter and the sweet on the parti-colored matzo that one of the young men broke in.

"What about the Hallel?"

His high-pitched, agonized voice carried all the way to Nathan Sobel, who answered with equanimity. "We have omitted it this year."

But the Pole had by now somehow gained the courage to rise. He was a scrawny, rabbinical fellow with a long neck, weak shoulders, and red-rimmed eyes. "Rabbi Hillel says that you must do at a Seder only four things. Drink four glasses of wine, tell the story of our redemption from slavery by the strong hand of Ha Shem, eat the bitter herb with matzo, and recite the Hallel." Then, without invitation, he sang:

Hallelujah, Praise O ye servants of the Lord.
Praise the name of the Lord.

Bela joined him, and so did Eleazar, who honestly loved the words.

Who maketh the barren woman to dwell in her house
As the joyful mother of children, Hallelujah.

No one else sang. Afterwards, there was a silence you could swallow. Then out came the first course of the meal.

The incident was forgotten in the chaos of the children's search for the Afikomen. If they didn't find it, the Seder couldn't end, and Bela had hidden it in the new chicken coop, under a nest. The five children were followed by forty adults. Bela kept a steady commentary: "Closer, yes, closer now—no far, dead cold, Gabi, over there to the left, you're hot, you're burning hot!"

Then it was very late. The Poles settled in their tents, and Ahmad and his wife and children took their leave. A few members tried their ragged Arabic which made the children laugh and pleased Ahmad's wife. She was a round, shy woman who hadn't raised her eyes from the table all through the meal, but now she smiled enough to show a dimple. Ahmad shook Bela's hand and said, "I didn't understand a word tonight, but that ugly young man loves God."

Bela replied, "He didn't sing because he loves God. He sang because he was afraid."

Later that night, when Dori, Nathan, and Bela sat in the kitchen eating leftovers and drinking coffee, Nathan said to Bela, "You shouldn't have encouraged him. He's going to see plenty of things here that Rabbi Hillel couldn't have imagined."

Bela laughed and thought, not for the first time, that Nathan was an ass. He exchanged a complicit look with Dori and said, "Mouse, where'd you come up with the poem about the woman watchman? It's awfully bad."

Stiffly, Dori replied, "I wrote it."

With the coffee cup in one hand, Bela rose from his seat and stood on one leg. He said, "Do not do to others what you would not want them to do to you."

Someone challenged Rabbi Hillel to summarize the laws of the Torah while standing on one leg, Bela wrote me, *and that was what he said. It's harder than it sounds. I told Nathan that we need to sum up the movement the same way and he accused me of wanting to turn everything into a slogan. Meanwhile, Dori was still put out because of what I said about her poem, and because I won't call her Arielle.*

I wrote Bela that, as his conscience, it was my place to inform him that his mother didn't want to go to Palestine and neither did his sister or her husband or my husband or my son, so he should stop badgering us about it. We would find Hebrew names absurd, and we had no intention of standing on one leg.

One letter caught me like a blow. He had been wounded, not badly, but enough to keep him from a visit we'd been counting on that spring. *I'm writing you instead of my mother or Adele because you'll know how to break the news. It isn't serious, but I think my knee will make me more useless than ever. I'm turning into an old man. Handling firearms was never my strong point, and they shot first.*

I wrote back: *They?*

A letter cannot consist of a single word, and my thoughts flowed in two directions. One took me, to be honest, straight to Palestine. How hard would it be to take a train and then a boat and find myself there? How much harder than staying here and not knowing how much of what he said was true? He might have gangrene for all I knew. Then there were Aunt Moni and Adele. Who did he think I was, to tell them?

Who did he think I was? Someone strong enough to write back, in rational German: *Can you still stand on one leg? Your mother will be hysterical, of course, but Adele is tougher than you give her credit for. Her husband's probably rich enough to buy an airplane and fly you to some hospital in Switzerland. As for my son, I know he would have liked to have seen a knee with a hole in it. Janos would have measured the hole. Since you have not met any of these people, you will have to take my word for it, just as I will take your word that this isn't serious. We have to trust each other, don't we? We have no choice.*

Of course, that letter wouldn't do at all. The last line gave away too much. It went into the box.

GABOR CAME IN FROM SCHOOL ONE day and caught me reading those letters. He was eight by then, and quick, and I couldn't manage to gather them together before he grabbed a page. "Did you write this?" he asked me.

"Yes," I said. I fought the urge to take it from him. By then, I knew it would only whet his curiosity. "I practiced my handwriting years ago, so I would copy out stories from books."

"Why did you take it out now?"

"Paper's expensive," I said. "I thought I could use some of the empty sides."

Gabor picked up a few more pages, turned them this way and that, and said, "No, Momma. They're covered all over."

"It was a good story," I said, without really thinking about it, and I took my son on my lap and said, "It's about a magic bear, a shaggy bear who found some magic bread. And as long as you ate the bread, time would stop, no one would get old, nothing would be lost. But it was such good bread, you had to eat it all up."

"I'm too old for your stories. I tell the stories now," Gabor said. He was also too old for my lap. His bushy hair made me sneeze, and his long legs took up most of the couch and knocked a lot of pages to the floor. That was fine. He wasn't reading them. Then he told me a meandering tale about an airplane, and he contradicted everything he said without apology, in the way of an eight-year-old who didn't need to make sense to anyone but himself.

LOUISA'S PROGRESS STRUCK THE

Israelis as miraculous. After less than two months in the transient camp, she spoke Hebrew without a trace of an accent. In the hat and shorts she looked less like a newcomer than an awkward, eager boy, and it probably seemed like a natural thing to the North Africans that she should take a seat in the cab beside the foreman. Leaning her elbow out the window, stray hair loose below the hat-brim, she would smile down at the black, dust-covered laborers who were left behind. She gave them a little wave.

"Queenly," one woman said to me in Yiddish. "She wasn't so queenly when she was eating grass. Must have been down on her luck by then. No one would have her. On her hands and knees like a dog. My husband almost shot her, but she looked too low to waste a bullet on."

Thankfully, most of the Europeans were gone now. They had been replaced by a group of Egyptians who did not take much notice of Louisa or, for that matter, of me. They were first-rate black marketers, and three sisters did a lively business in pink scented hand-cream. The place was beginning to smell like a bordello. I would pull my blanket over my head and write in the little notebook for Levin.

The camp personnel were fond of Louisa, particularly the language teachers. One day, when I was eating one of those strange cucumber salads at a table alone, a big, homely woman pushed herself right against me and began babbling in Hebrew, clearly beside herself with enthusiasm, and I could hear Louisa's name bob up and down on the flow of nonsense. She seemed to expect some response. I kept a bit of cucumber and mayonnaise on my fork suspended between us and let time accumulate. Then I put it in my mouth and swallowed.

I did not see her go, but as she pushed back her chair, I did hear her say, clearly: *"Sabonim."*

OV LEVIN HAD SENT A LETTER to Kibbutz Gan Dahlia and another old kibbutz called Beit Shemesh that had been established not far from Safed in 1908. A week had passed with no reply. Perhaps to get my mind off waiting, one afternoon, Levin found me coming out of the barracks and said, "Wear this." He presented me with one of those little white cloth caps. "It's getting towards summer now. Hot sun. I don't want you fainting on me."

"Why should I faint?" I asked him. "Are you going to show me something shocking?"

"No," he said. "Only my daughter."

I took the hat. It had a frilled brim and little strings to tie under my chin, and it was so clean and white and I was so grim and dark that the effect must have been comic. Or tragic.

"Levin," I said, "why am I meeting your daughter?"

"Miért nem? Some medical staff are visiting today. I told her about you."

I squinted below the brim of the hat. "She's a doctor?"

"A psychiatrist," said Levin. "Trained in Zurich."

He led me towards the medical tent they had set up on the outskirts of the camp. A thought occurred to me, and I stopped dead. I said, "You're not having me committed, are you, Levin?"

Levin didn't smile. "You don't think you're costing the state enough already?"

"You must admit, I'm a pretty interesting case," I said.

"You'd be surprised," he said, "how ordinary you are, Nora. Now come on." We pushed through the crowd to the shaded area where men had stripped down to their boxers and women's dresses were slung across a curtain. I hadn't a clue what a psychiatrist would do under those circumstances, and when we found his daughter, she looked equally bewildered, holding a clipboard, standing between two hampers of towels.

She shook my hand and said something in Hebrew. After one look at my face, she switched to German. *"Entschuldigung,* Frau Gratz. The day has been endless. Lunch is out of the question, a break is out of the question, life is out of the question." Her manner put me in mind at once of her father, as did her homely, sheep-like features.

"Nami," said Levin, "nothing is completely out of the question."

"For example." She thrust her clipboard at her father. "You see this? They want me to treat people who have been in the camps, ordinary, unhappy people. And their symptoms. You know, some of them steal cutlery. One woman hoards sanitary napkins and she hasn't menstruated in six years."

Levin threw her a gentle look of warning, which she shrugged away. I didn't begrudge her the need to blow off a little steam, and I was enjoying the shade of the tent and the girl's excellent, Pesti-accented German.

Then she said, "Frau Gratz, do you know who I'd like to meet? Your daughter-in-law."

The request took me by surprise. "What would you want with her?" I asked, maybe a little harshly.

Nami said, "My special field of study is the psychological foundation of pure altruism. I don't mean resistance. Resistance is a completely understandable response to save your own skin. I mean selflessness."

"Galut sentimentality," said Levin, with affection. "In my own daughter."

"Not sentimentality. It seems to me common sense that altruism has a completely selfish foundation. To create a whole self. To become a mature, productive citizen. I'd like to write up something for the popular press. And then we could arrange a tour."

Levin laughed out loud. "Nami, *kedvesem*, if you put that poor girl on a tour through Israel, she'll have to travel in a cage like a circus animal or she'll be torn to pieces. You haven't heard those Poles go at her."

Nami sighed and rubbed her hands straight up through her thick hair in a gesture identical to her father's. "There is no excuse for prejudice and barbarity. Frau Gratz," she said to me, "I am serious. My father's told me all about Louisa, and to me it seems like a typical example of displacement. Survivors look at her and see Germany. They can't believe in innocence anymore. But if they knew her story, she could be a symbol of—" She paused, and proudly found the right word. "A symbol of redemption."

"Don't get out of hand," her father said.

Nami was determined. "If she could tour the *Aretz*, if she could sing— just imagine that girl singing songs by men like your own son, men who have been martyred—"

"You don't want to hear her sing," I said.

Nami frowned. "But it would keep his name alive—don't you understand?"

"Nora," Levin said in Hungarian, "do you want to go somewhere and sit down?"

I continued in German. "I want to make clear," I said, "to your daughter the psychiatrist that she doesn't want to hear Louisa sing."

"But the power of music," Nami said, "the universal language—"

"Yes, music is a universal language, Doctor Levin. How much do you want to understand?"

"Sit down, Nora," Levin said again, but I did not sit down.

From our corner by the hampers, I could hear the mingled babble of those waiting to see real doctors, people who could heal them. There were distant groans of men whose bodies were pressed on sore points, and from far off, a sound unmistakable, a woman in labor.

Nami said, "Frau Gratz, I know I can't fathom what you've been through." She cocked her head and smiled at me as though I were a child. "Surely, music is a way to heal us and bring us all together."

Then I laughed. At that moment, medical personnel pushed in and started taking clean towels out of the hampers, and I kept on laughing, not quite enough to sound hysterical, mind you, but enough to meet the eye of a middle-aged lady doctor with blond hair who looked me full in the face for long enough for me to catch my breath.

I started to call out, but she'd propelled herself towards the mesh gate of the restricted area, and without thinking twice, I followed and almost knocked over a passing technician, who gave me an odd look and produced a telegraphic line of Hebrew.

By now, the doctor had opened that gate, and it had closed behind her. I gestured towards her. I must have had a really desperate look on my face because the technician called out to her.

She paused and turned. I got another look at her face through the mesh, and now I had the nerve to shout: "Dori!"

I had only known the face from the photograph of the chicken coop, but if I'd had doubts before, they were gone now; the small, bright eyes, the round cheeks, even the texture of the hair I'd seen only in black-and-white, though now it was clipped to a professional bob, and if that wasn't enough, the way she responded to that name as though someone had opened shutters on a window. She took a step towards me.

I approached the closed mesh with caution and very hesitantly spoke Hungarian. "You don't know me."

After a pause, she answered in the same language. "Is this urgent? I have a baby to deliver."

"Yes, it's urgent," I said. "Please, don't disappear. Give me a minute. That's enough. I'm Bela Hesshel's cousin."

What impact did I think those words would have? She said nothing for a moment, but gave a clearly false glance at her medical chart. Then she said, "My name is Arielle Ginzberg. No one has called me Dori in twenty-five years."

My God, what the hell difference could that make to me? I swallowed, trying to clear a path through the lump in my throat. "Couldn't you tell me, please, where he is?"

"Where who is?" she asked me, looking at that damned chart again.

"My cousin. Bela."

"No one calls him Bela," Dori said. "No one's called him that since 'twenty-three. I think he knows you're here."

"You think?"

"We forwarded your telegrams. Listen: You're Nora Csongradi, aren't you? Could you come back in an hour?" Just as I was recovering from hearing this woman say my maiden name, she tapped her fingers on her clipboard and said, "No, on the other hand, don't bother. I'll be gone by then."

Almost to myself, I said, "Where is Tilulit?"

"Not Tilulit," she said. "Gan Leah. We changed our name in 'forty-two. But you won't find him there."

My hand squeezed around the mesh. It was difficult to get words out. "Where is he?"

"No one knows. We forwarded your telegrams on through the military. I can't stay. It's a difficult delivery, and, frankly, I think you've done enough damage already."

Dori's tone remained businesslike to the point where I hadn't thought I'd heard those last few words correctly, and if I had sense I would have taken what she'd given me, not pressed for more. But I didn't have sense and so I shouted, "I don't care what you call yourself and I don't care what happens because I'm keeping you for five minutes to get a straight answer!"

"No," Dori said, maybe lightly. "You don't care. You didn't care about his mother or his sister either, or they'd be alive and here in Israel now."

Then, she pulled on her surgical mask, like a pale-green snout, and walked off into the restricted area where I couldn't follow.

I lingered by the gate, staring after Dori Csengery until I felt Levin come in behind me. He said, "Well, you've had a hell of an afternoon."

I still couldn't move. The sounds of the woman in labor filled the silence again, regular as the whistle and the pistons of a train. It must have been delusional; no real labor could have sounded so steady and musical.

"*Gyere,*" Levin said, as though he'd hoped Hungarian would cut through something. "Don't make an ass of yourself."

I let him take my arm and tuck it in his own, something he hadn't done before. Nami came towards us to lead us to a bench near the canteen. I was too stunned to put up resistance, and I even let her take my hand and look at me earnestly. She made a fuss about getting me a cup of lukewarm water. "You know, I really could help you both."

"No more, Nami," said Levin.

I barely heard any of this, and I was compelled to say, "You don't understand. Something wonderful has happened. I found the place I've been looking for since I got off the boat. And he knows I'm here. My cousin knows I'm here."

All of this came out in a soft, cultivated flow of German I didn't recognize as my own voice. Levin did not release my arm. As for Nami, her eyes grew as penetrating as her father's because in spite of her earlier manner, she was no fool. She could tell something didn't add up. Yet I had told the truth.

That's what I said to Levin as he walked me back to the barracks. The heat was intense and I felt sheets of sweat slide down my neck and gather between my breasts and thighs.

"You want to go to Gan Leah tomorrow?" Levin's voice was gentle.

I felt my head go white for a moment, and I realized I'd taken off the cotton cap. Levin was holding it. "No," I said. "To be honest, I don't think I'd be welcome."

A FEW DAYS LATER, LEVIN TOLD ME he had received a reply at last from Beit Shemesh. Dully, I took in the news: Yes, Tilulit had changed its name to Gan Leah, after a girl who'd died during a skirmish with the village. Of course, they remembered a Bela Hesshel, but he'd left the kibbutz in '44 and worked with the Rescue and Relief Committee smuggling Jews from Hungary into Palestine. No one had heard from him for over a year.

"Yes, that's what I gathered," I said.

"And?"

"They're not going to help me," I said.

"On the basis of some bitter woman he jilted? That's probably what that doctor is," said Levin. "Look, have a rest. Think it over. Have a cup of coffee."

"Coffee isn't what I want," I said. I had to get out of that office. I didn't want his help anymore. What had it gotten me?

His coffee was too sweet. It didn't make a dent in my headache and didn't make it any easier to believe what he said about Dori Csengery. Her anger came from somewhere, and the rest of them would share it. Perhaps with cause.

M AYBE I'D TAKEN LEVIN'S ADvice and had a rest, or maybe the heat made me dull-witted. All I know is later that afternoon, I sat up in my bed and there was Yossel Berkowitz. He sat just where he'd been that first night, on a bed recently claimed by an Egyptian grandmother, and there was a hard brown suitcase pressed between his knees. In spite of the heat and sunlight, he still kept his leather coat buttoned to the top, and sweat glistened on his eyebrows and his long, deep upper lip.

I said, "That bed belongs to someone else."

"Your interest touches me," he said. "I don't need much sleep. I don't need much of anything, except for what I need. We have that in common. Here." He pulled from his leather jacket a pack of Lucky Strikes, half-open, and he shook a cigarette into his hand.

"What will that cost me?" I asked.

"Ingyen van. All for free. *Nagymama,* you don't trust me? I've never lied to you. I don't take you for a fool. But I will tell you that you are going about this business like the Queen of Fools." He shook a second and a third Lucky from the pack. "How many?"

"Go to hell."

"I could leave a trail, and you could pick them up and see where it led you. It's easier to give you a few packs." He hoisted up the case, unlocked the clasp, and let it open on his lap. There was a rustle of cellophane, and he rooted around and said, "You want sardines? Whiskey? Cash? You want a new passport? You want to go to America? You want someone dead?"

"What I want is my business."

"But I'm a businessman. What? It's a telegram you want?"

All through this, he'd been riffling in that suitcase, but he looked up then with little black sparks in his eyes. One hand was pinned around a carton of Lucky Strikes. The other touched the suitcase clasp as though he weren't sure if he should close it.

"Maybe you want something I got," said Berkowitz. "Maybe you got something I want."

I stubbed the cigarette out and said nothing.

"What is she to you?" Berkowitz asked me. "You know why no one talks to you? You know why they look at you as if you're made of shit? It's because you carry a curse around with you."

Then, he closed the case with a crack and rested on top of it that carton of Luckies and on top of the carton his not-very-clean hands. He smiled a little.

"Tell me, why do you keep this girl?"

I didn't answer. He flipped the carton open and pulled out two packs.

"I mean, what does she give you?"

It was late afternoon. The barrack was full of people wringing out their underwear, brewing coffee, playing cards, but no one took notice of Berkowitz, and no one seemed to find our exchange of the slightest interest. He pushed one of the packs in my direction, and I didn't lay my hand on it but didn't push it back either. He added one more.

He said, "I could find this cousin for you. In an afternoon, in half an hour, I could find him."

I didn't answer, and I didn't lay my hand on those packs of cigarettes. No, he left them on his own, *szabad*, no strings attached. They lasted me four days, and then he left me more, tucked under my pillow, four packs this time.

He also said this to me. "She must have a nice time in those orange groves. She must have the time of her life. You want to know why?"

With that Lucky in my hand, I felt no need to answer. The information would present itself when its time came. All I had to do was wait.

"Because," said Yossel Berkowitz, "there's not a damned orange left on the trees. Harvest ended a month ago."

WO MONTHS AFTER GABOR HAD introduced me to Louisa, he took to spending more time at home. By then, it was October. He sewed the buttons on the other side of the lamb's-wool coat and modeled it for me, striding up and down the kitchen like a Russian prince. Then he puttered with the gas stove until I made him stop. One afternoon, I returned from work to find him with a notebook propped up on raised knees, and as I put some onions in the bin, he picked at the end of a pencil and watched me as though I were an animal in the zoo.

I asked him, "Don't you have somewhere else to go?"

"Of course I do," he said. "But I like being here. I think I'll sew the buttons on the other side of the coat again. Where's the thread?"

"You're exhausting me," I said.

"I wrote a sonnet about you."

"Did you finish it?"

"What's this obsession with finishing? I think it's death-worship, if you want to know the truth." Gabor sketched an open can of sardines and kept humming two dull notes over and over until at last he settled back against the windowpane and groaned. "Momma," he said, "I think I should move to Turkey. How much money do we have?"

"Why Turkey? Why not China?"

"She'd guess China."

"Why not just break it off?"

"She won't let me," Gabor replied, a statement I did not yet understand. Then he added, "I have to give her the song."

"You know," I said, "there's something appealing about that girl waiting for the song. She's like a clean slate."

"More like a hole," said Gabor. I made no reply. His mood changed, and he lit one of my cigarettes for himself, though he seldom smoked. He made a show of letting smoke drift out of one side of his mouth. We sat in superficial harmony, but tension sang. Clearly, he'd wished I hadn't met her, but the damage had been done. She'd been in our flat, and now it wasn't quite what it should have been, a refuge. I asked what I should have known better, in a thousand years, than to have asked.

"Are you supposed to be seeing her now?"

He seemed startled to hear my voice. "What does it matter?"

"If you lie to her," I said, "I'd sooner you didn't make it my business."

"What the hell are you talking about?" Gabor stubbed out the cigarette. "She's not your daughter and she isn't your business, and I don't have to stay here. It's damned depressing. It's too big. We just knock around here. Why don't we move? Don't you know he isn't coming back?"

It was uncalled for. Why did he need to bring it up now, out of the blue? I wasn't waiting for Janos. I'd faced facts. What would he have me do? Put a notice in the paper acknowledging that I was a straw-widow? Pawn all the clothing? Burn the engineering books? Besides, moving to another flat would cost a fortune. I said none of these things, but I did say, "I don't ask you to do anything against your will."

"Fine," Gabor said. "I'm going out."

 E WASN'T GOING TO LOUISA.
That was clear. In fact, Gabor got a tram to Nyugati Station. He often ended evenings there, I knew, watching trains come and go. Many a morning, he

came in to breakfast still stinking of coal-dust and axle-grease. Shivering and feeling more than a little ridiculous, he followed the tracks clear out of the station, through a wasteland of railroad ties and coal heaps, and tried to remember the first two measures of *Rocket*.

But what good was it without an ending? Everything he wrote trailed off or just stopped. It was as though an airplane, rather than swooping onto the landing field, fell from the sky like a stone. Stone, stone, he thought. He should take a stone and kill the girl. Wouldn't that be an ending?

Gabor looked over his shoulder at a train pulling into the station. Its headlight dimmed, and the light on its tail winked on and off like code. How could something so heavy look so light and so warm-blooded? He paused, and sat on an empty oil-drum, wondering if he should write a song about a train. Trains reach a destination.

Then something spun towards him and fell at his feet with a crash. It was an empty bottle of *pálinka*.

Gabor turned and saw two workers pass at a distance. "Hey!" Gabor called. "What's that about?"

One of them paused and spun around in Gabor's direction. "Didn't see you."

"The hell you didn't!" Gabor stepped forward into a beam of light, though his legs were unsteady. "You aimed!"

"The hell I did." The man stepped towards Gabor, a hulk with a mustache and a flushed face, clearly able to snap Gabor in two across his knee. "Why the fuck would I bother?"

His friend pulled at his arm. "Zoli, come on, don't waste time on that little kike. We're already late. You don't want to miss Judit."

Zoli gave Gabor one more glare, but turned his back and walked on, not so steadily, beyond the tracks, and even from a distance, Gabor could hear their brutal laughter. He pushed over the oil-drum, and it rolled downhill into a gully, leaving a black trail. He raked his hands through his hair.

Then, silence. He could make out the hum of the lights from the station, and very distant, another train approaching. From behind, feather-faint, a violin. Greasy, shaken, wrongheaded, he turned towards the sound of that violin and started towards some hint of glowing windows, a *kocsma*, a worker's bar, and now, unmistakable, the violin was joined by another, and he could hear laughter, feet stomping, a glass breaking, more laughter, and by then he stood at the threshold.

He had never been to that *kocsma* before. The brakemen and stokers kept their hats on, but they were down to shirtsleeves. The girls wore full black skirts, and their hair was loose and wild, and they were either stuffed onto the workers' laps or they were dancing. Men spun the girls and one girl on a table, with her skirt stuffed in her fists, screamed out a song about roses. The floor was sticky with wine and beer, and flames from candles singed the walls.

The fiddlers were both gypsies, skinny men in cheap felt vests, and they were playing something familiar. Gabor heard himself sing out: *Little dog, little dog you will lead the sheep to me—*

He swallowed the rest. The fiddlers kept playing. The two workers he'd seen outside were right by the door with their boots up on a plank table, and the one who wasn't Zoli gestured him over.

"What the hell? Dickhead, you think you come right in and join the party?"

Gabor said, "I never knew anyone in particular owned that song."

"So you're a lawyer too?" He raised a hand like a paw, and Gabor steeled himself to be struck, but that hand clamped down on his shoulder and pulled him towards him on the bench. "Hell, *anyone in particular*. You have too many words in your head. You need a drink."

"I'll take a drink," said Gabor, and the man introduced himself as Zsolt and poured Gabor a glass from his own bottle. Gabor put his chin in his hand and stared across the black table, over Zsolt's boots, to the floor where Zoli danced with the girl who'd sung about the roses; and in the blur of candle-light and liquor, he took in the sound of the fiddle, the tramping of the heavy shoes as couples danced. A song began and ended. Then another song began. It was all the same to the couples dancing. Their bodies pressed together like fat pressing against pork.

"What the fuck do you sit out there for?" Zsolt asked Gabor. "You look like a jerk."

"Sit out where?" Gabor asked Zsolt.

"By the tracks."

"I'm trying to commit suicide," said Gabor.

Zsolt laughed, or maybe retched. "What's the problem? Some girl won't let you fuck her?"

It was Gabor's turn to laugh then, though his head rang. He said, "No. Some girl won't let go."

"So throw her in front of the train," Zsolt said.

"Can't," Gabor said.

"Then, son," said Zsolt, "you listen to me. You want to get rid of her?"

Gabor nodded, taking it in and at the same time grabbing hold of the tune which had wandered through *Uncle Janos* and *Sweet Home of Mine* back to *Little Dog* again.

Zsolt pressed his mouth against Gabor's ear; he could feel the mustache. "If you want to get rid of her, give her everything she wants. That's the way it is. You treat a girl like shit, they worship you. You treat her like a queen, she leaves. Steal her a diamond bracelet. Shoot a fox and make her a coat. Nothing drives a girl away like that, nothing."

"It wouldn't work," said Gabor. "She doesn't want a coat."

Zsolt shook his head. "Look at that girl," he said, and he took Gabor's head in his hand and turned his face towards Judit, whose red cheeks and dazzling eyes made her look half-consumptive. "I treated her like a queen, and Zoli treats her like shit. Guess who has her now?"

Gabor didn't take his eyes off Judit as he asked, "Did you steal a diamond bracelet?"

"Who says I stole?" He pulled Gabor's face back towards his own. "You're the thief. I can see it in your face. I'm on to you."

"Are you?" Gabor asked, lightly. He reached for the bottle and poured himself another drink. "Maybe you are," he said. "So if I give her everything she wants, she'll leave me. But what if I can't give her what she wants?"

Zsolt pulled the bottle out of Gabor's hand and took a long drink. He said, "Then you're fucked. You'll never get rid of the bitch."

Smoke made a film on the windows and obscured the headlamp of another locomotive as it passed the *kocsma* and moved on through the dark.

WAS ASLEEP WHEN GABOR stumbled in that night, and as ever, he shed his coat first, and then his shoes, flung each sock free so that one landed on the hat-rack and the other on the kitchen table and just before the threshold of his bedroom he had peeled off his trousers. All of this I saw when morning came. He left more marks: Pulled out of the closet were the boxes of old sheet music he must have kept from his piano lessons years ago. They fell across the floor in a smudged white fan. I rubbed my eyes and listened for the sound of him sleeping, bedsprings shifting, something, but he had obviously gone out again. So early? Without his trousers? No, he had other trousers. It wasn't the first time he had come and gone, but I had an uneasy premonition. The shoes were muddy, flecked with gravel. I picked up those trousers which were smudged with oil, held them for a moment, dropped them again, and looked down at the mess he'd left behind.

Bending with difficulty, I began gathering it up. There were elementary finger exercises all marked up in grease-pencil by his old piano teacher; there were three pages of *The Eorl-King,* and on cheaper, badly decorated paper, bits of what looked like ragtime music. Then, I saw an overturned shoe-box and a page that made my heart stop. Another page. I backed away and almost stepped on the music box.

That music box lay in the middle of the floor. Kneeling now, I picked it up. The handle rattled. I gave it a single turn, and it came off in my hand.

*A*T DAWN, GABOR STOOD SHIVER-ing at the door of the Bauer house. He didn't knock. For a moment, he considered climbing in through the cellar door, but he felt foolish enough already, tired, anxious, soiled with the pencil and with perspiration that steamed off him even as he stood.

It was the maid, Eva, who opened the downstairs shutters. She asked in German, "You must be—you have to be the composer?"

Gabor said, "I have the song."

Eva closed the shutters. The silence felt eternal. Meanwhile, behind him, Buda came to slow, Sunday life. There was the faint sound of metal wheels on cobblestone, windows opening, and at last the first-floor window opened again, and there was Louisa.

Her face was brilliant, half-sleepy, young, pure. "Gabor," she said. *"Das gibt's doch nicht!"*

"Es ist fertig," Gabor said, and into her hand he pressed five sheets of crumpled paper smeared with pencil.

She didn't take her eyes from his face; it bore a look she'd never seen on a human face before. It must have been, she thought, the look of Goethe after he'd composed *Faust,* that distant and luminous. Her breath faltered into something close to a sob. *"Nein, nein,* it isn't mine to take," she said.

But now Gabor was turning, walking away, and with a cry she pulled herself half-out of the window in her blue quilted robe, and she called: "You can't leave me like this!" Then she hoisted herself over the white geraniums, slippers and all, waving those sheets of paper as she followed him up Castle Hill.

Gabor still found her behind him when he reached the business district some blocks away, where the first of the shops was opening its shutters. He gave in and turned, his head hanging with exhaustion. She was breathing hard under her robe, and the pages rattled as she held them towards him. It seemed impossible to Gabor that someone would not arrest them both.

She managed to put some words together: "This is the only copy?"

"Sure," Gabor replied. Somewhere, the grate of a shop door gave a hollow clang. He felt it in his stomach.

"But I can't let you make that mistake again. It isn't right."

Gabor told Louisa that he had to get home. His mother would be worried.

"Oh, *deine Mutter,*" Louisa said. "No one can feel the way about you I do."

"Look," Gabor said, "find someone at the Academy to copy it out on good paper, if that would make you happy. Make five copies. Make twenty."

Detaching Louisa from himself was, indeed, a delicate and imperfect process. There was her hand from his arm and her gaze from his face and finally her person from the corner, but she hadn't gone two steps before she rushed back and asked if he really meant he trusted her not to lose it.

"Lose what?" Gabor asked.

Louisa gave a disgusted little sniff. "You're just horrible!"

"Go home," Gabor said. "And I'll go home."

BUT GABOR DID NOT GO HOME. He made a day of heavy drinking. Beginning at a *cukrászda* with a *pálinka,* he went from *kocsma* to *kocsma,* moving through a succession of greasy tables. The company of strange men, the smell of bad tobacco, the absence, most of all, of any female was precisely what he needed. If he could only find that *kocsma* by the station, move in there permanently, with a bottle by his elbow and the flow of life around him acting like a cloak of invisibility.

Gabor took his time with each glass of *pálinka*. Even here, none of the men knew him and no one would expect him to be a genius. In fact, they had no expectations whatsoever. They finished what was in their glasses and paid for another. He'd done the same, yet again, and raised the glass paid for with the last of his pocket money when he heard a tapping at the window. He glanced; there was Louisa.

Her face was pressed to the glass, and her paste-white knuckles looked like teeth. He tried to give her a look of desperation; he was a man, he couldn't help it, that sort of thing. But she gestured him outside, and he managed to down that final shot before unsteadily appearing in the doorway.

She gripped his hand. "What's wrong?"

"Nothing," said Gabor. "What time is it now? I had no idea."

"Are you afraid to go home?" Louisa asked with knife-like earnestness.

"Nothing's wrong. Honestly, Angel, why are you here? I thought I sent you to copy my manuscript."

"But you don't even have a coat," Louisa replied. In fact, she'd somehow changed into street-clothes and what must have been her father's overcoat lay over her quivering arm, smelling of her so strongly that he shrank back from it, and she saw it and trembled, red-faced and clumsy, and sputtered out, "I tried to find you—all day—to give it to you—and now you—"

"Hey, hey," said Gabor. By now, they were walking together, and the liquor made him feel at odds with his own body, as though, try as he might to shake her off, he only got more entangled until he almost stumbled over his own feet and found her sticky arms around him.

"The coat—take it," she whispered. Her voice was full of wonder now because it caught up some of his own breath. To his appalled surprise, Gabor had kissed her.

Louisa went limp. Bracing his back on the lamp-post, Gabor managed to pull the two of them to something like an upright stance, and then he spoke hoarsely. "Go home."

"It's—" Louisa began.

Gabor cut her off with a push backwards. "I'll take the coat. Go home before you're missed."

Louisa's face was brilliant now. She turned to go. Yet she couldn't help herself. She had to turn and say, "Eva told me—translated—you must know, Gabor, you won't lose this. You won't lose me."

Those words, expelled with obvious effort, were the last she said before she turned and ran. The twilight was frosty. The whole day had been cold but he hadn't noticed until now, and he buttoned that reeking coat and looked after Louisa as she ran, fleeting between lamp after lamp like a bit of ribbon. He rubbed his head and wondered if he could find a trolley.

F GABOR HAD TAKEN A
trolley home to Prater Street that night, he would have arrived drunk.
I would have been slightly appalled, but I would have forgiven him,
worked off his shoes and socks, and helped him into bed. I would have
asked no questions; there would have been no need. We'd never lied to
each other. But Gabor walked. The five kilometers he walked were hardly
direct, though increasingly determined, as cold air wore down his intoxi-
cation.

By the time he arrived, he was sober. I was, of course, awake. I'd hardly
slept. The ashtrays were full; the dirty coffeepot was cold; the heater was
broken. What was the sense? He gave me a nod; his face looked unnaturally
flushed and his hands shook, but he didn't falter as he took a cardboard suitcase out of the wardrobe.

I asked him, "Going somewhere?"

He seemed to bear me no ill will. His tone was mild enough when he
said, "I meant to tell you. Somehow there hasn't been time. I found a room
with a friend, almost rent free."

"You have a room here. Rent free," I said. "Come on, Gabor. Put the
suitcase away. Tell me what happened."

"I'm almost twenty," he said, as he threw this and that into the case. "I
can't stay here forever."

"I wouldn't ask you to. Where is this room?" I asked him. "Take winter clothes for God's sake, Gabor. Take some of your father's sweaters."

"They're full of holes." Then he turned to me with unexpected tenderness. "You really ought to move out, Momma. It would give you an excuse to clean out the closets for good, get rid of all these old things."

"What are you talking about?" I asked Gabor.

"Sweaters, papers, those stupid drawings I made when I was a kid. Throw them away."

That was when I was supposed to ask him about what I'd found on the floor, but I could not bring myself to begin that conversation, so I only said, "That's why you're leaving? Because I'm untidy?"

Gabor picked up the suitcase and said, "My flatmate plays the clarinet."

"What do you want me to say, Gabor?" I asked him. "Do you want me to play the clarinet?"

"I'll leave you my address," said Gabor.

Then he did something surprising. He kissed the top of my head. His breath smelled of *pálinka*.

"You scare her, you know," he said. "The German girl."

He left then, and I lit another cigarette and listened for the closing of the door below. Then, I watched him through the window, walking off with that suitcase. He must have been exhausted. What was his hurry? What might I smell on him? I walked around the dinosaur of a flat with its greenish, lumpy walls, its warped floor, the gas leaking from the stove. It had been the flat, no doubt, that scared Louisa. Now, empty of the prospect of Gabor's return, it swelled. What were the rooms like with that mysterious clarinetist? I doubted they existed at all.

*B*UT THE ROOMS DID EXIST. IN fact, he got a full night's sleep there, and in the morning, a Monday, he met Louisa at school and told her about his new digs. She was delighted. Though of course, he added, there was no question of her visiting. Too small and too appalling. And the piano—

"There's a piano?" Louisa's voice hit a shrill note. Gabor, walking a careful distance from her, managed to reproduce the piano in a way that wouldn't offend her vanity. It was an old, clunking upright, though, of course, it was better than nothing. Now he could work at home. Louisa broke in: "There are wonderful pianos at the Academy."

"Angel, face it. I can't get real work done there." Whether Gabor referred to limited time or some other force of nature, who could know? A clever young man, my son; he managed to hold off on the address of his new room for so long that Louisa felt too ashamed to ask. He promised he would meet her after school. It would be wonderfully vigorous, after composing, to walk to the gate where girls in green jumpers clustered like the leaves of wild violets.

"It'll be too cold soon," Louisa said. She added, "You won't come."

Gabor didn't give those words the benefit of a denial. He said, "I expect you'd track me down."

Louisa felt his statement to be a rebuke, but what could she do? He appeared again on Tuesday and on Wednesday. Louisa kept running ahead and rushing back again. He caught himself in time to push her out of the way, knowing her face held the memory of that kiss.

The first afternoon Gabor didn't meet Louisa, she found the lodgings. She didn't say how. He was, to all appearances, glad to see her. The slight hadn't been deliberate, he said. He'd just lost track of time. She brought a sack of apples, past their season now and rather mealy. She looked out of place in the room. The clarinetist was cooking macaroni on a hot plate, and there was music paper thrown everywhere, and the window didn't close all the way, which was for the best because the central heating turned the air to lava. Still, Louisa smiled stoically and leafed through the sheet music on the piano.

"What's this?" she asked. It was a handwritten copy of three songs by Duke Ellington.

"Something I'm working on," Gabor said, not exactly a lie. He'd hoped to earn a little cash playing in clubs.

"Is it for Dramatic Soprano?"

"Angel, stick to Schubert."

"Old Schubert?" Louisa giggled then and said, "Professor Lengyel looks a little like him, you know. All chin and forehead. What a clown!"

"A powerful clown. He can make a career for you, you know," said Gabor. "When are you leaving for that tour?"

"Oh that. Not for ages. Besides, it's not even completely sure I'll go," Louisa said. "Really, the other girls will be the ones who get to show off. They're such divas."

Gabor took the pink ribbons from Louisa's hair, and two heavy locks fell on either side of her face. He shook his head. "You're not diva material. There's no pretense. That's the miracle of it. There's nothing but that voice."

He knew he shouldn't have touched her or said a word of encouragement because afterwards she stayed for hours, sharing the macaroni and margarine, though she ignored the clarinetist, and expressing opinions on art and music which he realized, as though in a dream, were things he'd said to her months before.

"Now you must go," Gabor said. "Tibi has to practice, and besides, it's late."

Louisa seemed prepared for this. "I won't go at all until you let me sing the *Lied.*"

"Let the girl sing," Tibi the clarinetist said from his bed.

Gabor spoke dully. "You've got the only copy."

As it turned out, she'd brought along a surprise: three clean copies in a hand so tidy and precise it brought on a chill. On the piano rack, in the dimmish light, he hardly recognized it. Before he could protest or fully prepare himself, he was seated at the piano forming the initial chords, and she sang the Hungarian words.

What is lost, what is lost
We can not have back again.
It is like a breath we've taken.
We can not breathe it again.
It is like good bread we've eaten.
We can not eat it again.
It is like a heart we've broken
Or our own heart, lost in vain.

Was it the same song? What had she done? Somehow, his hands built up the common melody and over it soared her voice, like light on water, swift and heartless. The high notes poured out of that girl with the loose hair and the empty face, and when she drew a hand to her throat, Gabor thought he would be sick.

By then, it was well past ten, dead dark and very quiet. Gabor raised his hands from the piano and rested them behind his neck. "They'll be wondering where you are, Lu. You'd better go."

"Aren't you glad I came?" she asked him.

"Of course," said Gabor, though too quickly. "I'm glad."

Louisa wanted more, he knew. She didn't move, but in her voice was the ghost of that second voice, the voice she sang with, not hesitant or modest. She asked, "Haven't I earned a kiss?"

Gabor didn't rise from the piano bench, and without otherwise touching her, he kissed her on the lips. Then he got up and led her to the door. "You'll miss the last trolley."

"No, I won't!" she said. She was an awkward girl again, racing down the stairs two at a time as though Gabor could take that kiss away.

Both men sat, saying nothing, for a while. Then, Tibi rose from the bed and scraped hardened bits of leftover macaroni onto brown paper. Without looking at Gabor, he said, "I didn't know you composed."

Gabor said, "We all have hidden talents."

"That girl's awfully young," Tibi said. He walked to the piano and picked up the copies of the song. "She's got a pretty voice, though. The real thing. It almost justifies what you did to that drinking song. And what was that text you adapted? It can't be yours. Awfully sentimental."

"It suits her. She's a sentimental girl," Gabor said. "Not like the dancer I met yesterday. She lives in the back of a candy store. Nice to indulge two tastes at once."

"Didn't you save any candy for your old friend?" Tibi said, laughing. He liked my son; he was happy for the company and an excuse to stop thinking about his own troubles. "I suppose now you'll take up dancing, like a Russian."

"I," said Gabor, "am going to be a fighter pilot and fly faster than the speed of sound."

The clarinetist set the music down, and taking up his own instrument, played a riff rather in the same style as the song. As he played, Gabor dressed down to his boxers and climbed onto the half-broken couch by the window. Cozy and well-exerted, he slept easily, as his companion practiced to make up for the time he'd lost that night.

THE NEXT MORNING, THE CLARinetist left for his office job and Gabor was putting on his socks and considering if he ought to go have a coffee, when Louisa arrived. Again, she brought apples, and this time also bread and cheese arranged in a neat, white basket. The next day, she came again and stayed. It became necessary to dress and wash before nine and leave the flat before she arrived. Then, she started coming later, when he'd already returned, or earlier, when even the clarinetist was asleep.

Once she was there, Gabor was forced to tinkle at the piano and scratch a few notes on paper. She would watch him as she peeled apples, sliced cheese, and stretched her long slim legs on the couch. Under her gaze he actually rewrote most of Ellington's "Satin Doll" and added three more measures of a swing number he'd heard on the radio, and then he hid them both in case she'd see them and, God forbid, try to sing them. Sometimes he'd just sit, thinking about anything but music; the overheated flat brought oily sweat to the roots of his hair, and his legs cramped under the piano, and not for a moment, as far as he could tell, had Louisa stopped staring.

He asked once, "Don't you go to school?"

"What good is school?" Louisa asked him. They were sitting on either end of the couch, and she had just peeled him an apple. The skin was on her skirt.

"Well, really," Gabor said, "you're just a kid."

"I'm not," said Louisa. "I don't sing like a kid."

"You're barely sixteen."

Louisa shifted herself up the couch and said, "I'm not a kid." Then she gave a bounce, and said again, "I'm not," and she liked the way the couch creaked so she bounced again and again, singing out: "I'm not, I'm not, I'm not!"

"Quit it!" Gabor shouted, moving to stop her, as the couch rocked and the contents of the basket tumbled everywhere, but Louisa was delighted and she called:

"Listen to it—it's singing, singing, singing!"

Then the couch gave way, and Gabor's head cracked against the floor, and in a white flash of pain, he was aware that half of him was caught against splintered wood and the other half against Louisa, whose moist, bare, scented arm pressed on his cheek and whose head was somewhere at his armpit. She laughed and laughed, her mouth vibrating like a soft harmonica, and through the spring and crossbeam, Gabor was conscious of his illogical erection. And what could he do then? Tell me, what?

Under such circumstances, Gabor told Louisa, he found it difficult to work. He'd see her at school, every afternoon. And, she asked, what about during the winter holiday? That was years away, Gabor insisted. It was best they didn't meet every day in his room. Tibi had been kind about the couch and together they'd repaired it as best they could, but he did hint that perhaps Gabor ought to pay some rent, or at least share the grocery bill. Louisa said she understood. But the next day there were her three quick knocks, and she stood in the doorway with bread, cheese, and apples.

"I'll just leave it here," she said. "You have to eat."

Then she'd look up with those pink cheeks and those sorrowful, excited gray-blue eyes, and he'd have to give her a kiss goodbye, which was no hardship. But she'd clamp one hand inside the doorway like a shoehorn, and invariably they would lurch inside, crack would go Gabor's head against the wall, and that slim, strong girl would wedge herself into that moment of vulnerability, and what could he do then? Another day lost, which he could not, at heart, begrudge her.

One morning, as he bent to tie his shoes, his skin prickled. Three heartbeats later, he recognized Louisa's three knocks.

Gabor did not so much as breathe. Three more. He could even make out the sharpness of the knuckles. After a very long time, he heard her footsteps as she walked away. He lay back with an old book on Dutch painting and didn't look up until Tibi appeared at the door with the basket in his hand. He ate all the apples at once so that when he picked Louisa up at school he could tell her how much he enjoyed them.

"I was out for a walk," he said. "I couldn't get a thing done so I went to the Academy to look for you. Then I ran into an old friend."

"Male or female?" Louisa asked, flirting bravely, though she must have felt some new note in the conversation.

"None of my friends can match your voice," Gabor said, and there was enough sincerity in his declaration to allow Louisa to blush.

She said, "Why won't you let me sing your song for Professor Lengyel?"

Gabor begged off with words about Lengyel's narrow mind, and the argument was so old that he could speak his part by rote and felt comfortable enough to walk her home. But this time, just as they reached their usual corner, she pulled him against her and buried her mouth in his neck. She whispered, "Come down with me?"

"Where?" Gabor asked.

"You've never seen the cellar." Her modulation told him she had practiced saying this. "It's dark there."

Gabor felt a shiver run through him similar to what he'd felt when she'd presented the three copies of the manuscript. They stood below a bare chestnut tree now, the Bauer house in plain sight, and Gabor felt so embarrassed and exposed that he actually pulled his coat closer. "It'll be cold there too," he said.

"It's a coal cellar." Louisa's voice faltered now; there was something moving in her, this young girl who'd propositioned him outright, and Gabor felt her hand slip into the pocket of his coat and drop something there: a key. "I could meet you tonight," she said, even less certainly.

Netted by anxiety, Gabor made certain promises that he didn't keep, and that night he went to bed very early, with the shade drawn and the covers over his head.

He dreamed of the cellar. It would smell like old blankets and its grainy darkness, like the darkness of the blanket, would smother him. Fleeting, white, enormous, spreading, Louisa pursued him through the heaps of coal, leaving a trail which smelled of scented soap and apples, and into the coal-dust Gabor sank slowly and by degrees, first his feet up to the ankles, then his knees, and soon he was wading through coal-dust. He woke up with the blanket in his mouth.

The next morning, she knocked again. Gabor kept still. She called in, "Hello?" Her voice poked through the door like a finger, probing the room. Gabor would have slid under the couch, if he hadn't been afraid to make a sound.

It took effort to meet her at school. Around the entrance of the yard, young girls milled in their green jumpers, with their smooth hair and their empty pretty faces. The cold drew puffs of steam from their lips, and inside of them each was a fire, but rather than feeling aroused, Gabor took all of this in with deep nausea. When Louisa appeared, the nausea deepened by an octave. Weakly, he waved to her.

This time, she had no speech prepared. Her jumper hung awry, her eyes were pink, and her voice was very raw. "Where were you?"

"I don't know." Gabor spoke as though the question didn't mean much. "I have quite a few pupils, you know."

"I thought you'd given all of them up."

"Oh. Did you think that?" Gabor smiled and all the time wondered why his lies were taking that direction; there were no other girls at the moment, though there would be by and by. For what was he preparing Louisa? The answer took this shape: "I need money. I'll be leaving soon."

Louisa blinked like a rabbit. She said nothing.

"After all," he said, "I need to get a broader view on life. Maybe I'll move to Istanbul."

Louisa asked, "But in Istanbul how will you write music?"

"What does music have to do with it?" Gabor asked her. He thought: What the hell is in Istanbul? He suppressed the urge to laugh, at life, at Louisa, or at the surprise of what might come out of his mouth next. "Why should I stay when you'll be singing in all the capitals of Europe?"

"I won't go!" Louisa threw her arms around his neck and kissed him with such depth and urgency he couldn't pull himself free without actually throwing her against the schoolyard wall, which he did. She fell with a mild thump. The gray in her eyes shimmered dangerously. Maybe her school-mates were watching. She didn't cry.

"Look," Gabor said, "there's nothing for me here. Budapest is a dead city. But if you don't go, you'll miss a real chance. Lengyel has influence."

"I thought," said Louisa, "that you hated him."

"Use the man. I would if I could." Gabor couldn't stand the way Louisa just sat there staring, so he gave her a hand up and brushed off her bottom as though she were his little sister. "Come on, Lu. Chin up. I won't be leaving for a while."

"I don't understand," Louisa began, but then her voice broke, and it took a moment for her to regain control. Then she said, "It isn't your mother, is it?"

"Momma?" The comment came from nowhere.

"She's jealous of me."

"What does that have to do with it?" Gabor made Louisa sit on a bench beside the schoolyard, and he made a pretty speech about me. "My mother probably is jealous of you, but that doesn't matter. She can't do a thing to hurt you. I don't think she even knows how to hurt someone."

Louisa took all this in. She said, "I think I understand her. She's like me."

The comment threw Gabor off-balance, but he let it pass. "I'll tell you something else. She's been through some pretty raw stuff in her time, but none of it's made her hard. You know, she told me never to hurt you?"

"But you will anyway," Louisa said.

"Probably," Gabor said, grateful she'd paved the way for him to say it. "I think her secret is, she speaks her mind. It makes her seem rough, but she's all there."

"We should go back to see her," Louisa said.

Gabor shuddered a little but dropped the issue. "Now I have to get to work."

"And what have you written?" It was almost an accusation. Gabor rose from the bench and walked off, fruitlessly pretending he hadn't heard her, wondering if he should have mentioned me at all.

A MONTH PASSED. GABOR NEVER again told Louisa that he was leaving, but he cut back his appearances at the girls' school. Once, when his roommate was on tour with a woodwind quintet, he came down with a cold and didn't open the door for two days running. When he emerged, he found two baskets of bread, apples, and cheese perfuming the hallway. They had been gnawed by mice.

One afternoon, I was making myself a coffee when the door opened, and there was Gabor. He'd looked better. His hair was matted and his nose was running. He brought with him a little of the dry December air; it hovered around his coat. I stood with the coffeepot in my hand and said, in a friendly way, "It's good to see you."

"Oh, hell, Momma," he said, tossing the coat over the couch, "I did look in a few times. You must have been out."

"Must have been," I said. "Want a coffee?"

"I could have left a note," Gabor said. It was as close as he would get to an apology.

Afterwards, we were both quiet for a while. I'd found a box of lemon biscuits that were so stale they broke in pieces. I knew I should offer him something more substantial, but I sensed that if I mentioned supper or even so much as pushed back my chair to warm up his coffee, he'd take it as a sign to go, so I stayed put. The crumbs clogged my throat, and the cigarettes roughed them up until I had to swallow hard.

As for Gabor, he seemed a little stunned. He'd slung himself into a familiar chair and observed a familiar kitchen with its mismatched tiles and its curtains faded down to ocean green. He must have wondered how he'd spent nineteen years in the place. Then, he turned those same measuring eyes on me and said, "How long would it take to get a pilot's license?"

At last, I broke down and said, "Gabor, don't talk nonsense. You know they wouldn't take you."

Gabor smiled a little; his teeth weren't clean.

"Do you love her?" I asked. The question startled even me, who'd asked it, and as soon as it was out of my mouth, it seemed absurd. Gabor rocked backwards on his chair and at the same time drew a cigarette from my pack and lit up before he answered.

"Let me tell you about this German girl. She's got a voice that will take her places. She's got a future."

"And she'd give up that future for you?"

That brought on silence, and even our coffee seemed to grow a shade paler until it was pointless to go on. Released from the prison of his lodgings, Gabor had returned, and I'd said everything I shouldn't have said. Even as he sat across from me, he was already receding.

But actually, he leaned across the table to kiss me goodbye. He said he'd be back soon. "Don't worry about Louisa."

"You said her name." I voiced the observation without thinking. It stopped Gabor in his tracks. "You never use their names," I said. "It's always, The Fat Lady or The Virtuoso or The Angel. Never names."

"You've lost me, Momma. I'm too slow to follow your logic." Gabor pulled on his coat and opened the door. "You know her name, after all."

*T*HAT AFTERNOON, HE MET Louisa at school. Perhaps he planned to tell her he was going to become a pilot. Due to his cold, he took a trolley. He hadn't seen her for a few days, and as the trolley rattled across Margit Bridge, he wondered what sort of greeting she would give him, but she only smiled, surprised to find him waiting. She didn't kiss him, but she didn't seem to hold back out of resentment. Rather, she simply fell in beside him as they walked together.

"You look like a rose in bloom," Gabor said. "You must have a new boyfriend."

Louisa only laughed; she did look fine that afternoon, particularly in contrast to Gabor, who should have been in bed. Her face glowed, and her laughter was so free and candid that Gabor wondered if he'd hit on the truth. Then, Louisa asked, "Why don't you meet my family?"

Gabor said, "I've never been invited."

"Well, I'm inviting you. Christmas Eve."

It had the edge of an announcement. As though someone had set upon his eye a sharper lens, Gabor saw everything again, and in as steady a voice as he could muster, he asked, "Lu, are you pregnant?"

Louisa blushed, but her lips turned pale. "How could you even think that?"

"Well, it's not impossible," Gabor said, reasonably enough.

"How can I be pregnant," Louisa said, "when I'm going on that tour?"

Nonplused at this series of revelations, Gabor took the young girl in his arms and held her close. He tried not to notice the rapid beating of her heart. She had invited him to her own farewell party, and the relief he felt was mixed with something sharper. He wasn't completely lucid when he said, "Of course I'll be there. With bells on!"

He thought: That angel, that kid. He ought to get her something nice for Christmas.

T'S AMAZING WHAT A STEADY
supply of Lucky Strikes will do. After the first pack, I discovered that my
everyday dresses had absorbed so much perspiration they might as well have
been made of wet paint. Louisa got me a new one. She'd bought a length of
rose-colored cotton with her wages, and one of the Egyptians did it up on a
sewing machine in an afternoon. Really, she did take good care of me. Cigarettes allowed me to put her in perspective.

If orange harvest had ended, that meant that Louisa had been lying to
me, and if she'd been lying to me, that meant I didn't have to tell her about
Dori or Gan Leah. After all, what did I really know about that girl? Consider: How had a child of seventeen arranged to stay behind in Budapest
when her family fled to safety? How had she hid me in that cellar? How had
she managed to live out the years between the war's end and the day she
found me at the border, wearing the fur coat and fancy earrings? These
were all mysteries, and I could let them go. Having something to hide is
simply part of the human condition. Those were the sorts of things I
thought when I was smoking: Platitudes that could make anything sound
reasonable.

I couldn't have said why I withheld information from Louisa. Perhaps I
didn't want to get her hopes up. After all, life at the transient camp seemed to

get harder rather than easier for her as winter turned to summer. Even after the Poles were gone, she was hated by the residents who flicked her breakfast tray into her face or threw her washing from the line. Israeli boys in shorts would intervene, less angry than embarrassed. They apologized to Louisa, and out came the word again: *Sabonim, Sabonim,* accompanied by a gesture of despair.

Louisa took all of this without complaint. What she couldn't bear were the Transylvanian girls. They left her gifts: a canvas sack of brown sugar that leaked all over the blanket, a transparent plastic pocket comb, photographs torn from magazines of blonde girls with dazed, serene expressions. Louisa obviously still found them unnerving, and once confided that she'd found a few pairs of her bloomers missing.

"What would they do with my bloomers?" she asked me. "They'd be much too big."

"Perhaps they don't have any clean ones of their own, dear," I replied.

"But then they give me all these dirty things." Louisa shook her head. "I don't want dirty things. It's hard enough to keep clean in this place."

One memorable gift came from the youngest of the girls, who caught us once at dawn, appearing by the cot and staring down right at Louisa. She wore what looked like a soldier's duffel coat which ended somewhere at her ankles, and her hair flew from her wide forehead like black feathers. Her eyes twinkled with malice. *"Mit csinaltsz, német lány?"*

Louisa lurched away and pressed herself to my side. She whispered, *"Mutti,* what is she asking?"

"Nothing of consequence," I said. "She simply asked what you are doing."

The Transylvanian girl leaned down a little farther, smelling of vinegar, cabbage, and blankets. *"Tetszik a csúnya kis baba, német lány?"*

To illustrate, she pulled from her coat a bald doll the size of the palm of her hand. It was missing a leg, and blue inkblots obscured an eye and most of a nose. She held it towards Louisa, whose face did some interesting things.

I explained. "She's offering you the doll. She says it is an ugly doll."

Louisa got out of bed so quickly that she got half-tangled in the bed sheet and stumbled up against the windowsill. The truck from the orange grove pulled in then, and she took a shallow breath and pulled up her shorts under her nightshirt with one hand as she felt for her hat with the other.

The girl leaned over my side of the bed and grinned. *"Itt van a völegény!"*

If there were no oranges to harvest, where did that truck go? I knew I ought to be a little afraid for Louisa, riding off in that unmarked truck with the compactly built Arabic Jew. Yet she seemed at home beside him, as though she had ridden off with strangers in the past, therefore procuring herself, say, a rabbit-fur coat, or expensive earrings. Speculation came easily to me, and cost nothing.

I sat up, lit a cigarette, and turned to the Transylvanian girl, whose heart-shaped, swarthy face was smeared with dust, and who still held that doll in her hand.

She said to me, *"A völegény, Nagymama. Öreg, csúnya."* A bridegroom, old, ugly. Like you.

*L*OUISA DID ONCE BRING ME BACK an orange. *"Himmlisches Apfelsine.* Have a taste."

I was bewildered, and not pleased. "Where on earth did you get that?"

She didn't seem to think the question out of place. She arranged herself on the edge of the cot, and I realized, for the first time, that she'd gone quite brown. "The manager said: Here, take this to your *Mutter,* so she tastes a real orange from Zion."

There was a half-crazed animation to the way she pulled the dull skin off that orange, as though it were essential that I believe it really came from a manager who really said those things and that he would think less of her if she didn't get to the flesh of the fruit as quickly as possible. She tore off a section.

"I don't like oranges," I said.

"How can you not like oranges?" Louisa sounded a little desperate. She held the wedge out towards me, and I let it dangle there to dribble juice all over her shorts.

*L*EFT TO MYSELF, I TOOK A LOT of walks. If I showered, wore that dress, and had some Luckies in my purse, I felt almost human. The rainy season had ended and the air felt different than any air I'd ever breathed: thin, dry, almost like smoke. Perhaps I walked because I wanted to avoid Levin. He'd probably try to give me back that stupid hat. I felt conspicuous in the hat and what I wanted most now was to move unseen. I liked to blend into tent-canvas or shadows behind the oil-drums, and from that perspective to watch goings-on with a degree of distance.

I found myself drawn to the Yemenites. Their tents were pitched in the north end of the camp, and they were small as children, black as dirt, and quiet as cats. If I lingered there for long enough, I could observe the women carry out pots of water and do wash together, and I was brought back to that gypsy camp in Barnahely. Did Yemenites read palms? When I looked at all those mingled robes and headdresses it put me in mind of the circus back in Vidam Park in Budapest. SEE THE EXOTIC ISRAELITES FROM AFRICA. HEAR THEIR BARBARIAN TONGUE. MYSTERY OF THE EAST.

During the early '20s, when I had first arrived in Budapest and Adele had hoped to make a normal girl of me, she'd arranged for a few excursions to the permanent exhibit, and six or seven of us tried to keep together as the crowd did its best to push us in six or seven directions. I remember Adele's fleeting, helpless wave, as she and David, or was it Andras, were swept towards the dwarf-swordfight, and I remained with one hand clamped to the protective bar in front of Monkey Boy.

In 1941, Adele wrote me from Szeged: *The circus passed through last week, and Matyas and I took our nephew. Monkey Boy has gone gray. What will become of us?* After twelve years of marriage, she still had no children, though she hadn't yet given up hope.

I never did visit Szeged, but from her letters, I can imagine their home near the town center, with Matyas and Adele's households meshing into a glorious clutter, china on the shelves and rugs strung on the walls, trays of hard candies everywhere, and all of Bela's books and maps stored in the attic. It would have been a wonderful place for a child. Matyas made furniture and carved wooden toys for a hobby, and the front yard was filled with a collection of miniature rocking chairs and horses and sheep and three-legged stools he passed on to his nieces and nephews. There was a constant battle between Adele's roses and Matyas's carpentry, with Aunt Moni wielding a broom in the middle, making sure that at least a path stayed clear so neighbors didn't think they were barbarians.

Of course, the neighbors thought no such thing. They came and went through the front door and the back, exchanging plant cuttings, homemade wine, and pastries. Adele didn't trust the cook to properly kosher the meat, so often those neighbors would find Adele standing over the sink, still in her nurse's uniform, with house-slippers on her feet and both hands full of rock salt. The cook, a local girl, resented the intrusion, so Aunt Moni would have to distract her by asking her to buy some lemons. You could get lemons in Szeged, unlike in Kisbarnahely. Perhaps that made all the difference.

Matyas was considered henpecked. He didn't drink or play cards. Sometimes he had to work until nine or ten at night, but the moment the light went off in his window of the factory, you could set your clock by the ten minutes it would take him to walk home. Adele was far more likely to go out with the girls after her shift at the hospital, and she never seemed concerned that Matyas would be angry. He was such a shy, unassuming fellow, peering over his wood-carving with his moist brown mustache, that it seemed obvious Adele could walk all over him.

Yet in the matter of religion, Matyas ruled. The house was strict kosher, with separate dishes for the milk and meat. On Fridays and Saturdays, he went to synagogue, and sometimes stopped on his way to work for morning prayers. Though he didn't insist Adele join him, he was pleased when she did, and sometimes, though it contradicted the whole purpose of the women's balcony, he would turn in his prayer shawl and try to catch her eye.

Aunt Monika was bewildered by what she called "this business with the dishes." She resented not being allowed to play her phonograph on the Sabbath. Still, she was willing to put up with inconveniences, particularly if she would get to spoil a grandchild. She was nearing seventy now, and it was getting harder and harder for her to sweep Matyas's wood-shavings from the path. Closing the drapes against the afternoon sunshine, she would write me spidery letters, full of questions about Gabor, and I'd do my best to answer them.

She also asked about Bela. How was he? I'd realized, then, that Bela had stopped writing his mother about the time that he stopped writing me, in '39.

*H*IS LAST LETTER HAD BEEN uncharacteristic. Somehow, it lacked buoyancy. With his bum knee, he wrote, he'd become little more than a schoolmaster, a position given to people who couldn't do anything else. Tilulit was growing too quickly, and it would be difficult to make do with their thousand dunam for much longer. Though no one minded sleeping in a tent, they couldn't fill all of their arable land with tents. They had to grow something on that land. That was the whole point.

It had been a hard month. First, there'd been a blight on the chickens, and he'd opened up the coop one morning and almost fainted at the stench. They burned the infected chickens and scraped the coop clean, and there was an all-night argument about whether they ought to bring in turkeys. Nathan Sobel had heard that turkeys got a wonderful price, this seemed to Bela reason enough to argue against it. Bela's animosity for Sobel was admitted in such plain language that I couldn't believe it ran deep, but in this letter in particular I sensed a new tone, as though Bela were a bowstring wound tighter and tighter until it hummed.

Sobel wanted to buy another thousand dunam from Taell al-Taji and had opened negotiations with the absentee landlord in Syria. Bela's objection to this was straightforward. "You know the village is never going to accept the exchange as legitimate."

"That was how we got the kibbutz in the first place," Sobel said, "though I know you don't like to be reminded of that."

This argument took place during a particularly relentless meeting, and though they were fueled by grape juice and cookies it was obvious they wouldn't last much longer. Bela knew the vote wouldn't go in his direction. But wouldn't they all expect him to explain the land purchase in Arabic in Taell al-Taji, painstakingly and earnestly, until he won them after-the-fact compliance?

Dori was on his side; Dori was always on his side. Though as ever she'd been assigned to take notes, she piped in: "We can't keep making wounds and patching them up. It's not good policy."

"Don't you want any kind of buffer zone around your clinic?" Sobel asked her. That clinic had been built close to the gate on purpose, so it could be open to Taell al-Taji. But bandits had somehow broken in just a month before and stolen three suitcases full of the equipment Bela had brought her back from Hungary.

Dori said, "Subjective motivations are irrelevant in this case." There went her doctor voice again, a sure sign of retreat. Bela put his arm around her and glanced at her notes; her handwriting had always been terrible. It made him feel affectionate and sad.

In that same letter, Bela added that he and Dori were now sharing a room. He didn't say anything about the negotiation which must have led him to this point after the twenty-some year courtship. Instead, he described the room. *It's in one of the new concrete buildings, and has two windows with shutters. We put up curtains too.*

Bela still kept watch at night. From his place in the tower, he could see the flat white rooftops of Taell al-Taji across the gully. Ahmad had returned the bicycle because he said he was too old to ride it. Bela told him to give it to his grandchildren. He said, *"Shokran gaeʒilaen, lae,* you give it to your own grandchildren." When he saw the look on Bela's face, he added, "Do you understand?"

"I don't understand," Bela said. He pressed Ahmad's hand, and said again, "Take the bicycle back."

"Ask me a thousand times," said Ahmad.

"I ask you a thousand times," Bela replied.

"Then someone will steal it and take it apart," Ahmad said, "and sharpen every spoke into a needle and plunge those needles in my heart and then maybe you will understand."

Bela forced himself to laugh, and did not let go of Ahmad's hand. "You sound like a bad poet, my friend."

"You sound like you don't want to have grandchildren," Ahmad said. "I think that's why you won't let me give you back your bicycle."

In the end, Bela gave the bicycle to the children's house and was stunned with how little interest the boys and girls showed in the machine. Well, of course it was old, and not in the best condition, but it was still capable of getting them from here to there.

They were wonderful children. Raised first by Bernadette, and then by two of the Polish girls who'd come back in '34, and finally by the whole of the kibbutz in rotation, they were fearless and affectionate, secure, Bela wrote me, in a belief that anyone could be their mother or their father. They ran from house to house, trailing behind them toys they'd made from discarded tin cans, twine, or chicken feathers, and they dug their hands into the chicken-feed or fertilizer and worked as though it were another game.

Bela knew he should feel honored, teaching such children. There were maybe thirty of them by the year of his last letter. Their ages ranged from five to twelve years old. Once, he matched the older and the younger children, and gave them free range of the library, and the older children pulled books from the shelves at random, in a way that implied intellectual openness. Out flew the texts with their ragged Hebrew bindings: *Principals of Geometry, An Introduction to Magnetic Fields,* Ben-Yehuda's lexicon, *The Old-New Land,* and somewhere in there that lone volume in German, Buber's *Ich und Du.* Bela watched them open the books, and wondered as those same books were placed upright, or with their spines like tents, or laid out flat with their titles upside down.

Moving in a little closer, he heard one boy of ten say to an eight-year-old, "See, if we put another watchtower here, we could see past the hills, but it'll have to be higher," and as he spoke, he moved his brown hand absentmindedly towards a pamphlet on pasteurization, and rolled it into a cylinder. He set it on top of three other books, and called to one of the other children, "Rena! Have you got something really thick!"

Rena swung her pigtails sideways, and called back, "I'm using everything here, blockhead!" In fact, she and her partner had lined up a row of volumes of the encyclopedia, and they looked very impressive against the dark-red floor of the library, like a well-paved road. She saw that Bela was observing her, and she smiled up at him. "Any good ideas?"

Bela smiled back, though he felt she could see through him. "No ideas at all."

"Well, it's clear we're not secure the way we are, with just the little path. We need a big road, no apologies."

"No apologies," Bela said, and he felt the ache below his knee throb without warning, so that he had to sit down. He knew it was within his rights to tell them not to abuse books, but were they abusing them? They didn't do anything worse with the things than he'd done many times before, when he was their age and had allowed dozens of volumes to accumulate on the floor. He had been reading for no real reason; they, on the other hand, were in the midst of a completely useful exercise. What would he have them do? Take turns riding that old bicycle?

It was on that poignant note that the letter ended, a rare note for Bela. He'd just turned forty. He had reached, he said, the middle of his life and given his family history he would live for forty more years, unless a jackal ate him or a bandit shot him or he fell off a bridge and drowned. Did he once tell me that he was afraid of ghosts?

Now that the kibbutz had eighy-five members, there was activity night and day. Whatever spirits floated between the concrete houses were scared away by children running up and down the stairs of the dining hall, or young men playing guitar, or maybe Eleazar smoking one of his hand-rolled cigarettes and stopping by Bela's open window and calling in a greeting, as if it were impossible that he wouldn't want to be greeted or would want to close his window and sit in the dark.

We've lived here for sixteen years. It has changed so much, especially since '35, that it's like that photograph you sent of Gabor on your knee and what Gabor must be now. They're the same person, but that's where the resemblance ends. The really remarkable part is that I don't know where this place ends and I begin anymore. Maybe you feel that way about your son.

DIDN'T REPLY TO THAT LET-ter. Or rather, by the time I got around to replying, Germany and England were at war and I wasn't sure a letter would get through. I suppose I could have found some way around restrictions, but by then Janos was gone and I was working twice as hard and was hardly free to stand in postal lines all day. Besides: He could have written me.

I did hear from him one more time. This was in 1944. It was a note, with no return address. The language was uncharacteristically telegraphic, to the point where I did not completely believe Bela was the author.

It gave a time, a location by the Duna, and a request to gather up myself, my mother, my son, Adele, Matyas, and Aunt Moni. The location was some hours east of Budapest, near the Romanian border, and trains did not go there.

I received the note by hand, and at that point was so distracted that I didn't even get a good look at the fellow in the doorway, though when I closed the door he was still standing there. Louisa was vomiting up what looked like pieces of her own intestines, and sobbing when she wasn't vomiting. She and Gabor were married. He could hardly leave her now. I hadn't heard from Adele and Matyas since Christmas. As for Aunt Monika, was Bela insane? She could barely climb up a flight of stairs.

No, we most certainly would not be meeting at the appointed spot at the appointed time. I didn't leave this weird, scrawled note for Louisa to discover; things were bad enough. I burned it. Louisa must have smelled something in the kitchen, because she wobbled towards the stove with that horrible blanket draped like bat's wings across her shoulder, and she whispered, *"Mutti,* are you cooking something for me?"

"Now how could I do that?" I said then. "You can't keep a thing down."

"Ah, no, I can't, not now."

Louisa's voice held a little of her singing voice then, light and sweet. She should have been singing in Vienna, in Paris, in Berlin, in Amsterdam, in Krakow, but instead stood in our miserable, freezing kitchen on Prater Street, watching a slip of ash drift from my fingers to the sink.

7

Rabbi Needleman finally admitted it; he didn't like Louisa. He didn't know why he didn't like Louisa. The feeling crept up on him at odd moments, when he was walking home from shul or playing with his son. He would feel a wave of dislike overtake him, a fluttering sensation, and he'd stop at a corner or set down the red plastic block and think: She had been sent to him, bright, sincere, open-hearted. In what he felt, there was no justice.

To his Sharon, he would say, "She's a sweet girl."

Sharon would nod and go on doing whatever she did around the house, vacuuming, picking up stray crayons, lifting up their youngest son to change his diaper, washing a bowl of fruit. Their two oldest daughters would help her, good quiet girls who could already cook a chicken or mend a pair of trousers. It struck Shmuel that what he disliked in Louisa was that he could not imagine her doing any of those things. He said to Sharon, "Do you know anyone who needs a maid?"

Sharon looked up from her mending. "You can't expect that German to keep house."

"And why not?"

"Shmuel," Sharon said, setting down the thread and needle, "she's not that kind of girl. She's used to having other people do for her."

"Now that's not true. She does everything for her mother-in-law. And I can't think of a better way for her to get to know a Jewish home."

"Her employer would have to be a saint."

"I'll find her a saint," said Shmuel, and for the rest of the week the matter was on his mind. When he passed by the grocer's, he looked at the face of the clerk hanging above the register, a pleasant enough face with thick horn-rimmed glasses suspended from red ears. He wondered how Louisa might do arranging the shelves. His cousin Hershel visited, not a bad approximation of a saint at that, so patient with that fat dumb wife of his that it was a wonder he had strength enough to teach at the seminary. He considered Louisa in each circumstance, rejected it, and moved on, and it was not until one morning, just before he laid *tfillin*, when his mind was at its most lucid, that he realized he was selecting a bridegroom.

"This won't do," he said out loud, to the east window. "Not at all."

H E   TOOK   TO   WONDERING   IF she'd appear without invitation, and as he wandered the neighborhood, he'd think he'd see a fair head of hair through the bakery window, or spot a slim girl by the butcher shop, and most uncannily, one afternoon he glanced into the kitchen, and there she was, shelling peas with Sharon. Sharon's hands were deft and precise and bobbing; Louisa fingered the pods as though in a dream. But it wasn't Louisa; it was his oldest daughter, who saw her father through the doorway and passed on him a smile which struck him as not belonging to her face.

Later, Sharon said, "She's not your business. She's got every pencil-pusher in that camp making her feel at home."

They were in bed, with the covers over them, and he rolled some distance from his wife and looked at the ceiling. He said, "She doesn't belong here."

In a rather rough voice, Sharon said, "Tell her to go."

"I can't," said Shmuel. It was far too late for this sort of conversation; they should have both been asleep an hour before. Shmuel felt torn between speaking his heart to her and protecting her from what was in that heart, which he had not yet named or mastered.

This on his mind, he rose from bed, walked in the dark to the room where he kept his books, and at once found what he wanted in a British anthology: "Ode to a Nightingale." Lighting the lamp, he sat and read the poem several times, returning to the lines:

> *Perhaps the selfsame song that found a path*
> *Through the sad heart of Ruth, when, sick for home,*
> *She stood in tears amid the alien corn.*

Then he pulled out commentaries on *The Book of Ruth*, which led to neighboring commentaries until, at dawn, his wife woke to find his side of the bed empty and cold. She wandered out in her nightgown and slippers to his study, where he sat amidst a hurricane of strewn books, reading and reading.

In the days when Judges judged Israel, the Lord sent ten years of famine. Elimelech, a man of Bethlehem, took his wife Naomi and his two sons and they came to the fields of Moab.

Elimelech died, and the sons took Moabite wives. One was named Orpah, the other Ruth. The sons died, and Naomi heard that the Lord had remembered his people and had given them bread, so she decided to return. Her two daughters-in-law went with her.

Naomi said to her two daughters-in-law, "Go. Return each to your mother's house. May the Lord deal kindly with you, as you have with the dead and with me."

Then she kissed them and they lifted up their voices and wept. They said to her, "No, but we will return with you to your people."

Naomi said, "Turn back, daughters. Why go with me? Do I have sons in my womb who can be your husbands? If I had hope, even if I had a husband tonight and could bear sons, would you wait until those sons were grown? Would you shut yourself off and have no husbands? It grieves me for your sakes that the hand of the Lord is against me."

They lifted up their voices, and again they wept. Orpah kissed her mother-in-law, but Ruth cleaved to her.

Naomi said to Ruth, "Your sister-in-law has returned to her people and to her god. Go after her."

Ruth said: "Entreat me not to leave you, and do not tell me to return from following after you; for where you go, I will go, and where you lodge I will lodge; your people will be my people, and your God my God. Where you die, I will die, and there I will be buried; the Lord do so to me, and more also, if anything but death parts you and me."

When Naomi saw that Ruth was determined to go with her, she stopped speaking to her.

It came to pass that when Naomi and Ruth came to Bethlehem, all the city spoke of them. The women asked, "This is Naomi?"

Naomi said, "Do not call me Naomi, which means pleasant. Call me Marah, which means bitter, for the Lord has dealt with me bitterly. I went out full and came back empty."

So Naomi returned, and Ruth the Moabite with her. They came to Bethlehem at the beginning of the harvest.

Naomi had a kinsman of her husband's, a mighty man of valor. His name was Boaz. Ruth said to Naomi, "Let me go to the field and glean among the ears of corn."

Naomi said, "Go, my daughter." Ruth went and gleaned in the field after the reapers, until she came to the portion of the field belonging to Boaz.

Boaz came from Bethlehem, and said to the servant set over the reapers, "What girl is this?"

The servant said, "It is a Moabite girl who came back with Naomi."

Boaz said to Ruth, "Hear me, daughter. Do not glean in any other field, but stay here by my maidens. Keep your eyes on the field they reap and go after them. The young men won't touch you."

Ruth fell on her face before him and said, "Why should you favor me or take note of me? I am a foreigner."

Boaz replied, "I have heard of all you have done for your mother-in-law since the death of your husband, and how you left your father and mother and the land where you were born, and how you came to a people that you didn't know before. May the Lord reward you, under whose wings you have taken refuge."

Ruth said, "Let me find favor in your sight, for you have spoken to my heart."

At meal time, Boaz said to her, "Come here and eat this bread; dip the morsel in the vinegar." She sat beside the reapers and ate the parched corn and was satisfied.

When Ruth rose to glean, Boaz said to his young men, "Let her glean even among the sheaves. Also pull out some for her on purpose and leave it."

Ruth gleaned in the field until evening and beat out what she gleaned and took it to Naomi. When Naomi saw what she had gleaned and heard what had happened, she told her to stay in the field of Boaz until the end of the barley harvest and the wheat harvest and not to stray to any other field.

One day, Naomi said to Ruth, "Daughter, shall I not seek rest for you? Tonight, Boaz winnows barley on the threshing floor. Wash yourself and go and do not make yourself known to him until he is done eating and drinking. When he lies down, go and uncover his feet and lay yourself there. He will tell you what to do."

Ruth went to the threshing floor and did everything her mother-in-law had told her. When Boaz had eaten and drunk and his heart was merry, he went to lie down on a heap of corn; and she came softly and uncovered his feet, and lay herself down. At midnight, Boaz was startled, and he turned over and saw a woman at his feet.

"Who are you?" he asked.

She said, "I am Ruth, your handmaiden. Spread your skirt over me, because you are a near kinsman."

He said, "Blessed is the Lord, daughter. You have chosen an old man. But do not fear. I will do everything you say. Everyone knows that you are a virtuous woman. There is a kinsman nearer than I. Stay the night and in the morning I will see if this man will do the kinsman's part. If he is not willing, I will be a kinsman to you. But lie down until morning."

She lay at his feet until morning, and she rose before they could tell each other apart. He said, "It will not be known that a woman came to the threshing floor. Take six measures of barley to your mother-in-law. Do not go to her empty-handed."

When Ruth returned, Naomi asked, "Who are you, daughter?"

Ruth told Naomi all Boaz had done to her, and showed her the six measures of barley, and Naomi said, "Sit still, daughter, until you know what will happen. The man will settle the matter today."

Boaz went to the gate and sat there. The near kinsman Boaz had spoken of came by, and Boaz said to him, "Sit down. Naomi, who has come from Moab, is selling land which belonged to our brother Elimelech. Buy it before witnesses. If you will redeem it, redeem it, but if you will not, I am after you."

The kinsman said, "I will redeem it."

"Then," Boaz said, "when you redeem the land you have also redeemed Ruth, the Moabite, the wife of the dead, to raise up the dead on your own inheritance."

The kinsman said, "I can not redeem it, for the Moabite is from a cursed people, and I will destroy my own inheritance. Take my right of redemption on yourself."

It was the custom then in Israel concerning redeeming and exchanging that a man will draw off his shoe and give it to his neighbor. So the kinsman said to Boaz, "Redeem it yourself," and he drew off his shoe. Boaz said to witnesses, "See that I have bought all that was Elimelech's from the hand of Naomi. Also,

Ruth the Moabite I have taken to be my wife, to raise up the dead upon my inher-
itance, that the name of the dead will not be cut off from his brothers and from
the gate of his house."

Those who watched said, "We are witnesses. The Lord make her like Leah
and Rachel."

So Boaz took Ruth, and she became his wife. The Lord made her conceive,
and she bore a son. The women said to Naomi, "Blessed is the Lord, who has not
left you this day without a near kinsman. Let the child's name be famous in Israel.
He will be a restorer of life, and a comfort of your old age, for your daughter-in-
law, who is better to you than seven sons, has borne him.

Naomi took the child and laid him on her breast and nursed him. The women
said, "A son is born to Naomi," and they named him Obed. He is the father of
Jesse, who is the father of David, King of Israel, from whose line will come the
Messiah, may it be in our lifetimes.

RECEIVED A LETTER FROM
Dori Csengery. It was typed and in Hungarian, with the accent marks pen-
ciled in. It began: *Kedves Nora, I got your address from Doctor Nami Levin,*
and hope I am not forward in writing to you after our meeting last week. I fear you
caught me by surprise. I knew you were in the country and suspected we would
hear from you before summer, but did not think it would be under those circum-
stances.

It seems unnecessary to tell you that we are all delighted that you are alive
and here with us in Israel. You have an open invitation to visit us at Gan Leah.
Why not come on Shavuot? Our celebrations are well known in our part of the
Galilee. Your cousin spoke of you often, and your letters were sometimes read out
loud to our great amusement. Sometimes, we would open them before they even
reached your cousin. On a more personal note, because I have no children of my

own, I found myself transfixed by the adventures of Gabor. Please convey to him my warmest greetings.

You should know that our resources are limited. We can offer you friendship, but little more. We also cannot help you find your cousin. He was here not so very long ago, during the War of Independence, and had just heard of the death of his mother and sister. He was greatly changed. Naturally, I asked how I could keep in touch with him, and he said that he had no address, and also no desire to keep in touch with me. I believe in my heart that he feels himself responsible for everything, and would forgive everyone but himself.

I put the letter down, and took a walk. It was the hottest part of the day, when anyone with any sense had found shelter. The perspiration burned off my skin and made my scalp feel like a cap.

So now I had my invitation, but I didn't have my cousin. What did I want with that cousin anyway? What did I think he'd give me? In the years since his last letter, he might have become someone I wouldn't even recognize. What had he given me anyway but a cigarette and a half, a beeswax candle, a lot of letters, and a photograph?

Dori Csengery was in that photograph, her hair thick as a lion's mane, her face so sun-struck it looked half-erased. She'd sat on that spool of chicken wire with her thick legs bare and her elastic shorts wrinkled up through the thigh, her grin square, her hands pressed to her knees. On one side knelt Nathan Sobel, and on the other Bela. Nathan laid one hand on the half-open gate of the new chicken coop, maybe to steady himself. Bela kept both hands on his thighs, so stable that he might have slept in the position the way a cow sleeps standing up, but his head was cocked a little towards Dori, which spoiled the symmetry.

I stood in that same sunlight now, the endless, drowning sunlight of the country now called Israel. I couldn't have known that back in 1944 when Louisa lived on Prater Street and rose from the couch with the blanket draped from her shoulders, confronting me with it like an accusation.

"You're going to leave me! You're going to the Holy Land!"

I'd said, "Dear, I'm not going anywhere."

"But look at all that sunshine," she'd said. "Here it's so dark and horrible. All I do is make you unhappy." Then a spasm of pain came on her so abruptly that she doubled over, and I helped her onto the couch and pressed the flat of my hand to her stomach, which was hot to the touch. I might have helped her to the bedroom that she shared with Gabor, but she was afraid to be behind a closed door, where she couldn't see or hear me. When I tried to put her there, she would struggle and knock over the bottles on the end-table; all sorts of brown oils and medicines would stain the bed.

The photograph got lost. I lost it when I left Prater Street for the Yellow Star house in June of 1944. Over twenty years of accumulated letters and photographs, I left behind. There were reasons. I had no time to sit and sort through box after box, winnowing it to a something I could carry. I also had a premonition that the house would be bombed; already the Americans had blasted the rooftops off some blocks of flats two doors away. I didn't want to linger. No, I took only the lamb's-wool coat and what I could stuff into the pockets of that coat; my identification, a comb, a lighter, and a few packs of cigarettes.

For some time, I stood in the middle of that flat, sweating in that coat with the lumpy pockets. A tram passed and rang its bell, and the sound reverberated through the window in a way that made no sense; it wasn't as though the flat was empty. I closed that window. I checked the gas. I did everything I would have done if I'd been leaving for an afternoon with the intention of returning. Janos's yellow scarf was still strung across the coat-rack, and I took a moment to even the ends, so it wouldn't fall.

I felt through the lining and tangled my fingers in a mass of keys before I located the one that locked the door. My God, what possessed me to lock the door? I had nothing worth taking.

8

ON CHRISTMAS OF 1943, MY SON, Gabor, approached the Rose Hill residence of Louisa Bauer. It is possible to understand why he'd accepted her invitation. She had looked pretty that day, and perhaps he'd felt a tug of conscience. Yet why did he actually go? That is still beyond understanding.

He had other options. His flatmate, Tibi, had an aunt in Varpalota and seemed to want his company; then there was the party in the Hotel Astoria, where he could play piano in the lobby and cadge glasses of champagne; his old piano student, the Giraffe, appeared on a street corner, tall and stately and stupid as ever, and he'd promised her that they would play a Christmas duet for her family. Then, of course, there was me.

But instead, he stood a few meters away from the front stoop of the Bauer house. The dark paint on the door and shutters looked so fresh it might have been reapplied that afternoon, and though the window-boxes of geraniums had been removed, light filtered through the curtains and made the stone front less imposing. It was no surprise that all the lights were on; it was a grim afternoon, with great frozen raindrops and a steady wind. Yet in spite of the weather, it was intoxicating to walk right up to the front door, ring the bell, and be greeted by the maid.

Eva addressed Gabor in German. "She's expecting you, sir." Then, as though he'd done it a thousand times before, he walked inside.

The hallway was astounding, all brass and mahogany, the striped white-and-gold wallpaper clearly imported from Germany. It was at once restrained and opulent. No, this was no Hungarian house.

Even the smell of dinner took him by surprise. Veal. When was the last time he'd had veal? Where had they gotten white asparagus in December? He'd been on a strict diet of macaroni for the past month and a half. If he'd had his wits about him, he could have saved Louisa and himself a lot of trouble and moved right in the day they'd met. No secrecy, no drama, nothing but veal and cognac and cigars and a mother to charm and a father to disregard completely.

There was a mirror in the hallway, and Gabor faced it as he shrugged his coat from his shoulders and without turning, gave the maid his warmest smile. He shook the rainwater from his hair, pushed a few strands back with his fingers, and asked her, "Am I very late?"

Eva said, "Everyone else has arrived, sir."

Gabor glanced towards the parlor as Eva disappeared with his coat, and through the doorway, Gabor saw Istvan Lengyel.

Lengyel was standing in front of the fireplace, rubbing his hands together and saying to Louisa's mother, "This is Goethe-weather. I wouldn't be surprised if Death himself was rumbling around on horseback."

Lengyel settled beside Louisa's mother on the couch and smiled with true affection. He liked the house, the fire, and Louisa's mother's cigarettes, which he admired as he accepted. That admiration took a moment, after which it was time for the other guest to present himself. Louisa's mother turned to the place where Gabor had been standing. He was gone.

"Eva!" she called. "Didn't you say the young man just came in?"

Eva confirmed that she had taken his coat and left him when she'd gone to fetch Louisa, but now the coat was gone and he had disappeared.

"There must be some mistake," said Louisa's mother. "People don't walk into a house and leave again. She'll be distressed."

"Will she?" Lengyel asked. "Hard to imagine. A most self-possessed young woman."

By now, dinner was ready to be served. Louisa appeared in the doorway, looking unusually elegant in a gold velvet dress. She paused with the air of making an entrance. Then she said, "Where is he?"

By now, Louisa's mother had lost patience. "It's almost nine, and there are other guests."

Lengyel smiled. "Perhaps he'll telephone."

"He has no telephone," Louisa said miserably. All pretense gone, she threw herself on a hard, plum-colored chair and made no sign of moving towards the dining room.

Eventually, they began without her. The first course was a goose-liver salad. At soup, Louisa stood at the table, puffy-faced and plain. Lengyel looked delighted.

"Well, hello, my young friend," he said. "I was afraid you spurned me."

Louisa said, "I'm fine, only I'm tired. Professor, do you think you could come back tomorrow?"

Her statement was met with embarrassed silence as it struck each of the people at the table that Louisa had asked Lengyel to leave.

Lengyel said, "Let me just finish this excellent supper. We'll see enough of each other next month when we're on tour."

Louisa sighed. She took her seat, though her plates were taken away untouched, and by the time she'd reached the veal in cream sauce, she had sunk down in her chair until her shoulders were level with the table and the conversation was in danger of sinking even further. Herr Bauer went on and on about the marvels of the Hungarian train system. "Really, it's a wonder of efficiency, a holdover from the great days of the Empire, and even the meanest provincial village has its little station." The subject was clearly of interest to no one but himself. Louisa's mother had given up on being polite and simply dragged her way through supper with thin lips. Finally, Louisa pushed back her chair.

"This is all wasted—wasted!"

"Louisa," her mother said, "sit down and eat your salad."

"What does that have to do with anything! You're all a lot of beasts!" She sprang from her seat and ran off blindly in the direction of the parlor. After a moment, a door slammed far away.

Louisa's mother rolled her eyes. "She's been difficult these days," she said.

Lengyel said, "Divas shouldn't fall in love. It's the opera in them. Marriage or death."

"Love, love. She'll have a new boyfriend next Tuesday. That's the way life is when you're sixteen."

Lengyel said, "That's a very modern attitude."

"You surprise me, Professor. You sound like a suspicious old woman." Louisa's mother wiped her mouth, blotting a little lipstick on the napkin. "Didn't you mention this young man once? I seem to remember—something about a composition Louisa left behind."

"Hungarian goulash," said Louisa's father. "All gypsy music."

Lengyel lifted the last morsel of veal from his plate and said, "Not quite. Some very interesting work being done by Hungarian composers these days. I'm sorry I missed the chance to see the young man again."

Soon, a cake studded with caramelized fruit was laid on the table, but nobody cut it. They could hear Louisa weeping in the practice room, and under the circumstances it was impossible to imagine moving on to coffee.

Lengyel said, "Would you mind? If it's a matter of music, perhaps I could be of service."

Both parents made a movement of protest, but they were clearly relieved as he left the table and started towards the practice room. He knew its location. He had been to the house before. The door was unlocked, and he opened it without knocking; though it was dark, he did not turn on a lamp. Still, he could see Louisa looking very young, illuminated only by the dirty-yellow secondary light of the hallway. She was crumpled on that piano bench with her face buried in the folds of her dress. He sat beside her.

"Come, young friend," he said. "This won't do." He touched her shoulder and she looked up at him. His voice sharpened. "You know it won't do and you know why."

Louisa frowned, lifting her head just enough for Lengyel to see a new line between her eyebrows. He combed her face for more profound changes as she pushed herself upright, arranged her skirt, and looked up again. "You might as well know, he's coming with us."

Lengyel asked, "Do you remember nothing?"

"Oh, that." Louisa looked as though something small had bitten her. She shook her head. "I don't know where you heard that, but it isn't true."

Lengyel's knees pressed hard against Louisa's now, and in that intimacy, he dared say, "You think that where we will be going, a Jew can be openly paraded?"

"It isn't true," Louisa said again, and disconcerted by her professor's nearness, she dropped her voice until it was a breath. "If it was true, how could he come for Christmas?"

"Louisa," Lengyel began, but she raised a hand to silence him.

"And don't the Jews mutilate themselves?"

Lengyel jerked away from her and looked down with a white face. He struggled to keep his voice low. "It isn't possible."

"But it's the truth. I'm telling you the truth."

"After the new year," Lengyel said, "you will leave Hungary, and if it's within my power, you won't return. You don't know what God has given you, and you don't know what you—" Lengyel's throat caught. "You don't know what you squander."

Louisa could only stare, uncomprehending. But one thing was clear; somewhere in Lengyel's broken words was fear; he was afraid of her. She said, "He'll come with us."

Lengyel read Louisa's face and said, "I'll tell your parents."

Louisa didn't answer at once. Then she said, "And so? What will they do? Put me in a convent? I know things too."

Mysteriously, she did. Even in the gloom, Lengyel could make out the malicious glow in her eyes.

"I know all about you, Professor."

Istvan Lengyel remained standing. From his pocket, he removed his cigarette case, and with a trembling hand, he dislodged a cigarette. The flame of the lighter erupted, and Louisa stared across at him.

She whispered now: "I know everything."

"No," said Lengyel. "You don't know everything. You know what others tell you. Would you like me to tell you everything? I think I could."

Louisa knocked the lighter out of Lengyel's hand. It fell flaming to the carpet, and while he scrambled for it, he reached, with his other hand, towards Louisa. But she had disappeared.

*J*ANOS AND I HAD ARGUED ABOUT circumcision. He insisted it was more hygienic, but while I was recovering in the hospital, I had the misfortune to pass by a room where a doctor was performing the procedure. Afterwards, I stood firm. Hygiene or no hygiene, no one would put a knife to my son. Janos's vehemence surprised me and, to my mind, bordered on barbarism. It was only when I accused him of reverting to a tribal mentality that he backed down. Personally, he said, his son's foreskin made no difference to him one way or the other.

Well, as it turned out, the foreskin did make a difference. When Gabor was five, he confronted Janos and said, "You're not my father."

Janos, reasonably enough, replied, "Of course I am."

Gabor smiled his broad, angelic smile and dropped his shorts.

Odd, that I should have been flooded that night with memories of my husband. Christmas was hardly a family holiday. Still, sometimes there would be chocolates or bottles of homemade wine from the parents of his students at the Katona Jozsef School. Perhaps because he had been raised near mountains, he had a weakness for the smell of evergreen. He didn't seem displeased when neighbors dumped a lot of branches down the fire-escape.

Where was Janos? Was frozen rain cracking against his window? For some reason, I imagined snow. During the years when he sent a little something through the mail, there was never a note, just the money folded inside a white sheet of paper. Perhaps it was the whiteness of the paper that made me think of snow, or maybe even the silence of that flat, the way the night stretched before me like an open field so deep and cold that nothing could cross over. Time would pass more quickly if I'd slept, but I only threw a blanket around my shoulders and turned on the stove to heat the coffeepot. From my purse I drew the last of the cigarettes I'd smoked with Gabor. I smoked them one after the other, and by the time I'd finished the pot of coffee, they were all gone.

By then, it was midnight. I was determined to go to bed and had just tucked myself between the covers when I heard strange footsteps on the stairs. Not Gabor. I didn't move. The neighbors to the right were in the Nyirseg for the holiday, and the old man to the left seldom had visitors. The steps stopped by my own door.

I rose and put on my robe, closing the belt with one hand, waiting, knowing he had a key, that I hadn't changed the lock. But there were three quick knocks. Standing in the hall with her hair loose and her face very pale, wearing only a soaking velvet dress, was Louisa.

She stood in the doorway for some time, saying nothing. As for me, I wasn't immediately certain I was going to let her in. Rather, I crossed my arms over the front of my robe, and looked up—I'm shorter than she is—and said, "He's not here."

"Nein?" Louisa looked over my shoulder.

"Try his flat."

"I'm not looking for him." Louisa shivered; her dress was half-frozen and her hair hung in dripping locks. "I came to see you, Frau Gratz. I didn't know where else to go."

Her answer took me aback to the point where I at last allowed her inside. She entered with hesitation, as though the whole flat could dissolve before her feet. "Excuse me, dear," I said, "but it is very late and I wasn't expecting company."

"*Ich verstehe.* I'm so sorry. I just—" Louisa stopped herself midway and took a breath. "I'm sorry if I—it's only—"

Another pause. She set a hand on her head and kept it there.

"Would you mind a lot if I sat down just for a minute? Then I'll go."

Well, of course, I had to let her rest on the couch. She slung a long, wet arm along the back. The dress was dark with damp and bled a little yellow dye onto her skin.

She closed her eyes and opened her mouth just enough to whisper, "I'll get out of your way soon."

It was a long walk from the Bauer house to Prater Street. I confess, I put on water for more coffee. As I ran the tap, I glanced over my shoulder more than once at the girl my son had called the Angel. She looked younger than ever, with her hair loose and her eyes closed and the small, thin nose tilted towards the ceiling. Her mouth was open like a baby bird's.

I brought over a cup and said, "Drink this. It's hot."

Louisa straightened so quickly that her hair fell in her eyes. "*Danke.* I wish you hadn't," she said, taking the cup. "I don't need anything. Do you have cream?"

"Milk," I said.

"Oh," she said. She let the cup thaw her hands for a while before lowering it. "You're sure you don't have cream?"

"Are you going to tell me why you're here, dear?"

She set the cup on the arm of the couch. "What do you mean?"

"I mean," I said, "why you're here. Why you aren't home."

"I have no home," Louisa said. "Not anymore. I couldn't think of where to go, so I just ran and ran."

"Ran here?" I shook my head. "Louisa, if you're here, you're here. But you'll have to speak plainly. I don't have much patience. It's too late—" I added, and by then it was one in the morning at least, "—to listen to lies."

Louisa looked stunned. To fill a space of hesitation, she reached for the coffee cup, which had sat on the arm of the couch long enough to leave a brownish indentation. Finally she asked me, "Is lying against your religion?"

Now I was stunned. "What religion?"

"Israelite," said Louisa.

I smiled, but not quite enough for her to see. "Yes, it is."

"Well," Louisa said, "then I'll tell you." So she told me what had taken place that evening. When she mentioned Lengyel, I held back my panic with some success, and she said, "I want them all to love each other. I wanted to help him. Would you mind if I cried now, Frau Gratz?" Though I didn't give her permission, she began.

I'm no good when people cry. I would have to learn the trick, it seemed. Louisa had sunk her head into her hands and she was sobbing, less with abandon than with endurance, and I had plenty of time to squeeze in next to her on the couch and put my arms around her and rest my chin against her hair.

"Honestly, dear," I said. "Don't try to protect Gabor. He doesn't need protection."

Louisa buried herself a little deeper into my shoulder, and she muttered something I couldn't understand.

"What was that?" I asked her. She raised her head and spoke again.

"He does," she said. She pushed herself upright, cheeks still damp, eyes still fuzzy.

From close range, I observed this strange young girl. Her slim feet in black low-heeled shoes, her gold dress dried into a mass of wrinkles but pulled tight against the breasts. "Louisa," I said, "you're pregnant."

Louisa said, "No, I'm not."

"I told you, no lies."

She didn't hold out for long, crossing her arms against her chest as though against a chill. Through narrowed lips, she said, "I won't tell him."

"Dear, don't you think he ought to know?" My hand, all by itself, rose to her hair and stroked it a little. "I'll tell him, if you won't."

"But he's going to Turkey."

"Dear, Gabor's not going anywhere."

"How do you know? Where is he, then?"

I pretended I hadn't heard her. "How far along are you?"

"I don't know," Louisa said. "Am I big?"

"Have you seen a doctor?"

"Do you have a blanket?"

Relieved to break off this fruitless sequence of questions, I crossed into Gabor's room and stripped a red wool cover from his bed. Louisa held out her arms to take it and she tucked it around her shoulders in a way that made me conscious she wasn't so far from being tucked in by her mother at night.

Sitting beside her, I asked one final question. "What are you going to do?"

Louisa didn't answer, but she stared ahead with tight lips and a fixed expression. I think I was the only one she'd told, and telling didn't seem to bring relief, in part because it led to that same question, which she couldn't answer.

I went on. "You're not the first girl to be in your position. There are ways—"

"Abortionists," Louisa said, not looking at me. I didn't contradict her. "I read a book that gave the number of Christian babies who'd died because of Jew abortionists. Do you know, Frau Gratz," she said, turning at last to meet my eyes, "you're wrong. No one has ever been in my position, no one ever."

Those eyes, gray and rimmed with stubby lashes, were dry and sharply focused. Above the red blanket, her face hardened. I didn't say a word.

She said more. "You think you know all about Gabor. Well, if he's not in Istanbul, where is he? I said I hadn't been to his flat, but I was lying. He's not here and he's not there and he's not at my house so tell me where he is!"

"He's not at his flat?"

"Then you don't know?" Her surprise was genuine. "I thought you'd know. Why don't you know?"

I held back a deepening panic and said, "Look, Louisa, it's going to be morning soon and life isn't going to get any easier for a while."

"You really don't know?" Louisa asked again.

I shook my head. In the wake of that bad news, Louisa put up little resistance as I pulled her to her feet and led her to the bedroom once occupied by Gabor.

I thought: Is that why she came here? To sleep in his bed? I returned for the blanket and took a moment to spill out the dregs left in her coffee cup. By the time I brought the blanket back, Louisa's eyes were closed, and she had curled up with her open hand beside her cheek. I threw the blanket over her and didn't fiddle with it, but took myself out of that room as quickly as I could before I gave in to the temptation to take off her shoes and stockings and lay them at the foot of the bed.

9

YOU MIGHT HAVE WONDERED HOW
a son of mine became a Gabor. Janos and I are, after all, hardly what you
might call artistic. Well, it could be pinned, once again, on Bela. He led me to
the Katona Jozsef School, to headmistresses in loose gowns and their
bohemian younger brothers who frequented cafés tucked into less reputable
parts of Pest and smoked and talked all night. Imagine these men—almost
all of them were men with a handful of ornamental women—ordering coffee and brandy after coffee and brandy or shouting across the upper balconies of concert halls or lounging in well-appointed homes in exchange for
the mention of a wealthy lady in a magazine. I did those things too. Unlikely
as it seems, I did those things too.

And I was hardly ornamental. No, I came along because one of those
younger brothers once appeared in the school office and said, "You're Bela's
cousin? My God—no resemblance whatsoever!" He was a grubby boy in a
loose tweedy sweater, and he could have used a bath. "Maybe around the
eyes," he said, almost as an afterthought. "You've got little sparks in them,
like fireflies."

I did not take my hands from the typewriter. By then, I was thirty-five,
and looked it, but there was no mistaking; this boy was flirting with me. I
asked, "How did you know Bela?"

"How did I know Bela? He practically lived in our kitchen before he went to Palestine. I was maybe ten when he left, and we went through a period of mourning. My sister was in love with him, my mother was in love with him, I was probably in love with him myself. I still have a hat he left at our flat," the boy said. "It's too big for me. Goes down to my nose." He threw himself onto a chair across from my desk and rolled himself another cigarette. "You've got a big head too," he said.

"Want to measure it?" I asked him, still not looking up.

"Draw it," he replied. "I want to draw it. What are you doing Thursday?"

I could have told him I was making dinner for my husband, but that wouldn't have been the truth. Lately, Janos had not been home in time to eat with us, and Gabor and I had often made do with a couple of egg and dripping sandwiches. Since Adele had moved to Szeged, I didn't have much in the way of company, and though I hadn't realized it, the invitation wasn't something I could honestly refuse. I did ask, "Can I bring my son?"

"Son?" He laughed. "Ah, there's a novel idea. Is he much trouble?"

"Yes," I replied. Gabor was eleven years old.

"Sure. Bring him," the boy said to me. "If we're lucky, he'll break something. That'll annoy the master of the house and when he heats up, things get, well, they get interesting. And bring some letters," he added. "You have letters, don't you?"

He'd meant letters from Bela. I hesitated for a moment, though there was nothing private about the letters, and though he would have no objection to my reading them to his old friends. I rolled back my office chair and took a moment to give the boy a second look. In spite of his deliberate air of originality, he seemed essentially harmless. I said, "You know, I'm nothing like Bela, even if I do have a big head."

"You do have letters," he said again.

"Will I need to dress up for this party?" I asked him.

After a pause, he said, "Well, you're not planning on wearing what you have on, I hope."

*S*O I BOUGHT A NEW DRESS, something I hadn't done in at least five years. It was chintz, cheaply made, and printed all over with little bluebirds. Gabor had helped me choose it. I modeled it for Janos one night, and he frowned. "Frivolous," he said. "And it won't be the end of it. If you start spending time with those sorts of people, you'll need new shoes and a new hairdo, and then a new address and a new set of ideas and—"

"A new husband." I completed the thought. It wasn't wise. Janos looked off somewhere so I wouldn't see his face. When had he stopped getting my jokes, and why did I always think he would? I added, "I could just give you a haircut and brush off one of your old suits. That would make you new enough for me."

"Don't bother," Janos said. I wondered if what I had said amounted to an invitation for him to come along, and if his reply was a refusal. He walked off to make himself a coffee. It pained me to see the back of Janos. He'd been a tall man, but he stooped now, and the chalk-dust had worked itself so deep into his skin that his neck looked bloodless.

*T*HAT THURSDAY AFTERNOON, and every Thursday afternoon for the next three years, Gabor and I took a tram together to a house on a steep hill in the Castle district. Once there, Gabor would shoot off through the hallway like a firecracker. I let him go with an ease I cannot now quite understand. Maybe it was because these people knew Bela. In spite of everything, that made the place feel like a refuge.

I would sit in an expensive chair, smoke cigarettes from somebody else's silver case, and pass around Bela's letters, old and new. Only once did I feel ill at ease, when a man stared at me for a good thirty seconds. I curled up like a hedgehog. In his handsome linen suit, he might have been a composer, an architect, or a politician. In fact, he was Istvan Lengyel.

"Charming," Lengyel said of me. "The Brooding Jewess. Someone ought to do a sketch."

"I did, of the head," the boy said to him, "but it didn't turn out. The proportions were all wrong."

"Perhaps it's the fault of the head," said Lengyel. I took an instant dislike to him. That should teach me to trust first impressions.

Later, of course, I'd tell myself that I had judged him too harshly. After all, the house itself belonged to Lengyel, and he let these bright young people drink his good liquor, play his three pianos, sleep with his maid, and generally make themselves at home. Afterwards, when they would drag me and my letters to a café, they would make fun of him, speaking through their noses and pouting and talking about mountain-climbing. I wanted to give them a smack. Once, I actually found him upstairs in the library, in his pajamas, smoking an Egyptian cigarette and reading poetry. How could I dislike someone who wasn't ashamed to get caught in his pajamas? What was wrong with me?

Most of what was wrong with me was this: I had come into this life too late. Here was the world I had imagined when I read Bela's letters in Kisbarnahely—the free talk, the wit, the sense of a closed, charmed circle, and I was not nineteen, but a woman with a husband and a son. I tried to imagine how Bela had conducted himself. Had he asked probing questions? Had he invited everyone to come to Palestine?

In 1936, I wrote to Bela in Palestine, *Do you actually know these people? They make fun of you, you know. They say you have a hundred wives, like Solomon, and are building a temple. Honestly, Borzas, they're unbearable, spoiled and headstrong, and they don't know how to end a conversation.*

Bela replied, *I'm glad you like them so much. Tell them I can't even build a WC, let alone a temple. I have some fond memories of little Jeno and his sister in particular. He can keep the hat. I have a new one now.*

I read that passage out loud the next Thursday, and even as they laughed and started in on what fond memories anyone could possibly have about Jeno's sister, I felt myself slowly recede, as I had many years before in that restaurant with Adele and our dinner dates. I floated to the ceiling of Istvan Lengyel's sitting room, and the distance between myself and the situation passed through me like physical pain.

What were my own fond memories? And where had they led me? What should I have been doing, when I was nineteen? I could have boarded a ship and sailed off somewhere new. Instead, I was stuck with leftovers, with people who tried too hard, and with a sense of loss I could not shake.

"Nora," one of the ornamental women said to me, "keep an eye on that son of yours. He's a heartbreaker."

Gabor was rushing past just then with a sandwich in either hand, and I said, "More like a plate-breaker."

"No, heartbreaker," the woman repeated, tapping her slim, white finger on my chest for emphasis, so close I could smell her cologne. "Plate-breakers always turn out to be heartbreakers. Trust me. I know. Your cousin broke plates too."

GABOR, IN FACT, WAS IN HIS element. To him, Istvan Lengyel's house was a personal amusement park. He climbed up arbors, turned the pages of music scores, and zoomed through the parlor with his arms outstretched doing his airplane imitation in a way that made everyone feel original. He also proved to have an ear for music. When one patroness played piano, Gabor overshadowed her, and she taught him basic theory. She would strike a chord, and Gabor would call out "Major" or "Minor" or "Augmented" or "Diminished." He was always right.

At this point, Istvan Lengyel had just recently abandoned his career in opera, but he hadn't lost his sense of musical engagement. He loved nothing better than to listen to a piece he couldn't understand over and over again until he formed a justified opinion. He wrote for several papers in Budapest, Vienna, and Berlin, and occasionally, he also reviewed art exhibitions. Many of the men present on those Thursdays had received favorable reviews from Lengyel. Back then, he still had a taste for what was new.

So it was no surprise that he would take his place at the edge of the circle around this little wonder. He asked the lady at the piano, "Who works with the boy?"

"Don't assume all of us can afford private lessons," she replied. That was her way of saying Gabor was a pauper.

Lengyel must have seen an opening. He found Gabor in the kitchen garden one afternoon and knelt to meet him face-to-face. Gabor had picked the vines clean of green-beans and filled the cook's straw hat. He looked up at Lengyel with an accomplished grin.

Lengyel wasted no time in plucking Gabor from the mud and taking him upstairs to the library for a talk. He asked him how he could tell "Augmented" from "Diminished."

Gabor laughed and said, "I just can."

"That's not good enough," said Lengyel. "Such an answer can only take you so far. If you give me an answer I like, I'll let you look inside the hood of my car."

Gabor was open to bribery, so he made an attempt. "Augmented's mixed up," he said, "and Diminished is mixed up and sad at the same time."

Lengyel made himself smile, though his true feelings were more complex, or rather, Diminished. He asked, "Do you like music?"

Gabor didn't think the question worth answering, and he dropped his hat full of green-beans and buzzed across the library to stare out the window into the sunshine. He wouldn't be kept in that room for long, not even if he got to look inside the hood of someone's car.

Lengyel followed with his hands in the pockets of his white suit-jacket; the sun turned Gabor's black hair reddish and his slender, restless shoulders pressed against the windowpane. Lengyel said, "Did you know songs could be taken apart to figure out what makes them run, like cars?"

Gabor turned then, and asked, "Like airplanes?"

"If you prefer," said Lengyel. "You like airplanes, don't you?"

Gabor walked away, straight through the hall to the verandah, where, by the time Lengyel found him, he was humming a tune that went nowhere and humming it with such natural confidence that Lengyel paused to listen. When I took Gabor home that night, he rested his head on my shoulder, and said, "Momma, you know that song you used to sing when I was little?"

"Which one?" I asked him.

"The one about the magic bear," he said.

"The bear wasn't magic," I replied. "He was just big."

"Oh," Gabor said. "I made up a song today about a magic wolf." And he sang it to me on the tram, about a wolf who flew an airplane, and all the while I was so full of my own troubles that I barely listened.

*T*HAT NIGHT, JANOS DID NOT come home. He'd been late often enough, but even after I'd fallen out of the habit of waiting up for him, I'd always woken up to the familiar pressure of his back against my own. That Friday morning, I didn't. I didn't see him in school the next day, and in fact, he was reported absent. When I returned, he was in his study with the door open and the scrubby hair on his crown damp with exertion. I knew how unusual it was for him to be at home so early in the afternoon, and I didn't want to break in and ask where he'd been; in that way, I lost my only reasonable chance to ask a few questions.

Because I didn't demand an explanation for the first night, it was an unspoken agreement that I couldn't demand one for a second or a third, and so passed two years speckled with those absences. Then, one autumn, when Gabor was fourteen, Janos disappeared for two full weeks. He returned with his mustache shaved and, I swear, smelling differently, like disinfectant.

I handed Janos his mail, which had piled up, and he frowned and leafed through it. I remembered a time when he'd read to me over supper, news of old classmates from the Polytechnic, paragraphs from the engineering journals. I'd never liked that habit; I couldn't keep my mind on what he read and usually had to pretend I'd understood him. Now, I found myself clearing my throat to get the attention of my clean-shaven husband, and I said, "I just got some news from Bela. Want to hear?"

"No time now," Janos said, carrying his work to his study.

Then, he closed the door, so I couldn't tell Janos that Bela was coming to Hungary for a visit, and he would stay with us overnight before traveling south to see his mother and sister in Szeged. I'd been curious to know how Janos would respond.

BELA WAS DUE IN ON A THURS-day. I was supposed to meet his train, so I would miss one of the afternoon salons. Gabor looked cross, but then he brightened. "Istvan could pick me up."

"Istvan who?" I asked. It never occurred to me to call Lengyel by his first name.

Gabor laughed. "I won't tell him you said that. He won't mind swinging by. He has a new Mercedes."

Of course, I should have asked him how he knew that sort of thing, but I'll admit to having plenty on my mind at the time, so I said, "Just don't tell anyone your cousin's here. They'll steal him away."

"Oh, him," Gabor said. By then, his natural sweetness had gained an edge of sarcasm which sometimes made him seem a little older than he was. He was already close to the height of Janos. He liked to stretch out on the floor when he did his homework. Chairs couldn't contain him. Of Bela, he said, "He's the farmer, isn't he? The bear who ate the bread?"

I knew I shouldn't play that game now, but I said, "That's right. *Borzas Medve*. You can't tell me you're not a little curious."

"Isn't he the one who's such a Jew?"

"Yes, he is," I said. "I'm making a roast."

"Well, I'll be back. No question," Gabor said, kissing me on the head. "A roast. You never make me a roast."

So he accepted my terms, and that Thursday, at five, when a midnight-blue automobile pulled up by the flat, he leapt up, threw on his coat, and swung through the door, calling back, "He lets me drive!"

Now I opened my mouth to say a thing or two, but Gabor was already out the door, and I stuck my head out the window and watched him climb into the driver's seat. I could barely make out Lengyel, who moved over to make room for him. How could anyone in his right mind put my son behind the wheel? I couldn't let myself dwell on it for long. There was a roast to cook, a train to meet, and there was Janos.

FOR THE FIRST WEEK AFTER Janos's return, he had come home every afternoon straight from school and at once locked himself in his study, emerging only to make himself a sandwich or open his mail. I noticed he'd switched from a pipe to cigarettes, a strong Bulgarian brand, and those cigarettes, along with his naked upper lip, gave me the sense that the man was an impostor. Finally, one afternoon when Gabor was out, I waylaid Janos, standing bodily in front of his study door, and I said, "What's going on?"

Janos frowned, and without his mustache, he looked all the more severe. "Nothing that concerns you."

"Janos, I'm your wife."

"I don't have time for this nonsense," said Janos.

A lump rose to my throat, and as I spoke through it, my voice came out all crooked. "I want the truth," I said. "I want to know the truth."

Janos sighed. He said, "All right. I wanted to wait until it was confirmed, but you were going to find out anyhow. One way or another." He motioned me towards the couch and sat me down, and he lit one of those brutal new cigarettes, a gesture that made my stomach turn. I knew that for me they had always been a way to stop time, to keep one moment from following the next, to postpone. Janos took a puff, blew it nowhere in particular, and said, "I've been offered a position. Abroad."

I stared. The blood ran out of me, and it was as though the old couch on which we sat was slipping down a precipice. I wanted to hold onto something, and without even thinking, the thing I grabbed hold of was my husband. "What?"

Janos broke free and said, "You heard me. It's been arranged."

"Where?" I asked him.

Janos stubbed out his cigarette, hesitating, and then he gave me a long look. "Has someone been asking you about me?"

My voice caught, and when I didn't answer right away, he pressed me.

"Has anyone been by? Tell me the truth." Now I know he was waiting for me to say: The truth is that we want you with us, that we need you here. But then, all I saw in that look was an accusation. I shrank back and made myself speak.

"You're having an affair, aren't you."

"I won't even give that the benefit of an answer," Janos said.

That's when I should have said it: Stay. But instead, I said, "I suppose you think I've driven you away."

"It's not about you. Why can't you see past yourself? You're like a child," Janos said. He got up and rubbed the place where his mustache used to be. "You think I'm a defeated man because we don't live a bourgeois life. If that's what you want, you're better off without me."

Then he walked off to the study and closed the door.

After that day, he was gone again for a week, and then he returned. He said a few words to me in passing. Once, he engaged Gabor in a conversation about jet propellers that seemed to go on for so long that I wanted to drop a tray of sandwiches or crack a window, do something to signal disaster. Afterwards, Gabor said to me, "He's in a good mood today. You know, he said he'd take me to watch the trains again? I don't think we've done that since I was a kid."

"You still are a kid," I said, heart beating hard. But all I could imagine was Janos and Gabor boarding a train and riding far away, leaving me alone.

*A*LL OF THIS PREOCCUPIED ME during the weeks before Bela's arrival. It was strange, the way something you long for happens and then seems almost beside the point. I bought the makings of a wonderful dinner and left the roast in the oven while I went to meet Bela's train. That train was late. That gave me too much time to think, and I deliberately kept my mind on that late train and on what might have happened to Bela. Did he catch malaria in steerage? Did they take away his visa? Did they stop him at the border? Worrying about Bela was like settling into a warm bath. I relaxed on the station bench, marked time by the announcement of new trains, and came to myself only when Bela shook my shoulder.

He took me up and hugged me, and when he let me go, I braced myself for my first look at him in fifteen years. I said, "You're still big."

But he wasn't. He'd dropped weight, too much weight, and rather than standing straight, he veered a little to the right. There was a lot of gray in his hair. I felt moved, somehow, by the sight of Bela approaching middle age, and I waited for him to tell me that I was still as small as a girl. He didn't. Instead, he hoisted a duffel-bag over his shoulder, an outdoor gesture that somehow looked out of place in a train station. "Uff," he said. "Should have gotten a porter."

"I made you a roast," I said, "but it's probably shoe leather by now."

"Nora, I'd love shoe leather," he said, "believe me. I can't remember the last time I had a decent piece of beefsteak. I'm sick of cucumber salad and eggplant pie and—"

"Milk and honey?"

"Honey," Bela admitted. "The hives are fine. I'll tell you more but I'm out of breath. Let's just go home."

That might have started it, the way he had said home, much as he had once said that when he was with me it was like having time to himself. I watched the way he doubled under the bag and thought, I should take up a strap, yet logically that only would have made the weight more awkward. The long train ride must have made him stiff. As we pushed our way into the open, he stumbled a little, but recovered himself.

At the threshold of the underground, he hesitated. It was then I remembered. I said, "Drop the bag."

"It's fine," Bela said. "I'm fine."

"We're taking a taxi," I said to Bela.

"I can roll it down the stairs," Bela said. He blushed hard, which made him look younger. "This is really embarrassing, but with my knee the way it is—"

"Don't you want to see the wonderful new taxis in Budapest?"

Bela shook his head. "I've been looking forward to taking the underground since I got off the boat."

"It's not necessary," I said.

"Since when did you turn into my mother."

I couldn't decide whether I felt insulted, and to be honest, I don't think I got over the remark until we'd managed to roll the bag downstairs and were seated in one of the cars. I lit a cigarette and said, "So here you are, on the underground. Is it everything you thought it would be?"

"I'm not a cripple," Bela said.

"Well, I'm not your mother," I said. "Don't call me that or I'll have to do something drastic."

Bela smiled. He'd set the duffel between his knees, and when he leaned over to put his arm around me, the weight was substantial. "Drastic? Like what?"

I said, "Like take my son and move to Palestine."

The underground gave a groan then, reaching its terminus. Bela laughed. "Well, that would be drastic, all right. And to think I wondered all these years what it would take to convince you."

"I'm serious," I said, and then the doors opened and we had to struggle with that duffel-bag again. It was harder to roll up than to roll down, and Bela pushed. All the while, he kept looking at me, earnest as ever, the lines around his eyes and mouth somehow making him look even more probing and gentle, and it touched something in me that for weeks now had been opening. Over each step the duffel rolled, and I thought about the way things climb, year after year, and go nowhere, and rising over the bag, that face of Bela's, really there, looking up at me, and when the bag came over the final step and Bela followed, I said, "We're going with you—Gabor and me. To Palestine."

"Hey, Nora, hey," he said, catching his breath. "Now what's up? What's the trouble?"

"You don't believe me," I said. "But we're going back with you."

He managed to calm me down, and that's when I told him Janos was going to leave me. He asked me if I was sure and how long there had been problems. He asked me if we had tried to talk it out or had spoken to a rabbi. This last question made me choke. By then, we'd reached the flat, which was a little smoky from a roast that had cooked for far too long, and Bela threw down the duffel, sat on it in a temporary sort of way, and looked at me.

"Nora," he said, "you know, it's not an answer."

I was opening a window when he said it, so I didn't think I'd heard him right. "What isn't an answer?"

"Leaving. Running away. That's not a reason to make *aliyah.*"

A little air blew the curtain over me, and I pushed it back. "I'm not running away."

"Just talk to him. You've always been so good at speaking your mind."

"That's not true."

I had spoken without thinking. I had no idea what I'd meant by what I'd said. Bela leaned his elbow on his knee, and put his chin in his hand, looking up from that pose of thoughtfulness in a way so heart-wrenchingly familiar that I lost my reason. He asked, "What's not true?"

"I don't speak my mind," I said. I was falling all to pieces, and I had to keep myself occupied, do something with the roast, offer him coffee and a biscuit, at the very least get him sitting on the sofa properly instead of on that duffel, where he looked as though he were ready to bolt. I knelt to open the deep drawer where I kept the quilts and pillows and said, "I'll make up your bed."

From behind, I heard Bela shift his weight. He spoke with some hesitation. "Maybe I shouldn't stay here."

What could I do then but rise with all of that bedding pressed against my chest and my flesh compressed to a fist in my throat. He was going to go to a hotel. After all, I had no claim on him, nor had he reason to think himself anything but a friend who'd walked into something that was none of his business.

Bela let the silence grow. Maybe he looked bewildered. I can't know, because I couldn't bring myself to look at him. Instead, I trained my eyes along the floor.

I said, "I have something to show you."

Then I knew what I'd intended from the moment I'd pulled the bedding from that drawer. There they were, twelve boxes lined up, striped, gray, or white, all stuffed with closely written pages. I dropped the bedding and bent to pull those boxes free. As I threw down an early box, the sides broke in a kind of explosion. The contents spilled across the floor. At last, I turned to look at Bela. He rose from the duffel now, and his knee gave just enough to make him wince. "What's this about?"

"You'll need some light," I said. I switched on the lamp, and there they were, spread at his feet, maybe two hundred pages scrawled on both sides.

By the look of the broken box, I'd guess the letters dated from the late twenties. He glanced up and asked, "You wrote all this?"

"They're yours," I said. "Just read."

Bela settled back onto the duffel with the page in his hand. The air in the room throbbed, and lamplight fell unevenly, filtering through Bela's hair, the stuff of his shirt, the closely written page. I could see the faint lines around Bela's eyes deepen. He turned the page over, and without looking up at me, kept reading.

Then I couldn't watch him anymore, so I checked the clock. It was well after eight. Gabor would be home soon, and we would pack our things. If we could go by airplane, he wouldn't put up much of a fuss. And it was easy to imagine Gabor brown and happy among the chicken coops, chasing away the rooster, baking cakes in the common kitchen, and it all seemed so natural that I didn't have to think too hard about where I would fit into the picture, and how a picture exposed to light would start dissolving. Time was short. I couldn't bear it. I forced a glance at Bela, but he had picked up a second letter, and I thought: I must fetch my son now, before it's too late.

I left Bela there. I wasn't running away, but running towards—racing against time—as though if I could present Gabor, hold him up like evidence, Bela would have to take us both. How could he not? That Gabor was nearly fifteen and could not be held up like a parcel didn't occur to me. Rather than risking a late tram, I broke down and took a taxi to Istvan Lengyel's house, and by then half an hour had passed. The minutes were like a trail of bread crumbs; I would soon be empty handed.

I rang the bell. No one answered. Yet there was a light in the window. I hesitated, and then I turned the knob. The door was open.

The foyer was dark; there wasn't a single coat on the rack, and a sharp heat flowed through the French doors. I stepped forward, almost called out Gabor's name, and hesitated. I could hear faint voices coming from a room far away, and then laughter, Gabor's unmistakably. A low voice. Then a few notes on a piano.

Slowly, I moved through the French doors and down the hall, feeling cold in my bones. A chord was played then, and another. Every room I passed had a fire burning in it, yet somehow I still felt cold, and I pulled the coat around me as I walked up the stairs to the library. Through the open door, I saw them.

Gabor was stretched out on his back on the piano bench with his head dangling upside down. His shirt was out of his trousers. One arm extended, hand resting on the keys. He lazily played another chord. Lengyel sat on the couch in his pajamas, reading a newspaper. Neither had noticed I was there.

I said, "Gabor, it's time to go home."

Lengyel put down the newspaper and rose. Gabor sat up and knocked his head against the piano. "Um, Momma?"

"It's late," I said. "I can't know—"

"Madam," said Lengyel, but then he seemed at a loss for words.

"I was only learning to play," said Gabor, rubbing his head and walking towards me none too steadily. "It was going to be a surprise. I'm learning—"

"I don't want to know what you were learning," I said to Gabor. I grabbed hold of his arm, hard. "I don't want you to lie to me either."

Lengyel took a step forward. "Don't draw rash conclusions."

"It's true!" Gabor said. "I'm not lying to you. Why would I lie?" He looked bewildered, but his voice caught in a way that made me doubt him, and I veered between anger and fear and something darker, knowing only that I had to get the two of us out of that house before I lost my mind.

We caught a tram, and the lights of Buda streaked by as we crossed the Duna and turned a corner into the heart of Pest. By that time, Gabor had calmed down, and I could risk a few questions.

"How long has that man been teaching you?"

"A long time," said Gabor. "It started with basic theory, and I was bored at first, but then I wasn't. We only started piano a few months ago. Don't be angry, Momma. I was only learning."

I stroked my son's hair, and he took my handkerchief so he could blow his nose. In ten minutes, we would arrive at my flat, where I would find Bela gone and this letter waiting.

Nora,

What I have read stuns me and makes me proud. You have shown me your heart. It is everything I knew it to be, honest, tender and brave. I do sincerely hope that you will one day bring that brave heart with you to Palestine, but I think we both know you shouldn't go under these circumstances. Nora, I can't save you from anything. There is too much I don't have the strength to do and too many things I don't understand.

You are my friend. That is steadfast. I trust you to trust it, and to forgive me.

Bela

P.S. I am taking the overnight train to Szeged, and have left a few things for you and your family. It makes the bag a little lighter. I'll write to you soon.

He did write to me as soon as he returned to Palestine, and we exchanged a few more letters before war put an end to our correspondence. Then there was the note presented by a stranger that called for me to gather his family and transport them all to Palestine, the note I burned.

As for Gabor, he did continue on the piano, taking lessons from the music teacher at the Katona Jozsef School, and through her he made friends at the Academy, and that would lead to another story, one you know, that moves on to a cellar and a train station where a girl would not let go, and forgive me if I don't have the strength to begin that story again. I am exhausted at the thought of reconstructing the look on Gabor's face as the tram rattled towards our flat on Prater Street, towards home, where Bela wasn't, where Janos wasn't, where I had to dump the burnt roast in the trash-bin and sleep long enough to face the office in the morning. Bela had left a dipper carved out of olive wood and three jars of honey. What would my life be, by the time those jars were empty? What could be sweet? What could be mine?

What do I have? I thought then, as the tram turned towards a street where lamplight filled many windows. I have my son.

THE MORNING AFTER LOUISA appeared, I woke up, and for a moment, I didn't know where I was. There was the mammoth wardrobe and the frozen window. There was the door, half-open, letting in a slant of dusty sunlight. From the pipes in the walls came a note which could only mean that someone was filling them with hot water.

I wanted to keep still. If I moved then I would be awake and if I was awake I'd have to take some action. Yet what choice did I have? When I pulled myself from bed, a red wool blanket fell to the floor, Gabor's blanket. I called: "Hello?" The flat seemed bigger than ever, and my voice couldn't carry past the room. Reluctantly, I moved into the open, and called, "Louisa!"

This time, I was met with a creak and a splash. The bathroom door flew open and there was Louisa wrapped in my husband's old white robe and shaking out a quantity of long, fair hair. With her free hand, she twisted that hair and pulled her face towards me with a dazed expression. "You're up?"

I couldn't even remember falling asleep but had a vision of someone walking me off the couch; the thought of being caught in such a vulnerable state disturbed me. Louisa squeezed a trickle of bath water from her hair, loosed it, and combed it with my own comb as she spoke.

"I've been up forever. I bought cream and rolls, and I made coffee too." She seemed very proud of herself. In fact, by the stove sat two of the Herendi teacups, and the pot itself, which by some miracle wasn't leaking very much.

"I expect," I said, "you didn't call your parents."

I'd hoped to keep the conversation on a level of irony, but Louisa continued to look at me with a kind of dizzy wonder. I turned towards the windowsill and was relieved to find my cigarettes. I lit one, which cleared my head considerably.

"It would help if you gave me their number," I said, "but I can track it down."

I pulled my cloth coat off the rack and felt the pocket for change, at the same time thrusting my bare feet into winter boots and wondering what I'd say to these strangers. Louisa cried out: "Don't call!"

Something in her voice stopped me short. I turned. Her eyes sparkled with panic.

"I want to stay here," she said. "Just for a while, please, Frau Gratz, until I can find Gabor."

All this came out in a burst. In spite of all my good horse sense I took the coat off and allowed Louisa to pour me a cup of coffee. The shepherdesses on that pot were rubbed down to a few raised blue and yellow smudges. Louisa's hand trembled as she reached for her cream. I said, "I'm flattered that you want to stay here, but your parents are bound to track you down."

She didn't answer. She stared into her coffee cup.

"When they do find you here, you'll get me into trouble too. I don't want trouble."

"It's true, what Gabor told me," Louisa said. "You don't hold back what you say. I can know where I am with you. You don't lie."

"I'd lie to save my own skin," I said.

"And to save your son?"

I didn't answer. She got up and took away our empty cups. Such a pretty girl, I thought, and such an odd fish. My husband's robe slipped down her shoulder, and the smell of her damp hair mingled with the coffee. It seemed, just then, as though she were toying with me in an unforgivable way and at the same time had no idea what she was doing.

She called to me from the kitchen. "I want Gabor to go with me to Turkey."

That stunned me. "To what?"

"Turkey," she said. "I've thought it through. We could escape together tonight. You could come with us."

As dryly as I could manage, I said, "Kind of you to think of me."

Louisa stuck her head out of the door so quickly that her hair flew in her face. "You think I could leave you to this? To what's going to happen? Because," she said, "it's going to happen."

"Will it?" I paused, and then I said, "I'll admit that I don't have the slightest idea what you're talking about."

"You're going to lose everything," she said. "Your job. Your home. Your family. Because Hungary will be part of the Reich, it must be, and the Israelites in the Reich—"

I interrupted her. "Hungary is not part of the Reich. We're Germany's ally. There's no reason why you'd invade—"

"Not me," Louisa said. "No, please, we can escape. I have money." And that's when she showed me the clump of Reichmarks she'd gotten from who-knows-where, maybe her mother's purse. Those banknotes, still damp, lay on the table like old rags. They had the feel of something secreted away for months, as though Louisa had known all along that it would come to this. The effort of revealing them seemed to exhaust her. She said, "I can't go back. Don't make me explain why. But it's not me. I can't even say what I am."

My perplexity deepened. Admittedly, I was a little touched too. "I can't accept that money."

"It's Gabor's," she said. "What good is it if it doesn't belong to him? He's given me too much—too much I don't even know what." Then she stopped talking, and her eyes grew moist again. It was a moment before she took possession of herself, and then she said, "I've never sung for you."

Embarrassed, I said, "This place doesn't have the best acoustics."

Then she sniffled or she laughed, and took a step away from the table, raising her arms a little away from her hips, and in an almost conversational way, she began:

What is lost, what is lost
We can not have back again.
It is like a breath we've taken.
We can not breathe it again.
It is like good bread we've eaten.
We can not eat it again.
It is like a heart we've broken
Or our own heart, lost in vain.

I felt the skin float off my bones, and did nothing until she'd finished. Then I asked her, "Where did you learn that song?"

Louisa said, "But it's your son's."

It took me a moment to relocate myself in the present where this pale, fair, pregnant girl stood wiping her hands on a tea-towel and also wiping her eyes. Could Louisa mark some change on my face? Or maybe she thought the song had moved me. Yes, I was moved, moved back, as away from some horrible thing. I could say that it was her voice that changed the words, but those were my words, and I could not tell where those words ended and her voice began. I could say: This isn't me, this isn't me, but I was going to be sick.

I said, "I'm going out for a while."

Louisa didn't look happy. She might have been disappointed that I said nothing about her voice or about my son's song. More likely, she was afraid I'd call her parents.

But I couldn't call her parents now. Previously, what happened to Louisa was not my doing. Now, somehow, it was. I said to her, "I'm going to get myself some cigarettes. Then I'm going to find my son."

*F*IRST, I TRIED THE CLARINET-ist's. Louisa had been correct; Gabor wasn't there. Furthermore, the clarinetist made it clear that he wouldn't be welcome back again. He'd returned from his aunt's to find the room in such a state of heroic disorder that at first he'd thought he'd been robbed. Now he'd piled Gabor's things on the broken couch; a paper sack of boxer shorts and socks and linen dress shirts, assorted magazines, a pitch-pipe. There were at least a dozen empty baskets stacked crookedly against the windowsill. "If he doesn't come back for them in three days," the clarinetist said, "I'll throw them out the window."

I also tried the Academy, where the lady at the desk asked for identification and wouldn't let me through the labyrinth of practice rooms. The padded doors, seen from afar, hardly seemed a place where once a young girl with a folder full of Schubert would have knocked and knocked. Finally, I had a premonition. I took a tram to Nyugati.

I had to walk the full length of the tracks to the place where the station ended, and there was Gabor sitting on a pile of railroad ties. I watched him from a distance before I made my approach. He was staring straight ahead at a cluster of mechanics gathered around something in a wheelbarrow. I started towards him with caution. He saw me, but he didn't rise. Instead, he leaned back and thrust his chin into his chest.

I was the first to speak. "Have you been here all night?"

Gabor didn't look up. "I wanted to get a job on the railroad, but I need my papers and I left them somewhere. Do you have them?"

"You know what papers I have," I said.

"What are you talking about?" he asked. Then he blew his nose.

"Your song. Louisa's song," I said. "The words from my letters."

Gabor looked up at me, and in his red eyes I could have read remorse or sleeplessness or the beginnings of another cold. He rubbed his face as though to force a little warmth back into it, and then he sighed. "All right," he said. "I'm sorry. You weren't supposed to know."

I said, "She's home, Gabor. In your father's robe. With a fistful of Reichmarks." And then I told him everything. He listened, at first baffled, and then appalled, and finally on his feet and interrupting:

"I asked her if she was pregnant, and she told me she wasn't!"

"Your angel," I said, "is very protective."

Saying this, I felt unaccountably happy, because Gabor laughed, weakly but genuinely, sinking back down onto those railroad ties and shaking his head. Perhaps, I thought, it was all over. He could go back to writing sonnets about sardine cans and posing in the nude and teaching piano. But then I realized the form that girl's protection might take.

I crouched on the gasoline-moist dirt so that my eyes were level with the eyes of my son. I asked, "Do you love her?"

This time, Gabor didn't laugh. Maybe because he was too cold or stiff, and laughter would have been literally painful. Anyway, he answered indirectly, "I can't shake her."

"Have you tried?"

"Yes, Momma."

"I mean really tried." And here I set a hand on his shoulder and locked my eyes with his own.

He shook my hand away. "Yes, yes, I really tried. And I can't, all right?"

I took a long look at my son, whose face was tucked back into the shoulder of that long-suffering lamb's-wool coat, and whose eyes were closed, so that his lashes brushed his cheeks. I said, "Marry her."

He opened his eyes. "You're not serious."

"She is. She's a very serious girl, and maybe she could save your life."

"My life's not in danger," Gabor said.

I said, "Yes, it is. It won't be long before you're called up for the Labor Battalion. This girl won't let you go."

I can only guess what Gabor thought as he sat on those railroad ties and stared past me at the signal light. His eyes hardened, but that might have only been the glare. His hair was in those eyes; I wanted to take a comb and push it back; I wanted to tell him to come home; I wanted to take back what I'd said as well because I didn't like the silence it brought on, thick and palpable.

Finally, Gabor said to me, "Momma, is it true?"

I asked, "Is what true?"

"That they won't draft men with Christian wives. What if I marry her in the church and get baptized. Would I get new papers? What are my papers like now? What am I?"

I finally put my arms around him and gave him a kiss. The poor boy shivered, but his forehead burned. I expect he had a fever. "What you really need is a passport. She wants you to go to Turkey."

Gabor pulled back. "Turkey? Turkey? Why not China?"

Then he started to laugh, and this time he didn't stop, but fell backwards, laughing and laughing until I was afraid the mechanics would hear and run over, so I hushed him and he pulled me to his side, and we both laughed at life's absurdity as though we knew it would be for the last time.

*I*N JANUARY OF 1944, THERE WAS a run on conversions. A line formed in front of the rabbinical office on Wesselenyi Street, where the apostates made their declarations and then the next stop was the Terezvaros parish office where for fifteen pengös one could get a little cardboard certificate from the Union of Christian Jews. There had been a rumor that by the end of the month further conversions would be invalid, but that same rumor had made the rounds many times before, and it had always proved false. Christians are very forgiving.

"So I got sprinkled. I'm a new man," Gabor said as we ate white cake to celebrate. "I don't know why I didn't do it years ago. Now I'm absolutely free." Louisa kept a piece of cake in her cheek for a long time until I thought she wouldn't manage to get it down.

The wedding took even less fuss than the conversion. One of the teachers at the Katona Jozsef School had a friend who knew a willing judge to bribe with some of Louisa's Reichmarks. The dark wood benches of the office and the chandelier with its tulip-like bulbs put me in mind of my own wedding. Louisa wore the gold velvet dress, steamed in our bathroom into something like its original shape. As she had no wedding ring, I gave her mine, though she had to secure it with a bit of twine to keep it from slipping off her finger. I arranged for a wedding portrait at a studio, and Louisa posed Gabor and herself dutifully in front of a tinted oval, but Gabor pulled away so suddenly that Louisa stumbled forward and overturned the camera and tripod with a crack.

Louisa asked, "Did something break? How much was it? Tell me. We have money!"

"No, we don't!" Gabor pushed her back with such force that she fell against the panel. I stepped in to help her to her feet and threw Gabor a look I hadn't thought myself capable of. Maybe he was also startled. He set a hand on Louisa's arm, and said, "I need some air."

"I'll come with you," Louisa said at once. Her eyelids fluttered and her mouth seemed to take on a life of its own, twisting this way and that.

It was senseless for him to object, as she wouldn't let go of his arm. In my cloth coat, she looked urchin-like. They went out together into the cold.

*I*T WENT ON THAT WAY FOR A while, Gabor escaping, Louisa trailing behind. He would try to slip away in the middle of the night, and there Louisa would be, running as she tried to work on a pair of my boots, calling out, "Gabor! Gabor!" and half-tripping down the stairs. I'd force myself out of bed and watch the two of them through the window. The streets would be deserted; and I couldn't think of where they'd go.

One night, Louisa shook me out of a stupor, whispering, "There were men following us!"

"From your parents?"

"They trailed me. Gabor got away."

I straightened up on the couch and tried to keep my temper as I asked, "Did they trail you here?"

"Bitte?" Louisa drew her hand to her mouth, and though her face was pink with cold the color drained from it slowly. She stared at the ceiling. "We'll move, then."

"Where to?" I asked her. "Dear, come clean. Tell them. You're married now. You're carrying their grandchild. What can they do?"

But Louisa didn't answer. She settled on the couch, still staring at the high, pale ceiling, and in that position she waited for Gabor, who did not return that night.

As for me, I shuffled to the kitchen to wash the supper dishes. Though I moved like an old lady, I was only forty-four. No gray in my hair, good posture and firm flesh. Yet within the year, my hair would fall out in clumps and I would lose enough flesh to make a whole other Nora. Within the year, Gabor would be dead and many other things would come to pass. Other stories; no time for them now.

No, now I will describe that year's beginning. As an added precaution, we managed to arrange a second wedding in a church, and Louisa and I waited for Gabor. He arrived drunk, mumbling something about missing an important appointment. He did give Louisa a fierce kiss afterwards, which softened matters.

Gabor asked the minister, "Do you do this often?"

The minister, a dim-bulb I'd been lucky to track down, gave Gabor a benign smile. Gabor clarified.

"I mean, do you marry two separate species? Our baby will have wings and horns. We'll sell him to the circus."

"Idiot!" I said, when we were alone again. "Do you want to die in a minefield? These people could save your life."

"All right! All right! Stop blowing your stinking breath in my face," Gabor said, wheeling away from me. "Give me a little room to do my own thinking for once."

"What thinking is that?" I asked him.

"I can't live like this, all right? I know my limitations."

"If you want your freedom, take it," I said. "Take Louisa and go."

"You mean you'd turn us out?" There wasn't an ounce of worry in his voice. In a moment, Louisa entered with her nervous smile, and that was the end of the conversation.

HE WAS OFTEN AWAY NOW, PLAY-
ing piano at a dancing school. The pupils had strong bones and straight backs, and there was a reality to them that Gabor relished. Louisa had begun, recently, to stoop. Her hair thinned and her features thickened and her small, bright eyes grew large and solemn. We spent a lot of time together.

"You know, *Mutti,*" she said once, "I think I could give singing lessons."

I poured out tea, and she drank it down not with her old apologetic sips but all at once. Then she folded her hands around the cup, a sad, plain woman.

"When we get to Turkey," she said, "we'll need more money. Especially once Gabor starts composing again."

What could I say to that? She practiced, sometimes, in the room which had once been my husband's study. She did exercises, with two fingers pressed to her mouth: *lu lu lu*. She sang about losing things. Then there was the afternoon in late January when, without warning, this flew across the room:

> *"I love you, your fair form allures me.*
> *And if you don't come willingly, I'll use force."*
> *"Father, father, now he's seizing me!*
> *The Eorl-King has hurt me!"*
> *The father shudders, he rides swiftly.*
> *Holding the moaning child in his arms.*
> *With one last effort he reaches home;*
> *The child lay dead in his arms.*

I didn't like the effect of that voice, but I also couldn't escape it unless I, like Gabor, fled and walked until my head was clear of who this girl might somehow be.

I did take a little walk once, in early February, and it led me to an old haunt, the Hovirag *cukrászda*. It was a mild day, and I borrowed Gabor's lamb's-wool coat. When I put my hands in the pockets, I felt a key. That key, I examined. It was small and rather new, a key for a cheap padlock, easily mislaid in a coat's lining, completely trivial. Yet it remained in my hand for some time as I let my cup of tea chill, and I remembered the days when I had a son whom I believed told me everything, when I could tell myself that every lock had a key. But now I knew better. I had wanted to be a woman to whom no one need lie. I was asking for something impossible.

*L*ATER THAT MONTH, LOUISA FELL ill. The household was upside down. Gabor paced the kitchen, slamming his fist against first the right wall and then the left, infused with an emotion that I couldn't classify. I sat by Louisa's bed myself, and she wouldn't let go of my hand.

Nor could she speak; she gasped and sobbed and the sheets were drenched with perspiration. The medicine Gabor had brought for her stood loosely capped on the nightstand, in an oily paper bag. I kept the hand she didn't grasp tucked behind her head; her hair was rank and slippery. Slowly, I pressed that head on the pillow, and reached out for the bottle to tighten the cap. The label was obscured by dark stains, and I turned it to the light and read:

PORTUGUESE TANSY WOMAN'S ELIXIR

RELEASES MONTHLY FEMALE FLOW

"Mutter," Louisa gasped now, "I'm bleeding. I—it's my fault. I'm bleeding on his bed."

I pushed a little hair out of her eyes, and then I said, "Do you want me to get towels?"

"Don't leave me," Louisa whispered. "I'm going to die. I don't want to die alone."

"You're not going to die," I said, but to tell you the truth, I wasn't sure. She looked as though she might die; she'd lost a lot of blood. Whatever overtook her had her now. Could I have called a doctor? I don't know.

But I did not let go of her hand. I didn't leave that bed. I missed two days of work, and didn't know if they would have me back again. In fact, I would lose that job soon enough, along with everything else, just as Louisa had predicted. I lined Louisa's legs with towels, washed her thighs with water from the dish-basin, and sponged her forehead. I watched her fine skin turn to rice-paper and new blue veins appear on her temples. On the third day, she said, again, "I'm going to die."

I said, "No, you're not. Let go."

Louisa looked as though I'd struck her. Her fingers froze around my wrist. I spoke again.

"Let go and open your hand. I'm going to read your palm."

What could Louisa do then but release her hand from mine and, with hesitation, open the fingers. The whole hand was flushed from the pressure of her grip, and there was a streak of blood by the base of the thumb, but I didn't look at those things. Rather, I turned that open hand towards the secondary light of the hallway—the curtains in the room were drawn—and I looked at what I saw.

"All right," I said. "You're not going to die. Or not for a long time." I knew it too. There was a perseverance to the hand itself, and to the lines, which seemed to change in character from subtle tracery to something strong. "And also," I said, "listen, Louisa, you're going to have a child."

I felt a tremor shoot up through the wrist. She started to say something, but I silenced her.

"You'll have a child one day. I'll be a grandmother. I swear, it's God's own truth."

I released Louisa's palm, and now she didn't speak, but turned her head from her pillow with her hair in her eyes and the hand still open on the bed. She drew her other hand to her mouth, and kept it there, looking up at me in a way I didn't want to bear. I went to get more towels.

On the way, I passed Gabor. He'd grown leaner; his face had hardened. I placed my hand on his arm and he shook it off like an insect, and with a sudden shudder of nerves, he went in to his wife.

I thought: This is all madness, a mistake, but mistakes have their own momentum. If only we were not held accountable, or could move on, or were commonly innocent or guilty. If only it were that easy.

PART
THREE

HE ONLY REAL THING ABOUT Gan Leah was the mud. It was blood-colored, rich, and so deep that a series of planks lay across the path between the parking lot and the administrative office. I paused to tie Levin's frilly white hat below the chin.

"Making a good impression?" Levin asked me.

"For who?" I answered, and I tried to smile. From the moment Levin's jeep entered the Galilee, I'd quickened with such foreboding that I'd three times almost told him to turn back, but didn't because it felt ridiculous.

He took my arm, an old habit by now, and he helped me negotiate the mud. I still didn't believe we were in the right place. For one thing, the topography was wrong. If there was one certain thing about Tilulit it was its placement on a hill, and as we neared the location Levin had circled on his map, I scouted hill after hill; telegraph poles linked them like charms on a chain, and sometimes there would be a flash of white rooftops and my heart would freeze over, but Levin would keep driving. Then those hills leveled off, and suddenly there was a brightly painted sign in Hebrew and Latin characters: GAN LEAH: EST. 1923

I said, "There's some mistake. This isn't it."

Levin took off his sunglasses, and said, "Nora, there's no mistake."

Beyond the sign there was a burst of garish sunlit rectangles, patches of bilious green and overlaid asphalt, and that mud. Nothing I recognized from any letter. Frankly, I was relieved. I let myself be walked towards that neat white shack at the end of the path and adjusted the hat as he rang the buzzer.

A young girl with blond pigtails opened the door; her face was pleasant enough, but of course she spoke Hebrew, so her conversation with Levin was incomprehensible. She left us sitting on folding chairs in a dark little office with a window-fan.

Levin reached for a water pitcher and offered me a glass.

"I'm fine. Drink the water yourself."

"You don't look fine," said Levin. "You're white as a ghost."

I lit a Lucky Strike, and found an ashtray weighing down some loose papers on a bookshelf. There were old notebooks on that shelf, some spiral bound, some with thick, cracked cardboard covers. The thicker ones had dates on their spines: *1927, 1928, 1932, 1924.* The oldest of them lay top-most, and its cover had been carefully repaired with masking tape. I pulled it out, and it opened of itself to the middle; the language was Hebrew, but the scrawl so wild and blotted that the pen had probably exploded. Beyond that point, a few of the pages had gummed together with something sticky that had crystallized around the edges.

All right, then. So someone took notes while she ate honey with her fin-gers. By the time I stubbed that Lucky in the ashtray I wasn't so surprised to hear the door open and see Nathan Sobel.

As with Dori, I would have known him anywhere from the photograph, though he'd gone fat. His eyebrows still grew together. He took maybe two steps into the office before telling us in Hungarian that he didn't have much time to show us around. Then he took two steps out of the office before say-ing to me, "Why didn't you come in 'forty-four?"

"It wasn't possible," I said.

"That's ridiculous," said Nathan Sobel. "But you're here now, you made it through hell, you've come home, eh? And where're you living? With this man?"

I was appalled to see Levin turn red. He answered for me.

"She's still waiting for housing."

"Well, you look just like I thought you would from your letters," Sobel said. "Nothing like that cousin of yours. How is your son?"

"He's dead," I said. I thought maybe he'd ask me how he died, but he only pressed his liver-lips together and motioned us down a path shaded by young trees.

"These saplings were planted in 'forty-two. We'd just doubled in size, and Leah and the other orphans lived in tents. Who had cement or lumber for new houses? At least after digging up a road and planting trees they didn't think a tent was so uncomfortable. It builds character," Sobel said.

Levin asked about the harvest and about kibbutz policy on using hired labor, and those questions allowed me to observe everything around me without fear of interruption. What could I know here? The laundry? The dining hall and library? They were a lot of ice-cubes freshly shaken from the tray. There was nothing I knew here, nothing.

In spite of myself, I broke in. "What about the bee-hives?"

Sobel looked surprised. "Bee-hives? Well, these days, we don't go in much for small industry. There's a hive in the children's quarters. Educational purposes. That's in the old part of the kibbutz."

"The old kibbutz," I said, "that's Tilulit? On a hill?"

"You could call it a hill," said Nathan. "Look, it's time for lunch. You must be awfully hot in that fancy pink thing you're wearing."

"Is it painted yellow?" I asked him, and he gave me a long look. I clarified. "The hive."

For some reason, he didn't answer me. He left us at the dining hall and I felt suddenly faint. Levin seated me at a table near the door and got me a plate of tomato salad and a glass of fruit juice. He whispered, "Nora, there's a guest room you can use, I'm sure, if you need to have a rest."

"No, no," I said. "Who needs to rest?"

"Why didn't you ask that fellow anything about your cousin?"

While we were whispering, our table filled up with young people who chattered away in Hebrew. One stocky boy with red hair gave us a friendly greeting. Levin answered him. Never had the language sounded to me so impossible to penetrate, or so artificial. Levin turned to me and said, "There's going to be a performance at the children's house in three hours. Then the kibbutz string quartet will be playing in the auditorium, and afterwards there will be a special dairy supper and a dance. This boy has been here for eight years, he says. These people might know something."

I doubted it. In their cotton shirts and shorts, with their sun-bleached hair showing under the brim of their cotton hats, they didn't look as though they could recognize their own fathers and mothers. They were like happy cattle.

I said to Levin, "Ask them," and after a little thought, I finished the sentence. "Ask them about the Arab village Taell al-Taji."

Levin did just that, and I watched their faces. One of them addressed Levin. He translated for me. "We're sitting in it."

This was what Levin told me: The villagers had fled during the War of Independence in '48, and afterwards most of the older houses had been bulldozed, but a few had been salvageable and could be absorbed into the kibbutz. The office where we sat when we'd arrived, for example, had once been a stable. Below the asphalt of the parking lot was stone, beautiful but badly cracked. Gan Leah made use of what they could: bricks, roofing, and beams. Such fragments had been incorporated into the new dining hall; the beams lined a verandah of gray slate.

"And the water," I said to Levin.

"What water?"

"There was water," I said, "between the kibbutz and the village. A gully with a plank bridge."

Levin shrugged. "Who knows? Maybe they rerouted it for irrigation. That would have been the sensible thing to do."

From the verandah, I could at last see what might have been old Tilulit. It wasn't a hill, precisely, more of a slope dotted with purple wildflowers.

The shaggy, forgotten look of that slope made me wonder if I had been mistaken. Perhaps there had never been a Tilulit; perhaps it wouldn't exist on any map at any time. It was like that telegram from Bela, something I might as well have never had at all.

Levin asked, "Did you want to go to the clinic?"

"I said I would be fine, Dov."

"You look like hell."

"Thank you. Why are you so protective of me? Do I remind you of your mother?"

"Someone else," said Levin. "Your hat's on too tight." He untied it, and as he fumbled with the string, his hands brushed up against my cheeks in a way that confused and alarmed me, and I might have pulled away if he hadn't gone on talking. "My daughter, sometimes. She's not as tough as she pretends to be."

"What do you think's in the clinic?" I asked him. "The fountain of youth?"

"It's possible," said Levin.

I knew what else would be in the clinic and why he wanted me to go. I'd been avoiding Dr. Dori Csengery since we'd arrived. "Listen," I said, "I don't want to be young again."

Levin didn't ask me what I wanted. He knew, from experience, that he couldn't give it to me. On that slate verandah, I felt in my purse for another cigarette, but somehow the matches had gotten damp, and I struck and struck but was left with a nose full of sulfur and three bent strips of cardboard in my fist, and then I realized that I was crying.

"What I want," I said, "is just a welcome. What the hell was I thinking?" To my appalled surprise, I found I'd buried my head in Levin's shoulder, and helpless sobs came of themselves out of my throat. His hand was in my hair, and then that old Pesti bureaucrat was kissing me. I pulled away. "How on earth—" I began.

But he interrupted. "You want to put your hat back on?"

"I can get it on myself, thank you," I said. I took it from him and tied the knot only with some effort. My hands weren't too steady.

The road between the dining hall and the clinic was another sea of mud, which meant yet more planks and also meant that Levin had to take my arm again. This, I allowed. As we gingerly stepped across yet another mud bank, he said, "It was my teacher in *gimnazium* you make me think of. A thousand million years ago."

I asked him, "What did she teach?"

"Hungarian History and Literature. She was an anti-Semite. Isn't that funny? But I had a terrible crush on her," said Levin. "She had a big bosom and the angrier she got, the bigger her bosom got and when she would call on me to recite, she'd always pick on me because I was a Jew. She had me in a state of complete erotic terror."

I'll admit that this description almost made me lose my footing on the planks. I had to say, though, "You've got a wife. I think I'm wearing her hat. You never mention her."

"How do you know I'm not a widower or divorced?"

I smiled. "Levin, you've got a wife."

"And you've got your cousin," said Levin. Then he paused to ask someone directions to the clinic, and by the time we were alone again, I'd forgotten how I'd meant to answer him.

The clinic was as new as the rest of Gan Leah. I think I had expected a shack, with Doctor Csengery stringing a stethoscope onto a nail in the wall. Instead, the doors opened into a busy waiting room with tan upholstered benches, framed paintings, and a receptionist. A little cowed, I whispered to Levin, "She's probably not here."

"She invited you," he said. "We've come this far. A few more steps, Norika."

His use of the diminutive astounded me. He pushed his way to the girl at the front desk and announced our arrival. There was an argument, I think, and he was clearly out of line; I enjoyed watching the scene he made on my account, I'll admit. I also knew that when the girl disappeared to get Dori's permission, she would agree to see me.

She did. Levin walked me around the partition, and then he released my arm and said, "Here, I leave you for a while."

"Leave me?"

"Little Echo, you'll be fine. You knew I couldn't stay for more than an hour or two. I've arranged for you to get a lift back with one of those young people we met at lunch. The girl knows you're gone?"

"She's with her rabbi," I said, "for Shavuot." Levin made a face, and I asked him, "Why don't you like her?"

"I don't have an opinion of her one way or the other," Levin said.

"I owe her my life," I said.

"You don't owe anyone your life. Get that straight, first of all."

"And second of all?" I asked him, wondering where that question would lead. I knew he was probably going to have dinner with his family in Haifa, and I wasn't sure if I was ready to let him go.

"Second of all," said Levin, "don't smoke so many Lucky Strikes. Find a local brand. They're cheaper." Then he gave me another kiss before I could stop him, though I'll confess it wasn't unexpected. He gave me a little shove towards the door and walked away.

ORI CSENGERY WAS NOT IN AN examining room but behind a desk. She got up when I entered and extended her hand. She said, "I wasn't sure if you'd come."

She looked less daunting now, maybe because she wasn't on the way to surgery. At the same time, she held less of a resemblance to the photograph. She'd pulled her hair back in a clip, and it made her look strained and exhausted. I gave her my hand to shake, and she held it so long that I wondered if she would ever give it back to me. Then she motioned for me to sit down, and I said, "You're busy."

"Oh—all that fuss out there? That's nothing for me. Nurses take care of them. I've become a desk clerk. Weren't you a desk clerk at some school for rich girls?"

"Something like that," I said.

"All the girls in that school wrote your cousin. It's a good thing Leah couldn't read Hungarian. You want a cup of something?" Dori asked me. "I have a hotplate here."

"Dori," I said, "it's true. I almost didn't come here."

"No one here calls me Dori. My name is Arielle," she said. "I married Yosef Ginzberg four years ago. Yosef's from Germany. He's a good man. So was your cousin. But there's one thing we learned and that was that he had his limitations."

"Of course he does," I said, and in saying it I realized I was forcing the reference to Bela into the present tense.

"You saw Nathan?" she asked me. I nodded and she said, "He's an ass, isn't he? Always was. But he's still here. Almost all of the old circle are still here. Unrecognizable, mind you, but immovable. And we all went through what he went through. Europe is a big graveyard. Why didn't you come in 'forty-four?"

The question hardly took me by surprise. In that dim room, I couldn't tell if she could read my face.

"All told," she said, "there were maybe fifty illegals he managed to get here. Five died on the way, and one of the ones who died was named Gabor, but it wasn't the same Gabor, was it?"

"No," I said. "It wasn't. That's not how he died."

"After Leah died, his family was all he had. He moved heaven and earth to save you," Dori said. "He'd left us by then, but he'd still come here to make sure you all had a place to go, and after the Germans invaded and they started with the ghettos in Szeged, I thought he'd lose his mind worrying about his mother, but he just made sure we had beds ready for when you arrived. That's the kind of faith he had in you."

Then she paused, as though what I said had just registered.

"Your son isn't here."

When I didn't answer, she said it for me.

"So he's dead—Gabor."

Again, I wondered: Would she ask me how? Would I have to tell the story? But she only dug her hand into her hair, a gesture of anger or exhaustion. I said, "Dori, look, where is he?"

She said, "I don't know. I told you. I haven't heard from him in two years. What makes you think he'd even want to see you now?"

"I got a telegram from him," I said, "with an address. I lost it."

I could tell she didn't believe me. I began to wonder whether I believed myself. "What do you expect from him?" Dori asked me.

I answered honestly then. "I don't know."

Afterwards, she paused, and I could see that she was searching my face for something and hadn't found it. She leaned across the table and asked me, "Could I have a cigarette?"

"Of course," I said, and I shook one from the pack for her and lit it with my own.

"I never used to smoke. Terrible habit but it steadies my nerves." She took a drag before adding, "Leah smoked too."

So then of course I had to ask at last: "All right, I don't know. Who's Leah?"

Dori said, "Leah was his wife."

*S*HE ARRIVED IN A TRUCK WITH
the orphans from Kiev, and like the rest of them, she spoke no Hebrew, and
like the rest of them, she smelled like garbage from the freighter where
they'd stowed away. The truck was a flatbed, and the thirty-some boys and
girls on board looked like dumb animals, with faces so empty of curiosity
that it was hard to remember what they'd risked to come to Palestine.

Bela helped unload them; it was hard to think of it as anything but
unloading. Hoisting body after body from the bed of the truck, he had to
steady himself against the wheel. After a while, he tried whispering a little
encouragement in Russian, but it had no effect. How could they give them a
welcome? It was too dark; the atmosphere was too tense. Since the land-
purchase, relations with Taell al-Taji had deteriorated beyond hope, and it
was probably a mistake to take in newcomers at all.

Lifting another human being down from the flatbed, Bela tried his Russian again. "You'll get a hot shower soon."

The answer came back in French. "Are you implying I stink?"

Bela almost dropped the girl, who shimmied out of his hands, grazing the front of his trousers with her breasts, and then she emerged and
shook out her thick dark hair. Somehow, though there wasn't much of a
moon, Bela had never seen anything quite as clearly as that girl. He rubbed
his chin for no particular reason, and then stepped backwards, though

there was nowhere to go, and finally spoke French back. "Your accent is excellent."

She rolled her eyes, which were shaped like almonds and fringed with thick lashes. "Yours is passable."

Meanwhile, the last three orphans had gotten tired of waiting, and they climbed down on their own. One of the young men gave Bela a long look; he could have been that girl's boyfriend or her brother, or maybe he was just sending a warning. They were herded to the clinic where Dori checked them for lice and then gave them leave to shower. As the boys and girls stripped separately, Bela stood by Dori's side and remembered the early days of Tilulit when the men and women showered together. There had been no ideological reason for the shift in policy, though he did notice that it coincided with the arrival of that first group of Poles back in '34.

Dori said to Bela, "They'll be a lot of work. I don't have a clue what they're carrying from that boat, not to mention psychological trauma."

"They're excellent human material," Bela said. "A little raw, but excellent."

"I can't tell when you're joking anymore," Dori said to him.

"No, I'm not joking really," Bela said. "They're young. How young are they, exactly?"

"The oldest is eighteen."

"That's the girl?"

"Which girl?" Dori asked him, though of course he'd only noticed one, and she knew it.

"The one with all that hair."

"She's got head-lice," Dori said. "We'll have to cut it off. She's seventeen. Or that's what it says on her papers. She's probably younger."

Bela helped Dori clean up, and they walked back to their room. They'd shared that room for three years now, and it had more of Bela in it than Dori; he'd hung up checkered curtains and photographs of his family, and there were his newspapers and dictionaries and the boxes of letters from Hungary piled in a corner. Dori contributed only her medical diploma mounted on cardboard, and a sewing kit arranged as precisely as surgical instruments on an end-table. Bela would occasionally borrow the scissors to cut an article out of a newspaper and forget to return them, or worse, he'd pass them on to someone else. She'd get no rest until they were back in place.

"How can you be so attached to a pair of scissors?" Bela would ask her.

"Well, what if I have the urge to burn all those letters from your girl-friends back in Budapest?" she asked him.

"Then there'd be a fire in the room," said Bela.

Dori shook her head and said, again, "I can't tell when you're joking anymore. Really, you didn't used to be this way."

WHAT WAY HAD BELA BEEN, exactly? He wasn't sure. The week after the arrival of the orphans, he found himself identifying strongly with the youngest, a thick-necked boy with rough red hair and a marvelous vocabulary of Russian curses. He wasn't popular with the others. He always pushed himself to the front of the line in the dining hall, and when he didn't get his way he'd raise his fist and shake it like a character in a bad melodrama. Bela tried holding him back, and telling him he had to wait his turn, but he wrenched himself free, and shouted: "Fucking sister-fucker! Don't you dare fucking lay your faggot hands on me again!"

Bela was grateful no one in his own circle understood Russian. He kept his voice low. "Look, there's plenty of food for everyone here."

"Plenty of shit!"

"Calm down," Bela said, and he realized he ought to leave the boy alone to make his own enemies, but he found himself reaching for his arm again. This time he felt someone grip him at the elbow, and he looked down and saw the orphan girl.

She spoke French. "Don't play favorites, just because he limps like you."

Bela hadn't noticed that the boy limped at all. He backed up and landed on the edge of the trestle table where he made some attempt to pretend he'd meant to sit there. Now that the girl's hair had been cropped off, she looked older, much older, in fact, than seventeen. Someone had dressed her in standard-issue shirt and shorts, but they didn't fit her well, and she looked as though she were in the process of climbing out of them.

She said, "I'm Lenore. As in the poem by E. A. Poe." She didn't extend her hand as she introduced herself, and she also showed no sign of joining the line for supper. Bela felt a sudden urge to fill a plate for her, and at the same time couldn't imagine her eating.

In fact, it was two weeks before he actually saw Lenore eat or drink. By then, he realized she was a little crazy, a case, as Dori would put it, of psychological trauma. All of the orphans had adjustment problems, and some took the form of nightmares or a perpetual stupor. A few, like the redheaded boy, had lost something deeper. It was as though they had forgotten how to live with other people. Reluctantly, Bela admitted that Lenore, too, was in this category. Nothing about her fit. She had no friends among the other orphans. She was incapable of ordinary conversation.

It was considered therapeutic for the orphans to be put to work at once. As they'd arrived during the rainy season, much of the work was in the dairy or the chicken coop. After a few weeks of classes, Bela had managed to teach the orphans enough Hebrew to follow basic instructions, and most of them seemed eager to learn. Left to themselves, they generally switched to Yiddish, but that was natural. Lenore never joined in.

There was a reason: Lenore spoke no Yiddish. Through one source or another, he pieced together part of her story. She'd been born in Moscow, and her father had been a professor of French Literature, and a translator of Symbolist poetry. He was arrested in '38, and given the atmosphere in Moscow, her mother had thought it best to return to her own people in Kiev.

What did they find in Kiev? Bela didn't know. It was considered bad form to bring up the past, and when Bela gave the orphans Hebrew lessons, he had to pretend not to understand the Yiddish conversations going on around him which would make reference, almost in passing, to outrageous things. Sometimes he would find his gaze lingering on Lenore, who sat in the left corner with her cropped hair and bare white arms, and who also seemed to be pretending not to understand.

Everything about the girl seemed studied, even her selfishness. When she'd manage to get cigarettes, she'd smoke them half-behind her hand, to make it clear that they were hers and no one else's. Blowing the smoke through her fine nostrils, her expression would be unreadable, as though possession were a mystery, and she had no responsibility to help anyone understand what he couldn't share.

 NCE, HE CAUGHT HER LEAVING the dairy, with plastic gloves on her hands and her hair in a net; she smelled like sour milk and iodine. A few girls strayed behind, and when they saw Bela standing there, they giggled and called out to Lenore in Yiddish. Bela couldn't quite make out what they'd said, and decided he didn't want to.

He asked Lenore in French, "Do you understand them?"

She frowned, as though it were the strangest question in the world. "Of course I do."

"So why do you speak French?"

"You said you liked my accent," Lenore said. She pulled off her gloves, removed the hairnet, and shook out her furry half-grown hair.

"But don't you get lonely?"

"You speak French," said Lenore. "Don't you have a cigarette?"

For some reason, Bela said, "I speak a lot of languages." It felt as though he were bragging. The two of them had started walking together from the dairy to the orphans' tents and as though to distance himself from her he mentally took note of the languages he spoke, and then he sorted them into Romance, Slavic, Germanic, and Finno-Ugric, and perhaps it was when they reached the threshold of her tent that he realized he didn't know what to say to this girl in any of those languages.

He was so distracted that he only slowly realized Lenore had slipped a hand into the pocket of his trousers. In French, he asked, "What are you doing?"

"Picking your pocket for a cigarette," said Lenore.

"Lenore, you don't know what you're doing."

"Yes I do," she said. They were in the open, under a drizzling sky, but he had to admit that she probably did know what she was doing. She dug that hand a little deeper, and cupped it, as she leaned up towards his ear. "There's a hole in your pocket."

"You did that," Bela said. He realized he was speaking Hungarian. It didn't seem to matter. She pulled him around the side of a storage shed to a muddy bank, and somewhere in there she had stopped pulling, and he had started until he was struggling to get her muddy shorts and blouse off, and she was still fumbling with the buttons on his trousers from the inside, with no sense of urgency, and finally he had to free her hands and unbutton them himself.

Against the mudbank, Bela entered her, and she rose to meet him, face almost impassive. He felt he had to close his eyes, and the cool mud and warm body of this girl, the stench of sour milk and iodine, came over him and let him not think long enough to lose himself.

Afterwards, he rolled off Lenore. She looked half-squashed. There was mud in her hair, and all over her cheeks and breasts, and she retrieved her shirt and pulled it over her head. Her face emerged from the collar, and Bela tried to read it and couldn't.

He said, "My God, this is terrible."

"Bullshit," said Lenore. She felt around for the shorts and panties and discovered they were still around her ankles. She stood up and pulled them back to her waist.

"I'm your father's age," said Bela.

"My father's dead," Lenore said. "Who says I want another one?"

Bela again was speechless. His private parts were still exposed. When he tried to rise to pull up the trousers, he put too much weight on his left leg and slipped, but Lenore caught him.

Out of breath, she gasped as she said, "Look at me."

He did look at her. She still bore his weight. Her muddy neck was red with exertion and he had never seen her eyes so bright.

"See how happy it makes me," she said, "to catch you when you fall?"

URING THE NEXT YEAR, DORI began to keep company with Yosef Ginzberg, a member of Beit Shemesh kibbutz, no stunner and no genius, but a man, Dori said, with a heart of gold. He courted her. She had never been courted before. He brought her coffee cakes he'd baked himself, and bottles of wine from the kibbutz vineyard. They'd eat the cake and drink the wine together in the room Dori was still theoretically sharing with Bela, safe in the knowledge that Bela wouldn't come home. First Yosef stayed until the cake was gone and saved the rest of the wine for later. Then he stayed until the wine was gone. After a few months, he didn't need any excuse to stay. He laughed a lot, and told her she was beautiful so often that she stopped thinking it was a joke.

Of Bela, Yosef said, "He missed his chance. He had you for twenty years."

"Thirty," Dori said. "We met in primary school."

"He's that old, eh?"

"That old," said Dori. "Old as me. Can you believe it?"

She could joke about it now, barely. Bela was that old. Lenore insisted she was twenty, and maybe she even looked it now that she'd learned how to button her shirt correctly, but the whole thing was still preposterous.

Being Bela, he knew it was preposterous. He couldn't shake off a life-time of self-consciousness overnight. Dori couldn't stay angry at him, especially after Yosef, but she was embarrassed for him, and their long friendship made her aware of his own embarrassment. There would be times at the dining hall when he'd be sitting beside that girl trying to get her to speak Hebrew, and she'd clearly be doing something nasty to him under the table, and suddenly, across the room, his eyes would meet Dori's, and they'd both blush.

When he decided to marry Lenore, he told Dori before anyone else, or at least that's what he claimed. He stopped into their room unexpectedly, and unfortunately Yosef was somewhere else that night. He broke the news, and then said, "It's the only way to get her out of that tent."

"Well," Dori said, "she could leave the kibbutz."

"Lenore? Where on earth could she go?"

Dori shrugged. She scooted herself back on their old bed, and hoisted up the first of his boxes of letters. "You'd better take these."

"Wouldn't it be possible for me to leave them here?" Bela asked her. "Just for a while."

"I don't think so," said Dori. She tried to smile. She had to admit; he did look younger. That bitterness he had developed in the past four or five years had fallen away, and underneath was something she was almost afraid to touch. He leaned hard on his right leg and cocked his head in the other direction, and he looked sad and lost. He was half-crazy, just like the girl. She suddenly wanted to sit him down for one of the talks they always had. She asked, "Are you afraid she'll read them?"

"She can't read German," Bela said. "Or Hungarian for that matter. I just think they're safer here."

Torn between love and self-respect, Dori wavered. Then she remembered Yosef, so she said, "I'm sorry. They can't be safe anymore."

B Y THE TIME LENORE AND BELA married, she was calling herself Leah, and spoke a poor but fearless Hebrew. The rabbi who married them was a stranger to Tilulit, and he said to Nathan Sobel, "It's good to see two of those newcomers settling in."

Nathan repeated the remark to Dori, who forced herself to laugh. "He's picking up her accent," she said.

"Well, maybe it's for the best," Nathan said. "He hasn't done any real leadership work in months anyway, and he's been restless. Leave him to his dictionaries and his wife and give some of the young people a chance. Maybe they'd be less likely to run off to some crusade in Europe."

In fact, the demographics of Tilulit were alarming. Many of the young men had volunteered for the British army, and the kibbutz was often short-handed at harvest. For the first time, that year, they had brought in hired labor from Taell al-Taji. The decision hadn't been easy, and Dori, for one, had opposed it strongly, though an Arab representative from the village argued, in good Hebrew, that it would be seen as a hand extended in friendship.

"It's not friendship," Dori said. "It's an economic relationship. It's inherently exploitative and it goes against bedrock ideology." But she knew she was putting on what Bela had always called her "doctor voice," and she was lost.

Bela would have agreed with her; she was sure of it. Ideologically, intellectually, they were almost always in complete accord. Even when they'd fought, at least he'd been there, with his chin in his hand and on his face that dubious and inquiring expression. She missed him.

*A*ND WHERE WAS HE? IN THE room he shared with his wife, a cluttered room far smaller than the one he'd shared with Dori, though possessing a hotplate, a wardrobe, and a little wash-basin. Leah accumulated things: She stole bowls from the dining hall and filled them with stones she liked; she picked wildflowers and dried them upside down over the window; she took other people's laundry by mistake and then she washed it in the basin so they couldn't get it back; she stubbed her cheap, strong cigarettes out everywhere. Amidst all this were Bela's photographs, dictionaries, and boxes of letters.

One night, he came in and found her lying belly-down in bed, with her feet on the pillow and her head facing the door, smoking a Black Cat cigarette. There was a Hebrew-German dictionary open and a letter in her hand. She asked him, "Who's Nora?"

Bela crouched and read the letter upside down. "That's very old. Probably older than you."

"Is she German?"

Bela said, "No, Lenore. She just wrote me in German. She was no more German than you are French."

Though they spoke Hebrew in public, French remained their intimate language, and as Bela settled in beside her, it was in French that he addressed her, and in French he told her about my husband and my son, his mother and sister, and his father who had drowned in Lake Balaton. He showed her the photograph of Adele in the Arab gown.

"She's beautiful," Leah said. "You can tell she's a saint. Where is she now?"

"Hungary," Bela said.

"Then she's dead," said Leah. She said this, smoking her cigarette and letting ashes fall all over the brown flax blanket. She spoke with no particular urgency. Bela would have asked her what she'd meant, but she at once turned over on her back, and her loose hair fell across that photograph, and he forgot what she'd said. After they made love, sometimes he would dream that she was floating away in a clear, bright ether, and then he'd try to run after her and he'd call "Nora!"

When he called that name, sometimes he'd wake up, stunned and terrified, and there would be his wife beside him, asleep, with the cover half-pushed off her naked shoulders and two fingers pressed to her mouth as though she were calling for silence, or perhaps silencing herself.

*H*E DIDN'T LIKE THIS BUSINESS
with the letters and the dictionaries. He also felt helpless to stop it. He did
remove the Hebrew-German dictionary from his room and gave it to the
library; then he felt ashamed. Once, she confronted him with something he
barely recognized, a leaflet he had copied twenty-five years before, with
Arabic characters that looked like raindrops, branches, birds in flight. Below
was his cribbed translation into Hungarian.

Unite with us, brothers. Show them we are not dogs, but men. If we walk out
together they can not set one against the other. Our common Enemy is the Class
System. Our common goal is freedom from Imperialism and a National home-
land for all peoples Native to this country.

"Awkward," Bela admitted. "Those capital letters—I don't know what I
was trying to reproduce. And so old. Why are you asking about old things?"

Leah asked, "Did you have brothers?"

"No," Bela said. "I didn't write that. Someone else did. Some of the
early Pioneers wanted to organize the Arab laborers."

"Communists?" Leah asked.

"Some of them," said Bela.

"My father was a Communist," said Leah. "He translated Lenin's works
into French, and also Trotsky's."

It was the first time she'd said anything about her father other than
acknowledging his death, but she spoke with such indifference that it was
difficult to know if she was entering new territory. She did ask him to teach
her to write Arabic. The request surprised him so much that he said, "You
can barely write Hebrew."

"Well, Arabic is more my style," said Leah. She lazed backwards when
she said that and at the same time reached for the last cigarette in the pack.
"Light this for me. And say something to me in Arabic."

Bela said, *"Limaeʒae tadhak?"*

"No," said Leah. "Something dirty."

Bela turned red and was speechless, and Leah loomed up with that cigarette between her teeth and her dark hair in her face, and she laughed.

"You mean you don't know anything dirty in Arabic? You've never had an Arab girl? I don't believe it. All your girlfriends, none of them Arab? You're lying to me."

"Lenore," Bela said, "don't tease me."

"And why not?" She suddenly spat the cigarette out and buried her mouth in his ear. "Tell me about the Arab girl. Tell me about the girl and tell me everything you did to her and everything you made her do."

Bela tore himself from her, and addressed her in Hebrew. "Leah, there's no Arab girl."

"Yes there is," Leah said, a little breathless. "You took her like a German."

"No," Bela said. "I'm not a German. I'm a Jew. I'm your husband."

Leah looked up, and her hair fell from her eyes. "Can't you pretend you're a German? If I want you to?"

Bela couldn't answer.

Then she sat up against the wall with her legs tucked against her chest. Bela sat beside her, though he was afraid to touch her. Then, imperceptibly, her head lowered, until her forehead touched her knees, and then her shoulders began to rock.

He gave in to his first impulse, which was to reach out and take her head from between her knees and look at her face. She didn't resist. His heart turned over, because it was the face of a child, unmistakably, with swollen features and round cheeks and a soft, vulnerable forehead.

She said, "I don't know if I can pretend either. What if they're not dead, my father and my mother. I never saw them die. I left them. What if they're still alive there?"

"But you're here," Bela said to her.

"Nothing that happens here matters."

Bela said, "You matter. Do you know how much you matter? Do you know what kind of a life I had before I met you?" Even as he spoke, he realized he hadn't known, until that moment, what kind of life he'd had.

"If they're alive," Leah said, "then what I did can't be forgiven. I have to find them. And not just them. You don't know how many, or what I've seen, and to know I've left them and to live, how could I live?"

Bela was tempted to tell her that she was better off as she had been, taking them for dead. But how could he say that to her when her anger and remorse had filled the empty place he'd always sensed in her. She took shape, and before him was not some sleepwalker, some Lost Lenore but a woman he didn't recognize.

She turned that new anger towards him, and said, "You don't know what I've seen, and you don't want to know. But I don't have a choice. Will you help me?"

The confrontation was direct. She all but spit the words, and he felt her face harden between his hands. He had the sensation of stepping off a precipice as he answered, "Yes, I'll help you."

E TRIED TO EXPLAIN THE PROM-
ise to Dori, who gave him a complete physical examination, and said, "They'd have to be crazy to let you into any army."

"And if I go to Europe independently?"

"Then *you're* crazy," said Dori. "Maybe you want to captain one of those ships leaving from Romania, the ones that fit maybe a dozen wretches and get turned back by the British. Maybe you'll rot in a detention camp in Cyprus and she'll be happy."

"You hear rumors about what's going on in Europe," Bela said. What rumors he referred to weren't clear. He ran his hand backwards through his hair, and it stuck up, in comic contrast to his face. He was naked with the exception of a sheet which covered his private parts, and Dori saw that since they'd shared a bed, the hair on his chest had turned gray.

"Look," Dori said to him, "if we thought about that stuff we would go absolutely crazy. We've got our work to do here. Powerful people in the movement are doing everything they can—"

"Like what?" Bela asked her.

"Like the illegals."

"A handful."

"Your wife was part of that handful," said Dori. "The *Yishuv* saved her life."

"We can't go on with a few dozen at a time."

"What do you want us to do? Get into our Jewish airplanes and bomb Berlin? We don't have Jewish airplanes. We don't have an army. We don't have a state. And that's why we're here—not to save Jews but to build a state where we can be Jews."

Bela shook his head. There was a finality to that refusal which Dori didn't recognize. How could it be the end of the argument?

"What does she expect of you?" Dori asked, as Bela put on his trousers. "Does she want you to declare a personal war on Germany?"

Bela turned as he pulled the trousers up, and his bare back felt like a rebuke, as did his hesitation. It was only after he had buttoned up those trousers and reached for his shirt that he said to Dori, "It comes to what I expect of myself. Finally, that. We both have family in Hungary. I haven't sent mine a letter in years. And Mouse, you know what I realized? I'd written them off."

Dori said, "I don't know what you're talking about." It was the spring of 1943.

"I'd written them off," Bela said again. "I can't now. Neither can Leah. She's trying to volunteer to go there, maybe to contact the resistance. And me, I don't know what I'm going to do. Maybe go back to Hungary."

"You're crazy," Dori said again, and now she was terrified because she realized, as certain as she saw that man buttoning his shirt in front of her, that if he went to Hungary, he'd be dead.

Then she found herself asking questions. What was the life of one man worth? What if, as a consequence of his death, lives were saved? Or what if, as a consequence of the deaths of five comrades, they gained a few kilometers of land? Or what, Dori asked me that day in her office in the clinic in Gan Leah, if as a consequence of six million deaths, we Jews got our state? These thoughts, Dori could admit to me years later, but then she could only see Bela, whom she loved, and she couldn't bear the thought of losing him.

Bela said, "I'm not crazy. I only know I can't keep living here at Tilulit, not like this. I can't accept the terms."

Dori, helpless, could only say, "Don't leave."

"I'll try not to," said Bela. And he did try.

*L*EAH, ALONG WITH TWO HUN-dred others, volunteered to join the paratroopers who would be dropped all over Nazi-occupied Europe. The British chose thirty, three of them women. One of the women was Hungarian. Her name was Hannah Szenes. She was a poet who had come to Palestine, like Leah, not long before, and almost immediately after she landed in Budapest, she was captured. She died under torture. I'd never even heard her name until Dori said it to me that day in Gan Leah. Though Leah herself was not chosen to join the paratroopers, she returned months later, greatly changed. She arrived at the gate in an army jeep, and gave the driver a kiss before she leapt out, wearing a khaki jumpsuit and calling: "Where's my husband?"

The first thing Dori noticed was that her Hebrew had lost the French accent, and the second thing she noticed was that she'd taken out a pack of Black Cat cigarettes and at once offered one to Dori, who was so surprised she took it.

Leah swung her way down towards their room, and there was a rifle slung across her shoulder, which somehow seemed to fit the rest of her. She laughed as she knocked on the door, as though the act of knocking on the door was, of itself, amusing. "Old man!" she called. "Don't tell me you've got some other woman in there!" Bela had been napping, and when he opened the door, Leah pulled him back into bed, still laughing, and her sun-bleached hair came loose from her ponytail. When Bela gestured towards the rifle, she thought that was even funnier, and she pointed it at him.

"I order you to take off those pajamas," she said.

Bela said, "It's not loaded."

"How do you know?" Leah asked, poking the mouth of it below the upmost button of the pajama-top.

Bela unbuttoned that top. The rifle eventually slipped from Leah's hands, and as it cracked against the floor, Bela wouldn't have been surprised to hear the thing go off.

*S*HE WAS ONLY BACK FOR A VISIT. She had joined the Palmach, and had made contacts which would prove useful in the months to come. Bela listened with a jealousy that stunned him, a jealousy of her youth. Kiev had been liberated. She would not drop there in a parachute, but she could shape the excellent human material she was into whatever she chose. There were sea-routes and routes overland. Pockets of resistance took shape even as the Russians liberated Europe from one end, and the Americans and British from the other.

In spite of himself, Bela said, "I've been miserable without you here, Lenore."

"Well, that's because you haven't been busy enough," Leah said. "You've been brooding too much. And you're too useful to brood."

"Useful?" Bela smirked. Lying there naked, with this beautiful strange girl beside him, he felt like a pornographic joke.

"We need money," Leah said. "We have to do more than smuggle out the Jews. We have to buy them. In American dollars, two hundred and fifty a head, maybe more. Or there's been talk about a deal, an exchange—in Hungary. Trucks for Jews."

"But that would prolong the war," Bela said. Leah put her hand over his mouth.

"There's been talk about saving a million Hungarian Jews. Listen, we need money. And we need all your old Zionist connections and your Hungarian connections too. In fact, we need you. Also," Leah added, as though it were an afterthought, "I need you. So put on your clothes and have some supper with me and Amos"—that was the jeep's driver—"and then argue all you want about prolonging the war. And about how useful you are. I love you, and you saved my life, and if that's not enough for you, you can go to hell."

*F*ROM THE WAY SHE'D TALKED, Bela expected Leah and Amos to drag him off to Tel Aviv that night, but in fact, Leah had counted on staying through the month and convinced Amos to help with the olive harvest. As ever, they were short-handed, and now, for the third year, hired laborers arrived from Taell al-Taji. As the kibbutz paid more than any other employer, the competition was fierce. Bela was startled to see so many men crowd the gate of the kibbutz. He didn't know any of them, but they knew him.

"*Histaresh—!*" one very dark boy called. "*Min fadlak, min fadlak!*"

Bela smiled uncomfortably. Because he couldn't help pick olives, he was supposed to guard the gate and choose no more than twenty workers. That day, because Leah and Amos had arrived, he could take in no more than eighteen men. He made this clear as soon as everyone had gathered. Then he chose the men and barred the gate after the eighteenth had passed. The rest kept standing.

"*Esmaehli, esmaehli,*" someone called, and they parted to clear a path for the same gentleman who'd spoken such good Hebrew three years earlier at the meeting. Bela hadn't been at that meeting, and neither man knew the other. He addressed Bela in Hebrew. "Is there a problem, sir?"

Bela frowned, and said in Arabic, *"Lahza min fadlak."* He didn't like the idea of speaking a language the other men at the gate didn't understand, and he didn't like the man's smooth, light tan face, or the weasel smile on that face, or the way the other men deferred to him though he was clearly not respected. He went on in Arabic. "We need only eighteen men. I'm sorry, but it will be that way for the rest of the harvest."

In Hebrew again, the man asked Bela, "No chance we can negotiate?"

Bela realized what was going on, and deliberately called over the man's head to the rest of the workers, in clear Arabic: "How much have you paid this agent? He's robbing you. Deal with the kibbutz directly and you'll get your full wages without lining his pockets!"

He was surprised to hear his own words. Something had happened. Three years ago, he wouldn't have cared. The words he'd spoken were the words of Bela Hesshel in 1923. He could feel real, warm blood rush to his head, and that head rang with the stupidity of what he'd done, and at the same time he wanted to run straight to the field, find Leah, and thank her from his heart for making him himself again.

Later, of course, he'd get a talking-to. Where had he been, these three years? Didn't he know the circumstances? It wasn't as if this was something they had just discovered, after all, or something the men in the village didn't know. Yet all the while, through Dori's tongue-lashing, and Nathan's, Bela did not let go of what he'd felt when he'd turned on the man and addressed those laborers. He didn't let go of it until that night.

OR THAT WAS THE NIGHT OF the worst raid they had seen in years, not so much a raid as an outright attack. A strong force rushed the gate and knocked it down, and Tilulit mobilized its own defense so swiftly that one moment, they were in bed and the next, rifles found their way into everybody's hands, including Bela's, and Leah took up her own. The clinic caught on fire that night, and so did the dining hall. Children hid in the root-cellar, sleepy and confused; Bernadette watched over the entrance of that cellar with a pistol.

Nathan Sobel radioed for help from Beit Shemesh, and Yosef was among those who came with fresh ammunition. Dori, paralyzed by the loss of the clinic, felt as though she herself were in flames. She stood as the wounded were brought to her, among them Gezer, Bernadette's son, a grown man now but still a boy to her, and she wanted to slap herself over and over, come to her senses, and at the same time she wished she could cross over into such a state that nothing would be expected of her.

But of course, Dori did come to her senses, and once that happened any grief she felt was lost in work. She gave orders to anyone close by; she flagged down any jeep to take the worst of the wounded to Beit Shemesh; she worked so hard that her consciousness fluttered above her like a hummingbird and she thought: If Bela and I had had a child, that child would have been fighting like Gezer; that child would be dead.

Just before dawn, they found three bodies in the gully. Two were Arabs, a young stranger with the beginnings of a mustache and an older fellow with a square jaw whom everyone at once recognized as Kamil, the son of one of the most prominent men in Taell al-Taji. The third was one of the newcomers from Kiev, Dmitri, a bright, sardonic, industrious boy who'd taken the name Ezra.

They knew they would bury Ezra in a graveyard they'd begun ten years before when Tibor had died of food poisoning. It had five graves in it now. There was some talk about what to do with the bodies of the Arabs, and they were laid out by the gully-bank. Before they could come to a decision, a truck appeared, and in the passenger seat was the agent. He got out, ran a handkerchief across his forehead, and took a few steps towards the dead men. He stood with his hands behind his back.

"A disaster," he said.

Somehow, it was assumed that the agent would take the bodies, but the back of the truck swayed a little on its tires, and from its depths came a pounding and a steady hum. Then everyone knew at once that it held eighteen men, that he'd come, as ever, with his quota for the harvest. As that sank in, a cry came out: "Open the truck!"

It had come from Boaz, once Boris, whose brown hair had turned blond, but who had regressed into ram-rod anxiety. He pushed his way towards the agent, shoved him against the back of the truck, and cracked his head against the door.

"Let those men out! You'll turn on the gas and they'll all die and we won't know where to bury them! Let them out!"

They pulled Boaz off, and he stumbled back a few steps, caught his balance, and mumbled an apology. The agent kept his head low as he got back into the truck and drove away.

$\mathcal{T}$HAT WAS THE END OF USING hired labor. To get the harvest in, they had to work half-through the night, and sometimes they pitched tents on the field, as in the first days of Tilulit. Bela held Leah close under the blanket, and sometimes she'd laugh and say that he was suffocating her, but he could not let go. He'd had such a strong premonition that he'd lose her the night of the battle that he had to keep his hands on her chin, her breasts, her hips, her bottom, and she would slip her own hands between his thighs and say, "I'm here."

Because they were so short-handed, Bela had to work beside them, and though it was hard for him to take the bending and to hold too much weight, he soon discovered that he had some skill as a foreman. He realized how much he'd missed getting dirt all over his face and under his fingernails, the rhythm of the olives hitting the buckets, the sheets of canvas on the floor. Leah combed leaves and twigs from her hair at night, and one day she said something astounding.

"Your family's still alive."

Bela wasn't sure what to do with what she'd said. He picked up a few twigs that had fallen from her hair, and rolled them around his hands before he asked, "How do you know?"

"Your sister's husband lost his factory, and she's not working at the hospital, but so far there haven't been deportations in Szeged. That will change," said Leah.

"Why didn't you tell me before?" Bela asked her, and at once regretted the question because it couldn't help but come out as an accusation.

"Because there's another side to it. I found out more. My mother's dead. She died three years ago. There were witnesses. She was shot and thrown into a mass grave outside of Kiev, maybe a month after I ran away. And my father—" She paused, and pulled that comb through her hair with a hand that suddenly shook. "Father died just six months ago, after the Ukraine was liberated."

She broke off then and let the comb fall, not crying but not able to go on. Bela pushed in next to her and brushed her hair out of her eyes.

She said, "As far as he was concerned there was never even a war. He was still a prisoner in some logging camp and he came down with a fever and that's how he died." She leaned her head on Bela's shoulder, and said, "Look, soon the war will be over, but there are some things that just go on and go on. My father wasn't a Jew, even if he was born a Jew. He was a Communist," she said, and the past tense forced itself through a thickness in her throat. "And maybe he died a Communist. He was arrested when I was so young that I couldn't help but be ashamed. What did I know? They told me he was a spy, and I thought about all the people from France and Spain in our apartment. I wanted to change my name to something very Russian, something unmistakable. I called myself Grushenka for years. Until I met you."

Bela said, "And now you're Leah?"

"Now I'm Leah," Leah said. "And this is what Leah will do. Amos and I are going to take some of the olives to the cooperative in Tiberious tomorrow, and I'll talk to some people I know. You've got contacts in Budapest?"

Bela nodded. "Old friends. Most of them stopped writing years ago, but they won't be so hard to trace. My God, Leah, all of those girls who wrote me letters, they must all have husbands and children by now."

Almost casually, Leah asked, "What about Nora?"

Bela looked at his wife's face and was stunned to see a ghost of her old impassivity. He said, "Yes, Nora too."

*T*HE NEXT MORNING, LEAH AND Amos loaded the truck with bins of olives and drove off to the cooperative. It was not Tilulit's best harvest; they felt the labor shortage. During those weeks, other parts of the kibbutz had suffered; the chicken coops needed a cleaning, one of the milking machines broke, and the children, who'd been recruited for the fields, had a hard time getting used to the inside of a school-room again.

Bela was teaching Arabic to five restless, handsome boys and girls, not quite old enough to join the British army, but the right age for the Palmach. They had all taken part in the defense of Tilulit the month before, and one of them, Gezer, had only recently removed the splint from his arm. His hand was still bandaged. He couldn't write.

"I don't care if I can't copy it down," he said to Bela. "You promised us the alphabet."

"My own strength is spoken Arabic," said Bela. "To be honest, you probably won't be writing much Arabic in your life."

Gezer said, "You always accuse us of being too practical, and when we want to learn something for its own sake you discourage us."

What did that boy think he would do with written Arabic? Forge military documents? Bela gave in and covered a chalk-board with Arabic characters, and as he watched these serious young people try to reproduce the curls and dashes, he suddenly found himself turning them into altogether different figures, the half-Hebrew of that old seditious leaflet, conscious that he was engaging in a kind of sabotage, or a private joke. He'd covered half the board when someone ran in with the news.

The truck had been waylaid four kilometers west of Tilulit. They found it with its windshield smashed, and two vats of olives spilled out on the road. Amos was dead behind the wheel with a clot of fresh blood still on his temple. Of Leah, there was no sign.

The search began at once: Gezer took part, and Boaz, and the red-haired bully who'd lost his limp and become a good strong farmer, and Bela himself was there, of course, though he hung back with Dori because no one wanted him to be the one who'd find her.

Dori held Bela's hand. The afternoon gave way to evening and the hills darkened and disappeared. Dori felt Bela's terror flow up through his hand, and she knew that she could not say anything to comfort him. She held a flashlight, but she didn't turn it on as they walked some distance from the road. Occasionally, someone would send up a flare, and then Bela would give a cry that was like a knot in her gut, a cry of complete helplessness.

It wasn't until morning that they found her, only a kilometer away from the kibbutz, well off the road. Bela at first thought they were mistaken, and he whispered, "It isn't her. Look in the water. She drowned there, I know she drowned."

The others examined the body. Leah had put up a fight; that was clear. The trousers bunched around her ankles had been pulled down by force and between her legs was a mass of dry black blood. There was a fragment of wood with a nail in it still clenched in her fist.

While they gathered around the corpse and tried to piece together its story, Bela looked at the fragment of wood. He ran his hand across the exposed nail, and then looked at that hand as though it had a message for him. Dori did not know if she ought to take him home or let him be. Yosef arrived, and she didn't even know he was there until he put his arm around her, and she took in his familiar smell of wine and coffee cake. His appearance and disconnection from the situation made her realize how much she loved him.

Yosef said, "You're shivering. Come back to the room. I'll make us some coffee."

"He was afraid of bridges," Dori said. "That always seemed funny to me, psychologically. After all, he was always the one who was our diplomat. He was always the one opening lines of communication."

"Don't say was. He's still alive, Arielle," Yosef said.

"I know, I know," said Dori. He pulled her closer, this fleshy materialist who wanted more from her than eternal friendship. Everything about the man felt moist and fertile, and when they got into the bed she'd shared for so long with Bela and they made love, she thought of pillows and of beer, of lying on the beach beside Lake Balaton, of playing with her dog Nikki as a girl in Budapest, of riding a bike with Bela through Margit Island, and then she thought of Bela staring at the palm of his own hand.

E NEVER TOLD THEM HE'D BE leaving the kibbutz, yet they all knew. First, he stopped teaching classes. Then he began to miss his shifts in the dining hall and laundry. Sometimes they'd find him talking on the telephone in a voice they didn't recognize: strident, ringing, a politician's voice. The calls would last for well over an hour, unheard of at Tilulit. Sometimes they'd discover him in the library surrounded by books they hadn't realized they owned, texts on the connection between Hungarian and the Semitic languages, and he would tell anyone who asked that he had been wrong to leave the seminary, that his work there was the most important thing in the world, and that he was going back to Hungary as soon as this business was over.

Perhaps two weeks passed this way, and then he caught a ride to Tel Aviv, taking only a change of clothing and a notebook. He left them with an enormous telephone bill, and it was perhaps characteristic of Tilulit that when they talked about Bela after he left, they talked about the telephone bill, and also about the state of his room, which took three days to clean.

A few days before he left, he was approached by two of the group they'd once called the orphans: a girl named Rivka and her boyfriend, Menachem. They were bashful and studious, and they had just turned seventeen. They'd observed the transformation of their Comrade and her heroic death, and now they felt drawn to the widower, the same big, friendly man who'd once hoisted them down from the flatbed truck. They found him in his room.

The air was stale and still smelled like Black Cat cigarettes. Most of the dried wildflowers had fallen from the windowsill and had turned into a purple dust that lined the floor. When Leah had returned, she'd scrupulously sorted out the clothes she'd hoarded, but somehow she hadn't gotten around to bringing them back to the laundry. As for the letters, they were spread on the bed, and Menachem caught Bela in the act of copying down address after address into a notebook.

Menachem spoke first. "We've been thinking about a memorial," he said. "Perhaps a plaque, even a statue."

Bela didn't look up from his work, and Menachem and Rivka looked at the letters from all over the world, with their tattered envelopes and beautiful stamps, and felt all their courage drain away in the face of the important work this old man must be doing. Rivka gestured towards the photographs: a thick, cracked tintype of a bride clinging to the arm of an enormous groom, a more recent picture of a dark-haired girl in an Arab gown with a mischievous smile on her face. Then there was the photograph of a woman holding a baby boy.

In spite of herself, Rivka said, "Oh, please, if we could only have a photograph of Leah!"

Looking up then, Bela set the pen down. "Get the fuck," he said, "out of my room."

Faced with this response, how could they help but obey, and they ran back to the dining hall where they told the other young people that Bela was a man of great feeling, emotionally honest, an authentic individual. Menachem and Rivka had never felt so small and foolish. What did the others think? They talked through supper, and then afterwards they had some juice and then some coffee, and then they took a brisk walk. They talked and talked, and then the redheaded boy took out his guitar and they sang until their voices gave out, and then they talked some more. They talked the way Bela and Dori had once talked instead of making love. Or did some of them make love? It's possible.

AVING LOUISA OVER ON THE
evening of Shavuot was unexpected agony. Rabbi Needleman admitted:
The girl tried. Yet the tension between her and his wife was undeniable.
They had never met before, and now they were deliberately thrown
together for hours, as Sharon tried to teach Louisa how to prepare the house
for Shavuot.

Part of the trouble was Sharon's Hebrew, which was stumbling and
abrupt. Rather than explaining things in the sort of detail Louisa preferred,
she could only say, "Don't open that."

Louisa would ask, "Why not? What's behind there?" in a peevish voice,
like a bored schoolgirl, and then she would add, "But how do you keep the
dishes clean enough? Your water isn't properly hot. I thought the whole idea
of kosher was to make everything clean."

Shmuel heard all this from the next room where he very deliberately
kept his nose inside a book. Meanwhile, he could also hear Naomi and
Shoshana, industrious and oblivious, arranging green branches around the
windowsills and doorways, and probably shoving Louisa out of the way.
Sharon didn't correct them as she should have, but only said to Louisa,
"Watch. Good girls."

"I can't tell what they're doing. Why are they bringing in those dirty
things?"

And so on. Once seated, the two of them seemed to have decided to say nothing to each other. Naomi prattled on about a friend's kitten, and Shoshana made Naomi eat all her beans, while Joshua sat at his father's side, discussing his day at school, and little Moshe fell asleep at the table with his chin buried in his tiny pieces of noodle pudding. All in all, it would have served as a picture of complete family harmony, if it weren't for the expression on his wife's face. Louisa didn't touch her own noodle pudding or sour cream and vegetables, but she did eat bread and honey and other things which hadn't come out of the kitchen.

They rushed through the Grace after Meals, and Sharon made it clear Louisa did not need to help wash up. This left her sitting alone at the women's end, with the stained, crumb-flecked tablecloth in front of her, pinned into place. Shmuel, Joshua, and the sleeping Moshe sat far away, and in the deep silence even Joshua stopped talking, and looked depressed.

Then Naomi stuck her head in from the kitchen, and addressed Louisa in Hebrew. "You want to see the kitten?"

Louisa looked as though she was going to cry. "Where is it, Naomi?"

"Next door," Naomi said.

Louisa said, "I would like very much to see it." She pushed her chair back and turned to Shmuel, and she asked him in German, "Is it all right? Am I allowed?"

"What do you think?" Shmuel asked, and at once he wanted to kick himself, but he added, quickly, "Of course you're allowed, Frau Gratz. No question."

So Shmuel watched Louisa take the hand of his youngest daughter. Naomi's dark hair hung in curls. She was a slight little thing with a sweet, round face, the image of Sharon when he'd met her. Next to her, Louisa looked like a rough, Teutonic giantess. Naomi led Louisa through the hallway and when Shmuel heard the door close behind them, he felt as though a weight had been lifted, and he pushed back his own chair and walked to his study.

He wasn't sure when his neighbors would arrive. There would be no more than six of them, and he'd already pulled books from the shelves and laid them on a table. Traditionally, the first night of Shavuot was spent studying the Torah. Lights burned until dawn, and then, in shul, the women scattered myrtle and fragrant branches in the aisle to keep them awake through the day of prayer and to refresh them for the second night, which would be spent reciting Psalms. Some time passed, and he was so engrossed in what he was reading that it took a moment for his eyes to focus on the figure in the doorway.

Louisa looked shaken. "I'm sorry," she said at once. "I'm going home now. I just wanted to say goodnight."

"Don't apologize," Shmuel said. "Not unless you did something wrong."

"Maybe I have. I don't know," she said. Then, as though testing water, she took a step into the study. "You and the men, your friends, you read all night?"

"All night," said Shmuel. He gestured towards an empty seat, though he at once had second thoughts. What would the others think if they found the two of them alone together?

Louisa arranged herself on the chair and asked, "What are you reading?"

"Why don't you guess," Shmuel said.

"It's in—is that Hebrew?"

"Aramaic," Shmuel said. "Commentary. But on something you know. Take a look."

Clearly, Louisa hadn't entered the study to try to read Aramaic, but dutifully she took the book and let her eyes pass over the characters. She asked, "Do all Jews know a lot of languages?"

Shmuel smiled. "Sharon only knows Yiddish. You've heard her Hebrew."

"I feel awful about your wife," Louisa said.

"Ah, she's no weakling. With four kids, you think she can't handle you, Louisa?"

Louisa fiddled with the pages of the book. "That's not exactly what I mean."

"You're looking at a commentary on the Psalms," Shmuel said, and he reached for the book. "Shavuot is the day King David was born, and it was the day he died. He was a singer, like you. And a composer, like your husband."

He opened the actual Psalter, and as he scanned psalm after psalm, he noticed how each seemed to lapse into a litany against the enemies of Israel. He paused at number Twenty-four, and read:

> *The earth is the Lord's and the fullness thereof;*
> *The world and they that dwell therein.*
> *For He has founded it upon the seas*
> *And established it upon the floods.*

Louisa stared across the table, and she seemed suddenly too big for the chair; perhaps it was the effect of reading too much Aramaic, or of nervous fatigue. He felt a sudden urge to ask her to sing. When had he first known that she was a singer? Had he been informed by someone in the camp, had she told him herself, or had he simply paid too much attention to the Keats and sensed in her a radiant song? *Kol Isha.* The Voice of Woman. The wise rabbis forbade a man from hearing *Kol Isha.*

Helpless, he said, "You must know the Psalms."

Louisa said, "I don't know anything, Rabbi."

"You shouldn't be so hard on yourself," Shmuel said. "This is all new to you."

Louisa said, "No. It's not new at all."

Her tone of voice shook Shmuel, and again he could hear, in it, a little of that singing voice. He sensed she meant more than she said. This time, he wasn't sure how he could change the subject.

"I've always done things wrong. I can't move without breaking something. I can't know my place. And nobody forgives me."

Shmuel said, "There's nothing to forgive."

"I don't know," Louisa said.

"Listen, listen to the rest," Shmuel said.

> *Who shall ascend into the mountain of the Lord?*
> *Who shall stand in His holy place?*
> *He that has clean hands and a pure heart.*
> *He shall receive a blessing from the Lord.*
> *Such is the generation of them that seek after Him*
> *That seek your face, even Jacob.*

He wasn't sure what effect he'd hoped the words would have on Louisa. What was meant by "clean hands"? Were clean hands even possible? Yet what he wanted most, he knew, was to pass the psalm on like a blessing. Let Louisa stand before Sinai, like the Hebrews in the wilderness, and if she would receive what God gave there, the way was open to her. She would be blessed. Shmuel might remind her, too, that King David was the descendent of a Moabite maiden named Ruth, a woman from a cursed people.

All of this he might have said, but Louisa spoke first.

"Rabbi," she said, "no one is coming here tonight."

Shmuel looked up then. He frowned. "What do you mean?"

"They're not coming into this house," said Louisa, "because I was here. Even if I go, they won't come, not tonight. You know, they left me on the sidewalk, playing with that kitten, and it was so small and warm and its heart was beating and all I could think was, why can't we be like the dumb animals?"

Her voice was ragged now, and Shmuel wasn't sure what he'd do if she started to cry. The whole situation was insanely inappropriate. He should not be alone in a room with this girl, not in an office at the camp, nor in his own home. She clearly expected something from him.

Perilously, Louisa went on. "I'm not a dumb animal. No one," she said, "will love me like that. For no reason. And no one will forgive me."

Shmuel forced himself to ask, "What is there to forgive?" And he thought: What does she want from me? At the same time he knew. She wanted love. It radiated from the girl like ozone.

"Christ would forgive me," Louisa said. "He forgives everyone. How do Jews live without that? What do they do?"

Helpless with pity and revulsion, Shmuel rose from the table, and said, "We forgive each other, Louisa." Then he left her in the strong light of the study, trembling and isolated. He hoped she would find her own way home.

 LEFT GAN LEAH AT SUNSET. Dori saw me off. First, she'd given me her own tour of the remains of the old kibbutz. She found us both pairs of high boots, which allowed us to tramp through the mud without fear. There wasn't much to the old Tilulit, no chicken coop, certainly. The children's dormitory was the only building that hadn't been bulldozed to make way for vineyards. "Good soil for grapes," Dori said. "You'd think, all us Hungarians, we would have figured that out years ago. But then again, we didn't have the valley or the other fields back then."

We watched the end of the children's show, a comic pantomime where a fat girl with one gigantic ash eyebrow was clearly imitating Nathan Sobel, and there was a lot of business with a milking machine and a carrot that I couldn't understand. We must have missed some sort of harvest-dance. Grains of barley still littered the stage.

The boy who'd offered the ride at lunch must have had second thoughts, because he seemed put out. He spoke Yiddish and had been less than two years in this country, but that didn't keep him from acting as though he were doing me the biggest favor in the world. By the time Dori and I made our way back to the parking lot, he had the motor running, and stood by the passenger door with a smirk on his face. Dori gave him a cuff behind the ears and said something to him in Hebrew, which she translated, for me, into Hungarian. "I told him you were related to Hannah Szenes."

I smiled. "That ought to keep his mouth shut."

"Nora," Dori said, "are you still going to look for him? Because you probably could find him if you went through the military. He was on active duty, last time I heard from him, and I'm sure he's still in the reserves. I'm surprised your friend didn't suggest it."

My friend? I realized she meant Levin. Levin was home by now, eating a dairy supper with his daughter and his wife. He would look in the next day, surely; how could he not? He'd wear his wrinkled shirt and trousers, with his steel-wool hair brushed back, and his thick eyebrows making him look ironic whether he wanted to or not. Maybe he'd take my arm as he led me to his office, and after that something closed on my imagination like a trapdoor, and I said to Dori, "If I was going to look, I'd need to know his new name."

"All those years," Dori said, "he wrote you as Bela, and no one else called him Bela. He must have wanted there to be someone left in the world who called him that. But I think I'd tell you his name now, if you'd ask."

Even as she gave me a kiss goodbye, I wasn't sure if I would ask that name. If I had his new name, I would have my cousin, and against that having, something, again, closed like a trapdoor. I felt blind panic for a moment as Dori released me and I climbed into the passenger's side of the car.

It was a small car, and smelled like horse-manure, or more likely the boy smelled like horse manure. He was a skinny boy, with no chin, buck teeth, and a long, hooked nose. He hadn't smirked since Dori had given him the line about Hannah Szenes. In Yiddish, he asked: "How far?"

"Less than an hour," I said.

"Ah good. I'll make it back before the party then, if the car holds out." He gunned the accelerator, and the bones of the automobile gave a shake. "You ever pray?"

I shook my head.

"Learn to pray now. It wouldn't be funny for either of us if this broke down in the middle of nowhere. Especially after dark. You get the creeps near all those empty villages."

In fact, as twilight deepened, the moon threw light on clusters of houses scattered among the hills.

"Villages without people," the boy said.

I asked, "Where are the people?"

He shrugged and said, "You're the people, the new ones coming here. But the trouble is, most of you don't want to be out in the country. You want your buses and your hat shops and your tobacconists. Not you, I mean," he said, turning a little in his seat. "I'm talking about the others, the *sabonim.*"

I asked him, "What is this *sabonim?*"

"The word means *soap,*" he said, showing some teeth. He shook his head. "Like the soap the Germans made out of the ones they gassed. What can you do but make a joke? I was in Treblinka. I know it was no joke. But we can't all be Hannah Szenes. We can't all die under torture. And if we go on and live, they think we're soap anyway. Pretty good joke, huh?"

"Pretty good joke," I said. I reached into my bag and took out the last of my Lucky Strikes. I could tell this young man wanted me to offer him one, but what was I supposed to do, break it in half? I had some trouble lighting up, what with the wind coming through the car window, and I cupped my hand around the match and sucked the flame in with all of my strength before it turned to smoke.

In the accumulating silence of the car, I took that cigarette between my fingers and its far end was a point of light, unreachable, yet close enough to singe my fingertips. Time thickened; how long could one cigarette last? Where would I be when it was gone? When we reached the camp, the boy gave me a nod. *"Goot Yawntev,"* he said. He didn't pull into the gate, and the minute I was out the door, off he went without looking back to see if I'd reached the barrack. Maybe he didn't think the gesture necessary. After all, what was it to him whether I lived or died?

It must not have been very late when I got back from Gan Leah, but nothing stirred. In fact, the whole of the transient camp felt deserted, like one of the villages without people, or like a cemetery. Somehow, I could not bring myself to go inside the barracks. It would mean opening a door and stepping into the dark, and I didn't have the strength. There was a cinderblock under a floodlight, and I sat on it, untied my hat, set it on my knees, and waited for I do not know what.

I felt dry heat behind me. I didn't want to turn around, but then the voice: *"Nagymama, Goot Yawntev.* You enjoyed your field trip?"

"Berkowitz," I said, not turning to look at him, "I have nothing to say to you."

"Too bad. I like a little lively conversation. *Gyere ide, Nagymama.* Come on. I've got a fire going." He gave my shoulder a tug, and I gave way and faced him. He was still wrapped in his leather jacket, with the fur hat pulled down low. His sour, cunning face glistened with sweat.

I said, "I'd sooner sit here. Too hot for a fire."

"Sajnos. Too bad. Those little girls from Transylvania are sorting through a few odds and ends," said Berkowitz. "Including something that might interest you." Now he gestured towards a faint shimmer past the barracks. "Cleaning house. They found a nice home at a religious kibbutz. Excellent human material."

"Soap," I said.

Berkowitz gave a powerful snort, and with both hands he wrenched me from my cinderblock. I resisted enough to feel a little rattled, and the cement grazed my hip. "Come on, *Nagymama.* Don't you want to say goodbye to those little *édes lányok?"*

"Sweet girls? What's your idea of sweet?" I asked him. Yellow light played off his jacket folds and his torso shimmered and blurred like butter in a pan. "I'm worn down, Berkowitz. I'm in no mood for sentimental farewells."

"They want to say goodbye to you," Berkowitz said, "and also, we have to have a talk, we should have had a talk long ago, because I need to know your intentions."

I managed to ask, "My intentions?"

"Don't sound like such a Jew with the questions. I mean your intentions." He stopped me short, pushed me at arm's length, and raised his hat a little, freeing his eyebrows, which stood up like a ruff. "I mean, why are you farming her out to such small cheese as rabbis and orange-pickers?"

I felt wary. "You've been following her?"

"How much time do you think I have? Her comings and goings are well-known."

Now I could see the ash-can and its lip of flame. Perhaps ten of the Transylvanian girls surrounded it, chattering in Hungarian and poking through crates and greasy paper sacks.

"Look," Berkowitz said, "take it or leave it."

"Leave what?" I asked. The fumes from the fire were thick and sour. One girl pulled out a pair of cotton bloomers.

"You know what. What they found," Berkowitz said.

What were those girls sorting through? Pages from magazines fluttered past, and on each was a picture of a blond woman with a serene smile. Then there were stockings dumped from a cardboard box, white cotton stockings from the charity bin, the ones that had been on Louisa's legs the day she'd found me there at Zalaegerszeg. I drifted past Berkowitz, drawn towards the items floating from that box: ticket-stubs, locks of fair hair, more bloomers, white, off-white, a clear horn comb, and there it was, unfolded, light and almost in pieces like the petals of a daisy, and by then I was close enough to catch it. So faint the type, if I hadn't known, I wouldn't have been able to read: *Das gibts doch nicht! Wann? Wo?*

One of the girls tried to grab it from my hand, but I stepped away in time and read those two lines of German. Below it was an address in an exact handwriting I recognized.

Close to my ear, the voice of Berkowitz. "You must have known."

My hands were shaking so hard that I couldn't at first read that writing. What was the address? It had been half-torn and I knew I would not be able to see it by this light.

"Where do you think she's been going? To pick oranges? No, you've known. And you've let it go on. Even this, she's taken from you."

The girls seemed to have forgotten about the telegram. To them, it was worth no more than everything else they'd stolen from Louisa, the undergarments, stockings, ticket-stubs, and bits of hair pulled from her brush, the images of her they'd found in magazines, all of which they burned with the other remnants of their childhood: sheepskins, tubes of cheap lip-stick, the limbs and heads of all those dolls.

I said, "I owe her my life."

"No, you don't," said Berkowitz. "There's something you're not telling."

"I owe her my life," I said again, and the soft, dark heads of all those girls bobbed close, and looked, to my mind, like the heaps of coal in the cellar where I hid through the siege of Buda, and the fire, too, put me in mind of that cellar, where by February I was in danger of freezing to death, but couldn't light a fire.

"Wash your hands of her," said Berkowitz. "She'll come back tonight, so innocent. What ties you to her? Wash your hands of her."

Never had his Hungarian sounded so rhythmic. Lulled to the point where I could hold the telegram open, I read the return address at last: *M. Lorenz LTD, 310 Hillel Street, Haifa.*

Then, almost as an afterthought, his new name: *Jonah Histaresh*

I heard myself say, "I wash my hands of her."

That was all I said. I made no promises. I signed no papers. And I didn't get a thing from him then, not so much as another cigarette. A wind blew through me, cold, from nowhere. Somehow I took a few steps forward and there I was in front of the administrative office, dark now, and padlocked, and it was a cool, ordinary night in June. I turned around, and there was the ash-can, smoking. One of the girls still stood there, looking at me through the hair in her face. She held a burnt stick. The rest seemed to have disappeared.

And Berkowitz was gone. With the sense of grasping at air, I closed my hand around that telegram, and when the paper crackled, I smoothed its folds and read again: *Nora: I don't believe it. When? Where?*

Then that name I must have thought belonged to a postmaster: Jonah Histaresh. Yet in those words I heard the voice of my *Borzas Medve,* the shaggy bear who'd hold me upside down as I plucked, from the tree, the sweetest apricot. There was the address in my hand.

"My cousin," I said, to no one in particular, "likes little girls."

The words deepened that chill that hadn't left me, and I longed for that coat I'd lost, the one Adele had given me on my wedding day. It had been such a good, soft lamb's-wool coat, and now it was gone.

"Go to him," I said, as though Louisa could hear me. Or was I talking to myself? I was face-to-face with that welcome I'd convinced myself my cousin wouldn't give me. I could go that night. I'd find him and he would crush me to him, clumsy and overwhelmed. He'd welcome me; I had the telegram in my hand.

Why did I sit on the stoop of that administrative building without so much as a cigarette to keep me company? All of this time, she'd known, maybe she'd seen him, and now I could see him too, yet I did not move.

I could not throw myself at Bela's feet. Once I had thrown a box of letters there, and come to grief. Now he had met this little girl, Louisa, the one who had saved my life. Why did I send her in my place? What was I afraid of?

IVE YEARS AGO, IN MARCH OF
1944, Gabor died. He died along with many young men pulled from trams or
found in train stations or airports in the days after the Germans invaded
Budapest. Now that the war was clearly lost, Hitler was afraid that Hungary
would make a separate peace with Britain and America; thus, by March, he
took a firmer hand. That spring, the Germans would begin the process of
gathering the Jews of Hungary's provinces for deportation east. The Germans worked against time, emptying villages before they could be liberated
by the Soviets.

Five years ago, in June, months after Gabor's death, I put on the old
lamb's-wool coat, stuffed cigarettes, a comb, and my papers in its pocket,
and moved to a Yellow Star House. The house was in the Kiraly district, and
other Yellow Star Houses were by policy scattered throughout the city so
that Jews would be spared no part of the Allied bombings. By then, a lot of
Pest was rubble. The flat I occupied was not so far from Aunt Monika's old
place. The owner remembered me and said, "Poor Moni. She was a lady.
She'd die if she saw the class of people they've got here now."

Perhaps I did look a cut above the rest, as I wasn't hunchbacked under a
life's belongings, but almost at once I sunk to their level. There were twelve
of us in three rooms, with our elbows in each other's faces, bickering over
where to hang the wash or who got first crack at the bath-water. We slept in

our clothes because we never knew what would happen in the middle of the night. There was no privacy for changing anyhow, though in the end, modesty gave way along with everything else.

Nine of the twelve of us were women. Most had sons or husbands in Labor Battalions, some in Romania and some in Serbia. A few of the husbands had been in the Ukraine when it was liberated, and their wives kept a little apart from the rest of us, as though they had something we didn't. Though they'd heard no word from them, they never stopped speculating on when they would appear at the head of an invading Soviet army.

What I wouldn't have given to get out of that place, even for an hour, but it was safest to remain indoors. Curfew was arbitrary. Sometimes they would give us two hours to see a doctor or buy groceries, and without warning we would have to drop our bags and run for shelter for fear of arrest. Still, for all the chaos of those months, there were a lot of rules. A list was posted in the house lobby with restrictions on entertaining guests, shouting from balconies, and disposing of rubbish.

Those rules were a great comfort. We reasoned: Someone must have taken the trouble to formulate those impossible sentences and post the list in every Yellow Star House. We had heard rumors about the provinces, talk of Jews from Debrecen and Szeged being deported to some desolate part of the Great Plains or to a labor camp called Waldsee. A few of us began to receive messages from family who'd been sent to Waldsee: *I have arrived. Am well.* These handwritten postcards were at first reassuring, but when they began to arrive in great numbers, all bearing the same message—*I have arrived. Am well*—we did not know what to think. I received one from Adele, whom I hadn't heard from since winter.

One thing seemed certain: They would not deport Budapestis. If someone cared about how we disposed of our rubbish, why would they bother to displace us altogether? Maybe we could just sit out the rest of the war.

By summer, Romania had been liberated and American bombs blasted the roof off a church not far from the house. Plaster rained into our soup.

That soup was muddy and foul, full of pumpkin-fragments and tallow dumplings. Plaster might have improved the taste. We used teacups for bowls.

A woman who'd just arrived looked at me over her cup. "So where's your husband?"

I said, "East."

"Perhaps he's escaped and joined the partisans," she said. She wanted to cheer me up.

It took a long time to chew through one of those dumplings. I swallowed hard and said, "Perhaps he has."

HEN THERE WAS LOUISA. I hadn't seen her since the day of Gabor's death, and as far as I knew, she had moved back with her parents on Rose Hill. We were not in touch. Then, in October, I returned from shopping and found her at the entrance of the house. Non-Jews were not forbidden to enter a Yellow Star House. A few even had rooms there because they refused to be forced to make way for us. Still, Louisa couldn't have looked more conspicuous. She wore a warm blue coat I'd never seen before, and with her pink cheeks and her glossy hair, she might have lived on pastries and cream.

Without preamble, she came to me and said, "I'll take your bag."

I didn't reply.

"I'll take it up for you," she said. "Let me."

"Go home," I said to Louisa. "This isn't the place for you."

Something in my voice must have alarmed her. She turned pale. Then, with no warning, she tore the bag out of my arms and stumbled back with a strange smile on her face.

I asked her, "How did you find me?"

"I had to talk to you," she said. "I couldn't—"

I broke in. "You want the groceries? Take the groceries. There's nothing I can do."

"Mutti," Louisa began. "I had to see you, that you're alive." She was so much stronger than me that she could cradle that heavy bag of canned milk and potatoes in a single arm, and she approached me with the free hand outstretched; I cannot fully describe the heat and nausea that radiated from her to myself.

With all my strength, I pushed Louisa back. She stumbled, whimpering, and spilled those pathetic groceries onto the muddy sidewalk, and before she could recover, I fled upstairs where I wrenched open the door and closed it behind me, holding myself against it, shaking so hard that I could feel it rattle in its hinges.

N OT LONG AFTER THAT, NEWS came to us by way of a radio three floors down. Hungary had begun negotiations with the Soviets. We actually believed it was the end, that the bombs would stop falling and the Germans would leave and the Red Army would roll into Pest. It was so sudden and so dazzling that we didn't know what to do with ourselves. Some of the girls tore off their yellow stars. Later, I heard that in the labor camps the men threw down their picks and danced.

In fact, the news was false. That was the day of the German coup. Hitler ordered the current government of Hungary to be replaced by the Arrow Cross, Hungarian Nazis. There would be no more quotas or curfews and no more laws about collecting rubbish. In a month, maybe two, we'd all be dead.

By evening, I was huddled in a doorway somewhere near the Duna with my heart in my throat. Gunfire at close range is unmistakable, even if you've never heard it before. I pulled tight that lamb's-wool coat and was thankful that I was well-hidden because somehow, even if I didn't care whether I lived or died, my body disagreed.

I shivered; the lining of that coat had disintegrated into a few rags crosshatched by soft threads. I dug my hands into what was left of the pockets, and by then I'd grown so thin I couldn't even find my own legs. Then, something bit my thigh. It was a key.

It was the key to the padlock of Louisa Bauer's cellar door. I knew that because once I had a son who told me those things. On my face was an expression of mingled grief and hostility, and then that face broke like an egg, or like Gabor's head broke the day he died. I will not describe that death in detail now. Save it for later.

This much I will tell you. I considered the possibility that I could manage to make my way across the bridge to Rose Hill, to the house with the green shutters. I had never seen the house before, but it had been described to me. I knew the way. And what would the Arrow Cross make of this thin, pale woman moving steadily down the lip of the Duna River with one hand across her heart, the other plunged into the pocket of her coat? Let them make a corpse of her. She is already a corpse. She finds that cellar door, and she opens the padlock and crawls into the dark. The door closes behind her.

5

How WELL HAVE I DESCRIBED
the Bauer cellar? It was damp and lined with coal-colored moss. It hadn't
been used for some time, though an ancient heating vent led up to the grid
which, as I'd mentioned, opened below the pedals of the piano in the practice room. When the grid was removed I could fit head and shoulders
through it, though that head was bound to hit the piano.

In happier times, the cellar had held wine; I could make out mossy,
bottle-shaped impressions on the floor. No wine now; for comfort, I made
do with horse-hair blankets, and, of course, cigarettes.

All in all, not so bad. When Louisa discovered me that night, she leaned
over that grid with a struck match; her face was lit ghoulishly from below. I
noted changes the few months had wrought. Her soft, pink mouth had a line
down each side now, and her downcast eyes looked dry.

She didn't ask me how I got there. At first I wondered if she'd speak at
all. But then she whispered, "You can't stay. We're leaving Budapest next
week."

I said, "I'm not leaving."

The match spent itself. There was a little second-hand light coming to
the practice room from the hallway, and I knew she was still there.

I said, "I'm staying here, and I'm not planning to die."

Louisa's voice caught. "What can I do?"

"You want to turn me in?"

Now my eyes adjusted to the dark and I could make out a faint shine in Louisa's eyes, almost fear.

"You're not leaving," I said.

So gray and indistinct did Louisa look, so sick at heart, that you would think it was she, rather than I, who would soon be forced to live down in that cellar and wait for death. You would think she had something to complain about. I could hear her harsh, treble breathing. I thought: She'll stay.

And she did. I don't know how. The *Deutsche Reichsbahn* had sent her father east to help transport war workers, and her mother was preoccupied with ordering the servants to roll up the rugs, pull trunks through hallways, and throw sheets over furniture to prepare to move to the relative safety of Austria. Did Louisa tell her mother she had unfinished business here? What sort of unfinished business would keep a young girl in this house alone through that explosive winter? Perhaps she lost her in a crowded station, slipping away as the train pulled from the gate. Perhaps she feigned sleep in the back of an automobile, and crept out just before the border. I did not ask her. She did not tell me. Nor was she sought, I think. Resourceful girl.

The grate remained between us, and it divided her face into twenty-four squares, each of which held her fine-pored skin, the down below her ears, and her light hair. That face, seen from above, hung off her bones. Sometimes she would remove the grate to pass down food, water, or cigarettes, and once or twice I thrust my own head up, and that gave her a real scare because she didn't know what I would do.

Later, she'd sing. The piano was no longer in tune, and to play must have been torture for her, so I made her play. From below, I could gaze diagonally across her narrow, skirted legs up to a chin trembling and bobbing with the music. Sometimes she'd hit a note so false that she would pause and look down at me.

"I'm still alive," I'd say then. "Sing more, dear. Finish the song."

So she would.

"Schubert!" I'd call up. She would sing Schubert's "Gretchen at the Spinning Wheel."

My bosom yearns
to go to him.
Ah, if I might clasp
and hold him!

and kiss him
as I would wish,
at his kisses
I should pass away.

Then I would call for that song I knew well.

What is lost, what is lost
We can not have back again.

Then it would be more Schubert.

My peace has left me,
my heart is heavy.
I shall never find peace, never again.

"I'm still alive," I'd say if she paused to catch her breath or to steady her hands. "Finish those songs, dear. Give those songs an ending."

So she would. Afterwards, she would crouch to get a better look at me, to make sure I was a real person, not some voice emerging from a hole below the piano. It's God's truth: She wasn't sure. Yet I ate everything she passed me: bread, tinned meat, apples, bags of dried apricots. I smoked so many cigarettes that I could light each with the last.

"Sing more," I'd say. "Sing everything my son wrote."

"There's just one," Louisa would say.

"Why just one? Surely you know more."

"*Mutti,*" Louisa would say, her voice breaking, "can I get you something? Are you cold?"

"I'm thriving," I'd say. It was true.

So passed some weeks, during which my body took the shape of that crawlspace, wide and low. I defecated into a bucket that I passed up through that grate. Around this time the cold gave way to an illogical heat that nearly peeled my skin from my bones, and my mouth turned brown from all the cigarettes. They were, in some ways, the most satisfactory weeks of my life.

What had become of all the others in the Yellow Star House? It was in those weeks that they began the marches to the border. The eleven strangers with whom I'd shared the flat probably figured I was dead. At this stage, I never asked Louisa what she saw on the street, and she never volunteered information. It was during that time, as well, that the Soviets took Pest, yet I never thought about the war. Nor did I think of Janos, or even, I'll admit, of Bela. My days and nights, even my dreams, were full of Louisa.

The girlish, flower-like scent of her wafted over the heat-duct. As she passed above, through the dark stuff of her skirt, her bloomers, white and loosened, swayed before my eyes. I said to Louisa, "Sing again. You sing that song you stole from me."

She crouched, blinked down, and said nothing. She passed more cigarettes through the grate.

"You must think little of that song," I said to her.

"I don't think at all," Louisa said. Dropping her voice, and looking at me between her own bent elbows, she added, "If I thought, I'd kill myself."

"Would you?"

"Let's not talk about it."

"Why not?"

"What can I get you?"

"More cigarettes. Are they hard to get?"

"Yes."

"Dear," I said to Louisa, "don't go to any trouble. Stay here. Sing for me."

So passed October. In November, the provisions dwindled. Sometimes there would be a little bread with lard, or loose tobacco. Also, I saw less of her. This galled me. I found myself capable of swallowing enormous chunks of Louisa, as though she were sponge cake, and if she wasn't there, my being was like a jaw snapping at nothing. Also, when she was gone there was always the possibility that she would die and I would live, or that I would die and she would live, neither of which would have suited me at all.

So I insisted on knowing where she'd been each day. I'm sure she lied to me; I wanted her to lie. She'd recite her route through Buda in a whisper which would fall lower yet as she spoke, though nobody could have heard her. "There's a hospital," she said, "with wounded children. No children should be left here. It's not right."

"Why not?" I asked her.

"Because they're innocent."

"And where should innocent people go?" I asked her, staring up.

"There are safer places than Budapest."

"And those safe places, they're full of innocent people?"

Louisa didn't reply. Almost without a sound, but unmistakably, she let tears fall. She hovered over the grate and let her fingers dip through four holes towards me. I didn't touch her. The rattle of the foundations of this Buda house as bridge after bridge blasted away allowed me to resist such temptations. Still, Louisa wept and soon forgot restraint. Her weeping had so little power over me that I could wonder at how novelists were wrong, how tears make no one beautiful and involve secondary fluids such as sweat and snot and even drool, which soiled Louisa's blouse.

"Dear," I said as she wept, "what can I do? You're out there and I'm down here and there's nothing more to say. Did you bring more tobacco?"

Lifting her red face from her hands, Louisa said, "No."

"Well, find some for me. Don't soldiers have tobacco?"

"I can't take anything from them."

"Why not? Because they're innocent?"

Louisa didn't answer. She looked down at the dark spot on her blouse, and pushed her matted hair away to free her eyes. I could read her face, and maybe if I saw there anything but emptiness I would have let her go, but nothing I said seemed to really touch her; nothing could change her. The worst of it was knowing there was no limit to how hard I could push because she would always give way.

"Sell them your body," I said to Louisa. "They'll pay in cigarettes."

Maybe she did. She brought me packs again, and then I made her tell me what they did and where they did it, in their quarters, below the bridge, in the backs of the old Turkish baths. She told me what surprised her and what was commonplace, who entered from behind, who made her use her fingers or her mouth. As she told me these things, which might have all been lies, I smoked. Plumes of that smoke rose through the grate and filtered through her golden hair.

*S*HE COULD NOT COME CHRIST-mas week. She filled my hole with bread, jam, artificial meat-paste, and water, and then she backed away with her coat draped around her shoulders. I let her go then because I knew she would be back. In solitude, I ate the bread smeared with the paste and sipped the water. I felt myself return to myself, and I thought: She is really gone.

Yet what I felt for Louisa wasn't gone. It was renewable as blood, recreating itself, cell by cell. All I needed to do was let my mind wander a little and I would be back on Prater Street, in late March, the day I had my last encounter with Istvan Lengyel.

He appeared on one of the rare afternoons when Louisa wasn't in the flat; she had gone to find Gabor, who had been stupid enough to actually go play piano at the dancing school during the third day of the German occupation. I'll admit that the knock shook me out of a stupor, and given what had been taking place in Budapest in those days, my first impulse was to bar the door. I hesitated and called out, "Who is it?"

"Frau Gratz, don't keep me on the landing. I'll catch my death."

It had been almost ten years since I'd heard his voice, but it was just like him to assume I'd recognize it. There he was, tall, long-faced, and underdressed in a thin overcoat. Before I could think of what to do next, he'd walked inside, and with a sniff, shrugged the coat open at the shoulders and looked down at me through foggy spectacles.

He asked, "How is the girl?"

Speechless, I gestured towards a chair. He shook his head.

"No. The motor of my car is running. This is very straightforward, the way you people like it, an economic exchange. You know they'll never let him across the border as things stand. But I have some papers here—" and now he dug into an inner pocket of that light coat, and took out something thick, wrapped in a brown envelope. "For him," Lengyel said. "It's taken some time, but here they are."

Just like that, he held it out. I waited half a beat and said, "Professor, her parents—"

"Her parents are fools. They'd sooner lose the girl than make a scene with the police. She is completely wasted on them. An accident of birth," said Lengyel. He frowned and thrust the package forward. "You don't want a passport for him?"

"Of course I want a passport," I said. "We've been trying to get a passport for him since December. He's been at five different embassies. He's been—"

"You have no idea where he's been," said Lengyel. In the silence that followed, he laid the packet on the end-table, and let his gaze wander around the flat, which seemed particularly empty that day, with every blanket folded, every door closed, and a thin, early spring light filtering through the curtains. "So she's been here three months. Tell me, how does she look?"

Something in his tone made me reply, "She isn't happy."

"Funny. She's with the man she loves," Lengyel said. "Does she keep up with her vocal exercises?"

"Yes," I said.

"Good. That's a good sign. I think this will work itself out nicely. You see," said Lengyel, "she's very young. Young people are fickle. And I'm sure," he said, giving me a strange smile, "that your son will weather the blow. Isn't there something about Istanbul? Perhaps your son would prefer Morocco. I've heard wonderful things about Morocco." He said, "My motor's running. I think you understand the terms. Goodbye."

The moment he was out the door, I tore open the envelope, and there was everything he'd promised, the passport with a picture of Gabor I'd never known existed, everything not too crisp, a remarkable job. When Louisa and Gabor arrived and I showed the papers to my son, he looked as though someone had hit him hard, and his eyes sparkled in a way that looked a little dangerous. He said, "They're frauds. I'll die at the border."

I said, "They're probably your only chance."

"But why go?" Gabor asked.

As for Louisa, she'd remained silent through this conversation. The outing had exhausted her; she was still not well. She had no proper clothes of her own, and my tan dress made her look jaundiced. She sat heavily on the couch and watched Gabor leaf through the pages of the passport.

"Why go?" Gabor asked again, looking at me. He sounded almost defiant. "You don't think he's going to try to trap me? You think he's a friend of ours all of a sudden?"

"If he wanted you arrested, he could have done it months ago," I said, realizing this almost as I spoke. "He's obviously held off Louisa's parents until he could find a dignified way—"

"I never thought you'd call that old queer dignified," said Gabor. But I noticed that he didn't hand back the passport.

Louisa spoke then. "I don't have my passport."

We both turned to her. She spoke almost in a whisper.

"It's in a safe-deposit box. It would be hard to get it."

"Lu," Gabor said, "what's the sense in all this? Your family knows where you are. They wouldn't let you across the border."

"And they'd let you?" Louisa asked him. "You're the one who's a Jew."

"I'm not a Jew," said Gabor.

"Yes you are. I don't care how often they baptize you. I know exactly what you are."

"And I know exactly what you are," Gabor said to her. "Isn't that amazing? Hell, I can't stay here. And I can't use that queer's passport. I don't know where I'll go, except to hell."

He was still carrying the passport when he slammed his way into the kitchen and thrust his head under the faucet. It was the same head I knew, with the mop of black curls, the black clear eyes, the clever mouth. His shoulders spread with relief as the cold water ran between them. He'd had fits of violent rage, lately; sometimes I thought he drank too much, and sometimes I thought he'd always had those fits, but I had never noticed. I was seeing too much through Louisa's eyes.

By then, Louisa knew not to go to him. If she touched him, he'd slap her. I said to her, "Dear, you shouldn't have gone out today."

Then she asked me something surprising. "How did he look?"

"Him? You mean Professor Lengyel?" I frowned. "He asked the same thing about you."

"He did?" Louisa blinked a lot, and drew her hand to her mouth. "I think I'm going to be sick," she said. Then I had to take her to the bathroom. She must have eaten something bad. Everything came out one end or the other.

After I'd laid her in bed, I walked out to find Gabor with his hair still wet, sitting back on the couch and staring at the ceiling.

Once, it had been easy to talk to my son; now it felt like a risk even to say something flippant like: "Handsome fellow in that passport picture. Friend of yours?"

Gabor closed his eyes. "No friend of mine," he said. His voice seemed to come from someplace else; he might as well not have been there at all. But then he said: "Come sit next to me, Momma."

I lit a cigarette. They were harder to get these days, particularly since anyone in her right mind would be afraid to walk the streets. I settled next to my son on the couch.

Without opening his eyes, he asked, "How much money's left?"

"I don't know. Louisa holds the money. You want me to—"

"No, don't," said Gabor. He turned his head a little towards me, and said, "I want you to promise me something. Don't let her go through my things when I'm gone."

There was such heavy anger in his voice that I couldn't answer. Then he said something else.

"I smell smoke."

"That's me," I said. "Open your eyes."

"No," Gabor said, and he was suddenly awake and on his feet and running towards the kitchen where Louisa stood over the stove, burning his passport. Her face had a stoic expression as the burner singed the pages. Gabor snatched her hand away and slammed her to the floor, and she didn't cry out. She propped herself up on an elbow.

"Don't you see?" she said in a voice which must have reverberated at least a little from the impact of the kitchen floor. "I'm saving your life."

"Stop saving my life!" Gabor shouted. Then he scrambled for the passport itself, which was half-consumed and worthless. He thrust it in her face. "What the hell am I going to do now!"

"We'll get a real one, the real way," Louisa said.

"There is no real way!"

"Then we'll die together!"

"Oh fuck you! Die alone! I'm getting the hell out!"

He crossed to the door and, without putting on a coat, left the flat, and two beats later Louisa padded towards that same door in her slippers, thrusting her head through and calling, "Don't leave like this!"

Then she went out after him. Down the street, to the tram-stop, onto a tram, she followed Gabor, and who knows what anyone made of that girl in house-slippers, touching that man's arm and making him leap from the tram onto the sidewalk. She called:

"You can't leave me!"

"I'll leave whoever I want to leave!" Gabor shouted back. Where was he now? Did he even know? Near Nyugati Station, probably, because he could hear trains. How much money did he have in his pocket? Was there a freight he could catch? Floating towards him through the exhaust of a street full of automobiles was his wife, and she called through traffic:

"You can't leave!"

Now he didn't answer, and he started towards what he hoped was a side entrance to the railway station. There was a faint hum and the sound of signal bells. Or maybe something else was ringing as he pushed open those doors and found himself in the great cavern of the train-shed, full of coal smoke, oily heat, and soldiers. There were Hungarian soldiers, German soldiers, and the ghost-faced Jews with white and yellow armbands, en route to the copper mines.

Gabor took a long breath. Something like drunkenness had overcome him, a mix of fear and complete freedom. He had no idea what would happen next.

What happened next was that Louisa came up behind him, and grabbed his arm. "You come back with me."

Still with the sense of being in a dream, Gabor turned his head. He even smiled. "Come back where, Angel?"

Louisa had trouble framing the next few words, but they sounded like: "Come home."

Gabor removed her hand from his arm. "And where's your home, Angel of Death?"

Her face contorted then, and Gabor took advantage of that moment of vulnerability to walk, quite calmly, up track three, where a dull-yellow train sat in its own grease, stretching well out of the back of the station.

He walked so far that he began to believe that the train never ended. Was it occupied? None of the doors were open. Such an amazing thing, a train; it could go anywhere. All you needed to do was board. He swung himself onto a door, propped his foot against the body of the train, and gave the handle a tug. When he glanced over his shoulder, he wasn't very surprised to find himself face-to-face with Louisa.

Sobbing, she cried out: "After what you made me do—after what—you can't—"

Then his foot slipped, and he fell with a crack to the concrete, because the train door had opened from the inside. He rubbed his head, and saw the bottom of a boot hovering above his nose.

There was a voice in German: *"Fräulein?"*

Gabor rolled to his side and the bells he had heard when he entered the station pounded their clappers on his skull. He gazed up at these two towering figures: Louisa and an officer whose clean uniform trousers rose like the trunks of trees.

Did Louisa say: *"Helfen Sie mir, bitte. Mein Ehemann—"* or did she say, *"Bitte, mein Jude—"*

Pulling himself onto his elbows, Gabor tasted metal in his mouth, and found himself suddenly surrounded by young soldiers who had drifted off the train. They were looking down at him, and he could just see past their boots to the first soldier who was holding Louisa by the arm and trying to make sense of what she was saying. He asked her, *"Fräulein, was ist los?"*

Everything seemed filtered through molasses, the warm smell of those boots, the bells, the grease he tasted, and the way Louisa reached out towards him. Slowly, her face tightened into something he couldn't recognize as she shouted words he didn't know, and those words split the brown thick pool of his stupor with the force of a rocket, speeding, bright, electric. She cried out: *"Ich habe es verloren, mein Baby!"*

Was it then the rifle cracked Gabor's head like an egg? Or did they drag him to the tracks? Louisa did manage one more time to pull him towards her before the force of a bullet tore him from her arms.

*Y*ou've lost weight," I said to Louisa. It was January now. Buda was rubble. Her hair hung in her eyes and she had a way now of crouching in front of the grate and looking at me for a long time. I stared back, mostly silent, with the last of the cigarettes clenched between my teeth and double strands of smoke rising from my nostrils as from the nozzles of pistols. My discovery that I could say anything to Louisa had run its course. Now I knew that all words were the same as no words, and the more she wanted me to speak, the less I had to say.

She too said little. Mainly, three words, whispered close to the grate. "Let me in."

At first this took me by surprise, though it made sense. After all, the cellar was the closest thing we had to a shelter. I made no reply.

"Let me in, please," she said, as though she couldn't have easily lifted the grid herself and entered. I didn't tell her so, though even if I had, she still would have pleaded with me, "Let me in."

Finally, I said, "It's not your place."

"I want it to be," said Louisa.

"Why? What's your life worth to you?"

"Nothing."

"And you want to be down here? Why?"

"I don't know," said Louisa. Just then, a blast made the walls give a rattle and the strings of the piano sounded in a way I felt clear through my bones. She made to speak again, and I drew a finger over my lips. She drew two over her own, implying thoughtfulness. A hum came through her throat, a *lu lu lu*. She lowered her face close enough to the grid for me to see her eyes press towards me like a child's.

I slipped away to bury my own face in my hands. Convulsions of hunger, anger, and disgust passed over me, and buried in blankets stinking of myself, I thought: I am drowning, I am already dead, and she looks at me like that, wants something from me, and I want a cigarette, I want my son, I want my husband, everything at once, like light breaking.

There was no light. Even the bomb-flares died now. Yet the aura of Louisa's tenderness lingered, and I knew she was still gazing down, with those two fingers at her mouth, staring into the cellar as into a well which might show her a reflection. How much could I even hate that girl? I knew then: not enough. How much could I love her or anyone? I also knew: not enough.

No one can love enough. We are all cowards who can't look each other in the face or tell the truth. Then I thought of Bela and his beeswax candle burning, and I wept.

AS EVER, JONAH WOKE SLOWLY, coming to himself a little at a time, first the crown of his head, and then his eyes and nose and chin, and as he turned his face into his arm, he stretched his legs to bring the rest to life. His feet hit something.

"Mah ẕeh?" he whispered. He thought it was his neighbor's dog. Propping himself on an elbow, he rubbed his eyes with his free hand, and the gray hair on his chest and shoulders filled with light. Then, he saw Louisa.

She was curled at the foot of the bed, above the sheet, with her damp hair fanned across her shoulder and her hands tucked under her cheek. Jonah shifted his weight, and the mattress gave a lurch that woke her at once. She opened her eyes, stared up at him, and said nothing.

It was Jonah who spoke. "How did you get in?"

"It was unlocked," said Louisa. Her voice shook. She was clearly afraid to move.

"That was a mistake," Jonah said. "There are supplies. They could have been stolen."

"I haven't stolen anything," Louisa said.

"I know." Jonah rose from bed, adjusted the waist of his pajama-bottoms, and looked down at her. She sat up at last, but she wrapped her arms around her knees and gripped them hard as though holding something tightly enough could keep her from being forced out the door. "Louisa, you can't stay here. It isn't right."

"I couldn't go back last night. There were no buses."

Jonah believed her, though as usual, she didn't sound convincing. Since the first day he had met Louisa and had heard her story, he'd been struck by her inconsistencies and also by her undeniable sincerity. She had a face like a doe lost in the woods. He asked her, "So do you want some orange juice?"

"I want to work again."

That statement must have cost her something. She did not look at him. He walked to the cool place in the corner where he kept a pitcher of juice and some Arab bread. Mice sometimes got to the bread. Like most of what his life was now, he'd gotten used to it. He took his time about pouring the juice; he had a single stone mug and also a single piece of bread. Without considering the matter much, he gave those to Louisa, who accepted them. Her whole will obviously turned on what Jonah would say next.

In fact, Jonah didn't give an answer for a while. He sat a little away from his bed where Louisa ate his bread and drank his juice, and he considered what could be done for her. He'd hired her through the harvest and then managed to find odd jobs in the office, but at points it was so clear that he was creating work for her that he would have thought she'd be embarrassed. Now this. Why had he given her that bread and juice? Did it imply an obligation?

"It's Shavuot," Jonah said. "It's a holiday. No one works."

Louisa said, "I'm not a Jew. I can work."

She'd roused herself now, piping up in that soprano voice he'd noticed from the first, and looking at him more directly. She almost reminded him of Mouse. Her hair was in her eyes, and before he could stop himself, he'd leaned over and pushed it behind her ear. The gesture was intimate. She looked surprised, and so did he.

*H*E DROVE HER IN HIS SUPPLY truck to the new site, only five kilometers from his room above the office. She'd already made him late. Officially, they were closed that day, but work still went on because most of the employees were Arabs. The foreman, Adam, knew how to handle them, but Jonah tried to make a habit of getting there before the first worker arrived and leaving after the last went home. Ever since he'd taken the job from Manuel Lorenz, the regular hours had made it easier for him to sleep at night. Before then, there had been a sense of perpetual unfinished business. Now a day began, and then it ended; workers were called for and were delivered; oranges grew and workers picked them; barley ripened, and it was harvested. Life could be simple if he let it be.

Adam was a very good foreman. He'd emigrated from Iraq with his wife and five children in '47, and there was no nonsense about him. If a worker fell ill and missed a few days, he would be replaced. If anyone slacked, he was given a single warning before being told to find work somewhere else. Before coming to Israel, Adam had lived in a Baghdad slum and had never learned to read or write, but he knew how to handle men. He had the gift of consistency. Even now, Jonah was a little afraid of him.

It had been Manuel Lorenz who'd brought them together. When Jonah first saw a job posting in Arabic with the Lorenz name, he'd assumed the orchard must have belonged to the gentleman's son, and he was stunned to see the man himself appear in the office, dapper in a sports coat and light trousers and still smelling of cigars. He had seemed old in 1917, when they'd first met. He had probably been the same age then that Jonah was now.

"Good Lord! The linguist!" Lorenz said, paralyzed at the sight of him. "What on earth are you doing here? This is the den of the enemy!"

"I can't believe you actually remember me," said Jonah as he shook his hand.

"I can't either. But I do. Young man, you can't actually think we'd hire you to pick oranges."

"Because I'm seditious?" Jonah asked.

Lorenz gave a slight smile under his mustache. "Because, young man, you're too old."

It took little for Manuel Lorenz to convince Jonah to join him for lunch at a café down the road. During the time he'd spent in the military, Jonah had developed stomach problems, and somehow he hadn't managed to get back to eating properly. The white rolls, mushroom omelet, and ice-water seemed to all be part of being recognized by another human being, something that hadn't happened to Jonah for months. Lorenz was careful with him. He didn't ask too many questions. Still, the old man—he must have been over seventy—had an agenda. After making small-talk about egg rations and the gray in Jonah's hair, Lorenz abruptly asked a question.

"Look here. How many languages do you know, exactly?"

Jonah found himself with a fragment of bread and butter in his throat, and he swallowed before saying, "Depends. You mean fluently?"

"Won't need to be too fluent," said Lorenz. "But if you have more than Hebrew and Arabic, you have no business picking oranges. I've got a regular Tower of Babel in the office these days, with those *sabonim* from the camps and the blacks from Morocco and who-knows-where. If you're not planning on joining the diplomatic corps, I can offer you a job and a room."

Jonah took the job without thinking twice. He had been living at a boardinghouse so filthy that squashed bedbugs made a pattern on the plaster wall. His days had become completely shapeless. After his lunch with Lorenz, he was introduced to Adam, and the young man gave his hand a forceful shake. Jonah felt Adam's vigor and his force like a distant bass note, a call from afar.

"Boss," Adam said to Jonah, "it's about time the old man found some-one to take things in hand."

Lorenz clucked his tongue like an old lady arranging a match. "Ah, he won't want to be called boss. He's a Labor Zionist, a Founder. Lived in a Communist kibbutz for twenty years."

"I like to show respect," said Adam. "Now, boss, first of all, we need to get the ground rules in as many languages as you can manage. Arabic, Ger-man, Jewish, Hungaryish, French. You know them?" When Jonah nodded, Adam gave a low whistle. "You're sent from God."

Jonah couldn't help but remember what they'd believed at Tilulit about work being therapeutic. He'd spent the whole afternoon copying out a monotonous, awkwardly phrased Hebrew list into seven languages, and then he went back and smoothed out the original Hebrew until it could not be willfully misunderstood: the starting time, the oranges per bushel, the pay per kilo, the consequences of damage, the penalty for sabotage, the penalty for theft, the penalty for speaking with unauthorized personnel who might be saboteurs or trouble-makers.

Adam disappeared after the introduction, and by the time he came back, the sun had set, and Jonah was still working. Adam switched on the electric light. "Don't go blind on me, boss," he said.

Jonah replied, "Your eyes adjust."

"Have you seen the room? It's not bad," said Adam. "Used to live there myself before I brought my family over. Plain, but clean. There's even hot water."

Jonah almost asked: Are you implying I stink? He realized that when he'd left Tilulit, he'd left, among other things, the only people in the world who understood his private jokes. He rose and said, "Do me a favor, Adam. Don't let me hole myself up in this office. I want to be out in the orchard too. Don't worry. I won't pretend I'm nineteen years old. Maybe I could make myself use-ful somehow, do some translating if someone doesn't understand directions."

Adam didn't answer for a moment. He looked Jonah up and down, his gaze lingering on his left leg. Then he said, "You won't faint on me, will you, boss?"

"No," said Jonah. "I won't faint."

*H*E HAD BEEN HIRED WHEN THE orange trees were still in blossom. There wasn't much for him to do except watch the seasoned workers trim back branches, stake bent seedlings, or drink Turkish coffees in the shade. Lorenz had other enterprises: a construction firm, a textile mill, and wheat and barley fields. Adam passed Jonah by-laws, contracts, and business letters for translation, but he also kept his promise and made sure he got a little work outdoors.

"You can take the Pioneer out of the kibbutz," Adam said, " but you can't take the kibbutz out of the Pioneer, eh boss?"

Jonah shrugged. He wondered sometimes why he'd made that request. The sight of the orange trees in blossom caused him physical pain. One afternoon, he was applying pesticide to the roots, and a wind tossed a storm of those blossoms into his hair. He showered that night, and the rut of the stall was white with petals. He couldn't get the perfume off him, and though now there were no bed bugs, he turned and pressed his face into his pillow and still couldn't sleep. His knee throbbed. At three in the morning, he finally gave in, pulled up a chair, and propped the leg onto the windowsill. Something fell to the floor.

It was a military envelope. Jonah's first thought was that he was being called up again, though that seemed unlikely. He reached out to turn on his desk lamp and opened the envelope. Inside was a folded telegram addressed to a place that no longer existed: Tilulit. But who did he know in Bulgaria?

Out loud, he said, "It isn't possible."

Electric anxiety made his fingers unable to open the telegram without tearing it. He moved his chair closer to the bed and pulled the flexible head of the lamp towards him, and by the time he'd arranged things, he was able to carefully separate the page. The words were in German. *Bela: I am en route to Palestine with my daughter-in-law. Please advise. Nora Gratz c/o Central Postal Station, Athens.*

He read it again. Sweat from his hands stained the paper. Nora? He knew his mother and his sister were dead; he'd found that out a year before. He could only have assumed I was dead too.

How long had it taken the thing to get forwarded? I might already be here, might be walking down a street with that eternal cigarette in my hand and my sour little face observing everything with amused detachment. A wave of longing overcame him, and he read again: I am en route to Palestine with my daughter-in-law. So someone else had lived; life had gone on. When he'd last heard from me, Gabor had been fifteen. Could anyone possibly have married during those years?

He knew he should answer at once, even wondered if a post-office would be open that time of night. He pulled on a shirt and trousers and went out. It felt good to walk; it was something to do with all the stuff that filled him at the prospect of seeing me again.

He hadn't gone five blocks before he found himself sitting on a stoop with the telegram crumpled and his chin in his hand. My God, what was he supposed to do? *Please advise*, it said. What sort of advice could he give? The terror he'd felt when he first saw that telegram from Europe returned, and he ran his hand through his hair and thought: She'll want to live on the kibbutz and they won't have her. Not after what happened in '44. The people at Gan Leah wanted someone to blame. And would he be expected to go back, serve as a translator? He didn't plan to return again.

 E'D BEEN THERE ONLY ONCE since '44. That hadn't been by choice. It was by order of the Haganah during the War of Independence, when he had taken part in several actions called

Operation Broom. He had been stationed in the Galilee, and that afternoon, he'd been commanded to evacuate five hundred and thirty Arabs from Taell al-Taji.

It took a while. The soldiers tried to keep the crowd moving, and Jonah's job was to prevent a bottleneck on the bridge across the gully. The commander soon realized he should have parked the trucks in the village proper, but he had counted on the cooperation of the kibbutz where villagers could wait until the last of them could be transported.

The evacuation had been Gezer's responsibility, and he had asked for Jonah because he was supposed to have an intimate knowledge of the village. But that had been years ago. Now Jonah stood at the far end of that bridge as families piled their belongings onto the flatbeds, and he was amazed at how few faces he knew. He'd lost all sense of who was who. He didn't even know the young man Gezer addressed, a sad, dark, lean fellow who smoked a cigarette.

"Hael taefhaem," Gezer said in the Arabic Jonah had taught him. "It's for the best. You're all in danger here."

The man had already placed his two carpetbags in the truck, and now he stood in the sun, smoking his hand-rolled cigarette and shaking his head. "I can't promise they'll keep quiet. Because they know what you're doing. Do you know what you're doing, Comrade?"

Gezer whispered to Jonah in Hebrew. "He's a Communist. It's important that we get his cooperation. He's well-respected."

The bridge lurched under the weight of too many people with too many trunks and sacks and mattresses. Yet they would only be gone for a few weeks until the danger had passed; they didn't need to bring so many things. They would be moved to another village well out of the way, where housing would be arranged for them. When the war was over, they would return.

Jonah knew it was his responsibility to tell them all these things in plain Arabic and then to cross over and check the houses to make sure no one remained. Ahmad, dead for ten years, was buried in that village. His wife was still alive, but she had moved to Jordan, taking her children and grand-children with her. And who was this man who kept his eyes inexplicably on Jonah now?

He said, "You know what you're doing? You're creating a ghetto." Through his fine nostrils, he blew smoke, and the look he gave Jonah was at once defiant and resigned.

*J*ONAH SAT WITH MY TELEGRAM for five hours, until well after sunrise. First, the street-cleaners appeared and washed off the stones near his feet. Then, a few bicycles with bells passed by, and a small fountain fed from an electric pump began to spill its contents into a marble bowl. The cool air softened enough to make his trousers stick to his legs, and he knew Adam would wonder where he was.

The post-office had opened an hour before, and a line had formed already. Briefly, he considered finding some way to get to Athens to meet me, but at the same time he had trouble phrasing even his three-line reply. He had too many questions, and to begin to ask them would mean never sending the telegram at all. The woman who typed out the message had a friendly face, and Jonah said to her, "My cousin has come back from the dead."

"Maʒel tov," said the postal worker. "She's coming here? I've got people living with me now I never even knew existed. I wish you luck."

Her flippancy made Jonah all the more firm in his belief that he was happy I was on my way. Yet for some reason, she was the only soul he told. If Adam noticed a change in his behavior after that night, he didn't mention it. As weeks passed, and the oranges ripened on the trees, there was plenty of work for him in the orchard, and his life began to settle into the pattern he had hoped for: clear goals, clear head. Every day, he expected the informa-tion about the arrival. Every day, he made an effort to look around the block for an empty room where I could live. He wondered if I'd managed to learn

Hebrew. Perhaps I could do some typing and book-keeping for Lorenz. It wouldn't be so hard, finding a place for me in his life, so long as I didn't expect that life to be anything special.

The second telegram was forwarded through the military again. Jonah tore open the outer envelope, perplexed. Again, the telegram had been sent to Tilulit. Hadn't I received his new address? Or, he thought, sinking into his bed, had I received it and not believed it could be true? He felt a flash of something deeper than annoyance. Then, he opened the telegram, read the arrival date, and buried his head in his hands.

"My God," he said. "That was a month ago." He felt a stew of conflicting emotions, relief, remorse, anger, and an edgy knowledge that I did have his new address, that even if I hadn't used it yet I could at any moment appear at his door. There was, in him, an urge to flee and also to find me at all costs.

"Adam," he said to the foreman the next day, "is there an absorption camp nearby?"

Adam nodded. "We'll be getting some of them working here whether we like it or not. You'll have your hands full, believe me."

"Hungarians, any of them?"

"Sure," he said. "But blacks like me, mostly. All the *Ashkanazim* are too good to work with their hands. They want the *Aretz* to be New York City."

Jonah did not go to the absorption camp, but he found himself taking long walks through the business district after dark and searching the windows of cafés. Every time he saw a small, dark woman, he felt his throat contract. For some reason, he was certain that was how we would find each other, by chance, in line for the cinema or on a bus or under a beach umbrella. The half-hearted search went on for a few weeks, and one night, as he passed a sweet-shop, he turned to find a pale old man holding a strawberry ice-cream cone and staring at him.

"Bela Hesshel?" he said. Then, in Hungarian, *"Nem, sajnos fáradt vagyok. Az nem lehet."*

"De lehet," Jonah said carefully. "That was my name."

"*Istenem*, I knew your sister Adele. I'm Kalman Nagy. I met you maybe three times before you came here." He didn't seem to know what to do with his ice-cream cone, and he bent over and laid it on the cement before approaching Jonah tentatively to shake his hand.

Because Jonah could not think of an adequate response, he said, "You've got a strong grip."

To Jonah's horror, Kalman gave a high-pitched giggle and said, "That's what comes of hard labor. I was in the copper mines in Serbia. I never thought I'd leave a desk. You want a cigarette, Bela?" He pulled out a greasy leather case, and when Jonah refused, he seemed so offended that in the end, Jonah accepted one and put it in his pocket.

They sat in a café, talking for some time. Kalman hadn't heard about Adele's death, though it didn't surprise him. That I was still alive did interest him though, and he asked whether Jonah knew if I was still married. I would be looking for a husband surely. Every woman wanted a husband now, and every man a wife. It was the most natural thing in the world. At the DP camps in Europe, they were going at it like rabbits, everywhere they could find a stable surface, and now that I was in Israel someone would have to make an honest woman of me.

"Of course," Kalman said, "she'll probably have her sights on you."

Jonah rubbed his forehead as though someone had struck it, hard.

Kalman's giggle got the best of him again. "Well, you can't marry her. After all, she's your cousin."

"Excuse me," said Jonah, pushing back his chair.

Kalman looked stunned and horrified as though he were being left in mid-ocean, and he all but grabbed hold of Jonah's trousers to keep him there, but it was no use; Jonah walked off at such a pace that he was conscious of the pressure he was putting on his knee, and the pain spread up his thigh to the hip. He could have doubled over easily, but he forced himself forward, finally pulling himself upstairs to his flat and falling onto his bed in a state of nervous exhaustion.

The first telegram I'd sent was where he'd left it: *I am en route to Palestine with my daughter-in-law. Please advise.*

He folded it three times, and then he found the second telegram which gave the date and folded that one too. Both, he stuffed into one of the discarded military envelopes, and then he threw them in the trash.

He didn't generate much trash, and it took a week for his little bin to fill with persimmon peels and wrappers from cheese, but eventually, he emptied it into a dumpsite. The stuff in the dumpsite would go where? To an incinerator? You couldn't really get rid of trash, but if you kept your distance from trash for long enough, it would disappear. Same with the past, he thought. Same with what people wanted from you which you could never give them, and what people gave you, which turned to ashes in the end.

So THAT WAS THAT, AND THE harvest began, and Jonah had other things on his mind. The pickers were mostly Arabs, but a proportion were from the camp, and the two were often at each other's throats. Adam considered the Europeans the worst, in every way inferior to the Arabs. Jonah occasionally wondered if he was too hard on them or if his standards were artificially high, but what it came down to was simple: The Arabs knew the work and the Jews didn't. Worse, the Jews looked down on the Arabs, and they had reason, as their pay was higher, they ate cold chicken dinners provided by the state while the Arabs ate plain bread baked by their wives, and finally, they spoke European languages.

After the first week, Adam was in a rare bad temper. "Boss," he said, "I'll tell you, it's no wonder that Hitler tried to gas them all."

Jonah, exhausted from a day of simultaneous translation, could barely move his body into the cab of the truck. "Look," he said to Adam. "He would have gassed you too."

Adam shook his head. "I wouldn't have walked into the ovens."

Jonah said, "Sometimes you can't know what you'll do with what life gives you. Sometimes, it's better not to think about it."

Adam agreed, and he told his boss not to worry, that he had everything under control, and that Jonah ought to get some rest because he hadn't wanted to say anything, but he hadn't looked so good lately. "You know what you need?" he said to Jonah. "You need a little female company."

"So find me some, Adam," Jonah replied, too tired to even know what he was saying. The next morning, Adam brought Louisa.

*W*HAT HE ACTUALLY DID WAS approach Jonah, who was sitting in the orchard gate-house with a cup of coffee and a newspaper. He said to him, "Boss, there was someone at the camp who says she knows you."

Jonah lowered his paper. "At the camp?"

"A lady," Adam said.

He put down the paper. "Hungarian?"

"I'd say not. A real lady. Probably doesn't know a bushel from a diamond bracelet. So is it a go?"

"Is what a go?" Jonah asked, a little annoyed now.

"Can I make an introduction?"

Jonah raised no objection, though he had the sense that he was doing something dangerous, and there at the door stood a blonde girl he had never seen before in his life. She looked a little sun-struck and a little lost, and Jonah was surprised to find himself rising to offer her his chair.

"*Danke,*" she said, and then she put her hand over her mouth and said in Hebrew, "I'm sorry."

"You're German?"

"Yes," she said. "But I'm almost a Jew now."

"There are German Jews," said Jonah, in German.

Of course, she knew that. To be in the middle of this bewildering conversation reminded him of something that he couldn't quite place. He turned over an empty bushel and sat, taking a better look at her. She was a little puffy around the eyes, and her hair was actually not blonde but light brown. He wasn't mistaken. He had never seen this girl before.

He wasn't sure if he should address her in Hebrew or German, and he finally settled on Hebrew, though it felt artificial. "This is a work site."

She said, "I want to work. I came here to work."

"But this is heavy, hard work. You're not dressed for it."

"That doesn't matter," she said. Then, she gave him a strange look. "You're not like the photograph."

Jonah gave her one more, swift glance which told him nothing. To cover his uneasiness, he asked her, "Would you like some coffee?"

"Do you have cream?" she asked him.

"No," Jonah said. "Just milk. I can't find work for you here. My foreman was wrong to bring you. Try the labor-pool. Maybe they could place you at one of the textile mills."

"But you're the one who'll help us," the girl said. "Why would anyone help a stranger? My *Mutter*—" she said the word in German, "—she saved my life."

What was it about this girl that made her seem so full of a story the way a tin is full of milk? Jonah knew that with a gentle push, what was inside of her would spill out; he felt his hand shake a little as he raised the pot to pour some coffee.

"My *Mutter* saved my life. I owe my life to her. I'm here," the girl said, "because our lives are worth nothing to anyone but you."

Jonah added milk to her coffee and handed the cup to her. "You're talking to the wrong man," he said. "There's some mistake."

"There's no mistake," she said. "I'm here for her sake and mine. I'm here in her place. I'm Louisa."

Then she began. She told him that while her whole world had passed away, she'd clung to me, that I was the only home she knew, that my people were her people, that my refuge was her refuge, and that if she were parted from me she would die. Jonah listened to what Louisa made of our story, with his chin in the palm of his hand, and once, mid-sentence, she stopped and asked him:

"Why are you looking at me like that?"

Flustered, Jonah asked her, "Like what?"

"Like that? Right at me?"

"I'm listening to you," Jonah said, and the answer obviously didn't satisfy her, but she went on talking until there was no more coffee left in the pot. Afterwards, he arranged for her to do some light work through the harvest. Adam looked conspiratorial, but he also didn't seem surprised that he sent Louisa back to the camp.

"Frankly," he said, "she's a little young for you, boss. She must be my daughter's age."

"She's twenty-two," Jonah said, "and she's the daughter-in-law of my last living relative from Hungary."

Adam nodded and looked a little tired. "So some Hungarians. All right. Look, if she's going to work here, she'll need to be on the books. What about the relative? You want him too?"

Jonah hesitated, and Adam took the opportunity to clap him on the shoulder.

"Boss," he said, "we've got enough Hungarians as it is, no offense intended. If you want a family reunion, that's terrific. Have it in a café. I'll bring some whiskey."

"I'm not sure," Jonah said. Somehow it was safer to leave it at that. He arranged for Louisa to be taken to the orchard every day and took no steps to meet with me.

He came close once. The harvest had ended, and now Louisa did light work in the office, filing and addressing envelopes. She had gotten into the habit of taking her lunch with Jonah. He knew it was inappropriate but also couldn't help himself. As he drank his yogurt, she would tell him more and more of our story, about how she had met Gabor that day and left her Schubert behind, about his lost song, treated lightly, and his new song, written for her sake, and about how he looked right through her sometimes as though he were angry but wouldn't say why. At points, she repeated herself or contradicted what she'd said a few moments before, yet two things never changed: I had saved her life, and only Jonah cared now whether she and I lived or died.

Jonah sometimes let those lunch-hours stretch, and as the heat grew more intense, Louisa's story took on a momentum that astounded him. There seemed to be no end to how much she had to say. On the crest of that story, his own past was like a little driftwood, not worth mentioning. Yet now he was a part of that story. He was a new episode, the cousin who was their final destination, a figure he could not believe himself to be. He wondered when she'd find him out.

It happened a month after her first appearance when she said to him, "I never sang for you."

"No," Jonah said. "You shouldn't, though. It's too hot."

"But Gabor wrote the song. It's all I have left of him," Louisa said. Then, she rose from the stool, clearing a little space around herself, and silence, as ever, rose around her in an oval; her lungs, those round, strong fuses, emitted light. She began:

What is lost, what is lost
We can not have back again.
It is like a breath we've taken.
We can not breathe it again.
It is like good bread we've eaten.
We can not eat it again.
It is like a heart we've broken
Or our own heart, lost in vain.

After she'd finished, she looked expectantly at the man who sat on the overturned bushel. She might have wanted praise or a kind look. What she got was a face like a mask. Helpless, she said, "I'm sorry."

Jonah got up and said, "Don't come here anymore, Louisa."

"But I have to work—"

"Work, then!" Jonah said, and he hadn't realized that he was shouting until his unfamiliar voice rattled at him from the walls. "Sing in a night club. Scrub floors. I'm not up to charity cases. What the hell do you expect of me?"

Louisa shrank back with her hand drawn to her mouth, and a strange hum came up from her throat as though she'd turned into a tuning fork. He wanted not to care that he'd hurt her. He could change his name, his home, even his nature, and he could tell himself a thousand times that he had been right not to take me to Palestine that night, that it would have been a false promise, that those letters had not addressed him but some stranger, that he had not run away, nor had he left his family to their death. He could even tell himself that I was capable of knowing all of this. But there were some things he could not face.

Before she left, he gave Louisa an orange. He pressed it into her hand before she left him and said, "Give this to your mother-in-law. Tell her it's a real orange, from Israel. Tell her it's all I have to give her."

*T*HE MORNING LOUISA APPEARED at Jonah's feet, he could have turned her out. Even as they drove to the barley field together, he wondered why he'd told her he would find something for her to do. She had caught him asleep, off-guard, and then there was the business with the mug of juice and the bread, simple things to give her. Somehow, the rest had followed.

But life wasn't simple. As they parked the truck, he noticed that there was a strange group at work that day, young Europeans chattering together in Hebrew and pointing to parts of the field as though they were preparing for a battle. Adam walked to meet them and said, "Pioneers. Jewish Agency sent them, God help us all."

Jonah frowned. "What are they doing working on Shavuot?"

Adam shrugged. "They'll get us in hot water is all I know. But they won't leave."

Jonah could already see what would happen. They would disregard all instructions, refuse to work with Arabs or make trouble over working conditions, and make life completely impossible. In spite of himself, he said, out loud, "Where do they think they are?"

He'd almost forgotten that Louisa was there, and she said, *"Eretz Yisrael."*

Jonah found his hands forming fists. "They'll pitch tents and plant things and eat what they plant, and they'll think it makes them new men, but in the end, they'll live in ugly cement houses with their radios on."

"They've lived in worse places," Louisa said, and it was then he took a closer look at those young men and women in their short-sleeved tops and saw the tattooed numbers.

Yet he persisted, speaking directly to Louisa now. "What kind of ending is that?"

Louisa looked up at him and asked, "Why is it an ending?"

E FOUND HER A FRESH SET OF work clothes and a sun hat, and he settled in to record-keeping, looking out at her too often. She was no good. The heat exhausted her. Barley grains caught in her hair and flax got in her eyes, and she stumbled over a pile of canvas sacks and landed, face-first, in the dirt. Watching her pull herself up and persist, Jonah fought the urge to intervene. Yet why sit there, passively watching her suffer? It was as though he wanted something in her to break down. Then she would know that he wasn't anybody's salvation, that he had

no wings, just arms and legs and a gut and a heart. He was a man. She'd climbed into his bed as though he'd been a eunuch. If he had proved otherwise and had taken her that morning, how would that fit into her beautiful story?

She approached him at the end of the day, and he poured her some water and made her sit down. He said, "You should go home."

Louisa held her cup of water in both hands and looked at him over the rim. "You mean I can't come back here?"

"No," Jonah said. "Home. Germany."

He thought she'd take the words hard, but she only gave a little shrug. "I can't."

"Your mother-in-law can take care of herself. I know you won't believe it, but it's true. She's been taking care of herself for most of her life, Louisa. If you let her alone, she'll be fine."

"Go home to Germany," Louisa said, as though she hadn't heard him. "They always ask me, why don't I go home to Germany."

"It's a good question," Jonah said.

Louisa blushed and said, "Don't look at me like that."

"Like what?"

"Like that. Like you think I'm lying."

Jonah turned red himself. He reached out and touched Louisa's arm. She flinched, and he felt a rush of confusion as he went on. "You're lying to yourself. You expect too much from this country."

Louisa said, "No. *You* expect things." She swallowed, hard, and looked down at her hands. "I can't go back."

"You have a mother and a father," Jonah said.

Then, Louisa's mouth turned up a little. "No. I don't. They think I'm dead."

Jonah said, "You're joking."

"No. They think I died in Buda. Bombs hit the house and they never tried—" She dipped her head low now, and her voice dropped to a whisper.

"I was ruined. I was better off dead." Her shoulders began to shake a little until she gave a hiccup so abrupt, it threw Jonah off guard.

He whispered, "Louisa, hush. You can't be right. They would have looked for you. They're looking for you now."

"No. They don't look for me. They don't want me. I'm better off dead to them. How could they want me back? They should have put me on one of those trains. I was ruined. Nobody wanted me." She paused to catch her breath. "And everywhere—all over Budapest—it snowed."

"Louisa, hush. It's all right."

"It wasn't snow, it was ash, and coal-dust, and smoke, first all those trains, and then bombs, and then it was just filth. It got into my coat, my dress—I had to throw them away. There's nothing clean—nothing. If I could have thrown away my skin, I would have. And my hair—I couldn't get the smell out of my hair. But men like that hair, it's so light. They'd always want the ones with hair like mine. Even later on, after I had no insides left, even when there was nothing there, they'd grab my hair and take me in. What choice did I have then?"

"You're here now. Don't do this to yourself. You're here with me now."

"Because I've got hair full of ash and a mouth full of grass," Louisa said, and she drew a hand to her throat. "It can't go down, but it has to because it's all I have. The leavings of the field, what paupers gather. At least they leave a little for the poor. That's what the rabbi said. You have to leave a little."

Neither could have said when they stopped the stream of words or when the words dissolved, and Jonah wasn't sure when he started to hold her, but he no longer cared, and couldn't remember why he hadn't done it long ago.

"I had to come to you," Louisa said. "What if she left me? I don't want to die alone."

"Hush," Jonah said. Why shouldn't he hold that girl? There were too many people in his life that he hadn't held and hadn't comforted because they'd died too far away, or because they had lived on but did not let him near them, or because he himself had been afraid. He was tired of being afraid. He said, "You won't die alone."

When she was in his arms, the past spun around them, a blur of flesh and light, and not for the first or last time, he saw ghosts; his drowned father, his mother and sister, his wife, passing across a bridge to a kingdom of exile, burdened under their life's belongings, slipping from his grasp. What could he hold? He could hold Louisa. And blinded by his own grief, as he held her, the light receded, dimming to irrelevance. Then it disappeared.

*S*OME TIME LATER, THEY STOOD IN the door of the gate-house with their arms still around each other. It was twilight now, though the moon was too bright for the stars. From far off drifted the sound of a mouth-organ and people singing.

Louisa turned. "Where is that coming from?"

"The Pioneers have made a camp," said Jonah. "They're dancing."

"Oh! Let's join them!" Louisa said, and she already started towards the firelight, breaking away and walking with quick steps. Her arms were raised, and her sticky hair rose a little from her back.

In his hand, Jonah held her sun hat. With a mournful smile, he put it on his head, and then he followed.

7

*T*HEY DIDN'T MARRY FOR A
year. First, Louisa had to complete her conversion. Rabbi Needleman found
her easier to talk to now. She no longer struck him as uncanny or mysterious
but as an ordinary young woman who served him tea Russian-style, in a
glass, in the kitchen of a drum-shaped cement house in the company of her
mother-in-law.

"Naturally," said Shmuel, "marriage isn't a sound reason for conversion
any more than wanting to convert to get Israeli citizenship."

"Naturally," said Louisa. "Would you like some apple cake? It's dry, but
I'm just learning to bake. I think you'll forgive me."

Easily now, Louisa could assume that people would forgive her. She
gave a slice to Rabbi Needleman, who agreed that it was dry but washed it
down with some of her good tea. That he ate in our home at all stunned me.
Louisa kept strict kosher, but how could he know for sure?

As for me, I said little. I refused the cake and tea and stuck to my own
coffee, looking past them out the window at the laundry hanging from our
neighbor's line. In a few hours, Jonah would come over and the two of them
would talk about the future.

I always saw Jonah with Louisa. It stood to reason. After all, the two of
them would soon be married, and to make a point of separating them from
each other would have felt absurd. Besides: Louisa was the one who always

arranged to bring the three of us together. She even organized our reunion. "He'd love to see you," she said to me. "He asks about you all the time." She said those things as though they were simple pleasantries.

This was back when we still lived in the camp, and on the appointed day, after Louisa left for work, I paced and fretted, sweating through one blouse after another, wondering if I ought to cancel, though by now there was no way to get hold of them, and in the cool of the evening, I planted myself on a cinderblock in the parking lot to wait. The road beyond the gate saw little traffic. Every once in a great while, I'd see a pair of headlights and feel their approach like physical pressure.

What would happen when the truck appeared? Would it come straight through the gate and barrel towards me like a steam-roller? Would I let it pass over me? What seemed most likely was that the truck would not appear, that they would have the good sense not to force a meeting that either would have taken place last winter or shouldn't take place at all.

I had once believed that when I saw my cousin, I would know why I was here. Well, now I would see him, and what great change would it work in me? At the very least he could see for himself that I was still alive. I could say, "Jonah, here I am at last," or would I say, "Bela, here I am at last." What should I call him? Who was he to me now? These were mysterious questions, and my heart bent just a little at the thought of addressing my cousin by any name at all, because a new set of headlights had approached the gate, blinding me briefly. It was the green truck.

The truck did not pull in, but idled, and a window cranked down. Louisa poked her head out and shouted: *"Mutti!* Over here!" She opened the passenger door from the inside.

I walked across the lot, all the while looking past Louisa into the dark, expecting my cousin to leap out of the driver's side and hoist me up into the cabin of the truck. But his door did not open, and when I was close enough to look through the windshield, I could make out no more than a shape behind the wheel. Then, Louisa yanked my arm and pulled me up beside

her, and the space between us was so thoroughly filled with her that I would
have had to climb across her to get a look at him at all.

Thus we rode, all three pressed together, myself, Louisa, and my cousin,
out of the camp for newcomers onto a dark road. Louisa leaned far into me
whispering something about where we were going, some fish restaurant in
Haifa that she and Jonah frequented. There was a pinch of silence, just long
enough for me to steal a glance across Louisa and see his hands on the wheel,
just a little too tight.

They were the hands I knew, square, generous hands. Yet they held onto
that wheel as though it were a life-preserver. Like a knife, it struck me. It
wouldn't matter what I called my cousin. He had become someone who
would never be close enough to be addressed by name.

O F C O U R S E , I S A W P L E N T Y O F
Jonah, but in the presence of Louisa, what we had to say was by its very
nature limited to what she knew, or ought to know. For example, there was
the matter of the letter Jonah wanted her to write her parents, letting them
know she was alive. I said to him, "You have your own letters to write. It's
been—what—two years since you wrote to Dori Csengery?"

Louisa laid a hand on Jonah's arm and asked, "Who's Dori Csengery?"

I felt Jonah's gaze on me then, hot and strong; he gave me those looks
often when the three of us were together, and I knew what they meant. I had
mercy on him. I answered as casually as I could. "She's a doctor."

"Oh," said Louisa. She touched Jonah's chin intimately and said, "You
think she could do something about your leg?"

"Probably not," said Jonah. He leaned back into the molded plastic
kitchen chair, and the urgency in his expression dissolved into tentative con-
tentment. He said, "It would take a surgeon."

"Then we'll get a surgeon," said Louisa.

"I've lived with it for long enough."

"That doesn't mean you have to go on living with it." Louisa spoke with absolute conviction. "Why should you be kept up half the night because you're too stubborn and lazy to help yourself? It's a good thing I showed up to take care of you."

This was Louisa's way of telling me that my part in her story was over.

OR THIS WAS LOUISA'S STORY from the start; she was its heroine. It was Louisa who threw herself into forbidden love, who saved my life, and who saved my cousin's life, I suspect. Yet what did she save us for? That question still remains; it has no simple answer. Now I will tell you what happened after I'd been liberated from the cellar, when I returned to Kisbarnahely.

What motivated this decision, I cannot quite say. It might have been the shock of Budapest. I faced it when I at last emerged from the cellar into the February sunlight. I still wore a horsehair blanket, and my face peered out of the folds like a mushroom. Naturally, the air smarted, and I couldn't take more than a step or two before sitting on a paving stone. Still, I hadn't had a cigarette in five days; need overcame vertigo.

It was impossible to get my bearings. The shape of a hill was visible under rocks and fallen beams, all black and white with frost, but the landscape didn't correspond with anything human; there was nothing to hang a gaze on, nowhere to go. All the while, I didn't know it, but parts of Buda were still under siege. In spite of this, I wasn't the only soul foolish enough to be out in the open. The Soviets had set up a communal kitchen and they doled out pea soup. How I managed to find a bowl and spoon, and how I managed to get even bread and cigarettes, is another story. Let me say only that by the time I'd found all of those things, I'd also been volunteered for a work crew.

Those crews were put together by the Soviets. A soldier in a white wind-breaker directed me to a wheelbarrow and gestured towards a cluster of old women. I think that's when I realized how I looked.

We were supposed to gather bricks and wheel them to a pit. It wasn't easy work, and without gloves, our fingers found it hard to close around the bricks, let alone pry them from the frozen mud. Each of those bricks had once been part of one of the houses that lay in ruins, and as we pulled them up, it was like emptying the ocean a drop at a time. We dragged the wheel-barrows through the icy slush. We'd been promised warm shelter for the night, but none of us believed it. Bundled, steaming with exertion, I lapsed into a stupor.

I did manage to light a cigarette. That kept me warm and got my mind working, but it also meant I had to pass it around, and by the time it got back to me, it was pretty much gone. I knew I had to get to Pest, where conditions were far less grim, or at least the dead had been buried. But that was a matter of getting permission and the proper papers.

I exchanged a few words with a wry little granny in a woolly sweater. She had more strength than I did and managed to keep up a steady stream of conversation, at the same time finding out my name, age, and hometown.

She'd come to the capital from a village near Sarospatak to stay with her daughter, and she'd been trapped in Buda all winter. Now her daughter was pulling every possible string to get them back home again.

"You think it's better there?" I asked her.

"There, at least, you can grow a little something," she answered. Abruptly, she asked, "Are you a Jew?"

She asked it in the same high, grating voice she'd used when she asked me the name of my hometown. I really had no choice but to admit it. She had already asked me about my son.

She pulled a bread and lard sandwich from her pocket and offered me half. She said, "You're lucky. Your people will own this country now."

 WO MONTHS LATER, I'D FOUND space on a train east. The cars were filled with Soviet soldiers who were all drunk before we even left the station. By then, I had crossed into Pest, seen what the bombs had left of my old flat on Prater Street, and served enough time in labor crews to get a small bag's worth of winter clothes. I even had a new coat with most of the lining intact. This, I wore, leaning on my elbows out the train corridor window, thinking how bare and blasted everything looked, even here. Then I remembered: I was on the Great Plains, where it had always looked bare and blasted in early April.

How strange it was, though, watching the towns pass, Cegled, Szolnok, Tiszaföldvar, some blown into gray rubble and some already half-reconstructed, with the mortar between the bricks sparkling. I disembarked, along with around two hundred soldiers, just outside of Szarvas. The sight of the suburban railway station brightened with a fresh coat of paint brought forth complex emotions. So did the mud. I hadn't tramped through this mud since I was a girl.

Kisbarnahely was some distance west. The convoys of soldiers passed me on the road without taking note of me. I don't know what I expected, perhaps some gentleman with a horse and cart who'd see me slogging along and insist I climb on board. I didn't give up hope until sunset, when I had yet to see so much as a tree, let alone a place to spend the night. Then I managed to wave a tin of beef to flag down a Red Army soldier on a motorbike.

He spoke no Hungarian, but the bike made so much noise that it didn't matter. With my arms gripping his waist, I hadn't time to wonder, yet again, why I was returning to my hometown. He shouted a lot of things in Russian, every once in a while shifting his weight so that the motorbike buckled like a horse, and I had to plaster myself against him to keep from flying off the seat.

"Staraja babas!" he called out: "Okay?"

Faintly, I said, "Okay." I arrived at an army base half a kilometer from Kisbarnahely not so long after dark, with a crick in my back, a ringing headache, and no idea what I ought to do next.

*T*HE LOGIC OF THE JOURNEY was as follows: I'd heard that the new authorities were returning confiscated property, and assuming that my mother hadn't survived the war, I was the heir to half of my uncle Oszkar's shop, as well as the house with the apricot tree. The brief, moonlit walk to the town center took longer than it should have because with every step, I grew closer to knowing the town held neither shop nor house nor tree.

Yet there it was: The steeple of the church. There was the town hall. They were intact and golden! As I walked on, the mud gave way to gravel, and I realized that the whole town square was brilliant with electric light. How could that be? More, from a distance, a breeze carried a sour smell, smoke from the brickworks. It was functioning as though the war had never been.

Even though the air was bitter-cold, I sweated through my coat now, needled with anxiety. Familiar house after familiar house gave way to familiar shop after familiar shop, Gyongyos Stationery, Sunshine Bread, the ice-cream stand. At the Kismacska, the windows were open. I heard mingled voices so close at hand, they might have been just at my back, and turning, I blinked wildly. Someone was beaming a flashlight in my eyes. It was a cocked-cap Soviet soldier who asked, in Russian, for my papers.

He was with another soldier who had his hand on a pistol. My documents were in order, but after the past year, who could help but feel a little rattled when you were asked to show them? I pulled everything out and they scanned it with an interest that made me feel even more uncomfortable. Then, one of them looked back up at me and burst out laughing.

"Gratz! Gratz!" he shouted. "Nora Gratz!"

The other pulled the papers from his hands and made him shine the flashlight on them. Then, he had him turn the beam, again, on me. He gave a long whistle. He did know some Hungarian, because he said, *"Gyere, gyere, "* and took my little suitcase from me.

By now, I was too scared to move. The soldier's whistle, the serene square, and the lazy voices emerging from the Kismacska, all blended together to give the encounter the feel of a dream that would lead somewhere I didn't want to go. The soldiers took me under the arm, and my heart pounded like mad as they frog-walked me beyond the shopping district, through the little green park, towards the brickyard. All the while, I had the least logical train of thought in the world. My name is on some list from thirty years ago. Somebody in that *cukrászda* spotted me and it's all over now.

I wondered if they could be bribed, and I called out: "Cigarette?"

The offer took them by surprise. The one who knew Hungarian said, *"Köszi, nem.* We have enough. You want?"

By then, we'd reached the brickyard. The town lay behind us like a fairy tale, and I didn't have a clue what I'd do next. A chimney nearby spouted occasional fire. The two soldiers were in high spirits now, and they took out their cigarettes and lit up, offered me one, and laughed because the thing snapped in half in my fingers. They conversed, smiling side-long at me and eyeing the railroad tracks. I heard the train approach, the rhythm unmistakable.

The soldier who spoke Hungarian said, "Many Jews here. Many, many. Now none."

The headlamp fell on the bricks scattered around a loading dock and shone against high weeds and the rails, as it had always done from the days of my girlhood, and in the days since when I wasn't there to see it. As it approached the yard, the train slowed and sighed, and then it stopped in a cloud of gritty steam.

Without warning, I was pushed forward, and I found myself standing in the open, not far from the tracks. A few men had emerged from the drying shed, and they opened the boxcars. They took no note of me. I rubbed my eyes, which smarted with dust and ash, and I didn't know whether to turn right or left, conscious of the soldiers still behind me.

Then, someone stepped off the engine-car, a stooped man in leather overalls. He was rubbing his whole face with a dirty rag, and he staggered off the train with a familiarity that meant he could have found his way with his eyes closed. Still wiping, he removed his hat with his free hand. Stiff, gray hair rose in a crest. It came on me at that moment.

I said nothing until he showed his face, and he almost walked past without seeing me. Then I called out, "Janos!"

E HAD BEEN STATIONED IN THAT
district since the fall. Later, he would admit to requesting it, but at first he
was still reticent, not certain if I wanted to hear that sort of thing.

"It's very hard," Janos said to me that first night, meaning it was hard for
him to talk then as he'd been awake for the past thirty hours, and more particularly that it was hard for him to talk to me. He'd cleaned himself up a
little with water from the boiler room, but grime still lurked in the deep
crevices on either side of his mouth and in the wrinkles in his forehead.

I said, "You shaved your mustache." His mouth looked vulnerable without it.

"I shaved it before I left, I think," said Janos. "I don't remember."

"Maybe you did. But I always think of you having a mustache."

"Would you like me to grow one?"

In spite of myself, I laughed. "Yes," I said.

We were sitting in his office. He was chief civil engineer for the south-
east region, a job less glamorous than it sounded. He was on the road most of
the time, overseeing projects, requisitioning materials, and visiting new
sites. He was good at his work and grateful for it. For most of the war, he
had been stuck behind a desk doing nothing in a town in one of the Repub-
lics whose name I could never pronounce no matter how patiently Janos
repeated it.

"Surely you weren't doing nothing at all," I said.

"As little as possible," Janos said. Then it was his turn to laugh, though that laugh sounded a little forced. He had been relocated from Moscow in 1940, not long after most of the men and women he knew from the days of the Commune had been arrested and executed, Bela Kun among them. He didn't say much about that.

We asked little of each other at first. That night, after he'd made us tea and arranged for my lodgings, he said, "I have something for you."

It was the deed to the house. I looked it over, line for line, not believing it existed. "It's not occupied?"

"It's only been six months since they started deportations."

"And my mother?" It might have been then I realized that if I took the house, it meant she wasn't there to take it and that I was holding my mother's death certificate in my hand.

"You think she might claim it? It's very unlikely she even survived the journey."

I knew about the deportations. The Soviets had liberated Auschwitz long ago. I changed the subject. "Can I see the house tonight?"

"Of course," Janos said, in an off-hand way that made me think of his old days at the Katona Jozsef School, but when I saw how he had to brace his arm on the desk in order to rise from the chair, I thought better of the idea.

I said, "It will still be there tomorrow."

"I don't see," said Janos, "why you should believe a word I say."

"Neither do I," I said. "But somehow, I do."

"You used to be such a sensible girl," said Janos, and he didn't kiss me then, but he looked as though he wanted to, almost as much as he wanted a night's sleep. There was a heavy sweetness to that look. My bed was at the Hotel Oasis. I slept on clean sheets for a change. There was electric light too, though I didn't use it, preferring the dark, the better to smell the faint breath of the brickworks and the railway station, the smell of home.

The house was vacant, as promised, though its furniture had all been stolen and couldn't be retrieved. Cleared of my mother's heavy credenzas and sofas, the rooms looked smaller, full of clean, spring light. Beginning at the wall of what had once been my room, I paced. Fifteen. Turning, I crossed my arms and paced again. I'd returned with the intention of selling the house and my share in the shop, and it hadn't occurred to me that I could actually move in, but of course now that I had the key in my hand, I considered the possibility. At least, I thought, until I could find a good price. Then I'd have a nest-egg to begin life somewhere else.

"If I were you I'd go to America," said the boy who'd given me the key. His name was Csaba, and he was Laszlo's grandson. I would have guessed that just by looking at him. He had his grandfather's golden hair and puppy-friendly face. He felt, to me, like a talisman, and under his protection I could bear the observation of the neighbors who watched me over their gates. Those neighbors knew who'd lived in that house, and they knew what had become of her; her hideous furniture was probably in their own parlors.

One man did say to me as I passed, "You know, that tree's diseased."

I answered casually, "Is it? I'll cut it down."

"Your mother should have hired one of us to do it."

I didn't ask why he hadn't simply lopped it off at the roots once she was in Auschwitz. With a backwards glance, rather suspicious, I noted that the tree looked the same way it always looked in early April, bulbous, dun-colored, and probably in better condition than myself.

Csaba took me to his house for breakfast. His mother had prepared a feast: a bowl of goose-fat, white bread, early vegetables, and something that almost tasted like real coffee. There were flowers in a vase and an embroidered cloth on the table. That house seemed as charmed as the rest of the town; every rug on the wall and clay pot on the mantel was the same as it had been when my mother and I spent the night there in 1919. All that woman wanted to talk about was my mother.

"She had an iron backbone," she said to me. "You can imagine what it took to get her out of that house."

"So why did she go?" Csaba asked.

"Kedvesem, they pulled her out. You know that."

"Why didn't she hide?"

"As far as she was concerned," Csaba's mother said, more to me than to her son, "that house was hers. And she didn't have to be ashamed to be sitting in the middle of it. More coffee, Nora?"

"Yes," I said, "I'll take more coffee."

There was more to tell, about her husband, who would be on leave soon and would be happy to pass on the deed to what was left of the business, and also about Laszlo himself, who'd died within three hours of his wife the same day that the Soviets had entered Barnahely. Nothing dramatic, Csaba's mother said. They just ran out, like clocks.

Laszlo had worked at the optics shop even during the German occupation. The Germans took one look at his equipment and requisitioned it and him. There was no real way that he could resist them. At least they let his family alone. They even made a mascot of him. They gave him cigarettes and hung around the entrance to his shop.

One of the Germans was fascinated by Laszlo's collection of lenses and prisms. He wanted Laszlo to cut him a set of his own, and he asked what Laszlo would like in exchange. "Maybe a motorbike? You'd have an easier time getting to your mistress."

Laszlo said, "I'm too old and tired for a mistress. If you want to know the truth, I'd like the Csongradi house."

"Old? Nonsense. You're younger than any of us," the German said. "If a man loves his work, he never grows old."

This was in June of '44, at the height of the deportations. Laszlo and his wife moved into the empty house. His wife was a light sleeper. She was often kept awake because the transit center at the brickyard was so close and she could hear the trains full of Jews from neighboring towns pass through.

They didn't pass like proper trains. They rattled to a halt and crawled a few meters before stopping again. They would wait for hours until new cars could be connected, and sometimes Laszlo's wife would make him get up and close the shutters.

By then, Kisbarnahely and Szarvas were both empty of Jews. Germans brought all sorts of things to Laszlo's shop now: little gilt clocks, watches from Switzerland, and once a chandelier with half the crystal missing. Laszlo often worked through nights, but he always returned to that yellow house so close to the trains, and thus the house was held through the remainder of the war until their deaths and found its way back to me.

Young Csaba seemed to be the only resident of Kisbarnahely who genuinely liked the Soviets. He picked up a lot of Russian, and as we walked from his house to the old optical shop he greeted many of the soldiers by name. The shop itself was dark and empty; the Germans had stripped it before their retreat. Laszlo's son hadn't yet decided what to do with the property, and I peered through the badly boarded window and tried to make out what was left of the interior.

"I think I was your age when your grandfather started working for my uncle," I said. "You know, I had a terrible crush on him."

"It's a good thing you didn't marry him," Csaba said. "Then you would have stayed here, and you would have been dead for sure."

That night, I was supposed to meet Janos's train, and I came early to the brickyard. I walked for a while among the broken bricks, looking for traces. Who knows what I wanted to find: a shoe, a broken comb, a pince-nez, maybe the handle of a suitcase. I'd been told that over two thousand Jews had been collected there from the whole region over the course of two months, but there weren't even footprints. The dirt had been raked over. So complete was my concentration that I didn't even hear his train approach.

Janos was in his army uniform that night. It wasn't until he'd come very close that I saw he was growing back his mustache. I felt appalled but also giddy, and without thinking about it much, I kissed him, just a friendly kiss.

He seemed taken aback, but only said, "You look rested."

"You can't say more than that?"

"What else should I say?"

This exchange took place in front of several other officers, the only consolation being that they probably didn't understand Hungarian. In Russian, Janos explained that I was an old friend and that our meeting was one of the miracles of the war. He translated for me afterwards as we walked back to the house.

The air felt soft that night, though it had been a spring slow to begin, full of false thaws and sudden frosts. I said to him, "You don't call me your wife?"

He didn't look at me as he said, "Ten years' abandonment."

"But I'd prefer it."

Then he stopped short and turned to me. He asked, "Why?" He looked almost angry. "I can't see how you can. We're strangers to each other now, aren't we?"

I felt suddenly tired. I realized I'd spent all day tramping around Kisbarnahely and that the last hour in the brickyard had worn me down. I said, "We don't have to be strangers."

*I*T COULD BE ARGUED THAT WE had never been other than strangers. Sometimes, when I'd find his pipecleaners on the table, I'd pick them up and wonder when he'd started using them instead of knocking the bowl against the furniture. His mustache was also a surprise, gray and vigorous. Then there was the camera, a German model the size of his hand that he drew out of a leather pouch one afternoon. He raised it to take a picture of the steeple, and I caught his hand and said, "What happened to the measuring tape?"

He glanced down, distracted. "What measuring tape?"

"I thought you didn't trust photographs," I said.

"I don't," said Janos, and then he took the photograph, stepped back, and took another. Then he put it down at last and said, "I don't trust measurements either."

"What do you trust?" I asked him, as we walked back home together. Rather than answering, he paused in the middle of the road to stare at an ink-black rabbit as it flashed across the grass. Then he turned with the camera and took a photograph of me.

*A*FTER SOME TIME, WE BEGAN TO share a bed again. Once, he had pulled up my little nightgown; now I was the one to reach for him and work the drawstring on his pajamas, feeling, below my fingers, something unfamiliar. He'd draw back, but I would not let him go, knowing that in this room, my parents made me, in this house, I dreamed of flight, and now I'd flown back to find this man who entered me at first as though it hadn't been what he'd intended, as though taken by surprise. I rocked with him.

Those good hands found me. I remembered nights long ago when those hands took me apart like a music box. Now they were less precise. They drew me in, but I had to draw myself deeper, carry him with me. I cannot describe what happened. It troubled and frightened me like an important conversation.

Then there was the morning I decided to find out why Janos sometimes left our bed just before I got up. I thought he might have gone out to take photographs, and after a few educated guesses, I tried the field where he had seen the rabbit. I spotted him in the middle of overgrown weeds, facing east.

He was alone. The weeds around him rustled; it was otherwise quite still. His back was turned to me, and his shoulders were hunched; it almost looked as though he were reading. He looked so meditative that I almost turned back. Then, he himself turned, and I saw that he was wearing phylacteries.

I was struck dumb. I'd never seen them anywhere but in the window of a religious store on Dob Street. The effect of the crossed leather on his arms and the thong around his forehead made me shiver, as though he were being drawn and quartered.

Janos spoke first. "Don't tell anyone."

I could only ask, "How long?"

"I began a year ago," he said. "They were passed on to me. They belonged to a man who's dead now."

His voice was a hoarse whisper. He didn't expect me to understand, and in point of fact, I didn't. What can you say when you find your husband bound in the *tfillin* of a dead Jew? He removed them, and he showed me their case, a bag made of dull, black velvet. It must have been richly embroidered once, though now most of the stitching was undone.

The man had been Hungarian, on trial in Moscow because he had known Bela Kun. When the trial began, there had at first been little evidence of association. Of course, Janos said, evidence could be manufactured, and it made little difference in the end whether the conversations actually took place, whether the café where they met existed, whether the room was crowded or they dined alone, whether the table measured one meter or five meters from the doorway where the informer stood recording what he heard.

In this case, however, there was a firm piece of evidence, a photograph taken during the Commune in 1919. Kun and five comrades, including the man in question, posed before a velvet curtain. Other photographs were passed around that day, more enemies of the state irrefutably associated with Kun and Kun's co-conspirators. Those photographs were so widely circulated that they reached even the obscure town where Janos sat behind his desk doing as little as possible.

"Useful photographs," said Janos. "Might still come in handy to somebody else one day."

I asked, "So you wear his *tfillin* because you have him on your conscience?"

Janos shook his head. "It's not his name that's inside of them," he said. "That's not what's written on the parchment."

I will confess that I did not know what was written on the parchment, and it came on me like a dizzy spell that Janos was telling me that he believed in God. Such a confession, made even obliquely, made me tumble backwards to the day he told me in a whisper that he was a Communist, and I wanted to make him swallow his words because I didn't know what I was supposed to do with them.

"From the day I turned thirteen," Janos said, "until I left my father's house, I wore these every time I prayed. Back then, I prayed the way you smoke, Nora."

I said, "I don't understand."

"I prayed," he said, "out of habit. And because it was the only way I knew one hour was different from another one, because I lived in a prison. You once told me you thought my politics was a trap. I thought it was a key, that I could become a free man."

By now, we'd reached the house again, and I was fixing coffee. He took out his pipe and looked inside the bowl.

"I couldn't believe my luck when I met you. I looked at you and thought: That girl could have anyone."

I didn't let myself laugh. I sat myself across from him as he felt in his pocket for a pipe-cleaner and looked at me under his ragged eyebrows. I only said, "Maybe you're right."

"You were smart, young. The world was open to you."

"And it wasn't to you?"

"I never told you," Janos said. He took a sip of coffee then, wetting the end of his mustache. Then he said, "I had a wife."

I let that sink in. It struck me that once you've decided to forgive someone, the choice stands; you must forgive them everything. Admittedly, I didn't find that one so hard to forgive. Really, I was more curious. "How old were you when you got married?"

"Sixteen," said Janos. "She's dead now."

"And your father?"

"Dead."

"Uncles? Cousins?"

"Of course they're all dead."

"How can you know?"

Janos had no more coffee in his cup, so now his hesitation took the form of cleaning out his pipe, and he did that for a long time before telling me that he had no reason to think they were alive.

"So you haven't tried to find out?"

"I've made no inquiries." Janos pushed his chair back. "I have to get to work. I'm already late."

"And me? Did you ask anyone about me?" I also rose from the table and was surprised to feel tears come to my eyes. "Don't leave yet. Let me know."

With the back of the chair still in his hands, Janos swallowed. "What would I have to say to those people?"

"What do you have to say to me?" I asked, helpless and barely believing I could ask such a question.

"What do you want me to say to you?"

"I want you," I said, "to tell me you're glad we're both alive."

Between us was the table and his chair, both Soviet issue. We felt the distance between us, physical and not easy to move. Janos's voice broke. "How can you ask me to be glad?"

"I don't know," I said.

Janos said, "I have to go," and in fact he would already be almost half an hour late for work. He'd gained control of his emotions, or at least his voice was steadier now. "I want to be a husband to you."

I almost asked: Why? For the same reason you wear your phylacteries? Instead, I said, "I want you to find out what happened to my mother and my aunt and my cousin. I want to know."

Janos nodded, and looked oddly relieved. His bicycle was in the garden, and as he rode to work, it drew a long rut through the mud, spattering the cuffs of his trousers. Alone, I wondered why I'd asked. He might think I'd done it to shame him. And in fact, did I really want to know at all?

*W*ITHIN TWO MONTHS, JANOS gave me the information. According to witnesses, my mother had not survived the trip to Auschwitz. Aunt Monika arrived, but had at once been gassed, as had Adele, who had been pregnant at the time.

"Her husband I could find no record of. You also might be interested," said Janos. "Someone else has also been asking about them. The Zionist cousin."

I tried unsuccessfully to hide the sudden rush of blood to my heart. "He's still in Palestine?"

"Apparently," said Janos.

"That's interesting," I said.

"The records aren't very detailed. You want his address?"

"I know it. Don't bother," I said. I already felt absurd enough, summoning up this information which was of no use to anyone.

In fact, one of the women in the neighborhood called out across her fence to me one day. "I hear you're bringing in relations."

I turned and tried to smile. She smiled back, or anyway showed some teeth. She was a handsome woman who must have been my own age. She was clipping roses, which grew all over her fence, pink and red. By now, some time had passed since I'd arrived in Kisbarnahely, time enough for my neighbors to more or less get used to me and make their judgments.

"I hear your mother's bringing her sister," the woman said. "From Budapest. And they're buying houses."

"You heard wrong," I said, with my smile frozen in place. It would have helped, had I known her name. All I knew was that her yard was more well-tended than my own and that her dogs strained at their ropes and barked all day. It was her husband who said my mother should have paid him to chop down the apricot tree.

She reminded me of this now and again; I always promised to get around to it and never did. He had been right of course; the tree was blighted. It stood in the dust of the yard like a useless sculpture.

"I heard," the woman said, still leaning on the fence, "that a trainload of Jews is arriving next week to force families out of their houses."

I should have said: Lady, they're all dead. Clip your roses. Rest easy. Instead I only shook my head.

She said, "Ask your husband."

In fact, Janos confirmed that there was a train arriving from Poland, one of many carrying survivors back to Hungary. He didn't know how many had expressed interest in returning to Kisbarnahely, but he had heard that some men freed from the Labor Battalions had inquired about lost property. "Rumors have some basis," he said. He looked worried.

"So what if they come?" I asked him.

"I think," he said, "it's time to cut down that tree."

To PAY IN CURRENCY WAS, OF course, impossible in those days. Janos came back from negotiations with the gentleman across the road in a mood even more taciturn than usual. "He'll be here tomorrow," Janos said to me. "He has a chainsaw."

"What are you giving him?"

"A position," Janos said. "He's deputy in charge of the reclamation of confiscated property."

"I'm not sure he knows how to read," I said.

"That doesn't matter. By the end of this decade, Hungary will be completely literate."

"And that's how it's done?" I asked him.

"That's one way it's done," he said. "There's another way."

We had this conversation in our living room. It was late June of that second year in Barnahely: 1948. By now, we'd been together long enough to talk in short-hand, like any married couple. I wondered if we had always spoken to each other this way, or if it was like what happened in bed, a language rooted in this place, where what we said mattered.

He said, "You know, we could have shot your friend Laszlo. He fixed their watches, and he took the house of a victim of Fascism. For such things we lined men up against the wall and shot them. You think I could find nothing on this other man? We'd get witnesses, we're very good at that, and probably most of what they'd say would be the truth. There's a place near the tracks where we did plenty of executions back in 'forty-five."

"So you silence him one way or the other? Those are the two choices?" I asked him.

"Those are the two choices."

"And you choose the merciful one." My voice sounded hollow, even to myself, because I wasn't praising him. He knew it. It wasn't dark and wouldn't be dark for some time; days stretched as we approached midsummer. Then those days would shorten and fog would lay over the houses and the shops and the steeple of the Reformed church. I would live out year after year in the town I was born, with a man who had crossed a continent to find me but could not tell me why, with a man who did not believe a thing could be false or true. There would never be a time when we could make a choice because we thought it was right.

"All right, then," said Janos. He picked up his briefcase. "I've got to get back to the office. My train leaves at ten tonight." He was going on another trip, north this time, to a village where a generator had just arrived. As ever, I watched him climb onto his bicycle. I wondered how he laid the phylacteries when he was on the road. I never asked him. There were too many things I still could not ask Janos.

I couldn't stay indoors; the house stifled me. I could hear a train approach. They were even more frequent now than in my childhood. Kisbarnahely was becoming a town, attracting new industries, and cement blocks of flats had been planned for the open space past the brickworks where the gypsy encampment used to be. No one could tell me what had happened to those gypsies. My first week back, I looked for the Jewish cemetery and found an empty yard overgrown with wildflowers and ivy, and now there was talk of turning it into a public park with a playground for children.

I lit a cigarette, the last in the pack. Then I took a walk to the Kismacska. As a respectable married lady, I wasn't quite a regular there, but I'd been known to stop in for a coffee. It hadn't changed; its pure dinginess, as ever, overcame me like sloth. The tables with half the plastic tops peeled off were oddly comforting. Of course, the place was crowded with Soviet soldiers now.

I slipped behind an empty table and ordered myself a coffee and a pack of cigarettes. The waitress, an unsmiling Hungarian, slapped both of them in front of me, shooting half the coffee onto the tabletop. I sipped what was left, though it was cold even before it touched my lips.

Csaba was there as well, one table over, pretending he was grown up and playing cards with two of the soldiers. He joked with them in his broken Russian. Then he glanced over and gave me a sloppy grin. "Hey, Mrs. Gratz, come join us. Don't you play?"

"Badly," I said.

"What do you have to bet?"

"An apricot tree," I said, "and a handful of pipe-cleaners. Maybe also a dish of vanilla ice cream bought by a Komsomol." I was in a strange mood. Csaba was too pleased with himself to notice.

Then a voice came from across the room. "She can't bet the property."

I turned, and there was a man I didn't even know, with a hat pulled over an unpleasant, fisty face.

"Come on, Comrade," Csaba called back to him. "We'll deal you in. It's no fun with just three of us."

"I'll be fucked if I drink with those Red Army shits. But I want the lady to know she can't bet the property. I don't care what the judge told her mother. It isn't hers."

Csaba gave an apologetic shrug in my direction.

The man called out: "It wasn't her father's. I tell you, in the village records, take a look sometime and she'll see our name on the deed from the time of the Turks!"

It was easy for me not to look at the man who addressed me as if I weren't there, and as I felt some distance from the situation, it struck me that he had an excellent point. The house was as much his as it was mine. What did I really have, if I didn't have that house? I made a little bet with myself, and I reached my hand towards Csaba and said: "Let me cut the deck."

Even as I set the edges of the cards neatly against the broken tabletop, I knew what I'd find. I raised half the cards with two fingers, and turned them over. The topmost card was Winter.

That old woman had the same solemn face I had seen when Uncle Oszkar read my cards when I was a girl. Her eyes were on the road before her, and the hand that did not hold the walking stick bunched the strings of her blue cloak between her breasts. The top of that walking stick was so jagged it was no wonder that she held it low, as she stooped to keep her bundle of twigs balanced between her shoulders. In contrast to that waste of snow and blasted trees, in the corners floated acorns so colorful, so fertile, that you could only hope they gave some sign of where she might be going.

But it wasn't winter in Kisbarnahely; it was midsummer. At nine at night the sky was still suffused with gray light which implied, to me, a kind of exhaustion. I asked Csaba, "Do you know the train schedule?"

"Mr. Gratz is leaving in an hour," he said.

"I know, but southwest. Which train goes south or west?"

It must have been Csaba who warned my husband, because I hadn't packed my suitcase yet when I heard him at the door, and before I even saw him, I called, "You'll miss your train."

"What are you doing? What have I done?"

"Nothing," I called, and I was telling the truth. "I just can't stay here anymore."

Then he appeared in the doorway, sweating so hard that beads of it gathered in his mustache. "What can I do?"

"Nothing," I said. "I just know I can't live where no one wants me."

"I want you," Janos said, with undeniable tenderness.

But I was ruthless. "Why?"

"To be a husband to you."

"That's not enough," I said.

"Where do you think you'll go? You're not a young woman."

"I don't want to have nothing," I said. "I can't live with nothing." I wasn't even sure what I was saying anymore. "I can't live in prison. I want to go somewhere where I don't have to be afraid."

"Oh, God, Nora," Janos said. "Listen to me." He sat on the edge of our bed, beside my half-filled suitcase. "It's a circumstance of life. You're going to take it with you everywhere. Can you name one place, one place?"

"Yes," I said.

Then Janos said nothing. He took his pipe out of his pocket and turned it around in his hand, though he didn't light it. I finished filling that suitcase under his observation and was just about to close the clasp when at last he asked me, "Is Gabor my son?"

My hand trembled, but without looking up, I said, "Gabor is dead."

Janos said, "I thought you'd leave, that time he came. I'll never understand—"

"There was nothing between us, Janos. I swear. That's not the reason."

"This Bela," Janos said, "is sure to disappoint you."

I couldn't deny it. Yet this time I vowed that I wouldn't disappoint myself. I pulled the suitcase from the bed. It was remarkably heavy. My train was due in half an hour, and I was hardly assured of a place, but it was heading in the right direction.

"You want something impossible," Janos said. "You're going to a place that doesn't exist. You're leaving me and you can't even tell me why."

*H*E WALKED ME TO THE STATION, taking his bicycle along the tracks, and he helped me up and passed me my suitcase. It was frankly dark by then. I could just make out his face, and it looked so mournful and confused that I wondered what had happened to that dry young man who had tapped his pipe on the table of the Hovirag *cukrászda* and called me sensible. I considered what I said next to be a rehearsal for the rest of my life, and I said it with the recklessness of someone stepping off the edge of a cliff.

"Janos, I love you. I'm leaving because it's so hard for me to say."

By then, the train had pulled out. I'd timed it that way. Janos jumped on his bicycle and followed, pumping and pumping in line with the tracks, and he called, "Jump off! Jump off!"

"I can't," I called back.

"Jump off! For God's sake! Jump!"

But by then there was no point in calling to each other, because that train had picked up speed and I could only wave with the hand that wasn't holding my suitcase as Janos was left far behind in the dark among the closed, shoulder-high sunflowers.

AFTER HER EXAMINATION BY THE
Bet Din, Louisa immersed herself naked in the ritual bath. They laid a sheet
on the surface for modesty's sake. It was a very old bath, constructed of gold
Jerusalem stone. Louisa rose with the sheet around her shoulders. She shivered a little and was handed a towel.

They couldn't believe she wouldn't take on the name Ruth. She wanted
to be called Leah. This was news to Jonah, who was there, but he kept quiet.
It was only later that he asked, "Can't it be some other name?"

Louisa said, "I like Leah. It's plain, and she had a lot of children."

She never asked him to explain his heartsick reaction. That was a comfort. Still, he never managed to use the name. It became a kind of joke between them, how everyone called her Leah—the grocer, the neighbors who
came by for tea and pastry, the pupils she coached—everyone but her husband,
who persisted with his "Lu" even when he introduced her to his friends.

He did have friends now, new ones, at their block of flats in Tel Aviv.
Jonah had used his connection to Lorenz to find them a spacious apartment,
and in return, he'd agreed to take a real management position at one of the
textile mills. But, Lorenz said, his real future obviously lay in politics. Jonah
decided it wasn't really an awful thing to wear a suit to work, as long as he
was allowed to pull off the jacket and roll up his sleeves. He put on weight
and took to smoking the occasional cigar.

Louisa directed children's choirs in primary schools all over Tel Aviv. The boys and girls looked at her sweet face and pony-tail and figured she'd be a soft touch, but soon enough, she'd be making each of them sing alone to hear who had gone off-key, or tapping the music stand with her reading glasses and saying, "Hebrew is a sacred language. The prophets spoke it. I want to hear every word, or I'll stuff your scores down your throats." Sometimes, a teacher would look into the auditorium during rehearsal and find twenty-five children with their fingers on their lips, humming out *lu lu lu*. The fixed expressions on the children's faces would be disconcerting, but they never looked that way when they performed.

After the marriage, almost at once Louisa was pregnant. I was the first one she called. By then, I'd moved into a rooming house in Tel Aviv. It was full of nice Hungarian ladies, like a little Yellow Star House. I never needed to learn a word of Hebrew. On one side of my room was a widow who'd lived around the corner from Aunt Monika, and on the other were two spinster sisters from Keszthely, one of whom picked up the hallway phone when Louisa called and shouted, "Nora! Your daughter!"

"Mutti, " Louisa said after she told me the news, "are you happy?"

"Of course I am," I said. "I couldn't be happier."

That was God's truth. I couldn't be happier. By then, I knew my limitations.

But Louisa wanted more. "You're happy for us?"

That was a more complex question. You see, what Louisa was demanding now was my blessing. She'd demanded it before, at the wedding. She wouldn't have many more opportunities. They might not have more children, with Jonah being well over fifty now. I said, "It's bad luck to talk about it now."

Louisa answered without hesitation. "No. This one will live."

It did too. Rather, she did, a girl they named Tamar. When Louisa came to visit me, which she does, regularly and without Jonah, she used to bring Tamar along, in part because she couldn't find a sitter and in part because it seemed important to her that I know the child existed. Tamar has a lot of curly black hair. As soon as she started crawling, I gave her the run of my room, and somehow she always ended up burning herself on the radiator or cutting her lip on the side of my bed-frame, so after a while, Louisa left her at home, but she remained the center of our conversations.

The other women in the house would gather around Louisa as she spoke in German about Tamar's playmates and her little boyfriend Ari, about how much she loves chocolate ice cream and how impossible it is to wash the stains out of her little Shabbat dress, and about her first day at the beach.

"She collected stones for her Nanni," Louisa said.

"Nonsense. She barely knows me," I said.

"She knows all about you," said Louisa. From her canvas bag, she removed a brown sack of pebbles, still sandy. She dumped them on my dresser and waited for me to admire them. I thought about a custom I had learned about only recently, to place a stone on someone's grave. Why was it done? To keep their spirit in the other world, I suppose, to give them some peace.

After Louisa had gone, the other women in the rooming house would linger by my bed and tell me what a jewel I had in Leah and how their own daughters, the flesh of their flesh, never so much as called them. They'd all wept when they'd first heard her tell our story.

"Tell me," I said to them, "how often do you think about the past?"

I asked the woman who'd once lived around the corner from my aunt. She was an ancient of days whose dyed red hair made her face as white as lime. She said, "If my story was as beautiful as yours, I'd think about it all the time."

I HAD A FEW MORE VISITORS.
One was Dov Levin. He came no more than once a month; after all, he lived in Haifa. Sometimes, he brought his daughter Nami, who continued to express interest in Louisa's case. They finally met at the wedding and set up a

series of interviews which Nami was in the process of transcribing. I found Nami's presence tiring and preferred it when Levin came alone. He always brought something I needed, like a new radio or a pot with a coil for making hot tea. Sometimes, he would just stay in the room for hours, standing on a chair and repairing the spring on my window shade.

"You don't know what the hell you're doing," I'd say to him.

He'd look down with a playful smile. "Why should you have to struggle with it?"

"Maybe it passes the time."

"Then find a better way to pass the time," he would reply from the height of the chair, a distance that made flirtation meaningless. Afterwards, he would lower himself by degrees, implying age, a sore back, and a hesitant nature. I knew that in another year, he would start coming once every few months, and in another year, he wouldn't come at all. As he drove off, I wanted to lean out the window and wave that old white sun hat at him, some helpless gesture.

Then there was Yossel Berkowitz. Without warning one night, there he was in my room, with the same stains on his leather jacket and the same deep wrinkles in his trousers. He'd removed the fur hat, though, and he'd combed his hair with brilliantine. Straddling a chair, he stretched his feet to the radiator and said, "There's a happy ending for you. Everyone gets his way."

I admitted some confusion and confessed I'd wondered if he'd thought we'd made some sort of bargain.

"Bargain? With you? What makes you think you have anything I want? I've got my own problems, *Nagymama*. Here. Have a cigarette. You probably don't get ones like these in this town." He was right, as ever. I couldn't scare up any Lucky Strikes. He lit mine with his own, and we smoked together for a while, something we'd never done before. "You know those Transylvanian girls?" he asked me. "Well, they're in the army now. Every last one a paratrooper. With those girls floating from the sky, I've got my hands full. Who knows where they'll land?"

*O*NE AFTERNOON, I WAS ABOUT TO go out for a walk when I collided with someone opening the door. It was Jonah, with both arms around a paper bag. He'd stopped by on his way to the dry-cleaners. It seems it was around the corner from the boardinghouse. He addressed me in Hungarian. "Are you busy? I could use a little company."

I probably tried to read something into his voice, but there was nothing to read. Although this was the first time we had been alone together, he acted as though it were something that happened every day, and now I tried to take it in the same spirit, and I said, "Sure, I'm busy. The girls are all going to the cinema. There's some Russian film about a woman aviator."

"Oh, well, then," said Jonah, but I led him up the street towards the café I frequented, a cramped place where the tables were covered with stained white cloths, but the coffee was as good as anything you could get in Budapest. He ordered a raspberry soda. There was something touching in this stout, cigar-smelling fellow drinking through a straw.

"So," I said, "dry-cleaning."

"Dry-cleaning," said Jonah. "What's wrong with that?"

"Don't you always leave the ticket somewhere. And if you leave it somewhere, do you have to retrace your steps and go to everybody's kitchen and if they find it first, do they pick your laundry up for you or hold it hostage?"

Jonah rubbed his chin, and maybe he smiled. "You wear me out, Nora."

"Good," I said. "Somebody has to wear you out." My own coffee was getting cold, but I didn't care. "If nobody wears you out, you'll keep on getting younger, and then one day, you'll disappear."

"No, I won't," said Jonah.

"Yes, you have," I said.

He didn't answer. Why did I say that? It was idiotic. Here was my cousin at last, and I make a fool of myself. Why can't I make peace with my own nature? When I open my heart, I drive people away. Well, I thought, so he'll go. What's done is done.

But although there was no soda left in the glass, Jonah showed no sign of leaving. His eyes, those heavy, soft, black eyes, he rubbed, and he had rubbed his chin, and maybe he was trying to confirm that he was still there. And he was still there, impossibly but firmly. It was a good thing I was sitting down, because I felt a little giddy.

Then he did something I hadn't expected. He put his hand in his pocket and took out something that looked as though it must have once been a cigarette. It was bent, and half of the tobacco had come out of it. He put it on the table and said, "There."

"What is this?" I asked him. "Is this your idea of a gesture?"

"It was in the pocket of a pair of work-pants I grew out of," Jonah said. "Got it from one of your old boyfriends I ran into around the time you came. Lu found it yesterday. I think she couldn't believe I hadn't washed those pants in all those years."

"So she told you to give this to me?"

"Nora, be fair," said Jonah. "You remember that day in Vidam Park when I said I'd pass all my cigarettes on to you when you came to Israel. I just wanted you to know, I keep promises."

I lifted that cigarette up between my thumb and forefinger. I couldn't even tell what brand it was. "I can't possibly smoke this thing."

Jonah cocked his head like a boy and asked, "Why not?"

"My God! Do you actually expect me to answer that question?" I asked my cousin. I'll admit we were both laughing. He looked for all the world like the boy he had been that summer in Kisbarnahely, who danced with me in the cemetery and sang, *We've come to rebuild the land, and be rebuilt by it,* and swung me around until we'd fallen with our breath knocked out. What did he want from me? To rebuild what we had, a half a cigarette at a time?

Well, then, I thought, I'll let him. I liked the thought of my cousin spending his twilight years in Israel as my source for cigarettes. Besides, it meant we'd go on having these coffees once in a while. I said, *"Borʒas,* why did you really come here? I hope you're not planning to try to teach me Hebrew. The girls at the boardinghouse tell me it's a miserable language. No vowels at all."

*A*CTUALLY, I HAVE OTHER PLANS for my cousin. Recently, I received a package in the mail. It was a press release for an upcoming exhibition in Jerusalem. At first, I thought they'd misaddressed the envelope, but then I saw the title: *Assimilation and Ashes: The Girls of the Katona Joʒsef School.*

Someone had attached a typed note to the letter, an apology. Apparently, they'd only recently managed to track me down. They would be thrilled and honored if I would be their special guest as the most long-standing surviving school employee. Perhaps I could shed some light on some of the stranger items in the collection.

From a glance at the catalogue, I believe I could do just that. They reprinted pages of their literary magazines, and alongside sentimental stories about the Galilee there was a comic poem about Janos. A partial list of artifacts: tickets to the Zionist Club's spring dance; a biology notebook, where some girl filled the margins with Hebrew; and a poster advertising Buber's lecture of October 1921. On the cover of the catalogue was a color reproduction of the mural of the blue-faced seamstresses worshipping the Crown of Saint Stephen. After the Germans invaded, some vandal painted in a Star of David.

I can't decide whether or not to go to the exhibition. Jerusalem isn't so far away, but I'm not up to traveling. It's hard enough for me to get up and down stairs these days. Yet if I could talk Jonah into driving down with me, it would be worth it. Maybe they'd even have the key to the boiler room.

The text of the press release for the Jerusalem exhibition contained the following in Hebrew, English, French, and Hungarian. *The martyrs of the*

Katona József School evoke the dilemma of Diaspora Jewry where one's sense of self can only be a hard-fought compromise and the clarity of vision which comes from a full acceptance of national destiny. Their ache for clarity, their love of people, their tragic story, is uniquely Jewish.

I showed that to Jonah and I asked him, "What the hell are they talking about?"

He shrugged. "Who knows? It reads worse in French, if you can believe it." Then he added, "I know they're not all dead. I've met a few. They all remember me."

Smiling, I said, "I'll bet they do."

I think of the photograph I lost some years before which showed Bela, Dori, and Nathan in front of that chicken coop. The remarkable thing is, everyone in that photograph is still alive, but the photograph itself is gone.

I SAW IT LAST IN FEBRUARY OF 1944 when Louisa found it with the letters and confronted me, weeping and weeping as though her heart were broken.

"You'll leave us," she said. "You're bound to leave and go to Zion, *Mutti.* You've got a place to go, and what about me? Where will I go?"

I comforted her, an act neither novel nor demanding. All it took was a pan of warm milk with sugar and a rhythmic stroking of her hair. In those days, it wasn't hard to love her because I knew how to please her. Maybe it's that simple. She asked nothing of me but that I stay, and I wasn't going anywhere; this in contrast to her husband, who was bound to leave, or at least wouldn't return until Louisa had already cried, been comforted, and sent to bed.

"Hush, dear," I said. "I'm not going to leave you." I tucked the blanket around her. "Certainly not for Palestine."

Louisa sat up among the pillows and said, "But it's the Holy Land."

I said, "Shh, shh, hush now. There's no such place."

HE AUTHOR WISHES TO AC-
knowledge the generous support and encouragement of: Rebecca Tannen-
baum, Juan Sebastian Agudelo, the Russian Teacher Retrainees of the
University of Veszprém, Jeff Georlett, Shankar Vedantam, Stessa Cohen,
Jeff Loo and the Loose Cannon Writer's Collective, Elizabeth Collins
Smith, Luise Hirsch, R. P. Burnham, Joshua Yanovski, Susan Viguers,
Zsuzsanna Gasparics, and the many friends and family members who were
this novel's first readers. The University of the Arts Venture Fund and the
Pennsylvania Council for the Arts made possible additional research and
revision. I am particularly grateful to my agent, Gail Hochman, and my edi-
tor, Laura Mathews, who helped me guide my readers through a complicated story while in no way compromising how that story had to be told.

Special thanks to Doug and Jane, who appeared just when my life had
turned upside down. It has been spinning ever since.